Pursuit Through Chaos

Pursuit Through Chaos

A REBELLION ROAD NOVEL

ROBERT J. SHADE

Sunshine Hill Press

Sunshine Hill Press LLC
2937 Novum Road
Reva, VA 22735

ISBN-13: 978-0-578-55628-4

Artwork with specific permission:
Front Cover: *Loading in a Tempest*
by Bryant White
(www.whitehistoricart.com)

Maps: Anthony Rozwadowski, K Art and Design, Inc.
(www.k-artanddesign.com)

To my wife,
Cathy Strine Shade

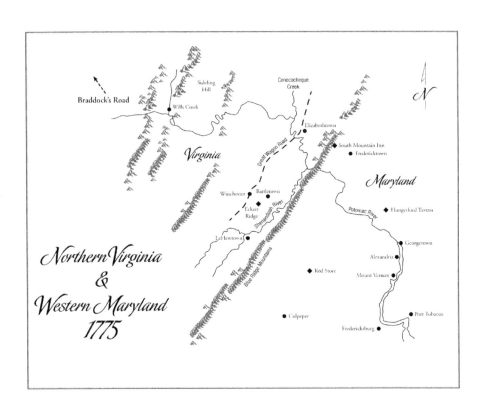

Braddock's Road

Sideling
Hill

Conococheque
Creek

Wills Creek

Elizabethtown

Virginia

Great Wagon Road

South Mountain Inn

Fredericktown

Maryland

Winchester   Battletown

Eckert
Ridge

Shenandoah River

Potomac River

Hungerford Tavern

Lewtown

Georgetown

Alexandria

Red Store

Mount Vernon

Blue Ridge Mountains

Northern Virginia
&
Western Maryland
1775

Culpeper

Fredericksburg

Port Tobacco

N

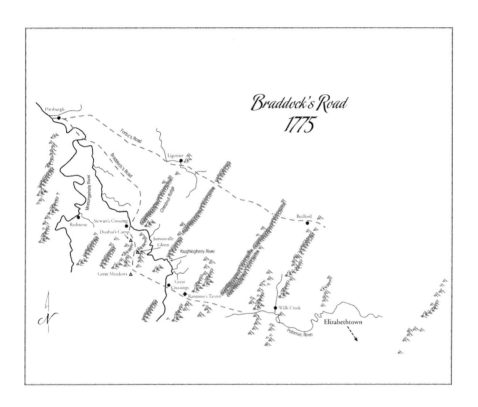

Braddock's Road
1775

Pittsburgh

Forbe's Road

Ligonier

Braddock's Road

Monongahela River

Chestnut Ridge

Stewart's Crossing

Bedford

Redstone

Dunbar's Camp

Jumonville Glenn

Youghiogheny River

Great Meadows

Great Crossings

Ransome's Tavern

Wills Creek

Potomac River

Elizabethtown

N

PLACE NAMES:
1775 VERSUS PRESENT DAY

1775	Present
Battletown Crossroads (East of Winchester)	Berryville
LeHewtown, Virginia	Front Royal
Red Store, Virginia	Warrenton
Hungerford Tavern, Maryland	Rockville
Fredericktown, Maryland	Frederick
Elizabethtown, Maryland	Hagerstown
Wills Creek, Maryland	Cumberland
Great Crossing, Pennsylvania	Somerfield
Dunbar's Camp, Pennsylvania	Jumonville
Stewarts Crossing, Pennsylvania	Connellsville

MAJOR CHARACTERS

Historical Name	Description
James Wood:	Member of House of Burgesses from Frederick County, Virginia
Jean Moncure Wood:	Wife of James Wood
John Murray:	Royal governor of Virginia, Fourth Earl of Dunmore
John Connolly:	Lieutenant colonel in Loyalist forces of Virginia
Dr. John Smyth:	Member of Connolly's conspiracy (spelled *Smith* in some accounts)
Alan Cameron:	Lieutenant in Loyalist forces, member of Connolly's conspiracy
Angus McDonald:	Member of Frederick County Committee of Safety, major in militia
Anna McDonald:	Wife of Angus
Daniel Morgan:	Militia captain, commanding Winchester/Frederick County rifle company
Abbey Morgan:	Wife of Daniel
Patrick Henry:	Colonel of First Virginia Regiment
Charles Hungerford:	Maryland tavern and innkeeper
Jonathan Hager:	Founder of the town of Elizabethtown, Maryland (later Hagerstown)
Jonathan (Jon) Hager Jr.:	Son of Jonathan Hager
Rosanna Hager:	Daughter of Jonathan Hager

Fictional Name	Description
Wend Eckert:	Gunsmith of Frederick County, Virginia; master of Eckert Ridge Farm
Peggy McCartie Eckert:	Wend's wife
Joshua Baird:	Militia scout of Frederick County, Virginia
Alice Downey Baird:	Common-law wife of Joshua
Simon Donegal:	Farmer, whiskey distiller at Eckert Ridge; formerly of 77th Highlanders
Sally Potter Donegal:	Simon's wife
Wilhelm Hecht:	Wend's journeyman gunsmith and shop manager
Andrew Horner:	Wend's senior apprentice
Henry Johann Eckert:	Son of Wend and Abigail Gibson, apprentice to Wend
Bernd Eckert:	Son of Wend and Peggy Eckert, apprentice to Wend
Jacob Specht:	Lead farmhand at Eckert Ridge
Jedidiah Ballantyne:	Captain, First Virginia Regiment
Horst Seidal:	Sergeant, First Virginia Regiment
Taddy Carlin:	Private, First Virginia Regiment
Johnny Carlin:	Private, First Virginia Regiment
Coleen Alison McGraw:	Proprietress of the Red Vixen Tavern-Inn
Emily Crider:	Maid at the Red Vixen
Warren Bradley:	Captain of the Anne Arundell Light Horse Troop
Richard Munger:	Pittsburgh Indian trader, member of Connolly's conspiracy ring
Tom Harley:	Youth recruited into the Connolly conspiracy
Henry Fallow:	John Connolly's servant

CONTENTS

Chapter One

THE RIFLE COMPANY

The July sun, just coming to its zenith, bore fiercely down on old Fort Loudoun, a derelict reminder of the war with the French and their tribal allies, now almost two decades in the past. There were large gaps in the once-imposing walls, the timber having been appropriated by the good citizens of Winchester for construction of houses and outbuildings in the adjacent town.

An open piece of land lay between the fort and the wagon road which led northward from the town, and in this area a large crowd of men, most of whom carried long rifles, stood around, talking and laughing among themselves.

Just off the roadway was parked a farm wagon pulled by a two-horse team. A table had been set up alongside the wagon, behind which two men sat on camp chairs. One was a clean-shaven, stone-faced, brown-haired man of about thirty. The other was a lean, rangy man with a brown, stubbly beard who appeared nearer to fifty than forty. Behind them, two more men leaned casually against the wagon. The older of the two, who looked to be in his midthirties, sported a faded and frayed blue cap, or bonnet, of the type worn by His Majesty's Highland regiments. The other man was actually a fresh-faced, blue-eyed, blond lad who clearly had not reached his twentieth year. Beside the table, sitting on his haunches Indian style, was another youth, even younger than the first. An observer would have noted that he was a near-duplicate of the stone-faced man and carried the same unreadable expression on his face. The boy sat rigidly still, only his dark eyes seemingly alive, but they played rapidly around the scene before them, taking in all the details.

The lanky, bearded man reached out and took hold of a tin cup that was on the table in front of him and brought it to his lips, draining the liquid within. Then, wiping his brow, he turned to the other man at the table and said, "Damn, Wend, it be hotter'n hell out here. When is Daniel going to get this show started?"

Wend Eckert turned and looked at a small group of men standing about fifty feet away, all engaged in conversation. "Joshua, you know Dan Morgan is as anxious as you to get started. And undoubtedly that will be as soon as he gets finished talking with the esteemed gentlemen of the Committee of Safety."

The older man retorted, "Hell, they've been jabbering for a fair piece now. Look at Reverend Thruston and Angus McDonald goin' at each other. And meantime, all them men out by the fort are sweatin' in this heat and gettin' restless."

Wend shook his head. "When did Thruston and McDonald ever agree on anything? At least since they had that big argument about vestry money for the church years ago? Look, James Wood is trying to calm things down."

Joshua responded, "Well, I wish they'd be done with it, whatever that be." Then he rose from his chair, standing still for a moment with a grimace on his face and his left hand on his hip.

Wend looked up at him. "Is that old hip wound bothering you more than usual?"

"Some days is worse than others. It ain't nothin' to worry about, and it don't stop me from doin' what needs to be done." He picked up his cup, and walked, limping, toward where the man with the Highland bonnet stood. He held up his cup, and said, "Here, Donegal, I've drunk up all my whiskey. Pray, give me another charge."

The Highlander waved toward the crowd by the fort and retorted, "Baird, I brought that stuff to sell to all these men once the recruiting is done. I'd 'na like to see you drink it all up before I have a chance to make some money."

Joshua looked peeved and pointed to the wagon bed. "Come on, Simon, you got jugs and jugs of that whiskey sittin' in there."

Simon Donegal waved at the men and grinned. "Look at all them lads. They're goin' to have a powerful thirst—powerful, indeed! I'm 'na sure there's enough to satisfy them as it is."

Then the young man leaning against the wagon, who had been listening to the conversation with a bored look on his face, spoke up. "Hey, Joshua, you got your wish."

Joshua carefully held his cup as Donegal poured, then responded to the youth, "Yeah, Horner, what do you mean?"

"I mean Morgan's heading for the fort right now with Humphreys beside him. And he's carrying his rifle."

Joshua Baird sighed in relief. "Finally all them committee windbags are finished. Now I'll wager we'll see some shootin'!!"

Eckert turned toward Horner and said, "All right, Andrew, if the contest is about to begin, we'll need to get our tools and parts ready."

Horner nodded. "Yes, sir. We'll do it right now." He called out to the young boy beside the table, "Johann, give me a hand getting the stuff! Donegal's got it all buried between his jugs."

The two youngsters went to work, lifting out of the wagon several boxes containing replacement parts and lubricants for the locks of rifles. Then Horner placed a long toolbox on the ground beside Wend.

Wend got up, reached under the seat of the wagon, and pulled out a leather apron. Donning it, he returned to the table and inspected the parts and tools. "All right, we'll be ready when the first man comes over."

Meanwhile, Morgan had arrived in front of the crowd of men. In a booming voice, he shouted, "All right, lads, gather about. Now listen sharp to what I'm going to say!"

The men, holding their firelocks grounded in front of them, coalesced into a tight crescent in front of Morgan. A silence descended as they waited for his words. As Wend looked at him standing there in front of the potential recruits, the size and bulk of the man became evident. At over six feet, he stood taller than all but one or two of the men. Even more imposing were his burly physique, massive shoulders, and head that seemed somewhat too big for his body.

"Now, men, you know why we're here. That congress sittin' up in Philadelphia has ordered up ten rifle companies to go help Washington and his army of them New England militia tryin' to throw the Redcoats out of Boston. Winchester and Frederick County is formin' one of two companies comin' from Virginia. And the Committee of Safety has given me the captaincy of this here company." He looked around at the men, then put his hand on the man standing next to him, who was perhaps four inches shorter than the captain and possessed a slim build. "This here is my First Lieutenant, John Humphreys." He waved for two men standing at the side of the crowd to join him. "And these two be my other lieutenants: Will Heth and Peter Bruin." Finally, he pointed to a tobacco-chewing man standing a bit to the side of the crowd. "And that there is Charlie Porterfield, who will be the first sergeant." He smiled and said, "You make it into my company, you best learn to listen to Charlie, or you'll be in big trouble!"

There was a smattering of laughs from the crowd.

"If there be any of you who don't know about me, listen sharp and I'll tell you 'bout the man you're here to march with. I came here from

Jersey long 'bout '54, when I was a lad of eighteen, and took up work as a teamster. Been doin' that ever since, more'n twenty years now. Round these parts they call me the Old Wagoner. Nowadays I own a whole freight line, and I got plenty of Conestogas and a herd of horses." Morgan shook his head. "Damn animals near eat me into bankruptcy during the winter."

More laughs from the men.

Morgan paused and gathered his thoughts. "Now if you're of a mind to fight the British, I'm the man you want to be with 'cause the one thing I've done beside run wagons is fight." He pointed to his nose, which was visibly crooked and somewhat flattened. "That's how I got this!"

The men stared as his face. Some muttered among themselves, and there was a sprinkling of laughs.

Joshua looked over at Wend and said from the side of his mouth, "He ain't gonna tell them it was in a brawl at the Old Battletown Tavern down at the crossroads."

Wend smiled. "Yeah, a brawl where he took a whipping, which even he admits."

Morgan picked up the story again. "I fought in every war that has come along. I was at Braddock's fight, and I went up again' the Indians during the French War right here in Virginia." He pointed to the left side of his jaw. "You look close at my face. You'll see that the left side don't match the right. And there be a scar at the left side of my mouth. That's 'cause I took a warrior's ball right through the back of my neck and it came out the front." Morgan shook his head. "Damn doctor did a fair enough job, but he couldn't put things back together quite right."

Morgan paused, and in the momentary silence, Eckert looked over at Baird and laughed. Then he said, "Daniel's building up to do the shirt thing."

The older man shook his head. "Naw, he ain't gonna do that right here in broad daylight. He's done it plenty of times in taverns, after a few cups, but not here in front of all these men."

Wend pulled out a coin from his pocket. "This says he does it."

Baird pursed his lips and shook his head. "All right, I'll take that."

Morgan started up again. He said, "I helped fight the tribes during that Pontiac War. And just last year I led a company in Dunmore's fight against the Shawnee, Mingo, and Delawares. A goodly number of you were with me then. We hit them at Wakatomica under our own Major Angus McDonald and at Seekunk with Major William Crawford."

He slowly scanned the crescent of men with his eyes.

"So if you want to fight and give the British a lickin', don't ever doubt I'm the man you want to be with. Now I'll tell you this: There be some who say we're fighting so the king and that damned parliament of his give us the full rights of Englishmen and stay out of our business. There be others who say we should just be done with it and declare our independence from England. But one thing is sure: We all hate the damned Redcoats, and the first thing that has got to be done is drive them out of Boston!"

There were great shouts of agreement from the men.

Wend leaned close to Joshua and whispered, "You're going to lose your money."

Joshua sighed. "He ain't done it yet."

Meanwhile Morgan had resumed his speech. "Now I'll tell you this: I learned to hate the damned British Army while I was driving a wagon in Braddock's campaign when I was still a lad. I had a trifling little disagreement with an officer, and the snotty bastards tied me up to a wagon wheel and gave me five hundred lashes."

Wend sat back and grinned. "Here it comes, Joshua. Get your money out."

Baird simply shook his head and said, "Shit."

Morgan turned around and pulled the shirt up, clearly displaying his bare back. There was an audible gasp from a number of the men. The captain's back was covered with long, raised scars, forming a crisscross pattern. Clearly they were old for they showed only a very dull reddish discoloration.

Eckert said, "He can't resist doin' that." Then he put his hand out to Baird. "I'll take your coin now."

"Damn, I ain't got any on me. Give it to you later after we get back to the farm."

Wend grinned. "Alice keeping you on a short rope with the money?"

Baird grimaced, then responded, "The woman is an absolute miser. I should've left her up in Carlisle when I finished with Bouquet's expedition in '64."

"Don't give me that, Joshua. You've gotten used to her keeping your bed warm and havin' cooked food ready on the table for you these ten years."

"Well, that part is easy to like."

As they talked, Morgan pulled his shirt back on and turned back to the volunteers. "Now I counted every damned stroke of the whip that Redcoat gave me, and I got to tell you, he counted short. They actually gave me one less! But I'll tell you this: I aim to pay the bastards back for all five hundred and then some! And I want a hundred good men to help me!"

There were loud round of cheers from the men, which persisted for some time.

When the cheers had finally died out, Morgan said, "So you lads came here to join my company. Well, we're only taking the best! So listen sharp now and look at this." He held up a wooden target. The circle was incredibly small. "This here mark is seven inches across. We're going to place it at two hundred paces." He motioned to a group of boys, one of whom took the target and ran down to where a post had been put in place.

As the boy put the target in place, the captain scraped a line in the dust. Then, with the lad out of the way, he checked the priming on his firelock, quickly put it to his shoulder, took brief aim, and fired. The boy retrieved the target and scurried back to Morgan with it.

Morgan held the target high so everyone could see. The hole was a couple of inches off to the right of center. "Not my best shot, lads, but listen close: anyone who wants to march with me will put his ball in the circle on his first shot." He stared at the men who stood silently in front of him, each undoubtedly assessing his ability to match the marksmanship they had just seen. Then he smiled slyly and said, "You can't do that—you might cogitate on goin' down to Berkeley County where Captain Hugh Stevenson is putting together another rifle company!"

Not surprisingly, some of the riflemen, shaking their heads, turned and left the crowd, individually and in small groups. Others set their jaws and prepared for the contest, or at least stayed to see who would succeed. A few, confident in their aim, jostled to get to the front of the line.

But Morgan was not finished talking. "So I'll take the first hundred men who can put the ball in that circle from a standing shot. No bracing or laying down, mind you." He paused and looked hard around the group of men. "And then, if you hit the target, you go over there to where sits Wend Eckert, the county's best damned gunsmith." He grinned and then continued, "And the county's second-best marksman—after myself, of course."

A voice from the rear of the crowd called out, "Come on, Daniel! If you're the best, how come Eckert keeps beating you every year in the shooting contest at McDonald's Spring Fair?"

There were scattered laughs.

Morgan glowered at the crowd and said, "Whoever said that is a *scurrilous* bastard. Fact is, he don't beat me *every* year." Then, considering discretion the better part of valor, he returned to his topic. "Point is, Eckert will look over your firelock and make sure it's in first-rate condition. If there are a few minor things wrong with your lock, he'll take care of it. And it's being paid for by the Committee of Safety. We want every man in the company to leave with his rifle in the best possible condition. But if Eckert says your firelock ain't in condition to stand up to a year's hard service, and he can't make it right, you ain't goin' along. Those are the rules!" He paused and then asked, "Who's going to be first?"

Adam Kurtz immediately stepped forward. Wend knew the man; he made his living hunting and providing game to local taverns and inns. He was the primary hunter for Winchester's most prominent inn, The Golden Buck, located right off the square. He stepped to the mark, checked his priming, raised his rifle, and fired. A boy ran the target back to Morgan, who took one look and slapped the hunter on the back. "There's the first rifleman of our company!"

The third lieutenant, Peter Bruin, held out a muster book, which Kurtz signed. Then Morgan motioned Kurtz to head for Wend's table.

As the rifleman approached, Baird, who had hunted with him numerous times, called out, "Good shot, Adam!"

The hunter replied, "Yeah, and soon enough I plan to have some damned Redcoat officer in my sights."

Joshua nodded. "I don't doubt you'll bag a few."

Kurtz turned to Wend. "Look, Eckert, I take care of my own firelock. Why do I need you to look over it?"

"Adam, I know you can take care of your lock, leastways around here. But there aren't many New Englanders who have ever seen a rifle. They use smoothbores. We can't be sure that gunsmiths up there even have parts for the locks we use. If your lock malfunctions, it may be hard to get it repaired."

Kurtz looked down at his rifle doubtfully, then with reluctance handed it over to Wend. "All right, since Daniel says I have to do it."

After a quick but thorough inspection, Wend said, "Your piece is in fine shape, Adam. The only thing I can find is that the vent needs a little cleaning."

"You're damn right it is. And I don't need your advice on cleaning it."

Wend suppressed a flare of irritation, and replied, "I was just telling you what I saw." He reached into a box and pulled out some flints. "Here, take these, Adam. They may be hard to find in the middle of an army." He looked up at the hunter. "Unless you've got a supply that will last a year of frequent firing."

Kurtz pursed his lips and hesitated. Finally he reached out and took the flints. "Won't turn down no supply of flints."

And then he walked off without another word. Wend looked over at Baird and grinned.

The shooting continued for hours, and finally, with the sun low in the west, Morgan had his picked company. Eckert had found four rifles with worn locks, which would need replacement parts, and was at work making the repairs.

Morgan called the company together. "Men, we'll set up camp here at the fort. The Committee of Safety is gathering up provisions and a supply of powder and lead for us. Now we're going to do a little drilling for the next few days while they get us what we need. But come hell or high water, we're leaving in four days. I aim to be the first rifle company that gets to Boston. And I'm damned well determined to beat Michael Cresap and his Maryland men."

There was a round of cheering and shouted agreement from the men.

Morgan looked around at the company and grinned broadly. "So lads, get your kit together and be ready to march when the time comes!"

Donegal stood up with a jug of whiskey in his hand and waved at Morgan, then pointed to the jug with his other hand.

Morgan laughed and shouted to the men. "And now that our business is done, and the sun is gettin' low, Simon Donegal has got some good whiskey for sale if you got the wherewithal!"

There was a final cheer from the recruits, and the entire crowd headed for the wagon.

—ɯ—

Peggy Eckert, her raven hair shining in the morning sun, sat beside Wend in the small, two-wheeled chaise as it bounced along the ruts of the road toward Winchester. She was dressed in a gown of her favorite color, medium blue, which matched her eyes and nicely complemented her hair. Perched rather precariously on her head was a small, flat, fashionable straw hat that was trimmed with a ribbon that matched the color of the gown. Wend was dressed in his black coat with gray breeches, topped by what he called his "church hat," which was also in gray. The chaise was drawn by an elegant and very young bay stallion with white stockings on his legs and a star on his face, markings that had earned him the name of "Boots."

Wend could see that Boots was quite frustrated at the slow pace at which he was pulling the little chaise, and he was tossing his head to show it. He was used to being at the trot or even faster when Peggy herself was driving. But today Wend was holding him back to match the speed of the three farm vehicles that followed behind.

Peggy turned and looked back at the little cavalcade and remarked, "This is the first time we've had everyone from Eckert Ridge travel into Winchester at the same time."

Wend laughed, then reflected, "Think on it, Peggy: Eleven years ago we came down from Pennsylvania with only Joshua and Donegal with us, and supposedly they were here only for help to start things up. And now we've got twenty-five people depending on us, and it takes two wagons and a cart to bring them along."

The wagon immediately behind the chaise was driven by Simon Donegal with his new, twenty-four-year-old bride, more than a decade and a half younger than the Scotsman, seated beside him. The pretty blonde was holding little Henry, her two-year-old son from a previous marriage, in her lap. Louisa, her four-year-old daughter, was on her knees in the wagon bed, holding onto the seat back and looking over her mother's shoulder. With them on the front seat was Alice Downey, Joshua Baird's common-law wife. Baird himself rode a powerful hunter alongside the wagon. Also in the bed of the wagon, joking and laughing, were most of the farm's field hands.

The second wagon was driven by Wilhelm Hecht, Wend's journeyman assistant in the gunsmithing trade. His wife sat beside him, and in the bed were their children and the shop apprentices. The third vehicle in the caravan was a cart driven by the former black slave, Albert. With him were his wife, Wilma, as well as his daughter, Liza, and his son, Billy. The two women performed the cooking duties for the Eckert household, and Billy also helped around the house, often serving at dinners when guests were present. With the servant family were three of the four Eckert children—ten-year-old Bernd, eight-year-old Elise, and the baby, Ellen, who had just turned five.

Bringing up the rear of the caravan were two mounted riders: Jacob Specht, the lead farmhand and primary caretaker of the horses, and Johann Eckert.

As the chaise hit a large bump and then shuddered its way through several ruts, Peggy steadied herself on the armrest. Then, when the ride became smoother, she turned to her husband, a serious look on her face, and raised a new subject. "So, Wend, as you said, we've got a lot of people depending on us. And I've been getting quite worried. When are we going to get paid for all this work you are doing for the Committee of Safety?"

He shrugged. "When they figure out where they're getting their money."

She retorted, "Well, they need to do that soon. You've refurbished over one hundred muskets from the Virginia stocks down in Williamsburg, and you obviously will never get paid by the royal government, whatever happens."

Wend laughed. "I might get paid by the royal government, but I won't get paid in money. There's no doubt Governor Dunmore considers me a traitor because I didn't deliver the muskets to his Loyalist forces. If he prevails and puts down the rebellion, my payment is likely to be the gallows, Peggy."

She pursed her lips. "If that happens, we'll flee to the border country. We've lived in the backwoods before. We can do it again." Then, after a few seconds, she returned to her subject. "You've also invested your own money to start producing new muskets for the committee. You put on two new apprentices, and they're using our own wood to carve the stocks for fifty firelocks. Plus you've started to make your own locks." She gritted her teeth and repeated, "And it's all at our own expense."

Wend sighed. "Dear, I'm all *too* aware of that."

"Then you and Donegal went in together to produce his whiskey on a large scale. And that has been mostly funded out of our resources. *Our* money to rent more land to produce enough grain, *our* money to clear more of our own land for grain, and *our* money to expand the distillery."

Wend said in a defensive tone. "Donegal did put what little money he had into it. And, my dear, don't forget it's his recipe and distilling knowledge that is key to the whole enterprise."

Peggy's anger intensified. "I'm not forgetting anything! *Damn it*, Wend, the whole point of going into the whiskey business was to compensate for losing the musket contract with the colonial government. It was to get us free of Governor Dunmore and that scurrilous minion of his, Barrett Penfold Northcutt. And now you're using what profit there is, which is little enough so far, to make more muskets for the Committee of Safety who can't pay us! We're right back where we started." She looked over at Wend, fire in her eyes. "No, that isn't right; the hell of it is, we're worse off!"

Seeking to calm her, he smiled at his wife and said in his most soothing voice, "Now Peggy, come on and put your worries aside, at least for today. Your words are beginning to sound more like Peggy McCartie, the tavern maid, than Lady Elizabeth of Eckert Ridge Plantation."

But instead of being mollified, Peggy's rage increased. She snapped, "And for God's sake, stop calling me Lady Elizabeth or Lady Eckert. You did that at the McDonalds' dinner party last month when we we're talking together, and I swear Jean Moncure heard it. She gave me a funny look from across the room."

"Remember, she's Jean Wood now. They got married right after James came back from the last meeting of the Burgesses."

"Don't bandy words with me! Of *course* I know they're married. We were at the wedding. It just takes getting used to. The point is, someday you're going to slip and call me Lady Eckert out loud in some important social occasion. I shudder at how embarrassing that will be!"

"I'll just be telling everyone the truth. You're a great lady to me." He paused, then gave her a devilish smile. "Last night after we went to bed, you were a *very* great lady."

"Don't give me that." She stared ahead for a while and then returned to her original theme. "Wend, promise me you'll talk to the committee. Tell them we must have some payment for all this work, or we're just going to stop it. The truth is, we could end up bankrupt."

"Yes, dearest. At the appropriate time, I will make a serious representation to them."

Somewhat mollified, Peggy became quiet and stared ahead, her Ulster-Scot temper slowly abating. They rode in silence for a few minutes. Then she looked up at the sun and asked, "Are we going to be in time? We left the farm later than planned. I heard that Morgan's company was going to leave in the early afternoon. And we're supposed to be at the Golden Buck for the Committee of Safety dinner at noon."

"Don't fret—we're in good time. And we're almost up to the drive at Glengarry now, and you know it's not much further into Winchester."

"I hope you're right. I surely don't want to be late for any of the festivities."

They came around a curve in the road and a large house with extensive stables and outbuildings came into view. "Look, there's Glengarry, and Angus and Anna are coming down the drive in their fine carriage that you are so fond of, Lady Elizabeth."

"Damn, Wend, just stop it!" Then Peggy rose slightly and waved vigorously at Anna, who was her best friend outside of the women of Eckert Ridge.

Wend said, "It's sure nothing's going to happen until Angus gets to town, so we're in good time." As they came to the end of the McDonalds' drive, he stopped the chaise and signaled to the rigs behind to do the same.

Then he called out, "We'll follow you into town, Angus!"

The Highlander waved in reply, then pulled the carriage, drawn by a team of matched blacks, out onto the road and headed for Winchester. Behind the carriage rode the old family retainer, Evan McCleod, who had come to Virginia with Angus thirty years before in the aftermath of Cullodon. Wend waved at the horseman and then slapped the reins on Boots's back and signaled to the vehicles behind to start moving again.

In a short time, the roofs and church spires of Winchester were in view, and minutes later the cavalcade entered the town itself. As they arrived at Fort Loudoun, the McDonalds' carriage and the Eckerts' chaise turned left and headed down Market Street while the farm vehicles headed for the grounds of the fort.

Wend glanced at Peggy and said, "The wagons are going to park at the fort. But Phillip Bush has reserved room for us and the McDonalds to park in the courtyard of the Golden Buck. We'll go right in for the midday meal with the members of the Committee of Safety and of course Daniel and Abbey."

Peggy smiled. "It's been a month since I've seen Anna and Jean Wood. And it's even longer than I've been able to talk with Abbey. I've been looking forward to today for a fortnight."

The two vehicles pulled into the Golden Buck Inn, and a pair of boys waved them over to a spot next to the stable. After he pulled up the horses, Wend jumped down and handed the reins to one of the boys. Then he went around to help Peggy.

Putting on a show of gallantry, he reached up with one hand to help her down and swept his broad-brimmed hat off and across his chest with the other. "Lady Elizabeth, pray accompany me. Your repast awaits you!"

Peggy took his hand and stepped down gingerly. Then she looked at her husband and said quietly so no one else could hear, "Damn you, Wend Eckert. Will you never stop this insufferable teasing of me?" But there was a grin on her face as she spoke.

Wend gave her his arm and led off toward the inn.

Meanwhile, Peggy smiled broadly, waved at Anna, and called out, "I'm so glad to see you! We must get some time to chat today!"

—⚓—

The Committee of Safety dinner was being held in the inn's largest private dining room, located at the rear of the building. The proprietor, Philip Bush, had all the windows wide open in respect of the summer heat and the large number of people crowded into the room. Wend could hear the hubbub of the crowd out on the square over the voices of the gathered diners. He stood in the corner, the only open space, and observed the members of the committee and their wives talking as they waited for lunch.

Angus and James Wood stood with Morgan, who was dressed for the march in the uniform of his company, which was a long linen hunting shirt over leggings. Once in a while, his voice boomed out in a hearty laugh. Reverend Thruston and David Rutledge, who had been the county lieutenant under the royal government, conversed with Sheriff Smith.

Meanwhile, the women were clustered in a large group, happily talking and laughing.

Rutledge's voice was the loudest among the men. Wend remembered seeing him at the bar in the inn's common room when they arrived and wondered how long he had been there. Clearly he had had his share of spirits, and he was perspiring heavily in the heat.

Wend reflected that he and Peggy were included in what constituted the upper circle of Winchester's society only by several matters of chance. First was his friendship with Daniel Morgan, whom he had first met in 1763 at Pennsylvania's Fort Bedford when the wagoner had delivered a load of provisions to the garrison. Knowing Morgan had led Peggy and him to choose Winchester as their home when circumstances had necessitated that they leave Pennsylvania. Second, and more consequential, was Peggy's friendship with Anna McDonald. The two had bonded for a couple of reasons: Anna was of the same age and similar personality to Peggy's younger sister, Ellen, and both women were from rural, humble beginnings and somewhat in awe of their rise in fortune. That friendship had led to the Eckerts' inclusion in social gatherings well above normal for a tradesman. The third reason for their presence in this particular meeting of the upper crust was Wend's possession of one hundred muskets formerly the property of the colony's royal government and now of great value to the forces of the burgeoning insurrection. Moreover, at the committee's request, he would soon be in a position to manufacture additional firelocks necessary to equipping the rebel militia.

Proprietor Bush officiously entered the room and called for attention. "Gentleman and ladies, we are ready to serve you." He smiled at the gathering. "I'm honored you've chosen my inn for this meeting of the committee on such an auspicious day, when we send our finest men off to war. It is actually quite appropriate that you meet in this room, for it might interest you to know that it was more than once used by General Washington, when he was colonel of the Virginia Regiment, to host his officers."

James Wood, who was the official host of the meal, nodded to Bush and then said, "Thank you, Phillip. Everyone, please take your places."

There was a general buzz among the group as they moved to their seats.

As the guests finished settling in, Bush announced, "The centerpiece of your meal today will be some excellent roasted venison. It is very fitting for the occasion since it will be the last game we'll have from Adam Kurtz, who has been our main hunter for several years and is leaving with Daniel today. So enjoy!"

When he finished, attendants entered the room, carrying large platters of food, and began serving the diners. There followed a good half hour of hearty eating and polite talk as they enjoyed Bush's fare, which, Wend reflected, was always satisfying.

When most had finished, Wood rose, glass in hand. "Gentlemen of the committee and your ladies, this day is most assuredly a memorable occasion in the history of Winchester and Frederick County. Today, at the request of Congress and Virginia's own George Washington, we proudly send our most accomplished marksmen to join the forces besieging the British. And as captain of this company of stout lads, we have appointed one of our most redoubtable citizens, Daniel Morgan."

There was a round of applause.

Wood continued, "I don't need to remind anyone here that since he arrived in Frederick County, Captain Morgan has been a stalwart of our defense against the ravages of the tribes. And it was in particular his actions during the recent conflict against the Shawnee and Mingo in the Ohio Country that added to his repute and made him the undisputed choice to lead our company of riflemen as they do their part to drive the Redcoats out of Boston."

There were cries of "Here, here!" around the table.

Wood smiled at the assembly. "Let us now raise our glasses to Captain Daniel Morgan and the brave lads of his company!"

The entire assembly stood and raised their glasses.

As they seated themselves, Peggy leaned over and whispered into Wend's ear, "Daniel is loving every minute of this."

Wend nodded. "Of course he is."

Meanwhile, Morgan, his face flushed, rose to speak. "I ain't real good at speakin' like this, but I do got a few words to say." He bit his lip as he organized his thoughts. "Here's the truth: I aim to make the name of Winchester known to all those New Englanders around Boston. We're going to march straight for that town, goin' overland if the roads don't lead in the right direction. I call it travelin' in a *beeline*. And we're set on being the first rifle company to arrive, even though those Pennsylvania boys got less way to go." He paused and then said, "And when we get there, we aim to show them what Virginia riflemen can do."

There was another round of applause.

Morgan finished up by raising his fist and saying with determination, "There's no doubt we'll chase all them Redcoats out of Boston or make them fly the white flag in short order. And then we'll be marching back here post haste!"

Morgan sat down to a final round of clapping.

Then there was a moment of quiet, which was suddenly broken by Rutledge's loud voice.

It was slurred, and now Wend was sure the man was in his cups.

"I have a question," Rutledge announced, in an almost belligerent tone. "We talk all the time about driving the British out of Boston. But what happens after we do that? Can someone give me a straight answer?"

Jean Wood said, in a manner calculated to mollify Rutledge, "Why, sir, our men come home."

Rutledge would not be denied. "Good lady, you miss my point. Are we to declare independence from the crown, or simply try to negotiate for our proper rights as Englishmen?" He shook his head. "Where is this all leading? The truth is, nobody can answer that question—not the Virginia Convention in Williamsburg, not the Congress in Philadelphia." Rutledge looked around the table. "Does anyone even know? Or are we truly adrift in uncharted seas?"

Angus responded, "My dear David, the question is really not what *we* do after the British in Boston are driven out. The real question is what the *British* do after they are forced to leave. You all know I fought the king in '45. If I know the king and parliament, they will be obstinate, and I can assure you that they will be in no mood to end things at that and leave us to our own devices." He looked around the room, then added, "Mark my words: Boston will not be the end of this affair. It will be but the beginning."

A sober silence descended on the room. Wend looked at the faces and saw many furrowed brows.

Wood, seeking to deflect the question and get on with the ceremonial business of the day, said, "Now David, your question is important, but we know that the Congress has been established to work through that problem. For the moment at least, let us leave it to them." He waved to the door. "Now ladies and gentlemen, the good citizens of our town are waiting for us. And Daniel's men are anxious to start their march."

Morgan nodded. "As is their captain."

The party began to shuffle out the door. Wend and Peggy, their seats at the table being far from the door, stood waiting for the others to leave.

As they waited, James Wood joined them. He put a hand on Wend's arm and said quietly, "Wend, we've gotten a letter from the Committee of Safety in Williamsburg that concerns your stock of firelocks. After things are over on the square, please come back here for a meeting to discuss the disposition of them."

"Certainly, James."

Wood nodded and then quickly left to catch up with Jean.

Peggy put her hand on Wend's arm and looked into his eyes. "Now, husband, things have come to a head. There is no choice; you must talk to them about payment. If you release those firelocks without getting our money, we'll never see it."

Wend sighed and resorted to the only words he knew would preserve domestic tranquility: "Yes, dear."

—⁂—

As they stepped out of the Golden Buck, Peggy said in astonishment, "My God, Wend, look at the square. The entire population of Frederick County must be here."

Wend nodded. "Pretty much of it, that's for sure."

"And the sound is near deafening. I thought Winchester was crowded and noisy on Court Day, but this is way beyond that."

Wend took some time to look around and examine the press of people in the square and its environs. Many of the vendors who came out monthly on the day the court met had set up their displays. Most of the town's shopkeepers had also put out tables of their wares, and people were browsing the merchandise. Children, often in laughing gaggles, ran up and down the streets and played games, brazenly displaying their boundless energy even in the face of the oppressive heat. Most adults, whether town inhabitants or from the surrounding rural areas, were dressed in their best apparel. The members of the rifle company, recognizable by their long hunting shirts, were scattered among the crowd.

The drummers and fifers of the Frederick County Militia were assembled, and the sound of their tunes wafted over the square, lending a martial spirit.

The sense of optimism and joyous celebration was palpable.

Wend pointed to a spot by the courthouse. "Look, Donegal has set up a table to sell his whiskey. And he's got a goodly number of people surrounding it, including a fair number of Morgan's men." He grinned and looked at his wife. "I expect they're laying in a supply in prospect of the march's hardships."

Peggy's face brightened. "Well, at least we'll see some measure of profit out of today."

Wend agreed, then pointed to a gaggle of people around Morgan. "Let's go over and bid goodbye to Daniel. I didn't have a chance at the inn."

They pushed their way through the crowd to where Daniel, Abbey next to him, stood talking to well-wishers. Also standing with them were their children, Betsy, a pretty sixteen-year-old, and Nancy, who was twelve. As they approached, the burly rifleman turned and grinned broadly.

"Wend! Peggy!" he shouted with exuberance. "Git on over here!" He turned to the group around him and said, "Good people, let me have a few minutes with my neighbors, the Eckerts."

Once they were alone in the midst of the crowd, Morgan said, "Damn, Wend, I still wish you were going along as my first lieutenant, like I asked you at the beginning."

"Come on, Dan. John Humphreys is a good man, and my place is in the shop building muskets."

Peggy wagged her finger at Morgan. "And if he had even considered going with you, the fight with the British would have been nothing compared to the one you'd have had with me."

"Still, Wend, it's a damn shame." Then Morgan had another thought. He reached over and put his arm around his wife. "You two look after Abbey 'til I return next year. I hate leaving her alone on the farm for all that time and havin' to run the freight line at the same time."

Wend shook his head and smiled. "Better you tell her to look after us. After all, she's the spirited woman who turned a vagabond wagoner into a respected citizen of Winchester."

Daniel threw back his head and laughed. "You got that right!"

Peggy moved over beside Abbey and touched her friend's arm. "And she knows the wagon business as well as you, Dan. Certainly the financial end."

"Hell, she knows that a damned sight better than I. Keeps me from goin' bankrupt." He thought a moment. "Between her and my man Jake Cather, I ain't got much worry about the wagon trade. And it's sure that with all this warfare goin' on, there'll be no lack of business for haulin' goods."

Just then, the drummers began tapping out "Assembly." Wend looked around and saw that the riflemen were beginning to gather at the center of the square. Lieutenant Humphreys was ushering them into formation.

Morgan looked around at the crowd and his men forming up. He sighed and said, "Well, now all we got to do is listen to another round of speechifying by these politicians, and then we can git on the road."

Wend and Peggy said their final goodbyes and then went to join the McDonalds and Woods at a spot across from where the riflemen now stood in a company front of two ranks. Morgan took his place in front of his men, and then the speeches Morgan had anticipated proceeded, accompanied by rounds of loud cheering from the crowd.

Wend looked over the company. Most of the men were veterans of border warfare. Many had been with Morgan during the prior year's war against the tribes in the Ohio Country, a war led by Governor Lord Dunmore. All but a few were wearing hunting shirts, but there was little uniformity in the cut or color of the garments. Below the long skirts of the shirts, some wore high leggings while others affected breeches with shorter leggings. All had broad-brimmed hats, most with the brim turned up on the side with a bucktail attached as decoration. Their packs were most often held by a single tumpline across their chest, but a few affected more traditional military-style packs with a strap over each shoulder. Besides their rifles, all carried long hunting knives in their belt or slung at their side. Their equipage was completed by various pouches on slings for ammunition and other necessary items and a powder horn. One thing about the company was uniform: all the men were lean, muscular, and tanned by long days in the sun and wind. Wend concluded that he had never seen a better band of border fighters.

Finally, the speeches were over. Morgan mounted his horse, and Humphreys ordered the company to step off. They paraded around the square, music being provided by the fifers and drummers who led the column. Wend had to admit their marching was ragged, with rifles at differing slopes and their step far from uniform. But then he reflected that no one expected parade-ground precision, and there was little doubt they would demonstrate that they knew their business as sharpshooters at Boston. Soon they were marching northward on Market Street. Behind, a private led a small string of packhorses that carried a supply of provisions. The crowd roared a send-off, with young boys running alongside the company. As they reached the corner where Piccadilly Street crossed Market, the fifes and drums turned aside, and the company continued northward on the Great Wagon Road past Fort Loudoun and the scattered buildings on the outskirts of the town.

Wend watched as the column faded into the distance. Once the drums ceased beating, the men abandoned marching in step and settled into the easy, swinging stride of border hunters accustomed to covering long miles every day. He could see them moving their rifles into comfortable carry positions in the crook of an arm or holding them at the trail in one hand. At one point, Morgan turned around in the saddle and called out something to the company, and Wend thought he saw a ripple of laughter pass along the line. In another minute, the shimmering heat waves blurred the shapes of the men, and a few seconds later the column disappeared behind the tree line of a bend in the road.

For a moment, just as the company went out of sight, the crowd that had been so raucous stood still and became unnaturally quiet. But that pause lasted only a few brief seconds, and then everyone returned to the business of visiting merchants' booths or heading for their wagons—or one of the town's taverns.

Peggy turned to Wend and said, "Abbey, Anne, Jean, and I are going to have refreshments and cool off at the Golden Buck while you men have your meeting. Don't take too long. We need to get back in time to put dinner on the table."

—⁊⁊—

The meeting took place in a back room at the Golden Buck. Everyone had a drink at hand—ale, rum, or whiskey. Wend nursed a small whiskey and looked at the members of the committee. Wood sat at the head of the table, with the letter that was the subject of the meeting in front of him. Thruston was on his right, and Rutledge, now having sobered up somewhat, was sitting on his left and dabbing his forehead with a handkerchief. Angus McDonald had set his drink down beside Rutledge but was actually leaning against the wall near the fireplace, lighted pipe in hand. Sheriff Smith was seated further down the table, across from Wend.

Wood took a sip of his drink, then picked up the sheet of paper. "The Committee of Safety in Williamsburg says a new regiment of foot is about to be recruited and wants the muskets you've got, Wend, for part of their armament."

Wend was a bit cranky and anxious to get home. And well aware that he would have to bring up some contentious matters. His answer reflected those feelings. "James, how the *devil* did Williamsburg find out that we had the muskets? Did Dunmore leave some government papers behind when he fled to that warship?"

Wood was silent a moment, looking around the room. Then he said slowly, "Actually, Wend, I told them. I thought they should know about what is obviously a major military asset."

Wend shot a look at Angus, then at Rutledge. "My understanding, James, was that we were saving them for use by our own militia, in the case we needed to field a battalion for protection."

Wood nodded. "I'm aware that we had contemplated that, but the fact is this new regiment is intended to help fight Dunmore's growing force. We must consider that the greater good for us—and Virginia on the whole—is to see him driven out." He paused and then looked around the table. "And once that is accomplished, Virginia's governing body plans to offer the regiment to Congress for use in Washington's army."

Wend's hackles were getting up, and he said in a voice louder than he had intended, "So, let us be clear. Despite a decision made by the Winchester committee, you took it upon yourself to inform the central committee about the muskets, without consultation with the rest of this group?" He motioned to the other men.

"Look, Eckert, I had to make a quick decision in the middle of an important discussion that was in progress." Wood was not used to being contradicted, and his tone was now getting defensive. "And it is becoming clear there is no imminent threat to Frederick County from Dunmore's forces."

Angus intervened. "Now, gentlemen, let us calm down. The first question, which is more relevant, is whether the muskets are in condition to ship. Perhaps we are arguing about the wrong point." He turned to Eckert. "Wend, what progress have you made in getting them ready for use?"

Wend looked around the room. "The situation is this: early in the year, I received two lots of fifty each, which were sent up from Williamsburg before the rebellion began. They were to be shortened and reconditioned under my contract in the same way I have done to hundreds of others in the past. Now these were among the last that were in possession of Dunmore's government, and they were in the poorest condition of all that we received over the years. I have completed work on the first lot, and they are ready to distribute in any way you decide. I have completed the work on the muskets of the second batch, as far as the weapons themselves. However, they came up without bayonets or cartridge boxes. I have contracted, months ago, with Zane's Ironworks for new bayonets, but they haven't been delivered. I also contracted with a leather tradesman, James Hauck, for the cartridge boxes, which also haven't been produced. Thus I don't consider the second lot ready in any way to ship."

Thruston wrinkled his brow. "But all the muskets themselves are ready for use? They could be fired?"

"Yes, Reverend, they could be fired. But they aren't ready for use in combat, primarily because of the lack of bayonets. I won't ship a weapon unless it is a complete stand of arms, which includes the bayonet."

The minister shrugged. "Is the bayonet so important? We just sent a hundred rifleman off to Boston without bayonets. But each one had a great hunting knife. Isn't that the same?"

"Riflemen are light infantry and sharpshooters. They aren't intended to stand up to regular foot soldiers. And in any case, the rifle can't accommodate a bayonet. Moreover, because of their lightness of construction, using them with a bayonet or as a club in close combat would likely destroy their alignment." Wend thought a moment. "My experience is that a soldier of the line is not ready for combat unless he has a bayonet."

Thruston looked bemused and then continued to press his point. "But still, if the firelock can be fired, isn't that the most important thing?"

Rutledge shrugged. "Now Wend, aren't you cutting things a little fine? Surely this is about a minor detail."

Wend gritted his teeth and looked around the room. "Gentlemen, you know I fought as a scout with Bouquet at Bushy Run."

Everyone nodded.

Wend gathered his thoughts, then said, "Well, on the first day, when the tribes ambushed us from a high hill in front of the column, they rained vicious rifle and musket fire on us. Bouquet's soldiers returned the fire. But it was only when they assaulted with the bayonet that the warriors were driven off the hill, allowing us to take up positions to defend the convoy of supplies for Fort Pitt. Then, on the second day, the charge that actually drove the Indians from the field was primarily based on the bayonet. The warriors tried to stand up against the Highlanders but found that with tomahawks and knives, they were no match for bayoneted muskets. Many died learning that lesson, and the rest flew in panic from the field."

Angus spoke up. "Gentlemen, let me speak in support of Wend. Now, you know that I fought against the king's army at Cullodon thirty years ago now. We learned on that field, to our great regret, the lesson Eckert is explaining. We advanced with a varied collection of firelocks—mostly pistols—and had great faith in our long broadswords. But when we actually got within close quarters of the British infantry, we realized our fatal mistake. The reach of a musket with a bayonet attached was greater than that of a Highlander with his sword. The British had been trained to wait until we raised our sword arm, then drive their bayonet into our sides. The result was devastating. Many of my clansmen died from such a mortal wound."

There was a silence around the room, broken by Wend. "I will tell you now that some of our citizens and I are alive now because of the bayonet. You are aware that last year I was part of a mission to a village called Hart's Store, which had been destroyed by a war party of Mingoes and Shawnees."

Smith nodded. "Everyone knows you were ambushed while escorting women and children to Wheeling Island and made a gallant fight to drive off the savages."

"Yes, we were caught in a crossfire between warriors ensconced on two hillocks. My force was a detachment from James's company."

Wood nodded. "Yes, you had Sergeant Calvert's squad."

"Yes, but the point was, we were outnumbered, and if we had stayed where we were and tried to shoot it out with the war party, we'd all be in our graves now. But because Calvert's men had bayoneted muskets, we were able to charge and drive the main body of Indians off their hill."

Wend stared at each of the men in turn. "Gentleman, what I have learned is that decision in battle most often comes down to the use of the bayonet—or the threat of its use. So I will not send muskets out without them."

Thruston sighed in resignation. "All right, let us concede the point. We will not ship the muskets until the bayonets and cartridge boxes are delivered to you."

Wend turned to Wood. "James, I have requested those items from the tradesmen several times. I believe it is time for members of the committee to build a fire under Zane and Hauck."

"All right. We'll do that." He thought a minute and then asked, "But let us be clear: Once those are delivered, there is nothing to keep you from shipping the muskets immediately?"

Wend gave Wood a hard look. "Yes, there is one other *very* important matter that must be addressed."

The politician looked puzzled. "One more thing? Pray, what would that be?"

Thruston added, "Yes, we have agreed with you on everything you have brought up."

Wend set his most steely-eyed look. "There is the matter of *payment* to me."

There was a sudden silence around the room, broken finally by Wood clearing his throat. "Wend, we told you last spring we would work out payment when things became clearer."

"Yes, you told me that. And that was in early May. Now it is July— over two months later. I have personally borne the cost of rebuilding these muskets. I received payment from the royal government for the first lot in the form of a bill of credit, the normal method over the years. But immediately afterward, the insurrection began, and Dunmore and his government fled Williamsburg. So the credit became worthless. Based on the word of you gentlemen, I proceeded with the work on the second batch, but I have yet to receive one pound of payment."

Thruston stammered out, "Well, well, uh, Wend, in this time of travail, need I point out that we all have to make sacrifices for the cause."

Rutledge spoke up. "Yes, indeed, Wend, what the reverend says is true. And certainly once things become clear, we will find a way to recompense you for your efforts."

Wend stared directly at Wood, but what he said was meant for all in the room. "Sacrifice? A word easy to say, but considerably more difficult to bear if you are the one called on to sacrifice. Let me point out that I am a simple tradesman and farmer. I have a mere two hundred acres—a tiny fraction of the land and resources each of you possesses—yet I must support upward of twenty-five souls. But now I am the one being told to make a noble sacrifice." He smacked his hand down on the table. "And let me remind you that at your request, I have also begun fabrication of new muskets. I have fifty stocks already carved out, waiting for locks and barrels, also at my sole expense to date."

Wood's face reddened, and he raised his hands. "Wend, my dear Wend, we recognize and appreciate what you have done, but you must be patient."

"Patient? Well, if *patience* is the word of the day, it will damn well have to be shared among us. Let me make this clear—the muskets are in my possession, and there they will stay until the Winchester Committee of Safety finds a way to provide some form of payment. And I don't care whose pocket it comes from."

James Wood sighed and looked down at his hands. "All right, Wend, we will pursue this matter with diligence and urgency."

Wend looked up at McDonald, who was still standing by the hearth, and thought he saw a glint of amusement in his eyes at Wood's discomfiture.

—⚅—

The sun was well down in the west, and the shadows were lengthening as Boots pulled the chaise eastward on the road toward Battletown Crossroads.

Peggy held Wend's arm and snuggled close to his side, her cheek on his shoulder. "So they agreed to make payment?"

"Yes, in the end that was the sense of the meeting. In any case, I had to be rather forceful and adamantly assert that I would not release the muskets until they found a way to pay."

"Well, I'm proud that you stood up to them."

"I can tell you that they weren't happy. There were a lot of irritated faces around the table when the meeting ended. They were contemplating having to take money out of their own pockets. Wood was particularly unhappy."

"James especially unhappy? Why so, Wend?"

"James Wood is a fine man; he's a competent soldier, and he runs a well-managed estate. But he's first and foremost a *politician*. Politicians like to make rousing speeches. They enjoy making promises that don't have to be kept and are very happy to perform easy favors for people. However, they decidedly don't like to have to do hard things or force people to take uncomfortable actions. Now Wood doesn't like the idea that he's going to have to go around Winchester and compel people to contribute money to pay us."

Wend guided Boots around some ruts, then said, "You should understand that I was rather direct and rough with James. I suspect he will be rather cool to us, at least in the near term."

"Oh, dear. I hope that doesn't sour things with Jean. I do so enjoy her company."

Wend looked over at his wife, her beautiful face now wrinkled in concern. "Well, my dear, you can't have it both ways. You were insistent that I demand payment for our work. I did so, and now there may be consequences. Let us never forget that James is the son of the founder of Winchester and the most influential man in Frederick County."

Peggy bit her lip. "I won't let this hurt our standing with the Woods. I'll make special efforts to court favor with Jean. She's relatively new in town, and up 'til now I've been her best friend. I shall cultivate that friendship."

"I wish you success in that effort. We don't want to be on the wrong side of the Woods."

Peggy tossed her head and responded, "Let's put this out of our minds for the moment. Now that the sun is low, it's cool and very pleasant. Give me the reins. I want to let Boots out."

Wend did as she asked, and his wife slapped the reins down hard on the horse's back, bringing him up to a fast trot. He looked over and saw her eyes gleaming and her face flushed with pleasure at the joy of speeding along the road.

At least for the moment, Peggy Eckert was a happy woman.

Chapter Two

THE FIRELOCK PLANTATION

It was a bright, sunny morning in early September as Wend, Joshua, and the lead hand, Jacob Specht, rode southward down the wagon track that passed Widow Callow's farm. Wend and Jacob were intent on checking the status of the crops in the widow's fields, which had been rented to help supply various types of grain for whiskey production. Joshua was along mainly to get away from the farm and the list of projects that Alice had made up for him.

After a pleasant ride of twenty minutes, they rounded a bend and the widow's farmstead, consisting of a well-built wooden house, stable, and assorted outbuildings came into sight. They had already passed some of the fields, and it was evident that the wheat and rye were ready for harvesting.

Wend and Specht were discussing the number of men and wagons that would be needed when Baird interrupted. "Take a look at the widow's house. Somethin's toward." He pulled up his horse, and the others followed suit.

Specht said, "He's right, Mr. Eckert. There's five men there, all armed. And look at that—the widow's standin' there at the door with a firelock in her hand and her black—that man Selby—is beside her, and he's got what looks like a musket."

Wend nodded. "It's some sort of confrontation." He took stock for a moment. All three of them were armed with pistols, so they were capable of intervening. "All right. They haven't seen us yet. I'll ride on in as if on normal business and find out what's going on. You two ride through the fields and come up behind the outbuildings. Get into position to cover those men if it comes to that."

Joshua grinned and said, "Easy enough, Wend." He motioned to Specht. "Come 'long Jacob. We'll work our way into place."

Wend sat his horse on the road while the other two rode through a patch of trees that would cover most of their approach to the farm buildings. As he waited, he pulled his pistols from their saddle holsters and slipped them into his belt. Then he trotted his horse right into the widow's yard and past the men, who turned in surprise. His immediate intent was to keep them distracted while his compatriots moved into position. He swung to the ground just below where the widow and her servant stood on the front steps, then doffed his hat to the widow. "Hello, Mrs. Callow. I just came by to check on the crops. I hope I'm not disturbing your business here."

"Wend Eckert, this is business I'm mighty glad for you to disturb. These here men aim to chase me out of my holdings."

Wend got his first good look at the men. One—apparently their leader—stood on the ground holding the reins of his horse. He was tall and burly, and he sported a full beard of reddish brown hair. He wore a curious mismatch of clothing—a black coat that had been converted into a jacket by cutting off the tails, a green pair of breeches, and a brown floppy hat with the brim down over his eyes. Wend looked up at his four mates, all of whom had remained mounted. They were all dressed in similarly scruffy clothing and armed, three with nondescript long-barreled firelocks, the fourth that Wend thought might be an old dragoon carbine. Eckert said, "Chase you out? By what authority?"

The leader spoke up in a loud voice. "We be here from the Frederick County Militia, and we aim to confiscate this here farm on account of they be a nest of Loyalists."

Wend smiled at the men. "Now that's very interesting. It happens that I am Lieutenant Eckert, quartermaster of Major Angus McDonald's battalion of the militia. And I can't recall seeing any of you at musters. Whose company are you in? Who is your captain?" He motioned to the leader. "And who am I talking to?"

"My name be Carlin. And you know that every able-bodied man is part of the county militia. Don't need to be part of a company to do our duty."

Wend put his right hand on one of the pistols. "Ah, I see. So, Mr. Carlin, you have declared yourself to be on a mission for the militia in general?"

"You could rightly say that."

"And what makes you think Mrs. Callow here is a Royalist and too dangerous to remain in her farmstead?"

"Everyone knows her husband was a Redcoat officer. The captain of a company of British soldiers. What else would she be?"

"Her husband was indeed the captain of an independent company in the Carolinas. They manned forts and fought war parties that raided settlers. In other words, they protected people like you and me, Mr. Carlin. And most of the men in that company were colonists, just like us." He turned to the widow. "Isn't that correct, Mrs. Callow?"

"It certainly is. Many were Ulster-Scot, just like a lot of the people around here."

Wend nodded. "And the captain left the British Army more than ten years ago, after the war with the French, and the two of you came up here and settled this farm." He smiled at the lady. "Just a year or two before I started my place."

Mrs. Callow grinned. "I remember when you and that pretty wife of yours took up that land just to the north, sure enough."

"And you certainly helped us many a time as we were getting started."

"It was the neighborly thing to do. I remember when everybody got together to raise that first cabin of yours—the one that's now your cookhouse. My man and Dan Morgan and that rogue Joshua Baird got drunk as skunks that evening." She shook her head. "Damned if I didn't have to drive the wagon home that night while the captain slept beside me."

"Yes, that was a great day."

Carlin scowled. "All that don't make no difference. We say she's on the governor's side, and I'll wager she's spyin' on us and sendin' messages down to them Tories in the tidewater."

Wend looked up at the man. "That's foolishness. She's minding her own business, tending her farm, just like the rest of us around here."

Carlin gritted his teeth. "Now listen. We're here to do the business of the Patriot cause. And we intend to carry through." He moved his firelock into a more menacing position.

Wend shook his head. "What you mean is you intend to use the fact that her husband was British to steal her property. And where do you suggest Mrs. Callow go once you take her place?"

"Ain't no worry of ours. Serves her right for not supporting the cause."

"Well, Carlin, this is damned foolishness and you know it. I suggest—no, I insist—that you and you friends get on your way."

"Eckert, those are mighty brave words. There be five of us, and all I see standin' there is just you, an old woman, and a black, who shouldn't be holdin' no firelock in the first place. The truth be, the widow needs to gather up a few things, and then we intend to take over the place."

Wend smiled. "Not so quick, Carlin. I suggest you look to your left, toward the hay barn."

Joshua stepped out from behind the building, both pistols in his hands.

Then Wend said, "Now take a look to your right."

A grim-faced Specht appeared from behind a wagon shed, pulled his pistols from his belt, and cocked them.

"So, Mr. Carlin, the way I see it, we have three armed persons in front of you and one on each side." He looked at Mrs. Callow. "Now I'm sure your husband would have a military description for that?"

"You're right, Wend. He'd say we got them flanked on both sides. It comes to shooting, they'll be in a crossfire."

"The very words I was thinking of, Mrs. Callow." He looked up at Carlin and simultaneously pulled his pistols from his belt. "Not to mention, sir, that four of you are mounted and make superb targets."

One of the mounted men said, "He's right, Taddy. They got us in a bad position."

Wend said, "Anyone know these men?"

The widow said, "I never seen them before in my life."

Specht called out, "I seen two of them before. It was at that tavern down by Keyes Ferry."

Wend grinned. "Jacob, what are you doing at a place like that? A man could get in trouble down there."

"There's a special good-lookin' tavern girl, Mr. Eckert. I been tryin' to pass some time with her."

"Like I said, you're courting trouble."

Baird laughed loudly. "Wend, if anyone should know that, it be you."

Eckert shot a look at Joshua but then asked Specht, "Now, Jacob, what do you know about these men?"

"The one on the ground is Taddy Carlin. And the one who just spoke out from his horse is called Johnny, and he's Taddy's brother." He waved a pistol in the direction of the river. "They took over the old Pettigrew place last year, Mr. Eckert."

Wend nodded. "That's swampy land close to the river. Terrible place for crops—gets washed out all the time. Nobody's ever been able to last down there."

The widow spoke up. "Now I say there's the real reason they want my place."

"Undoubtedly, Mrs. Callow." Wend pointed a pistol directly at Taddy. "Now listen carefully: you get out of here, Carlin. And mark my words: if anything at all happens to Mrs. Callow or her place here, I'm holding you responsible. I won't ask any questions about who did it. I'll just get men from my farm and come down to the river and burn you and yours out. I'll put you out onto the road just like you wanted to do with this woman."

Joshua walked toward the five men, pistols aimed. "You heard him. Now it's time for you to get!"

Taddy Carlin slowly backed up to his horse and mounted. "I ain't forgettin' this, Eckert. It ain't over. You made yourself an enemy you don't want to have."

Wend responded in a hard tone, "Just remember what I said, Carlin."

Carlin spoke no more, simply mounting and riding out to the road, followed by his compatriots. They headed northward along the wagon track.

The widow leaned her fowling piece against the door and said, "Bless you, Wend Eckert, for coming along when you did."

Wend grinned. "Well, it looked to me like you and Selby were holding your own, but maybe we tipped things a little bit more in your favor."

"Indeed, you did."

Wend looked at the firelock in the black man's hand. "Selby, I'll be damned if that isn't an old Doglock musket."

The widow answered. "You know it is, Wend. My husband's had that for near fifty years now. But it shoots as well as it ever did."

Wend took the musket in his hands and examined it. "Well, it's been well kept, that's for sure, and a man is just as dead from its ball as from a newer Tower Musket like we use now." Wend thought a moment. "Now, Mrs. Callow, as soon as I get back to my farm, I'll send a rider in to Winchester to tell Sheriff Smith what happened here today and who they were. And Jacob, with a crew of my hands, will be here early tomorrow to start harvesting the grain in your fields. And they'll all be armed. So you don't have to worry about that rabble trying to come back."

"Thank you, Wend Eckert. The craziness that is goin' these days is somethin' to behold. But the captain and I settled this place near enough fifteen years ago, and he's buried on this land. There ain't nothin' or nobody who is goin' to separate me from this place, 'cept the Lord callin' my soul home, and by God, when he does that, these old bones are goin' to stay right here beside my man's."

"Pray, Mrs. Callow, that won't be for a long time."

Widow Callow smiled warmly. "I'll agree with that sentiment. I loved my man, but I'm not in any hurry to join him." Then she stopped and reflected a moment. "But now I worry you have made yourself a gang of enemies, Wend. I see no good in those men."

"You know, Mrs. Callow, I think they're basically cowards. I doubt we'll see more of them around here."

—⁓—

Darkness had finally settled in over Eckert Ridge, and Liza had just come around to light the candles in the sitting room. A low fire, barely above embers, flickered in the hearth.

Wend opened the cabinet where he kept the liquor and poured a second glass of whiskey for himself and a first glass for Peggy. He put one on the side table beside the comfortable chair he liked to use and one beside the settee where he expected his wife to sit when she came down from settling the children in for the night.

He settled into his chair to await Peggy's descent from the upper floor. But almost instantly he heard the sound of hoofs coming up the front drive at the gallop. Sighing, Wend rose and went out into the hall, opened the front door, and walked out onto the covered porch. As expected, it was Hardt, the man whom Jacob Specht had sent riding into Winchester to advise Sheriff Smith of the events at Widow Callow's place earlier that day.

The farmhand pulled up in front of the porch steps and dismounted. Holding the reins, he looked up at Wend. "Mr. Eckert, sir, I found the sheriff, just like Specht told me to. He was at the Golden Buck."

Wend laughed. "That's the first place I would have looked."

"I told him 'bout what happened down at the widow's place."

"So what did he say?"

"He's going to send some of his riders down to the Pettigrew place tomorrow to check on those men you had words with, sir. He don't think they're supposed to be there, 'cause he ain't heard anything about that land changing hands. And he'll make sure they don't take it upon themselves to hassle people at their farms."

Wend nodded. "That's good, Hardt."

"And there's more news, Mr. Eckert."

"Yes? What would that be?"

"Sheriff Smith told me that some members of the Committee of Safety would be coming out here two days hence, sir, in the forenoon. They want to check on your progress with the muskets and discuss some other business with you."

"Did he say who would be coming?"

"Mr. Wood and Mr. Rutledge and some others. That's all he said, sir."

"All right, Hardt. Thank you. Take care of your horse and get some supper at the barracks. And get some good rest tonight. You're going to have a long day in the fields down at the widow's tomorrow."

"Yes, sir, Mr. Eckert."

Wend slowly walked back to the sitting room, mulling what he had heard from Hardt. Then, as he was about to sit down again, he heard Peggy's soft steps and rustling petticoats as she descended the stairs. Momentarily, she appeared at the door, and then, in a way only she could, swept into the room and took her seat by the whiskey.

Wend reflected that it was an effect she had perfected years ago when acting as a serving maid at her father's tavern in Sherman Valley, Pennsylvania. Then, she knew every eye would be on her and the beauty that made her one of the most remarked women in the Cumberland Valley. He smiled to himself. And now, when she made entrances at affairs in Winchester, her fair-skinned, high-cheekboned face, raven hair, flashing blue eyes, robust bosom, and long graceful legs, tantalizingly evident below her skirts, turned many heads and drew the covert stares from men throughout the room.

Of course, none of her female friends or the infatuated men of Frederick County even guessed at the Eckerts' most guarded secret: in those days as a tavern maid, Peggy had succumbed to the promise of easy money and had become one of the most celebrated prostitutes of Pennsylvania's border country, known to virtually every peddler or other kind of traveling man. Many had made it their business to come to Sherman Valley to partake of her favors, usually in a corner of the tavern stable. Her price had been hard coin when she could get it or a pretty item of clothing or other payment in kind when she couldn't. Now, her history had become the Eckerts' deepest secret for if the gentry of the county became aware of it, the stigma would undoubtedly lead to the loss of friends and patrons of Wend's gunsmithing business and the new venture of whiskey distilling. Aside from Wend and Peggy, only Joshua, Alice, and Donegal had any idea of Peggy's past, and it was a subject never raised in their circle.

Peggy seated herself and picked up the whiskey. "I take it that was

Hardt?"

"Yes. He talked to Smith, who is going to send some of his men to check on the Carlin family."

"From what you told me, they're nothing but Ulster trash."

Wend took a sip and grinned at his wife. He said playfully, "I seem to recall we have a good deal of Ulster-Scot in our family. Our daughters are half Ulster, and Bernd, for reasons we both are aware, is fully Ulster."

"For God's sake, Wend, there's Ulster and then there's *Ulster*. My family settled in one place and made themselves a good life, becoming a valuable part of the village. There's no better kept tavern on the border than my father's. But there's a strain of Ulster people like those Carlins who never make good anywhere; they're always on the move, always looking for something better."

Wend said, "I could not but agree with that."

Then, after staring into her drink for a long moment, Peggy's face reddened, and she said in a serious tone, "Wend, why did you bring that up about Bernd? That was unnecessary."

Wend looked at his wife's face and the set of her mouth, and he realized he had without thinking stumbled into a sensitive area. Bernd, now eleven, had been fathered by Matt Bratton, Peggy's former lover and the Sherman Valley bully. He had ultimately proven to be a scoundrel involved in illegal trading with the Ohio tribes as part of an outlaw crew headed by the rich merchant Richard Grenough. Wend had settled his dispute with both men in a violent and permanent manner only a few months before. He said, "I meant nothing by that remark except to spark some humor about our family's heritage."

"Well, it reminded me of something I've been meaning to speak to you about. I've noticed that, ever since Johann arrived, you have been slighting Bernd, particularly over in the workshop. You've been giving that Indian boy more of your time."

Wend sighed. He thought this subject had been settled months ago.

"Now, my dear, you are very much aware that Johann is *not* an Indian boy. He is half German and half English." He paused a moment. "The fact that he was raised in a Mingo village because his mother was a captive doesn't make him an Indian, but it simply has given him some mannerisms that he learned by living among those people."

"All right, forgive me for being *imprecise*. But my point remains: you are favoring Abigail Gibson's child over Bernd." She took a deep sip of whiskey. "Just because that woman grew up in the drawing rooms of Philadelphia society doesn't make her son any more valuable than Bernd."

"Peggy, I would say that Abigail's privileged youth has been paid for by fifteen years of hard living in a Mingo village. I've seen the sunbaked lines on her face and the scars on her hands from working in the fields and wielding the skinning knife. And the white teeth she once had have been yellowed by chewing on hides to soften them." He paused a moment, then continued, "And if I've been giving more attention to Johann, it's because the only time I've ever had with my first son is the few months since he came back with me from his mother's village in the Ohio Country last year. I've had ten years with Bernd, and you know I have great feeling for him. But mostly, I'm giving Johann more time because he is older. He's fifteen now and needs to make up for lost time in learning his trade. Bernd has many more years for that."

Peggy drained her whiskey. Then she raised her glass to Wend for another. He complied and brought the recharged glass to her.

"All right, Wend, I understand what you are saying about Johann. But promise me one thing—you'll make time to pay special attention to Bernd to make sure he doesn't feel slighted."

"Of course, Peggy. I'll take special care." He looked over at his wife. "And keep in mind, Johann and Bernd have, in just a few months, become close friends." He said very carefully, "I think it is not too much to say that they are handling things better than we."

Peggy looked at Wend for a long time, then took another sizable taste of her drink. Afterward, she changed the subject. "There's something I've forgotten to mention, which is related to your confrontation with these Carlin people. On the day when Daniel and his company left, while we women were having refreshments and you were meeting with the committee, Jean Wood mentioned to me that there had been a similar but more violent incident down in the southern part of the county toward Stephensburg."

"What happened? So-called Patriots giving Loyalists trouble?"

"I would call it more than trouble. Someone burned down the Silcotts' house when they were away. And they left a message nailed to a tree: 'Tories must get out.'"

"My God, George is a good man and a good customer. He bought a fowling piece from me two years ago." He shrugged. "But I can't deny he has been very outspoken that there is no authority for what is going on and didn't mind bespeaking his loyalty to the king and the governor." He shook his head. "But he's taken no action to support the governor, and in any case, it was simply criminal to burn them out."

"Jean says the family has cleaned out part of the stable and that they are living there while they rebuild."

"And I suppose Smith has no idea who did it?"

"Jean didn't think so."

Wend took a sip and thought for a moment. "You know, Silcott is right about the matter of authority. We have thrown out Dunmore and his government. We are in defiance of the king. What now is the basis of our laws and structure of government? Remember Rutledge's intoxicated questioning about what we are fighting about—independence or simply our rights under the king? It is all of a piece."

Peggy shrugged. "The Committees of Safety are the government now. They make the decisions."

"But don't you see? There is no central document or charter guiding them. There is no governor and these committees have appointed themselves. They decide affairs under their own rules based on what they are thinking at the moment. And each committee, in each county or town, has its own policies."

"But Wend," answered Peggy, "what about the Virginia Convention? Aren't they working to draft the basis of a new government?"

"Yes, that's true. But as of now, they've produced nothing definitive. So what I said about no foundation for government is accurate."

"I hadn't thought of that." She shrugged. "But things do seem to be working out just as before."

"When I was confronting those men at Mrs. Callow's place, something came up that I have been reflecting on. Carlin claimed that he and his men were part of the militia. That was patently not true, but in reality, who is to contradict them now?"

"Wend, I'm not sure what you are getting at."

"Think on this: Sheriff Smith and the county lieutenant, Rutledge, who manages the militia, received their authority from the governor. So, too, did our judges. Now all that has gone by the board."

Peggy cocked her head. "I'm beginning to see your meaning."

Wend walked over to his writing desk and, opening a drawer, pulled out a sheet of paper. He took it over to where his wife sat. "Do you recognize this?"

"Why, it's your commission as a lieutenant in the militia."

"And who signed it?"

"Lord Dunmore, of course. You were directly appointed by him last year to serve in the war against the Ohio Indians." Then it hit her, and she opened her mouth wide in shock. "My God, it has no more validity, unless we recognize the royal government."

"Precisely, my dear. The truth is, at the moment, we recognize the authority of the sheriff, the county lieutenant, the judges, and our militia to act in their capacities only by force of habit and our consent, but there is no longer an underlying legal basis. And at some level our friend Taddy

Carlin realizes that—he has as much right to call himself and his crew a militia as that which is organized by Rutledge."

Peggy shook her head. "Good Lord, this opens the door to...to..." She wrinkled her face in puzzlement as she sought the right word. Finally she had it: "Why, it opens the gate to *chaos*."

Wend sighed and nodded. "That is precisely the right word. And we shall have more and more of it, more incidents like at Widow Callow's and the Silcotts'. There will be more and more people like Carlin who will realize they can take the law into their own hands for their own purposes. He who has the most strength at a particular place or time will rule. And that will pertain until Virginia forms some basis in the law for its government."

—∞—

It was midmorning two days later, and the workshop was noisy and full of wood dust when the members of the Committee of Safety arrived at Eckert Ridge. Wend, at his bench, worked on a gentleman's fowling piece that Gerson's store in Alexandria had ordered. Around him the shop crew—journeyman Wilhelm Hecht and the apprentices—were busy working on muskets. The exception was Horner, who was focused on another order from Alexandria, a set of horse pistols.

Bernd, who had just taken some trash out, came running into the shop. "Father, there are people coming up the drive."

Wend walked out to look down the hill and saw four riders followed by a wagon. He quickly noted that the horsemen were Smith, Wood, Rutledge, and McDonald. In the wagon seat were a black driver and Reverend Thruston. Wend took off his apron and handed it to Bernd. "Here, son, take this back to my bench and then run over to the house and tell your mother we'll be having five for the midday meal."

Wend greeted the men as they dismounted and tied their horses to the hitching rack in front of the shop.

Rutledge looked around and remarked, "This is the first time I've been out here. You have quite an establishment, Eckert. More than I anticipated. It's like a small village."

"Well, David, you have to remember there are two farms here and five families, plus our apprentices and farmhands." Wend took in the buildings with a motion of his hand. "As you can see, the drive continues along the crest of the ridge. Generally, my two hundred acres is to the north, and Donegal's land is to the south."

Rutledge nodded. "So that wooden house across from us is yours?"

"Yes, we built that about six years ago. Behind it is the place we built when we first arrived, a log cabin that now serves as the cookhouse and the residence of our house servants."

Rutledge looked around. "What's that rather unusual long building just south of the drive?"

Wend smiled. "We call that the 'barracks.' The far side is the home for our apprentices and field hands. The near end are the rooms where Donegal has lived for the last ten years." He paused and pointed to the south. "But his new house, you can see, is almost finished. You can rest assured that his bride can hardly wait."

"I should think so." He pointed down the drive. What are the other two houses?"

"The one just on the other side of the barracks is for my journeyman, Hecht, and his family."

"So the one at the very end is Baird's place?"

"Yes, his and his wife, Alice's. We have a lot of children here on the ridge, and she serves as the teacher."

Rutledge looked around, a puzzled expression on his face. "Where are the cabins for your blacks?"

"David, the only blacks we have here are my house servants, the family of Albert, and as I said, they live in the cookhouse. I bought them as slaves from an estate, and James got them freed by action of the Burgesses, based on Albert's long service to his former master."

"But what about your field help; don't tell me you have paid men for all your work. How could that be economical?"

"Since we raise mostly grain, not tobacco, our need for hands is more modest than most farms. Most of my people are redemptioners, working off their passage to America. That way I support their living needs rather than paying wages." He paused and continued, "Some stay here after they have paid for their passage. My apprentice, Andrew Horner, and the lead farmhand, Jacob Specht, are two such." He paused a moment. "And when we need more men, such as during harvest, we put on day laborers."

Wood spoke up. "David, you might be interested in the distillery. It's over there near Donegal's house."

"Ah, yes, I see. And what's that large building beyond the distillery?"

Wend answered, "That's the warehouse for the whiskey barrels. We just put that up in the last couple of months—since we stepped up production."

Wood motioned toward the wagon. "Speaking of production, we've got something you've been asking for: the cartridge boxes from Hauck's leatherworks."

Thruston interjected, "And there's more good news. Zane has promised to deliver the bayonets you spoke of within the next week."

Wend shot the minister a look of doubt. "He's told me delivery was imminent before. I'll believe it when I have them in hand."

Wood shook his head. "No, Eckert. This time he means it. We were over at his works two days ago and saw some actual bayonets in the process of being forged. He's finishing them now."

Wend grinned. "Well, in any case, the proof will be in the delivery. I shall be very satisfied when they are in hand." He waved his hand toward the gunsmith shop. "Gentlemen, come on in to the shop. You'll find we've expanded it to facilitate production of the new muskets."

—ⁿⁿ—

With the meal concluded, Wend and his guests adjourned to the sitting room, where he served drinks around.

While he was doing so, Smith cleared his throat and said, "Eckert, I don't think you'll see anything more of the Carlin brothers around here."

"I sincerely hope not."

"After your man Hardt told me the story, I checked on the status of the Pettigrew place. The records show that the property is still owned by the Pettigrews, even though they've moved to the west. They've paid their taxes on it."

Wend thought a second, then said, "That means the Carlins are squatting there illegally. Am I not correct?"

"They were, indeed, but yesterday I went down there with several men and sent them on their way—the two brothers and a very shabbily dressed woman who purported to be the wife of Johnny. They were last seen near Ashbys Ferry, and if they crossed, they'll be out of the county."

Wood said, "The sheriff told us about the trouble you had down at Widow Callow's place with those people. But this isn't completely isolated. Have you heard what happened to the Silcotts?"

"Yes, my wife informed me. A regrettable situation."

James shook his head. "We cannot allow this to get out of hand. Ne'er-do-wells trying to take advantage of this unrest and uncertainty. For God's sake, I've known the Silcotts since I was a child."

Thruston added, "And Mrs. Callow—dear Lord, there is no more upstanding woman in the county. Despite the distance, she comes to my church every proper day of worship, weather and the roads permitting."

There was a round of agreement, followed by a long moment of quiet as the men imbibed their drinks to their own thoughts.

Then Wood cleared his throat and said, "Wend, we have some business to transact."

"I didn't expect you had ridden down here just to look around the shop and have dinner."

"As you are aware, the Williamsburg Committee of Safety has ordered the formation of a new regiment. I've just received correspondence that they've appointed Patrick Henry as the colonel."

The name struck a chord with Wend. "I seem to have heard that name somewhere, but I can't particularly place it."

Wood responded, "He's a lawyer from Hanover County. I know him from my time in Burgesses. He's represented defendants in a couple of high-visibility cases, and he's been in and out of the Continental Congress over the last two years. His particular claim to fame—and probably why you know of him—is a fiery speech he made back in March at the Virginia Convention down at Richmond. It was in the *Gazette*."

"Ah, yes, now I remember." Wend looked around and said, "Something about 'Give me liberty or give me death.' Rather extreme sentiments."

David Rutledge smiled and said, "And back in April, when Dunmore seized the powder at the Williamsburg magazine, he rounded up a band of armed ruffians to march on the capital. They were still on the road when Dunmore agreed to send the powder back, but Henry claimed credit for influencing the decision."

Wood nodded his head. "The important point is that now he's been made commander of this First Virginia Regiment. He's planning to start recruiting in October at Culpeper, and then he's going to march down to Williamsburg to finish recruiting and formally establish the regiment."

Wend raised his eyebrows. "I'm beginning to see how this affects us."

Wood nodded. "Yes, Williamsburg wants us to send as many muskets as possible to Henry in Culpeper. And Wend, we have agreed to do so."

Wend sighed and said more forcefully than he had intended, "Now *look*, gentlemen. I told you what must happen before I release them. No amount of cajoling on your part will do it."

Wood, Smith, and Rutledge looked at Thruston. The reverend put his drink down and reached into his pocket. "Yes, Wend, we quite understood what you said at the Golden Buck, and we are sympathetic to your position." He held out a leather coin purse. "Here is a sum that we hope will satisfy your immediate needs."

Wend took the purse and emptied a substantial pile of coins into his palm. Calculating quickly, he said, "As a rough estimate, this covers my expenses, but it provides very little above that. Not much support for my family."

Wood said, "That sum was contributed by members of the committee and other local citizens of means in the county. They want Williamsburg to understand we are doing our part. Accept my word that it was the best that could be managed in these difficult times." He looked around at the other members of the committee and took a piece of paper from his pocket and handed it to Wend. "Eckert, this is a letter from the Frederick Committee to the Virginia Committee of Safety explaining what you have done and supporting any claim you make on them for additional recompense. It may ultimately help you when Williamsburg secures some level of funding."

Wend thought rapidly and almost immediately recognized that he was seeing the best deal the committee could offer. He placed the bag of coins and letter in a drawer of his writing desk and said, "All right, gentlemen, I accept. I will prepare the lot of one hundred muskets for shipment as soon as the bayonets are received from Zane's Iron Plantation." He looked around and continued, "I'll contact Abbey Morgan to arrange shipping down to the First Regiment at Culpeper."

The four members of the committee looked at each other, and then Wood spoke up. "Actually, Eckert, as part of the arrangement, we are requesting that you personally take the muskets down to Culpeper with enough of an escort to make sure they are safely delivered. We know that was your policy when you were working for the governor."

"I fail to see why that is necessary. Morgan's foreman, Jake Cather, is as hard a man as you can find. He and his drivers always carry firelocks and should be enough to secure the arms."

Smith shook his head. "We don't agree. There is more lawlessness in the countryside than you understand. Witness the events at the Callow and Silcott farms. I assure you that those events are not isolated. I've got letters from other sheriffs saying that there are armed bands afoot on the roads, trying to take advantage of the unsettled times. It is essential that an adequately armed escort accompany a valuable shipment of this nature."

Wood smiled warmly at Wend. "Now, my dear Eckert, there is another reason I believe you should accompany this shipment. It will afford you the opportunity to become acquainted with Henry. As I read the trend of events, I believe the man is likely to rise in the government of Virginia, and being known to him may serve you well in the future. It particularly may assist you in getting payment based on that letter we have given you."

Angus raised a finger. "And then there's the new muskets you are making. It may do you well with the government of Virginia to have assisted Henry in this moment. Both to get payment for them and to contract for further deliveries if the need arises." He shrugged. "And the way things are going, I see little doubt of that need."

Wend considered for a long moment. He realized Wood, ever calculating the political angles, had a good point. But as he was thinking, something else occurred to him, something that would provide the opportunity for more immediate profit. He nodded to Wood. "All right, I will accompany the musket shipment, and I will provide some of my men as escort."

All the men in the room smiled. Thruston folded his hands in his lap and said, in the manner of a minister intoning from the pulpit, "We are glad that our faith in you has proven out. Be mindful that you are doing a great service to Frederick County."

Wend smiled. "Thank you, Reverend. Shall we cement this agreement with another round of Donegal's very fine whiskey and speak of more pleasant things?"

Thruston looked down at his near-empty cup and said, "Most decidedly, sir!"

—⚌—

That evening, long after the visitors had left and Liza had lit the candles, Peggy Eckert sat at the writing desk. She had moved one of the candles near to hand, and in the flickering light, her eyes agleam with pecuniary enthusiasm, she carefully scrutinized each of the coins from the Committee of Safety. She had long ago, at her tavern-keeper father's knee, learned the value of the disparate coinage in circulation in the colonies, specifically how much each piece of metal would be worth in exchange. As she looked at each coin, she made a tally on a piece of paper. Meanwhile, Wend sat back with a whiskey, enjoying the excitement with which she worked. Presently she finished the counting and, reaching into a drawer, pulled out a ledger. Quickly scanning the pages, she set down some figures on the paper, then turned to Wend with a broad smile on her face.

"Well, my dear husband, this covers our expenses on the muskets and provides us with the merest of margins for ourselves." She raised a finger and continued, "That is, assuming the committee paid Hauck and Zane for their work."

"Yes, they confirmed that to me before leaving. And they said they would arrange payment to Abbey for the wagon transport down to Culpeper."

"And you still have payment coming from Gerson down in Alexandria for firelock orders."

"Correct, Peggy. And we'll be sending off a fowling piece and a brace of pistols from his most recent order in a few days, so that will bring in some more payment. In other words, we're solvent for at least the near term." Then he grinned at his wife. "But while I was talking with the committee, I got another idea that will definitely bring in more money rather rapidly."

She bit her lip and looked askance at Wend. "Pray tell, what would that be?"

"I'll recruit Donegal to come along and bring a wagon load of the whiskey."

Peggy's eyes opened wide, and she grinned broadly. "Of course! All those men in camp with time on their hands. And they're bound to have at least a little money in their purses. And in that situation, they'll spend their last coin on good whiskey!"

When smiled even more broadly. "But wait, my dear. I am one step ahead of you. Think on this—a regiment is obliged to provide periodic rations of drink to the rank and file. If this Patrick Henry has any cash in hand, we might persuade him to buy a good part of the wagon load for the men."

"My God, yes!"

Wend held up a hand. "And then there are the officers. Individually and as a mess, we may find some interest there. And they will certainly have money to spend."

"You are beginning to think like a tavern proprietor, my husband." Then a thought hit her. "But do you think Donegal will leave Sally for a trip that will last perhaps a fortnight or longer?"

Wend shot Peggy a devilish grin. "I don't know, but it's been five months since they were married, and he's spent every day with Sally and little Louisa. He might be ready for a few days out with the boys."

She gave him a severe look. "As might you, my husband?"

Wend just smiled, then said, "It will only be a couple of weeks at the most."

"That's why I'm not particularly distressed that you're leaving. It's not like last year when you went out with Dunmore's army for over six months. And besides, we need the money."

Wend put his hand to his chin. "I'll also take Joshua."

"Are you kidding? Just try to keep him from missing a trip like this. And Alice will be glad to get him out from underfoot."

"And I'll include Horner and Johann to help with distributing the firelocks when we get there."

A thoughtful look came over Peggy's face. "Take Bernd, too. It will do him good to travel a little bit—to see what a different town is like and what happens in a big encampment of men."

Wend, mindful of their earlier conversation about the boy, nodded. "All right, that's settled. I agree it will do him good." Wend considered for a few seconds. "All told, including Abbey's two teamsters, that will give us eight men with firelocks. That should be enough to discourage any brigands we encounter along the way."

"Eight? Are you going to arm Bernd?"

"He's eleven now. I'll give him a fowler. He's handled one of those often enough for hunting. And it will make him feel more grown up. Isn't that what you've been urging?"

Peggy put her hand to her chin. "Yes, that's a good idea." Then she asked, "When will you be leaving for Culpeper?"

"Well, we still have to wait for Zane to deliver the bayonets for the fifty muskets that don't have them. But we can start boxing up the other muskets tomorrow. According to Rutledge, Henry has announced that recruiting at Culpeper will start in a couple of weeks. It will take at least six days to get down there with those slow Conestoga wagons. So we'll leave in about ten days if everything goes as planned."

CHAPTER THREE

SUSPICION AT CULPEPER

The forenoon sun was high in the sky and had completed its job of eradicating the October day's early chill. Wend Eckert pulled up his horse, slid to the ground, and doffed the heavy gray overcoat he had put on in the cold of predawn just before they had taken to the road. Rolling it up, he then strapped it to the rear of the saddle. As he did so, he looked back over his little caravan and then back along the wagon track. Far behind he could see the mountains of the Blue Ridge stretching completely across the western horizon. Much nearer were the foothills that they had navigated just the day before.

It was their sixth day since leaving the farm. They had headed southeast along the well-worn wagon track that led to Ashby's Ferry. After crossing the Shenandoah, they had journeyed down the broad valley to the growing settlement of LeHewtown, or as some had taken to calling it, Front Royal. Just south of the town they had entered a pass through the Blue Ridge, which had taken them the better part of two days to cross, having encountered some steep places where it took all the horse and manpower they had to get the heavily loaded wagons through. But now they had left the foothills behind and entered the gently rolling land of the Piedmont.

Wend scanned the little column of wagons as it made its way eastward. Directly behind him were Abbey Morgan's two canvas-covered Conestogas with their six-horse teams. The lead wagon was driven by her foreman, Jake Cather, who walked along the left side of the vehicle with his reins in hand. Jake and the driver of the second Conestoga, Elijah McCartney, were well known to Eckert, for they had been part of his group of quartermasters during Dunmore's War the previous year. Behind the last Conestoga came one of Wend's own farm wagons, loaded with whiskey, and its four-horse team was driven by Simon Donegal himself. On the seat beside the Highlander rode Bernd. Several spare horses were tied by lengthy leads to the rear of the wagon. Bringing up the rear rode the two youthful apprentices, Andrew Horner and Johann Eckert, at the moment laughing at some joke.

Wend swung back up into the saddle and resumed his position at the head of the column. They had gone only a short distance further when a rider appeared on a slight rise about a quarter of a mile ahead. Under the bright sunshine, the details of horse and man stood out even in the distance—a tall and rangy rider, wearing a hunting shirt that extended down to nearly his knees with a floppy hat jauntily turned up on the left from which a bucktail protruded. The man sat the horse as naturally as if he had been born in the saddle. A longrifle was slung over his right shoulder, the butt alongside his head. The horse was a bay-colored hunter, highly muscled but graceful, with long legs that would make any fence an easy jump.

The rider was, of course, Joshua Baird, who had gone ahead to determine how much further they had yet to go to Culpeper. Now he pulled up his horse at the top of the hillock to await the arrival of the caravan. Wend spurred his horse and rapidly covered the distance, pulling up beside Joshua.

The scout said, "I found a farmer in his field 'bout a mile ahead. He says we'll be at Culpeper by late afternoon if we don't waste no time."

Wend nodded. "I knew we were getting close. Was he able to tell you anything about Henry's camp?"

"Sure enough. He said it's just this side of the town at a plantation. On a piece of land called Clayton's Old Field."

"This side of the town? That's good news."

"There be other news. There be two regiments there."

"You mean another besides the one Henry is recruiting?"

"Sure is. This other one is called the Culpeper Minute Men, part of the local militia made up of men from three of the counties 'round here. They been called out to go south to help fight Dunmore. Farmer says there's eight or ten companies of them."

"If you figure fifty men per company, that's a lot of men—maybe five hundred or more. Not to mention however many men Henry has recruited." Wend turned and looked back at the wagons. "Donegal is going to have a lot of business. And we might not have brought enough whiskey."

As they had been talking, the wagons had come up. Jake Cather wrapped his reins around the brake handle and walked up to Wend and Joshua. "What's the word—how far to Culpeper?"

Wend waved to the east. "Not that far. Farmer just ahead says we can make it before dark."

Baird looked up at the bright sky. "We'll need to push hard if we're going to get to the camp and get set up before nightfall. Now it's October, the sun is goin' down earlier."

Cather pursed his lips. "Horses been goin' hard for days now. We got to be careful they get enough rest along the way. I'm sayin' that's more important than gettin' there by a certain time."

Wend looked eastward and then said, "I don't disagree, Jake. But it is important we get to the military camp today if possible. So we'll skip the midday meal and make brief stops at whatever intervals you say for the horses. The men can eat cold food while we're resting the animals."

Cather nodded. "That's fine with me, Eckert. So let's stop talkin' and get movin'."

—∞—

By the time the town of Culpeper and the military camp came into view, the sun was indeed low in the western sky. While it was still brightly il-luminating the tops of the Blue Ridge, farmstead buildings alongside the road were casting long shadows. As the day progressed and they traveled further eastward, the land had flattened out even more so that they were now advanced on what was essentially a plain.

Wend and Joshua rode side by side, and as they approached the field where the military units were encamped, the two apprentices urged their horses forward to join them. Wend noticed that a creek ran between the encampment and the town itself.

Joshua looked over the ground and said, "Well, that farmer was right. It's plain to see there be two regiments here."

Wend looked over the field. There were indeed two distinct camps—one right near the road and the further beyond a large oak tree. The dis-tant one was clearly well organized and under discipline, with a goodly number of tents set up in rows, while other groups of men were in the open, grouped around lines of fires. Most of the men were in green hunt-ing shirts, which served as something of a uniform. Several squads could be seen marching, while others were drilling with their firelocks. How-ever, the nearer camp, which was quite smaller, lacked any semblance of precision. There were few tents—most of the men were sleeping in the open. However, some men had improvised ramshackle shelters of logs and tree limbs against the weather; these were randomly clustered around a large central tent with a fly in front.

Wend said, "Well, I'd say there's one real regiment and a collection of disorganized men." He motioned toward the near camp. "These must be Henry's recruits. I would guess the others are the Culpeper Minute Men." He signaled the wagons to stop and then pointed at the creek. "Joshua, why don't you ride ahead and locate a good place for us to camp near that stream, where we'll have good water for all the horses. Meanwhile, I'll go try to find Colonel Henry." He turned to Horner. "Andrew, you came with me in case I need a messenger." He said to Johann, "Lad, go back to Donegal's wagon. Give him your horse so he can come with us, and you drive the wagon to our camp." He thought a second, then said, "And ask Simon to bring a jug of the whiskey with him. It might be useful."

Johann nodded, "Yes, Father." Then he rode back along the line of vehicles.

Wend turned his horse and rode to where Cather stood beside his team. "Jake, hold the wagons here until Baird has found a good campsite. Then take them down and get set up for the night."

Cather looked to the west. "Yeah, we better do it fast. We ain't got much light left." Then he called out to Joshua, "Hey, Baird! Get us a good flat space. We're going to have to jack up the Conestogas tomorrow and grease the axles and hubs. We can't start back until that's done."

Joshua called back, "Don't worry, Jake! I'll get us a good spot right near the water. You just be ready to roll when I get back."

As the three approached the camp, Wend was surprised to see no sentinels or guards. However, just at the outer limits of the bivouac, they encountered an officer in the blue uniform of a captain of the Virginia militia.

The officer smiled and raised a hand in greeting. "Welcome. Can I presume that you fine fellows are here to enlist in the First Virginia Regiment?"

Wend responded, "Sir, that would be quite incorrect. We're from

Winchester, and we're bringing some items I'm sure your commander will be glad to see."

"You mean supplies? Well, we've indeed been expecting some provisions, and it's damn well time they were here." He waved toward the Conestogas. "Are those your wagons? I'll get the quartermaster for you."

Wend shook his head. "I don't want to see the quartermaster—at least not yet. I want to see your colonel, who I understand is named Patrick Henry."

"That's correct, but I should say he's got better things to do than deal with a matter of provisions."

"Look, Captain, hear me out. We're *not* bringing provisions. I'm a gunsmith, and we've got one hundred stand of muskets in those Conestogas sent by the Committee of Safety of Frederick County."

The captain's eyebrows shot up. "You say one hundred muskets?"

"You heard me."

"I'll take you to the colonel directly. May I ask your name, sir?"

"Wendelmar Eckert."

"All right, Mr. Eckert, follow me." The captain swung on his heel and led the way toward the large tent.

Wend and his compatriots dismounted and led their horses as in the captain's wake. Wend looked around at the newly minted soldiers. It was evident that these recruits came from a wide array of backgrounds. Some wore the coats and breeches of town residents, others the rough clothing of farmers, and a great many wore hunting shirts of various cuts, indicating they came from the border country. He also took in that there were a variety of firelocks in evidence. He saw fowlers, rifles, and even some muskets and fusils, which their owners probably had retained from earlier militia service. The recruits, sitting around at their fires or working at constructing shelters, were staring at him and his party. Clearly it was curiosity at new arrivals by men who had too little to keep them occupied. Wend said as much to Donegal.

The Highlander looked around and said, "There's 'na doubt of that. The officers here don't know their business. These men should be kept busy out in the field learning drill or making a proper camp with a sergeant kicking their ass."

Wend winked at the former corporal of the 77th Foot and sergeant major of the Frederick militia. "Simon, I wonder if they've even been organized into companies or appointed sergeants and corporals. They've only just started recruiting in the last few days."

"Now listen, laddie. If the officers knew anything about runnin' a regiment, they'd have started all that right away. You've got to make the men feel like soldiers from the start."

"Perhaps the esteemed Patrick Henry thinks that seeing squads of men marching around in a field, being shouted at by corporals and sergeants, might discourage potential recruits."

Donegal made a face, but before he could answer, they arrived at the headquarters tent. A young lieutenant, dressed similarly to the captain, sat at a writing table, busy scratching on parchment with a quill. A sentinel with a shouldered musket but no uniform stood guard beside the fly.

The captain said, "Jared, these gentlemen want to see Colonel Henry. They've got a load of muskets for us out there in those wagons on the road." He turned to Wend. "Sir, this is Lieutenant Coble, the adjutant."

Coble looked up at Wend, then over at Donegal and Horner. His eyes moved down to the jug that Simon was carrying. He pointed to the container and said, "What's that, sir?"

Donegal smiled. "Just a little something we want to present to Colonel Henry."

Coble's face wrinkled in puzzlement, but he said nothing, instead rising and walking into the tent.

Wend's eyes followed him, and he could see the back of a man in uniform sitting at a desk. Coble approached and whispered a few words. The man quickly turned around and stared at the three of them standing

ROBERT J. SHADE

there. He was hatchet faced with a high forehead and reddish brown hair. The officer nodded in reply to Coble, who came out of the tent and waved Wend and the others in. "Colonel Henry will see you now."

Wend motioned for Horner to wait outside. Then he and Donegal went into the tent, and Wend introduced himself and the Highlander. Henry looked at Wend with sharp, squinting eyes. "My adjutant says you have muskets for my regiment. Now, Williamsburg has sent me word that they were looking for muskets, but they had no idea where they would get them." He shrugged. "How is it that Winchester has muskets to spare? Are they from your militia?"

Wend shook his head. "No, Colonel. These are muskets directly from the former colonial government's Williamsburg armory. They were shipped to me before the insurrection began."

"Now why would they do that? Ship muskets to a gunsmith hundreds of miles away from the capital?"

"Four years ago, based on a proposal I submitted, the government awarded me a contract to refurbish all the muskets from the old Virginia Regiment. The order called for me to cut the barrels down and, in all respects, convert the firelocks to the current short land pattern."

"So you have been performing this role for years? You must have worked on hundreds of muskets. Where have they gone?"

Wend thought a second, then responded. "Ask your sentinel to bring his musket into the tent. I believe I can show you some information that will help explain."

Henry called for the adjutant to send the sentinel inside.

When he arrived, Wend had the man hold the firelock up with the top of the barrel facing Henry.

"Look here, sir. That mark near the rear end of the barrel indicates it is a tower musket. Now look just a little further up the barrel."

Henry stood up, then looked closely where Wend had indicated. "I see some letters and numbers. The letters are WJE and then the numbers 3-011."

"Exactly, sir. The letters are the initials of my name, Wendelmar Johann Eckert. And the numbers show that that musket was the eleventh musket refurbished in the third lot we received. That would have been in 1772. Once we finished with each lot, it was shipped back to the armory or, in some cases, directly to militia units. Last year, we shipped one hundred muskets to Pittsburgh for the Virginia militia there."

The colonel examined the musket and then dismissed the soldier. "So we can assume your muskets are all over the colony." He thought for a moment, then said, "In any case we are grateful for the arrival of these firelocks. I will call the call the quartermaster so he can take custody."

"Before you do that, and before I am ready to release the firearms to your regiment, Colonel, we have some business to transact."

Henry cocked his head. "Business? I'm not sure what you mean."

Wend reached into a pouch at his side and pulled out two documents. He handed one to Henry. "This is a letter from James Wood, the head of our Committee of Safety."

He took the paper from Wend's hand. "Ah, yes. I have met James and watched him in the Burgesses. A practiced and eloquent speaker who represents Winchester well. And I once had the honor of sitting beside him at a dinner at the governor's palace."

"Sir, let me summarize James's letter. It explains that the Williamsburg Committee of Safety learned about these muskets from Wood himself and that he volunteered to send them to this regiment for the fight against Dunmore. Most importantly, it points out that I have performed the work on these firelocks without receiving full recompense. The only payment I have received is in the form of donations from the citizens of Frederick County at a level substantially below what I would have received from Dunmore's administration." Wend hesitated and looked Henry directly in the eye. "So James's letter requests that you support me in the recovery of the remaining payment due from Virginia's government." Wend passed the second document to Henry.

Henry looked at the paper, quickly scanning the contents. "I take it that this is your accounting and request for reimbursement?"

"Precisely, sir. Once you have a chance to read James's letter completely, you will see that it suggests you send that invoice along with his letter to Williamsburg with a personal endorsement from yourself."

Henry raised an eyebrow and hesitated momentarily. Wend realized that, like any politician, he was quickly analyzing the pros and cons of taking the action requested.

The moment stretched out, silence permeating the tent. Wend made sure to keep his eyes fixed on Henry's face.

The colonel responded slowly in a manner that indicated he was choosing his words with great care. "Certainly you deserve recompense, Mr. Eckert. But you must be aware that finances are precarious in these times. The Committee of Safety in Williamsburg is even now assessing its resources and the derivation of future funding for its operations."

Wend knew the moment for him to be insistent had arrived. "Mr. Henry, surely the committee will be the beneficiary of tax revenues that would formerly have flowed to the royal government?" He paused a second and then continued, "And surely matters of warfare will have first claim on such revenues as are received?"

Henry tapped his fingers on his writing desk, then sighed. "I cannot deny the logic of your argument. It will be my honor to second this request. Clearly Frederick County and yourself, sir, have performed a great service to Virginia."

Wend smiled. "I greatly appreciate your decision, sir." He turned and looked at Donegal. "And now, sir, we have a second—and I believe you will find it to be more enjoyable—piece of business."

A wariness immediately appeared in Henry's eyes. "Other business?"

Simon spoke up. "Colonel, do you consider yourself a good judge of spirits?"

A twinkle appeared in Henry's eyes, and then he laughed outright. "Gentlemen, I should tell you that in my formative years, circumstances led to my involvement in the governance of a tavern. Obviously I had the opportunity to develop some considerable experience in matters of spirits."

The Highlander held up the small jug he had brought to the meeting. "Now, Colonel, your honor, perhaps you would 'na hesitate to sample this libation?"

Henry's eyes lit up, and he smiled conspiratorially. "I would never turn down such an opportunity." He reached for a cup, then thought for a second and took two more and handed one each to Wend and Donegal. "It would be ungracious to drink alone in front of other gentlemen."

Simon filled each of the cups.

Henry raised his in salute and said, "Here's to our great cause and the contribution of Winchester in furthering it."

Wend and Simon joined in the toast and then watched attentively as Henry first sniffed the liquid and then took a sip.

The colonel's eyes opened wide, and he quickly took another sip. "Whiskey, by God, and damned fine whiskey! Where did you procure this?"

Donegal grinned broadly. "There's 'na *procure* to it. We make it ourselves—from the creek water and grain of our farm."

Wend said, "Mr. Donegal and I are partners in the distilling business. He has combined an old recipe from Scotland with his own mix of ingredients and distilling techniques." He held up his cup. "This whiskey has pride of place throughout Frederick County."

Henry took another sip. "You should get no argument from me on that."

Donegal placed the jug on Henry's desk. "This is for you, Colonel, with our compliments."

"I am exceedingly grateful."

Wend smiled. "Now, Colonel, it happens that we have a wagon full of that whiskey out on the road."

Henry paused with his cup before his mouth. "The devil, you say!"

"It's quite true, sir. We thought perhaps your officers' mess would like to purchase some quantify from their funds."

"I will directly make that recommendation."

Donegal spoke up. "Now, Colonel, what arrangements have you made for a spirit ration for your men? Of course, rum is the army tradition, but that has become increasingly difficult to obtain. And as a veteran of many years of service in a marching regiment, I would say that without a proper ration, the morale of your men will not be as desired."

"Quite correct. My quartermaster is even now endeavoring to obtain suitable spirits. I will put him in touch with you."

Wend coughed delicately. "Sir, given our costs in distilling, we would settle only for payment in hard coin. I'm sure you would understand that position."

There was a prolonged silence, and Henry put his hand to his chin. Finally he said, "Am I to understand that a promissory letter will not suffice?"

Wend shrugged. "You have yourself, sir, already alluded to the uncertainty of financial matters in Williamsburg. Regrettably, I must insist on actual payment prior to delivery. We have produced and transported the whiskey at considerable expense from our own pocket. I should not long remain in business if I released it on simple promises."

Henry's face hardened. "I will discuss the matter with the quartermaster, and he will be in touch with you."

Wend raised a finger and an eyebrow. "In the interim, Colonel, I assume you will have no objection to our selling some of our stock to individual men of the regiment? Particularly since it seems that at the moment you have no supply of your own?"

"Not until I've had time to discuss arrangements with the quartermaster. For obvious reasons I prefer to control the flow of intoxicants to the men."

Donegal interjected, "Now, my Colonel, I know you've just begun to recruit. But it will not take long for the lack of some form of spirits to lead to discouragement in the ranks."

A flare of irritation showed in Henry's eyes. "I take your point, Mr. Donegal. Let me repeat: I shall immediately talk to the quartermaster."

Wend added, "We will defer to you for this regiment, but I have no doubt we will find numerous men from the militia across the field who will be eager for our whiskey."

Henry bit his lip. Clearly he was not happy. But he said, "Of course I have no authority to restrict your sales to the militia." He was about to say something more when suddenly there were loud shouts outside the tent.

All of them turned to look out the flap and discovered that a large group of soldiers had gathered before the tent fly and the adjutant's desk. Coble was on his feet, and several men in hunting shirts were in heated discussion with him. One of them was pointing into the tent. Wend could see other men arriving momentarily, and the gathering was becoming louder.

The colonel turned to Eckert and Donegal, puzzlement in his eyes, and quickly remarked, "Wait here. I must find out what this is about."

Patrick went out and addressed the crowd of soldiers. Wend saw him using hand gestures to quiet the men. Then he engaged in serious discussion with a bearded man dressed in a hunting shirt who appeared the leader of the angry men. The discussion lasted several minutes, and then Henry turned and came back into the tent, followed by the bearded soldier.

To Wend's surprise, Henry motioned toward him and asked, "Are you sure this is the man, Lieutenant?"

The bearded man stepped so close that Wend felt exceedingly uncomfortable and inadvertently took a step backward.

"There's no doubt in my mind, Colonel. He's the one I told you about."

Henry stared at Wend for a long moment, his eyes running over him as if he were seeing him for the first time.

Wend looked from the colonel to the lieutenant. He had never seen the man before in his life.

The colonel finally spoke up. "Mr. Eckert, this is Jedidiah Ballantyne, a militia lieutenant who has recruited a company of men from the far western reaches of Culpeper County. They came as a group to join the regiment. Last year he marched in Colonel Andrew Lewis's brigade during the war in the Ohio Country. He says you were one of Lord Dunmore's intimates and that you played a central role in keeping Lewis's column from getting to the Shawnee villages and joining the main army at Camp Charlotte."

"It's true that I am a lieutenant in the Frederick County militia, and I was appointed to Dunmore's staff. Naturally I performed my duties as assigned by the governor."

"So you admit your closeness to the royal governor. You've already indicated that you received very significant payments for a musket contract from the former government."

"Look, Colonel, being on Dunmore's staff wasn't my idea. I was appointed because they wanted an officer from the border country, not just dandies from the tidewater."

Ballantyne could contain himself no longer. "That damned Dunmore sent Colonel Lewis's brigade—which we were part of—to the mouth of the Kanawa. He was supposed to bring his force there to join us. But when we got there, he was nowhere to be found. Then we got a message to come join him at a place over a hundred miles up the Ohio. And while we was getting ready to move north, hundreds of the savages hit us by surprise. We lost over two hundred men that day. I lost people in my family and close friends. Every man at that battle knows damn well if Dunmore and his men had been at the Kanawa like they was supposed to be, the Indians wouldn't have dared attack."

Henry held up his hand and started to respond, but Ballantyne would not be interrupted. "But it was after that when the real betrayal happened. We mourned our dead and gave them a decent Christian burial. Then Lewis led us across the Ohio, and we marched fast for the Shawnee towns on the Pickaway Plains. We were nearly there when a small skirmish occurred with a band of Shawnees. Then Lord Dunmore arrived, accompanied by this man and a few other riders. The governor ordered us not only to stop but to turn around and go home." He paused, then pointed at Wend and continued, "Dunmore left this man with us to make sure that we actually turned around and marched back east. It was like we was little children—little children that needed watching and he was our governess."

Wend turned to Henry. "Colonel, he's only telling half the story. The reason the governor asked them to turn back was that peace negotiations with the hostile tribes had already been concluded, and the treaty was about to be signed. The chiefs feared that the men of Lewis's column would get out of control and attack the villages."

Ballantyne's face turned red, and he almost shouted, "The truth is we were aimin' to make sure that the savages paid for their dastardly attack and the killing of our men." He hesitated a moment, shaking. Then he resumed, "And we were right—damned right—to be worried about what Dunmore was negotiating with the chiefs. When we got home, we found out that his treaty—if you cared to call it that—didn't do nothin' but make the Indians do what was required in the old Fort Stanwix Treaty of '67. All it did was declare peace on the same terms. We left our homes, marched hundreds of miles through the roughest country in Virginia, and lost hundreds of our friends and neighbors, and there wasn't no punishment of the Indians for their raids on the border or their treachery!"

Ballantyne stopped to gather his breath, and Henry seized the opportunity to speak. He said in a measured voice, "Mr. Eckert, what our friend here is working up to say is that he and his associates suspect you may be here as an agent of the royal government—a spy, if you will—to report on our activities."

Wend stood frozen in astonishment and was momentarily unable to speak. Then he said, "This must be some atrocious jest. For God's sake, does this man know I'm here to turn over a hundred muskets? Would I be doing that if I was loyal to Dunmore's government?"

Henry gave Wend a crooked smile. "Possibly."

Wend's anger flared. "What the hell do you mean, Henry?"

"Call me *Colonel* Henry if you please, sir. And it could be a ruse to cover your activity as an informant." He put his hand to his chin. "Perhaps you figure to safely gather information for the Loyalist forces at the same time you're getting payment from the Committee of Safety. That would be very clever, indeed."

Ballantyne said, "You know it's clever. And the man's a Dutchman to boot, and everyone knows they ain't too excited about our cause. There be lots of them down where we live who just want to attend to their business and support the king's government." He shrugged. "But Colonel, you ain't got to just take my word on this or the word of all those other border men out there. We got witnesses that this man—this *Eckert*—has actually been working against Patriots."

Henry raised an eyebrow. "Witnesses?"

Ballantyne nodded. You're damned right, sir."

Wend shook his head. "That's impossible."

Ballantyne laughed, then stepped back to the tent flap and called out, "Sergeant Seidal, bring in those men!"

A wiry sergeant in a hunting shirt led two men into the tent.

Wend gasped at the sight of them.

Ballantyne motioned to the two. "These be the Carlin brothers, Taddy and Johnny. They just enlisted a couple of days ago. But they come down from Frederick County where Eckert lives, and they say he's been protecting known Loyalist spies." He turned to Taddy. "Tell him what happened, Carlin."

Taddy pointed at Wend. "A group of us from the militia was rousting out a nest of Tory spies. It was on the farm of a British officer—everyone know'd they was sendin' word down to Dunmore. Then Eckert here and some of his friends come along. They stopped us at the point of firelocks and drove us away."

Donegal spoke up. "Now that's a bold-faced lie. These men are Lowland Ulster scum who were squattin' on an old worthless farm, and they wanted to get the Callow place for themselves. They were new to the county and ain't never been in our militia. And Widow Callow's husband was the captain of an independent company who left the army ten years a'fore he died. And she was born in the colonies. Everyone in Frederick County knew she wasn't takin' up for the British. Why, I watched her cheer Morgan's Rifle Company when we sent it off to Boston."

Johnny Carlin took a step toward Donegal. "You bastard. You got no place to call us scum. Look at that bonnet he be wearin'. I've no doubt he was a piece of shit carryin' a musket in a British regiment. Like as not he's as much a Loyalist as Eckert and that Callow woman."

Simon bared his teeth. "I wasn't in no damned British regiment. I marched with the 77th Highlanders. Callin' that British is fightin' words. My father and uncle fought at Culloden." He grabbed Johnny by the front of his coat and drove a right-handed punch square into his face. Then he released his hold and Carlin dropped to the ground, all but unconscious.

Taddy went for Donegal, who parried the Ulster man's blow with his left arm and then got in a glancing blow on the man's face with his right. But before things went further, Sergeant Seidal quickly stepped in between the two Scotsmen, keeping them separated.

Henry said in a calm voice, "Thank you, Sergeant, for that timely action."

Wend quelled his rising anger. "Colonel, Simon Donegal chose to stay here in the colonies when the 77th was reduced and sent back to Scotland. He's been a Virginia farmer for more than ten years and is as much a supporter of this insurgency as anyone."

Henry gave Wend a knowing smile and stepped over to his desk. He picked up a piece of paper and held it up. "It might interest you to know, Mr. Eckert, that I have here correspondence from the Committee of Safety in Williamsburg that reports large numbers of Highlanders, particularly in North Carolina, are organizing military units to support the king's cause. On balance, it's easy to suspect Mr. Donegal, with his unbounded fists, is of the same sympathies as his brethren in Carolina and that he is on the same spying mission of which you are accused."

Ballantyne spoke up. "Colonel, I say we put these men in chains. I think you got enough evidence to send them to a court."

Taddy Carlin joined in. "The lieutenant's got the right idea, sir. These be dangerous men."

Henry made a calming motion with his hand. "Lieutenant, I concede that you have raised some serious questions about these men and their intentions. I thank you, but to be honest, I must examine the case more closely."

"You ain't gonna arrest these men?"

"*Arrest* may not, at this moment, be the right word, but rest assured we will...should I say...*detain* them appropriately." He waved his hand. "You and your men may withdraw with my thanks and return to your company area. Meanwhile I will be investigating this case immediately."

Ballantyne looked around, his jaw set, obviously not satisfied. But after a moment he waved the Carlins and the sergeant out. "I thank you for listening to us, sir. And I've got no doubt you'll find these men damned well guilty of what we say." And with that, he left the tent.

Henry looked at Wend and said, "Well, Mr. Eckert, you've certainly received more attention this day than you could ever have bargained for."

Wend shook his head. "Surely you don't believe all this, Colonel? James Wood knows my background and certainly wouldn't be sending me with a letter of introduction if he thought there was any chance I had royalist beliefs. For God's sake, he was a captain in the same battalion during Dunmore's War."

Henry raised his hand to indicate silence. Then he reached for a pipe on his desk and walked out to the fire. Having lit the pipe from an ember, he walked back in and took his seat at the desk. He took a pull on the pipe and only then spoke.

"Eckert, to be honest, I don't know where the truth lies. I can see arguments for either side. As I told Ballantyne, I will have to investigate. I'm going to send an officer courier to Winchester to query Wood and the committee on your background and discuss this insinuation raised by the Carlins. On a fast horse, the courier might get to Winchester in two or three days. We could have an answer back in a week. So you need to stay here until we have information from your Committee of Safety."

Wend burst out in frustration, "This is absurd, sir! Those Ulster men—the Carlin brothers—were squatters of the lowest type and are not to be believed. The fact is, Sheriff Smith and his men drove them out of the county because of the trouble they were causing."

Henry stared at Wend for a long moment, taking a draw on his pipe. Finally he responded, "Eckert, you're a German, and the Ulster-Scots and the people of your ancestry share something of a mutual animosity." He waved his hand toward the camp. "At least half the men who have enlisted are Ulster, and generally speaking, they despise the English. That makes them a valuable asset, and you must understand that I'm not going to do anything that will dampen their enthusiasm or lead them to believe I don't have faith in them."

Frustrated, Wend said, "Look, Colonel, you don't have to lecture me on understanding the Ulster people. When my family was killed by a Mingo war party, I was raised by an Ulster minister and his wife and grew up in an Ulster village."

Donegal laughed. "Not to mention his wife is as Ulster as you can get!"

Henry raised an eyebrow and thought about what he had heard. Then a smile came over his face. "Now that's interesting—a German married to an Ulster woman. Well, given your situation, Mr. Eckert, you should completely understand why I must show support for the claims of these men and fully investigate. And you will also realize that I must carry out what I told them about keeping you under some sort of restraint."

"Restraint? What do you mean by that?" Wend held out his hands. "Are you going to clap me in chains and manacles?"

"Oh, come now, Eckert. Be serious." He laughed and said, "As a matter of fact, I don't think we even have a set of shackles in the camp. I assure you it will be minimal. I'll simply keep a sentinel in your camp to keep track of you and ensure there are no midnight departures." Henry hesitated as he thought of something. "And you know, Eckert, given the anger of Ballantyne and his men, you might be glad to have a sentry there to...shall we say...discourage any excess of enthusiasm on their part."

"You mean you can't be sure of controlling your own men?"

"Eckert, let's just say that the process of imposing discipline has only just begun."

Donegal shook his head. "Not by any standard I know."

Henry shot him a stern look.

Wend sighed and said, "All right, we'll prepare to unload our wagons. But I ask for this accommodation: once you have taken possession of the muskets, allow me to send the wagons and the rest of my men back to Winchester. The wagons belong to Daniel Morgan's freighting business, and two of my sons are with me. There's no need for them to sit around as part of this idiocy."

Henry raised his hands. "I have no objection at all as long as you and Mr. Donegal remain. In fact, I encourage you to get unloaded as soon as possible. And in any case, I would consider that a week of your time is a reasonable price to pay for humoring my brave fellows and restoring your reputation."

As he turned to go, Wend said, "You will understand that I differ with you on that."

Henry shrugged. Then, raising an eyebrow and smiling, he tapped the jug. "And gentlemen, my deepest thanks for the whiskey."

—⁓—

Shortly after dawn the next morning, the quartermaster lieutenant of Henry's regiment came down to the creek where the Winchester party was encamped and made arrangements to receive the firelocks. He told Wend to unload the wagons and that he would organize a working party of recruits to carry them to the main encampment. Jake Cather supervised as they worked to hand the boxes down from the wagons and stack them ready for the soldiers to take them away.

Meanwhile, as promised, Henry had assigned a detail to watch Wend and Donegal. The sergeant in charge was Seidal, the man who had broken up the fight between Donegal and Johnny Carlin. He was in his middle thirties and very businesslike, comporting himself in a manner like someone who had actually served in a disciplined unit. He treated Wend in accordance with his militia rank, addressing him as "Lieutenant" or "sir." Donegal speculated that he had perhaps served in the old Virginia Regiment during the war with the French.

Seidal had organized a relay of guards who stood watch in rotations of four hours each. The current one sat on a stump, carving on a long stick with his knife, a firelock leaning up against a nearby tree.

By midmorning they had emptied the Conestogas, and Cather and

McCartney had begun the process of jacking up the wagons in preparation for greasing the hubs. Jake had hopes of getting that labor-intensive job done by the next morning and starting back to Winchester in the afternoon.

As the two wagoners worked, Wend, Joshua, and Simon sat at the fire, cups of coffee in hand, making plans for the return trip of the wagons.

Joshua said, "I should stay here with you two. Look, Cather knows the road well and can get the wagons and the others back to Winchester without me. And I might be able to help keep you two safe. I don't trust Ballantyne and the Carlin brothers to leave you alone."

Wend responded, his words reeking with irony, "How could you possibly think that Colonel Henry and the sentinels he's posted might not be enough?"

Baird spat. "Well, you said it, Wend. Henry ain't no soldier—he's a lawyer and a politician who ain't got no business runnin' a regiment. Look, at least I can be ready to ride hard for Winchester if Henry pulls somethin' on you before word comes back from our Committee of Safety. I don't trust him."

Wend shook his head. "No, Joshua, I'll feel better if you go along with the wagons. You'll be better off telling our side of the story to Wood and the others, and I know you'll do a better job explaining things to Peggy and Sally than Jake would. You know they're going to be upset."

Donegal added, "Joshua, I'm with Wend. You'll be able to comfort the women. Sally will be at her wits' end if she thinks I'm in serious trouble."

Baird was about to respond when Seidal walked into the camp and approached Wend. He cleared his throat and announced, "Lieutenant Eckert, you're wanted by Colonel Henry. I'm here to escort you to his tent, sir."

Wend looked at his companions and then back to Seidal. "What is this about? I thought we had pretty well talked everything out yesterday afternoon?"

Seidal shrugged. "I ain't got no idea, sir. Colonel Henry don't take me into his confidence. That adjutant, Lieutenant Coble, just told me to get you up to Henry's tent posthaste."

Donegal asked, "He doesn't want me too?"

"Nope. He just said Eckert."

———

Coble showed Wend into the headquarters tent. Henry, in shirtsleeves, had fired up his pipe, and the interior was filled with tobacco smoke. His desk was cluttered with correspondence, and he was staring at a stack of two or three sheets directly in front of him.

The colonel looked up at Wend. "Well, Eckert, you got here promptly enough."

"I had lots of encouragement from Sergeant Seidal."

Henry motioned for Wend to sit in a chair across from his desk. Then he said, "Seidal is very efficient. And he knows discipline. He keeps that band of border ruffians who came in with Ballantyne pretty much in line. I heard somewhere that back in the French War, he had some time in either a provincial regiment or an actual British battalion."

Wend shrugged. "Interesting. I've observed the same thing about him myself. But more to the point, may I ask why I'm here?"

Henry didn't immediately answer. Instead, he took a draw on his pipe and then exhaled a stream of smoke high into the air. Finally he spoke, countering Wend's question with one of his own. "Do you know a man named John Connolly?"

"Yes. Under Dunmore's authority he organized a militia and then seized Pittsburgh from Pennsylvania in early '74. Then he became the administrative authority for that area, which Virginia classified as the district of West Augusta."

The colonel nodded. "Yes, but do you know him personally?"

"Certainly. Last year I took a load of muskets up there for his militia. He and his wife, Susanna, showed me great hospitality in a dinner party in his quarters at Fort Pitt."

"And then you would have had occasion to associate with him while you were on Dunmore's staff?"

"That's true enough. He led a battalion of militia in the northern brigade during last year's war."

Henry smiled broadly. "Excellent, Mr. Eckert. I had dared hope you had personal contact with the man."

An alarm bell was ringing in Wend's head. "Sir, may I again presume to ask what this is all about?"

Henry reached down and picked up the papers that were directly in front of him. "A courier who came up from Williamsburg last night brought these. The committee felt it was of sufficient urgency for him to exhaust several relay horses getting here as fast as possible. I saw the one he rode in on, and I can assure you the animal had been pushed to the limit."

"So what news was so important, and how does it happen to affect me?"

"Patience, my dear Eckert, and I will make it all clear." Henry paused and exhaled more smoke into the cloud, which hung in the air. "It happens that a patrol of our militia near Norfolk captured a Loyalist courier en route to Dunmore. He was carrying a very interesting dispatch. It was from Lieutenant Colonel Northcutt, who leads a battalion called the King's Loyal Virginia Regiment, and it was private correspondence to Lord Dunmore himself."

"Did you say Northcutt? Barrett Penfold Northcutt?"

Henry immediately shot Wend a sharp look. "You know Northcutt?"

"He's long been Dunmore's chief aide, advisor, and confidant. He also happens to be the one who arranged my musket contract."

Henry stared at Wend for a very long moment. "Mr. Eckert, for a country gunsmith, you seem extremely well connected with the former colonial administration." He cocked his head. "That would seem to lend some additional credence to Lieutenant Ballantyne's accusations."

Wend mentally kicked himself. It had been a mistake to blurt out that he knew Northcutt. And he realized he must now explain the relationship. "Colonel, I found out that Northcutt arranged to give me the musket contract because he had heard of my service as a scout for Colonel Henry Bouquet at the Battle of Bushy Run."

"My God, you were at Bushy Run? You do get around. But you must have been very young when that happened."

"I had just turned nineteen."

"And why did your participation in that action make you so interesting to Northcutt?"

"He felt my notoriety among frontier country people for that, along with the fact that I had contacts in both the German and Ulster-Scot communities in the Shenandoah Valley, would make me useful in influencing them for crown political purposes. He arranged for that contract so that I would be dependent financially on him and the governor and inclined to do their bidding. Basically he set a trap to induce my loyalty."

Henry sat back and smiled. "Now that indeed fits the style of the Barrett Northcutt I know. The man's a supreme manipulator. And from my time in Burgesses, I share the common belief in Williamsburg that Dunmore doesn't make a move without his advice."

Wend shrugged. "Once again, sir, how do Northcutt's dispatches relate to me?"

"They're about your friend Connolly."

"I said I knew Connolly. I didn't say he is my friend."

"Well, Eckert, your acquaintance, then. At any rate, the letter from Northcutt says Connolly is ready to embark on a secret mission that has been approved by both Dunmore and General Gage up in Boston." He paused to gather his thoughts. "It's a conspiracy to rouse the Indians in the Ohio Country against the settlers in the border areas."

Wend thought about it for a moment. "That could be extremely detrimental to the colonial cause."

"That's a hell of an understatement, Eckert. It would be a damned *disaster*! Attacks on the border settlements would lead to men staying home to provide defense instead of enlisting in our regiments for the fight against the British. Even worse, it could lead to us having to send armed units to the frontier to help defend against the tribes and thus greatly weaken the effort against the king's forces. And it could be accomplished at little cost to the British."

Wend was puzzled. "This could be extremely dangerous for Connolly. If the plot fails, he could be hung as a spy. He's a trained military officer. Why doesn't he put that experience to use in Northcutt's regiment?"

"Undoubtedly, Eckert, it's a matter of personal wealth. Last year I was at a meeting in Williamsburg concerning Virginia's western lands, which was chaired by Dunmore himself. Among the people there were Northcutt and Connolly. Connolly requested and received a grant from the governor of four thousand acres at a place called the Falls of the Ohio River. Does that mean anything to you?"

"I've never heard the term, Colonel."

"There are rapids and falls on the Ohio, down in Kentucky, hundreds of miles below Pittsburgh. Connolly spent some time there years ago. He knows that anyone going down the river must portage around the falls. He wants the land to start a town there in order to capitalize on the needs of settlers and eventually the passage of cargo boats. He figures it will make his fortune as the region develops."

Wend nodded. "That explains Connolly's extreme loyalty to Dunmore—why he worked so hard to take Pittsburgh from Pennsylvania last year and why he's cast his lot with the king now." Then he thought of something. "Why was it so urgent for Williamsburg to notify you about this? Are they expecting you to do something?"

"Good for you, Eckert. That is *precisely* the point. Northcutt's letter says he has made arrangements for Connolly and two other men with connections in the Ohio Country to travel by boat up from the Norfolk area to Port Tobacco in Maryland. Then they are to ride northwestward through Maryland to Fredericktown to join up with some compatriots and proceed from there to Pittsburgh along Braddock's Road. There they have identified other men and certain tribal chiefs who are ready to help foster this uprising."

Henry looked meaningfully at Wend. "Because of our northerly position here in Culpeper, Williamsburg has ordered me to send a group of men to intercept Connolly and his companions. So I intend to mount an officer and several men to dispatch on the mission." He hesitated a moment and then broke into a grin. "And I intend for you to be among that number."

Taken aback, Wend blurted, "Me? Pray tell why?"

"Because, Mr. Eckert, you are the only man in this camp—other than myself—that I know of who can recognize Connolly."

"But I'm not under your command. What if I refuse to go?"

"I believe it's very much in your interest to assist in this assignment. It will tend to validate that you are in fact on the right side in our insurrection. I'll go further than that—if you agree to ride with my men and are able to stop Connolly, I vow I'll clear you of any suspicion of being a Loyalist."

"So what you're saying is that your price for clearing me is cooperation on this expedition." Wend shook his head. "Now, Colonel, who is engaging in manipulation?"

Henry pounded his hand on the desk. "Look, Eckert, it's essential we stop this tribal uprising before it gets started. And I should think someone from Winchester would appreciate that."

"There hasn't been a war party raid near Winchester since Pontiac's War over ten years ago. Even in last year's war, the raiding was considerably further west. I doubt the town would be in danger."

"Regardless, I'm presenting you with a choice. It's undeniably in your personal interest to accept my offer."

Wend stared at Henry for a long moment, turning the situation over in his mind. "All right, Henry, I don't seem to have many options. And just which of your officers and men do you intend to send on this mission?"

"Lieutenant Ballantyne and four men from his company."

"Good God! Of all the officers in your command, you select Ballantyne? You expect me to ride with a man who hates my guts? This is a mission fraught with danger by its very nature. But with him in charge, I would be facing as much danger from my back as from my front."

"Ballantyne is the natural choice for this assignment. His settlement and his very home will be directly threatened by any tribal uprising. He'll be determined to stop Connolly." He shot Wend a hard glance. "And come, now, are you actually saying that Ballantyne might attempt to take your fate into his own hands? That he would commit murder?"

"If I were killed in a fight with Connolly's party, who could say where the ball had come from? Particularly since all the men in the party are under his command."

"Perhaps, for your reassurance, I should include someone not from his company to keep an eye on him."

Wend shook his head. "That's not good enough, Colonel. Not at all—I'll stay here and take my chances. Besides, when your courier gets back from Winchester, there will be no doubt about my loyalty."

He stood up and prepared to depart. "With your permission I'll return to my camp."

Henry raised a hand. "Eckert, hold on. What *would* it take for you to accept?"

Wend thought about it for a moment, then put on his hardest, most unreadable face. "First, I go with my rank of lieutenant in the Frederick County militia recognized by you in writing. Second, I'm allowed to take Donegal and two other of my associates with me—they're all members of the county militia. One of them, Joshua Baird, has been traveling the border country we'll be traversing for decades and was Bouquet's personal scout. He knows Braddock Road like the back of his hand. Third, you ensure that one of the men in Ballantyne's group is Seidal, who is old enough and sufficiently disciplined to reign in the rest of those firebrands."

Henry said, "You're asking a lot." But then he stared into the distance, obviously thinking it out. Wend could almost hear his brain grinding like a gristmill at work. Then a grin came over his face. "All right, Eckert, that's done. And as a matter of fact, there's no guessing how many men Connolly will have in his party by the time you catch up with him, and nine men will be better than six in a fight."

Wend stood up. "I'll make preparations."

"Do that. There's no time to lose, and I want the party to ride out by early tomorrow."

—⁂—

Lieutenant Ballantyne stood in front of the fire where the entire Winchester contingent was seated. Wend had been explaining the situation when the officer had approached.

Ballantyne looked down at the circle of eight men and boys, then spoke directly to Wend. "Eckert, you and your three men better be ready to ride for Alexandria at dawn. And make sure you got good, strong horses. I intend to move fast. And bring your own provisions. I ain't got no intention to feed you or your animals. That understood?"

No one said anything for a long moment. The animosity in the air was palpable. As the silence persisted, Wend calculated the best way to respond, one that would put a burr under the lieutenant's saddle.

Finally, he said, "Don't worry about us. We'll be ready when you are. And just remember that I'm carrying my rank of lieutenant on this expedition, as approved by your colonel. And Donegal here is a sergeant in the Frederick County militia. Is that clear, Ballantyne?"

Ballantyne scowled. "You two can call yourself anything you want. It won't make no difference to me. Just remember I'm the one in command."

"I would say the decision-making is to be shared if we're both of the same rank. At the least you'll have to give some consideration to my opinions."

"Look, Eckert, you're along for one reason only—to identify Connolly." He raised an eyebrow. "And Colonel Henry made sure that's the way things will be. He just appointed me a captain on account of how I brought in enough men to make a full company for the regiment." With that he smiled triumphantly, turned on his heel, and strode back to the main camp.

Joshua said, "That damned Henry crossed you, Wend."

Donegal spat contemptuously. "This is what happens when you put a conniving lawyer in charge of a regiment instead of a proper soldier who has got some honor."

Wend looked after Ballantyne silently for a moment, then said, "When I was a schoolboy back in Lancaster, my teacher had us read plays by a writer who lived a long time ago in old England. It was in the days of Queen Elizabeth. His name was Shakespeare. Anyway, he had a fine turn for phrases. In one play, I remember a line something like, 'First thing we do is kill all the lawyers.'" He shook his head. "Seems appropriate now."

Donegal laughed out loud. "Some things never change! They hated the double-dealin' bastards even way back then."

Jake Cather stared after Ballantyne, then stood up. "Well, me and Elijah got to get back to work on the wagons." He looked at Wend. "Eckert, I don't like your chances havin' to ride with that bastard."

Joshua said, in bitter tones, "Don't worry, Jake. Donegal and Horner and me will watch his back."

Donegal nodded. "That's the truth." Then he turned to Horner. "Come, give me a hand with the whiskey." He pointed to a group of men approaching. "There's more of them minutemen comin' to buy jugs."

The two of them walked over to the farm wagon, leaving Wend with his two sons.

Johann sat for a moment with a very serious look on his face. Then he spoke up. "Father, I should be coming with you on this journey. I am old enough to be a warrior, and I am as good a tracker as Joshua. It makes more sense for me to go than Andrew."

"I know you could be useful if you went with us. But Horner is five years older and has been on the warpath before. Remember, a good warrior follows the orders of his war chief. And you have an important job to do, driving our wagon back to the farm. Besides that, Jake says he will also use you as a scout. That will be essential because you saw the unsettled conditions we came through on the way here, and you can warn him of any trouble. Your journey may be as dangerous as mine." He turned to Bernd and put his hand on the boy's shoulder. "You also have a man's job to do. Since Johann will often be riding ahead of the caravan, you will be spending a lot of time handling the wagon all by yourself."

Bernd beamed and squared his shoulders. "Don't worry, Father. We will get the wagons through to Winchester."

"I know you will." Wend looked around the campsite and saw that everyone else was busy. Then he continued, "And there is an even more important thing I'm trusting you with."

The faces of both boys showed puzzlement. Johann said, "What is that, Father?"

Wend motioned to the boys. "Come with me." Then he led them to a wooden box that sat just outside one of the tents.

He looked around at the boys. "You know what this is."

Bernd said, "Of course. That's the tool box that goes underneath the seat of our wagon."

"Exactly. Now watch this." Wend opened the lid and pulled out a screwdriver. He used it to remove some screws on the side of the box and handed them to Bernd. "Here, hold these." Then he used the tip of the screwdriver to wedge open a panel of wood at the side of the box.

Johann exclaimed, "Why, there's a double bottom in the box!"

Wend smiled. "Exactly. It runs under the whole length of the box, and it's about two inches deep. Now listen: we're going to pack all the money we're making from the whiskey into that compartment, wrapped in cloth so it won't make noise, and then reseal the side." He looked at them. "Only the two of you will know it's there. I'm counting on you to get it back to Peggy. She'll split it with Donegal's wife." He looked Johann in the eye. "Now, is that a duty worthy of a Mingo warrior?"

Johann stood up rigidly straight and assumed a stone-faced, expressionless countenance. But Wend saw the shine of pride in his eyes.

"Father, I will get that box to Eckert Ridge no matter what we encounter along the road."

"I know you will, lad, and I'm counting on it."

—⁂—

Early the next day, with a streak of dawn visible in the east, Wend and his companions were saddling their horses and affixing their accoutrements. Horner had finished earlier and had started loading provisions on the packhorse that would accompany them.

Jake Cather and his compatriot still had a little work to do to finish their maintenance on the Conestogas, but they expected to begin the return journey to Winchester by midmorning.

As he worked, Wend reflected that at least the whiskey sales had gone well. They had sold a significant part of the wagon load to the Culpeper Minuteman Battalion. Then, late in the afternoon, Lieutenant Coble from the First Virginia had come over and paid coin for a supply intended for the officer's mess. Finally, the regimental quartermaster had arrived just before dark, seeking to buy the balance of the load with cash to furnish rations for the rank and file. He and Donegal had haggled over the price for some time and finally settled on an amount somewhat below what individual soldiers had been paying since it would empty the wagon. Later, by the light of the fire, Wend and Donegal had, with great satisfaction, counted the coins and packed them, wrapped in rags, in the bottom compartment of the equipment box.

Now, after saddling, they all sat at the fire, eating a robust breakfast and drinking coffee that Johann and Bernd had prepared.

Joshua was griping about the need to drink coffee. "Dammit, I wish we had some tea. Just can't get used to this coffee shit."

Jake said, "I'm with you on that, Baird, but tea is near impossible to get at any price. And then there's the boycott—there's people who will call you a Tory for drinking it. Might as well get used to this stuff."

As they finished, Ballantyne and his men came up from the main camp, leading their horses. Wend saw that Seidal was indeed with him, and another man—really a youth about Horner's age—whom he had never seen before. Ballantyne pointed to Seidal. "You know the sergeant. And this lad here is Caleb Jackson."

Then, to his disgust, Wend sighted Ballantyne's other two men: Taddy and Johnny Carlin. He looked over at Joshua and said quietly, "Oh, shit."

Baird saw them at the same time. He shook his head. "What the hell is this? There must be one hundred fifty men in that camp, and they pick those two?"

Wend stood up as the soldiers arrived at the fire. He pointed at the Carlin brothers. "What the hell are you thinking, Ballantyne? I didn't sign on to ride with these two liars who have a grudge against me. Is this your idea of a jest?"

Taddy Carlin laughed. "What's the matter, Eckert? I guess you ain't happy unless you got a pistol held on a man."

The captain looked back at the Carlins and said, "They volunteered for this trip. They said they'd be glad to keep an eye on you."

Donegal stood up. "It's all right, Wend. Joshua and me will keep these two Lowlanders in check."

Johnnie Carlin said, "Keep us in check? Horseshit. Soon enough it's we who will take care of the whole lot of you, Highlander."

Ballantyne put a foot in his stirrup and mounted. "Enough of this. All of you, put your damn arguments and threats aside until we have Connolly. Then you can do what you want. Right now it's time to ride. It be more'n seventy-five miles up to Alexandria, and I aim to make at least twenty-five of that a'fore dark. So let's get started."

Wend looked at Baird, Donegal, and Horner. "Go ahead and get started with them. I'm going to say goodbye to my sons, and then I'll catch up."

Ballantyne glared at Wend for a moment. "Don't tarry long, Eckert." Then he kicked his horse and took off at the gallop, followed by the others.

Chapter Four

ACROSS THE POTOMAC

It was well into dusk when they came to a tiny village astride the intersection of two roads. The main feature was a wooden store painted in a faded red. The rest of the village consisted of the store owner's house and several other very small cottages—some of them were wooden framed, others were log, and various were barns and sheds. In the distance were fields and pastures and a couple of farmsteads.

Ballantyne ordered the party to encamp in a small grove of trees just past the store. In reality, each faction set up their own camp close beside each other. Wend and Donegal worked at getting the horses secured on a picket line and then grained while Horner got a fire started and set a pot to boiling for some salt beef and another for coffee. Baird took it upon himself to walk over to the store on what he called a "little scout."

By the time Joshua returned, Wend was squatting at the fire with a cup of coffee in hand. He grinned up at Baird and asked, "Well, *scout*, what did you find out?"

"This place is called 'Red Store.'"

Wend threw back his head and laughed. "I'll bet that took some hard work to ferret out!"

Joshua gave Wend a sharp look. "The proprietor says it's just under fifty miles to Alexandria from here." Then he smiled. "And it happens he's got a pretty good-looking blond-haired daughter."

Horner perked up. "How old is she?"

"Looked to be maybe fifteen or sixteen." He winked at Wend and Donegal. "Turns out they use the place as a tavern in the evenings. Andrew may want to go over and take in the sights."

Donegal grinned, then looked at the young apprentice and said, "I'd say Horner is too tired for that. We've had a hard ride today."

The apprentice took the bait. He looked over at the store and said, "Well, I'm not that tired."

All the other men laughed, and Horner flushed red when he realized that he had been set up. But he persevered and said, "I might go over there after we eat and see what an old man like Joshua considers a pretty girl."

Donegal said, "Yes, indeed, you go take a look."

Horner didn't answer, but instead said, "Our meat is ready" and handed out tin bowls to the others, then took one himself. But after the meal was finished, he did head for the store, where bright lights were shining and several men from the town had been seen to have entered.

After the youth had left, Donegal said to Wend, "In case you haven't noticed, your apprentice has recently taken up an interest in females."

Wend shrugged. "The boy has been the most industrious apprentice I've ever had. He's really single-minded about learning the trade. And he's damned good with tools, particularly the carving knife. But it was bound to happen sooner or later."

Simon wagged his finger. "The truth is, the lad met a German farm girl at McDonald's fair last May. Family name is Haldorf. She's also a blonde and not hard to look at."

Joshua said, "I've seen that Haldorf girl. She's pretty in the face and broad down below—no doubt she'll drop babies easily."

Wend grinned to himself. "Well, that explains all the excuses Horner's been making to go into Winchester on market days."

The three of them nursed their coffee, and presently Baird said, "When I talked with the proprietor, he mentioned that the other road here runs southeasterly down to the port at Falmouth." He paused and looked at each of them in turn. "And if you go northwestward on it, eventually it joins up with Ashby Ferry Road. In other words, it takes you to Winchester." Joshua poured himself another cup of the coffee. "Now, if we was able to very quietly saddle up and sneak out of here—say a little after midnight—when all them others were asleep by their fire, we could be well on our way home by dawn."

Donegal furrowed his brow. "That's a pleasant thought, but I've 'na doubt Ballantyne and his men would be after us by first light. Sooner or later we'd face a fight."

Baird sipped some coffee and then said, "We're better at this game then they are, and we've got finer bred horses. They're mounted on whatever nags Henry could round up. We'd ambush them on the road, and that would be the end of that."

Wend shook his head. "I suspect they wouldn't follow us. Ballantyne knows how important it is to catch Connolly, and he'd continue on his way to try to finish the job himself. But whatever else these men are, they're good woodsmen. I doubt we'd get away without waking them, and anyway, they might post a watch. Then there'd be real trouble—we'd have that fight right here."

"If it came to that, we could take them," said Donegal.

Wend sighed. "Maybe, but at what cost? Look, I promised Henry I'd take on this mission, and I intend to carry through. I appreciate that you two and Horner have agreed to come along and cover my back. And since we've fairly started, we must persevere. If we can cut Connolly off in Maryland before he joins up with other supporters, the plot will collapse, and we can be on our way home in a few days. So our best bet is to work with Ballantyne and get it done."

Wend looked around at his companions for their reaction.

Donegal cocked his head and glanced at Joshua. "I'd like to go home, but the lad is making sense, like he always does. So I guess we're in all the way."

Baird shrugged. "I was just thinkin' out loud. And the fact is, if we go home, Alice is going to chase after me with her damned list of chores." He looked over at the other fire, then said, "Of course we'll go along and bring in Connolly. I never really liked that man in the first place."

There was a long silence, with all three looking into the flames. Then Wend stood up. Joshua asked, "Where are you going? To join Horner in the tavern? Now that sounds like a good idea to me!"

"No, I'm going over to confront Ballantyne. I want him to explain his plans for intercepting Connolly."

Donegal gave a short laugh. "You sure he's got a plan?"

"That's the point. I want to make sure this doesn't turn into a futile chase that stretches out all the way to Pittsburgh, where we could find things hostile to us. Besides that, I had a short conversation with Sergeant Seidal at a rest stop today, and he said Ballantyne has both a copy of the order to Henry from Williamsburg and a copy of Northcutt's letter to Dunmore, which started all this. I mean to force him to share the complete information with us."

Donegal got up. "Come on, Joshua. Let's go with him."

Baird looked over at the store. "I still think the tavern is a better idea. Let Ballantyne worry about all this on his own." But reluctantly, he rose to follow the other two.

Then Wend had an idea. "Donegal, bring along a little of the whiskey. Things might go better if we have a peace offering."

Simon made a face. "I wish we had some other whiskey along. I hate wasting good stuff on those bastards. They wouldn't know enough to appreciate it in the first place."

Wend smiled. "You're probably right, but bring it along anyway."

When they arrived at the other fire, they found the men just putting away their meal things. All five looked up suspiciously at Wend and his companions.

Ballantyne growled, "What do you want, Eckert?"

"I thought we should have a little talk."

"Look, let's do this another time. We was just gettin' ready to go over to the store to see what kind of spirits they have."

Wend motioned to Donegal. "You can have a drink here at no cost. We brought some whiskey along. And the talk I had in mind should be private."

A suspicious look came over the captain's face. "What do you want to talk about?"

"It seems a good time for you to tell us about your plans for catching Connolly's party."

"You don't need to know anythin' right now 'cept we got to get to Alexandria and into Maryland as soon as possible."

Wend stared at him for a long moment. "Look, I know that you have some detailed information on Connolly's plans, which were in the dispatches from Williamsburg. We ought to know that."

Ballantyne scowled, but before he could respond, Seidal spoke up. "Jedidiah, there's some sense in what Eckert says. Suppose somethin' happened to you. Lieutenant Eckert might have to take over."

"I don't consider him no officer. If that happens, you're in charge, Horst."

The sergeant shook his head. "That's not right, and it ain't my job. And you know the colonel gave you a letter sayin' Eckert is an officer in the militia." He pointed at the jug. "Besides, the word around the camp was they're carryin' some pretty good whiskey, and I want to try some."

Ballantyne gritted his teeth, then said, "All right, sit down. We'll taste your whiskey, and Horst can give you the information from the papers I got." He picked up a pouch beside him and tossed it to Seidal. "You read better than me."

The sergeant took out several papers from the pouch. He looked around, then said, "This is the dispatch from Lieutenant Colonel Northcutt to Dunmore. Right off, it addresses Connolly as a Lieutenant Colonel."

Wend interjected, "That makes sense. Dunmore made Connolly a captain when he took over Pittsburgh and then a major during the Indian war last year. Undoubtedly he's now commissioned him as a colonel to give weight to his words with the tribal sachems."

Seidal nodded and continued, "There's two other men with him. One's a lieutenant in the Loyalist forces named Allen Campbell. The other is simply identified as a John Smyth, spelled with a 'y.' Plus it mentions they got a couple of servants along."

Ballantyne said, "So I figure we're looking for a party of maybe five or six people."

Wend asked, "Sergeant, does it say when they were leaving?"

"Not exactly, Eckert. The dispatch was written eight days ago and just says they'll leave as soon as they assemble some provisions and weapons."

Wend said, "Henry told me that they were going by boat up to Port Tobacco on the Potomac."

Seidal looked up at Wend. "Yeah, it says that."

Wend thought a second. "Port Tobacco is just about due east of us over on the Maryland side of the river." He did some quick estimating. "If they got away a day or two after that message was written, they could actually be above Alexandria by now. We might already be behind them by the time we cross into Maryland." He gave a quick look at Seidal. "Does it say anything about his route through Maryland?"

"They're supposed to ride northward from Port Tobacco to a place called Fredericktown." He put the paper down into his lap. "And it says that other men will join them there. But it don't say anything about who they are or how many."

Wend mused, "There was no need for Northcutt to identify those people in the dispatch. Dunmore undoubtedly knows who they are." Then he looked over at Ballantyne. "Captain, it might be better for us to just head for Frederick by the fastest way possible."

Ballantyne had been sipping on his whiskey. He lowered the cup and responded, "I'll decide on where we go and when. Like I been sayin', we'll get across the river at Alexandria. There be a little tobacco port on the Maryland side called Georgetown that I 'spect Connolly might have to pass through. We'll ask around there and then decide where to go after that."

Seidal held up the dispatch. "That's all it says that is useful to us. The rest of it is just some reportin' from Northcutt to Dunmore about his battalion."

Wend asked, "You got other papers there. What do they say?"

"One is Henry's orders to us and the letter sayin' you're a lieutenant in the Frederick County militia, and the other is the colonel's orders authorizing the taking of Connolly."

That triggered a thought in Wend's mind. "What are we supposed to do with Connolly and his men if we catch them?"

Ballantyne said, "If we get him alive, we're to take him back to where Henry and the regiment are. Could still be Culpeper—or if this takes a long time, it might be Williamsburg."

Wend exchanged looks with Donegal and Baird, then said to Ballantyne, "If we catch Connolly, I'll have done my job. As you've said often enough, my purpose is only to identify him. And by doing that, I clear my name."

Taddy Carlin said, "Clear your name? That's your opinion."

Wend shot back, "I got that agreement directly from Henry, and you've got no say in it." He motioned to his friends. "I'm telling you now, Ballantyne—the moment we get Connolly, we're going home by the fastest way possible."

Ballantyne stared at Wend for a long, silent moment. The Carlin brothers, Seidal, and Jackson stared at the captain. Finally he spoke. "Eckert, we'll see about that when the time comes."

Wend returned his stare, and said, "Yes, Jedidiah, indeed we will."

Donegal picked up his jug. "I think it's time we get back to our fire. 'Na doubt we'll be startin' at first light."

They had no sooner returned to the other fire when Horner came out of the darkness.

Joshua grinned and said, "Did you get a sight of the young lass with her golden locks?"

Andrew smiled a little self-consciously. "Indeed, I did. She sat down with me, and we talked for a while." He bit his lip, then looked over at Wend. "Sir, are we coming back through here on our return?"

All three of the others broke into laughter.

Donegal said in a knowing tone, "Looks like the lad got on well with the maid."

Wend put his hand to his chin and said, "It seems, Andrew, that you are easily distracted from your pursuit of a certain young Miss Haldorf of Frederick County."

Horner flushed. "Don't mean no such thing. I just had some fun with the tavern girl and thought I'd like to spend some more time with her if we passed through again. It's nothin' serious."

—⁓—

Wend and his three friends sat on the ground, their backs up against the side of a small warehouse situated on a wharf along the Potomac waterfront. The horses were hitched nearby, and Ballantyne's men stood around, arms crossed, listening while their captain argued with the owner and mate of a blunt-bowed, wide-beamed, flat-bottomed scow with a low freeboard that was moored alongside the wharf.

They had arrived in Alexandria in midafternoon after a hard ride and, following inquiries about the availability of ferries, had been directed to the vessel of a certain Jeremiah Kirby, who was one of the few watermen in the business of getting horses, wagons, and heavy freight across the river. Wend thought that the contrast between the backcountry garb of the soldiers and the nautical clothing of the two ferrymen was intriguing. Kirby was dressed in a short, heavy blue jacket, canvas trousers, and high boots, topped by a round, broad-brimmed hat with a low, flat crown that had been glazed to shed spray and rain. Next to him, arms folded in front, stood his mate, who also wore canvas trousers, but instead of a jacket wore a tight-fitting, knit wool sweater and a knit, tassel-topped cap. Both men wore scarves around their neck, which Wend presumed were used to shield their sun-burnished faces from strong winds.

The conflict between Ballantyne and Kirby was about money. Kirby was demanding coinage to take the party across the river. While Henry had provided some money to Ballantyne for incidental expenses—principally provisions for the men and animals—he didn't have enough to pay the ferryman's price.

Ballantyne said, "Look, Kirby, I got the authority to sign a letter that will get you your money from Virginia. Let's go inside your place, and you can write it out."

Kirby shook his head. "What is it goin' to take to make you understand? I got to pay ten men to work the sweeps and help with the sails. They won't take nothin' they can't bite down hard on with their teeth. Plus I got to pay my mate—McPeak here—and put food on my own table. A piece of paper from you ain't gonna do that. So unless you come up with hard coin, the old 'Potomac Endeavor' ain't movin' from her moorings."

Exasperated, Ballantyne said, "Well, if you won't help out in a matter of urgent necessity, we'll have to find another boat."

Kirby smiled and spat. "Good luck with that, sir. Right now there ain't but one other boat workin' that's big enough to take them eleven horses of yours, nine men, and all your gear across the river. And I wager Captain Dan Handley ain't gonna do it for a piece of paper either." Then the ferryman turned to the waterfront and pointed toward where a brig and a couple of schooners were moored. "Or perhaps you'll be able to convince one of those seagoing captains to take you up to Georgetown, though I rather doubt that, since they're here to load tobacco."

Ballantyne's anger was flaring. He stamped his foot. "Damn you, stop baiting me! For God's sake, Kirby, we're on an essential mission for Colonel Patrick Henry of the First Virginia Regiment and the Committee of Safety in Williamsburg. How will your conscious let you sleep at night if you turn us down!"

Kirby shrugged. "I'm a far sight more worried that my good wife will be after me with a sharp stick if I take you over without getting paid. Now, we been through this before, Captain. I don't much care what your big mission is, and I sure as hell ain't never heard of this Colonel Henry or the First Virginia Regiment."

Wend looked over at Joshua and said quietly, "They could go at it for hours, and it isn't getting anywhere."

"So what's going to stop it? Ain't any of our concern. Ballantyne already told you just to mind your own business 'til he needs you to point out Connolly."

Wend sighed. "Yeah, but I want this whole thing over with and to get back to the farm."

At that moment they were interrupted by Ballantyne, having lost his temper, shouting out, "Dammit, Kirby, I could just seize this boat in the name of Virginia! And I'll just do that if you don't take us across forthwith!"

Kirby remained calm, a slight grin on his face. He shrugged his shoulders, put his hands on his hips, and said, "Sure enough, Captain, you could seize this boat. You got lots of men with firelocks, and neither McPeak nor me is armed. But what are you going to do for a crew? Your men know how to pull long sweeps? You know how use the sails and navigate the scow upstream through the current? Or do you think you can hire rowers without any hard money? Seizin' the boat ain't gonna get you anywhere."

Ballantyne's face went red with frustration.

Wend turned back to Joshua and said, "I've got to stop this." He stood up and walked over to the men. The captain and the ferryman stared at him, and Wend said, "Gentlemen, perhaps I can help break this impasse."

Kirby looked him over. "And who, sir, might you be?"

Ballantyne glared at Wend, then said, "Don't pay him no mind. He's got no part in this discussion."

Wend smiled and said, "Say what you want, Ballantyne, but I'm the *nobody* who may be able to provide the wherewithal you need to get across the river."

Kirby pushed his hat back on his head and grinned broadly. "Well, Captain Ballantyne, it seems like this gentleman *should* be part of the discussion."

Ballantyne said, through gritted teeth, "And just how, Eckert, are you going to get the money we need? You carrying it with you?"

"No, not enough. But I do business with a merchant here in town who owes me money. Let me go see him, and I might be able to come back with the fare Kirby is demanding."

Kirby's eyes opened wide. "Now we're talkin'! And just who is this merchant?"

"Charles Gerson, whose shop is up the hill on King Street."

The ferryman's face lit up. "I know Gerson well. He sells firelocks and good steel blades. His store is quite prosperous. Many gentlemen from plantations along the river patronize him."

Wend nodded. "I'm a gunsmith from Winchester. He sells my firelocks. Right now he owes me for some weapons I sent him." He turned to Ballantyne. "Jedidiah, let me go over and see Gerson, and I should be able to return with Captain Kirby's fare."

Ballantyne stared at Wend for a long moment, then finally said, "All right, but I sure as hell ain't lettin' you go alone." He turned to Seidal. "Horst, you go with him and make sure he ain't tryin' to pull anything."

Wend laughed. "Ballantyne, why would I leave behind my friends and property?" Then he said, "There's one more thing. Mr. Kirby, I request that you write out a receipt addressed to the government of Virginia saying that I furnished the money for this crossing, and then have the captain here sign his confirmation. When I come back from Gerson's, I'll give you the money when I'm handed that receipt."

Kirby nodded. "That would be my pleasure."

Wend gave Ballantyne a sharp look. "Are you in agreement?"

The captain's eyes were burning with anger, but he said, "I ain't got much choice."

Wend said, "Good, that's done." He turned toward the warehouse and waved to Horner. "Andrew, come along. It will do you good to meet Mr. Gerson and see his shop."

—⟋⟍—

Wend led Horner and Seidal along the wharves and warehouses until they came to where King Street met the waterfront. Then the three turned and walked up the hill past shops and taverns, which became more prosperous appearing the higher they climbed. Just after they reached the crest and crossed a busy street, he pointed to a store with a large front window and a sign that read "Gerson's: Fine Firelocks and Blades."

The window contained a well-arranged display of merchandise. On the left was an elegant brace of European dueling pistols, and on the right was a heavy set of horse pistols. Spanning the window was a light gentleman's sword with its scabbard below it. But there was an empty display stand where the centerpiece of the exhibit, a long gun by the size of the vacant space, was meant to be. Wend looked inside and saw Gerson himself talking to a well-dressed man who was holding a long-barreled firelock.

As they entered the shop, Gerson looked over and said, "My God, Wend Eckert! Good to see you, sir, unexpected as it is."

Wend nodded, "Good to see you, Charles, and let me say, my presence here in Alexandria is quite by chance."

Gerson turned to his customer and said, "Mr. Compton, you will be pleased to know that Mr. Eckert is the very man who crafted the fine fowling piece you hold in your hands." He turned to Wend and said, "This is Mr. Edward Compton, the master of Pine Grove Landing Plantation, which is a short distance down the Potomac."

Compton looked up from the fowler and at Wend for a few moments. "Well, sir, I must say I was taken by the elegance of your firelock. The wrist is particularly delicate and fits my hand perfectly. And the carvings and scrollwork are beautifully conceived and executed."

"Well, sir, I am gratified by your appreciation of the gun. But I must tell you that the man who did the carving is standing beside me." He put his hand on Horner's arm. "This is my senior apprentice, and he comes from a family of woodcarvers in the old country. It was a lucky day for me when he first walked into my shop."

Andrew blushed faintly and bowed his head slightly at the planter. "I'm glad you are pleased with my work, sir."

Compton said, "Well, lad, I congratulate you on a delicate hand with the knife."

Wend added, "I should also draw your attention to the lock. I import the finest quality from Germany. I assure you it will be extremely reliable."

Compton gazed at the lock, then ran a hand over the finish of the stock. He turned to Gerson and said in a decisive tone, "Charles, prepare your billing for this firelock, and I will return later to pick it up after I conclude some other business." He handed the gun back to the shopkeeper, nodded to Wend and Horner, and left the shop.

Once the door had closed behind the planter, Gerson said, "Eckert, undoubtedly the timely arrival of you and your apprentice here helped make that sale. And send me another fowling piece as soon as you can get one ready. That's the second we've sold in the last six months."

"We'll get started as soon as we get back to Winchester, Charles. But this isn't just a friendly visit. I need your help."

"In any way that is within my power, Wend."

Wend grinned. "You may regret that statement, Charles. I'm here as part of an urgent mission for the Committee of Safety in Williamsburg. As part of that assignment, we need to get nine men, eleven horses, and considerable baggage across the river to Georgetown this afternoon. The leader of the group doesn't have enough hard money to pay the fare of a certain ferryman named Kirby."

Gerson raised an eyebrow. "I'm beginning to suspect why you're here."

"As you can well guess, I need to collect my account with you to pay our passage." Wend told him the amount required. "I believe there is considerably more due to me than that."

"Yes. However, it occurs to me that you might not want to carry the full amount with you on a journey that might, shall we say, feature uncertainties?"

Wend thought a moment. "That makes sense. If I could have the amount for the river passage and then ask you to send the balance in the form of a letter of credit to my home in Winchester, I would be grateful."

Gerson raised a finger. "Here's a better thought: I actually know Jeremiah Kirby very well. I'll provide a letter of debt to him for your fare and deduct that amount from the letter I'll send to Winchester."

"He'll accept paper from you instead of coin?"

"There is no doubt, Wend. When he's ready he'll come along and collect the hard money. Let me prepare the letter. I shall return shortly." He then disappeared into a small office at the rear of the shop.

Seidal had been standing by quietly, taking in the conversation and looking around the shop. Wend noticed he was staring with great interest at an ornate Jaeger rifle that was displayed on a wall rack. In the silence after Gerson left, Wend asked, "Well, Horst, what do you think of this place?"

Seidal looked at Wend and said, "I've never seen anything like this. I've been to plenty of gunsmith shops, but I've never seen anything of the quality and variety of these firelocks."

"Yes, Gerson imports weapons from all over Europe. His clientele are the wealthy of the northern part of the tidewater. I feel honored that he displays my wares alongside some of the most valuable imported pieces and that his customers are satisfied to purchase them."

Seidal nodded slowly and looked down at the fowling piece that was laying on the counter. He ran his fingers along the stock, feeling the smoothness of the oiled finish. "Yes, this is a beautiful piece of work. You can be very proud."

Wend pointed up at the Jaeger rifle. "I saw you looking at that. As Germans, that is something of which we can all be very proud. An earlier generation brought that over from the old land, and it is the father of the rifles we use now."

Seidal grinned at Wend and then very carefully said, "Ja" instead of "Yes." He pointed to a long rifle on display. "The Ulster men on the border often make fun of us Germans, but would be at a loss without their rifle."

Wend said, "Indeed." Then, in the moment of budding companionship, he quietly asked, "Horst, why do you think Ballantyne is so determined in his hatred of me?"

"Jedidiah is my neighbor. His farm is next to mine, and I have known him for years. He has always been a man of strong opinions, yet until recently, he has been very fair. But occurrences over the last year changed him greatly. First was the battle at Point Pleasant. His brother was killed, and so was the colonel of his battalion, a man named John Field, with whom he was great friends. Soon after the encampment was surprised by the Indians, a part of their force tried to take our line on the right flank. Field led his battalion in a counterattack, but he was shot in the head at the first volley. Ballantyne's brother died a few seconds later—he shot down while standing right beside Jedidiah."

"Yes, I see. The experience was very personal for him."

"But there is more, Eckert. When he returned home, he found out that his woman, whom he had married the year before, had died in childbirth. The child died with her. So I think he sits alone in his cabin after the farm work is done, brooding and nursing his bitterness."

"Clearly life has dealt him some misfortune."

Seidal nodded. "So ever since the war, he has harbored a great hatred for Dunmore, blaming him for the loss of his friend and brother. I have heard him talk about this many times in the last year. It led him to raise the company so that he could fight the governor."

"So you think he has extended that hatred to me?"

"Yes. I've thought about this often in the last few days. He recognized you immediately when you came into the camp, and so did many others in our company who went to the war last year. I believe you became his target because he can't get directly at the governor himself."

"So that's why he raised a mob to come after me?"

"There was a lot of talk about you among the men after you passed our camp. Then those two Carlins, who had joined our company while we were on the march to Culpeper, told him about you stopping them from punishing those Loyalists."

Wend interjected, "Which is a lie. There were no Loyalists."

"Truth or lie, I don't know. But it was the final thing Ballantyne needed to rouse the men and lead them to Colonel Henry's tent."

"I'm grateful for you telling me all this, Horst." Then Wend asked, "But something puzzles me. How come you don't seem as angry as the others?"

"Well, I'm older, and of course, I wasn't at Point Pleasant."

Wend was surprised. "No? I had assumed you had marched with your neighbors."

"I stayed behind to lead a group of militia that was to protect our settlement while the others were gone to the fight. So it is logical that I don't have the intense feelings of the others who were there."

"In any case, I'm glad you are along to act as a restraining factor on Ballantyne and the Carlin brothers."

"I try. Fortunately, because I am older and have known him for years, Jedidiah often listens to me. But I must warn you to be watchful. There may come a day when Ballantyne's madness takes him over completely, and I won't be able to hold him back."

Wend sighed. "I understand. And I appreciate your frankness, Horst."

—⁓—

Dusk was coming on when the *Potomac Endeavor* approached George-town. In addition to her ten long sweeps, Endeavor was rigged as a ketch, and at a voice command from Jeremiah Kirby, the mate McPeak bus-ied himself taking in the sails on both masts. When they were in, Kirby swung the tiller over to the left and turned the *Potomac Endeavor* to starboard toward a low pier in Georgetown. A few seconds later he called out to the men at the sweeps, "Toss oars!" And to McPeak he said, "Get the lines over when we're alongside."

The scow slid alongside the pier, and McPeak, who had recruited a couple of the oarsmen to assist with mooring, leaped to the pier to put the lines down around pilings and cleats.

Wend, standing near the boat captain, looked over at the tobacco port and realized it was a tiny place compared to Alexandria. There were a few warehouses along the waterfront, and a brig was moored alongside a wharf. He could see only a few houses, stables, and outbuildings.

He turned to Kirby and asked, "Is there an inn or tavern in Georgetown?"

"Not a proper establishment. But there's a man named Suter who uses his house as a part-time tavern. He sells some spirits, and his good wife will cook a meal for travelers."

"Will he allow us to camp out near his place?"

"I 'spect so. It would make sense if he thought he could sell some rum or whiskey to your party." Kirby smiled. "He's been talking about going into the tavern business full-time for years. Might make sense if the town grows a little more."

Meanwhile McPeak and his men had finished mooring the boat and had gotten a wide brow over to the pier. Kirby shouted out, "Unhitch those horses, and get them off before anything else! And be damned careful getting them across the brow! We don't need animals in the water."

The *Endeavor* had two thwartship hitching rails for horses, located between the two masts, and Wend had been surprised at how quietly the horses had borne the crossing. Ballantyne signaled to the Carlin brothers, who began unhitching the animals and leading them onto the pier. Meanwhile Seidal organized the rest of the party to unload the balance of their gear.

Wend bid goodbye to Kirby and went down to the pier where Ballantyne stood observing the offload of horses, supplies, and equipment.

"Jedidiah, it's near dark. What's your plan?"

"We need to find a place to camp. Then ask around and see if anyone has seen a party that might be Connolly's."

Wend nodded and then told him about Suter and his informal tavern. "It's only a short distance from here." He pointed. "You can see it. Why don't I walk over there and see if we can camp close to his place?"

Ballantyne bit his lip and looked like he would prefer to tell Wend to mind his own business. But probably with the events of Alexandria in mind, he said, with reluctance in his voice, "All right, Eckert. We'll join you there once we've unloaded completely."

Wend was at the Suter house in a few minutes. He knocked on the front door and was greeted by a chubby woman with dark hair. "Are you Mrs. Suter?" he asked.

She smiled. "For these past fifteen years and more, that I have been."

"I'm told that you allow travelers to camp in your pasture. There are nine of us who need to spend the night."

"Oh, yes. That's perfectly all right." She grinned pleasantly, "And my husband keeps a spirit chest he'd be glad to open if you would like some refreshments later. Our charge is very reasonable."

Wend laughed. "I'm sure at least some of the party would find that attractive." Then he continued, "We're coming off a ferry at the moment, and everyone should be here shortly."

Mrs. Suter added, "There's some firewood stacked at the edge of the pasture. Help yourself to it, and Mr. Suter will be along presently to collect our fee, which, like our spirits, is very reasonable."

"Well, ma'am, it seems the Suter family is very reasonable in all things."

The woman laughed heartily, and then her face turned very serious. "We are, indeed. Frequently I tell my husband we are too reasonable!" She nodded to Wend, then turned and went back to her chores.

Later, with the camp set up and two fires burning cheerily in the night, Suter himself came by. He was thin, sharp-faced, and prematurely balding. After collecting money for the firewood, he announced he would be opening his bar directly.

Ballantyne struck up a conversation and presently got around to inquiring about Connolly. "We're interested in a party of three men and two servants who might have come through here, riding up from Port Tobacco, heading for Fredericktown."

Suter shook his head. "Well, if you expect to get word of them here, you've come to the wrong place. It's unlikely anyone coming up from Port Tobacco by horse would pass through Georgetown. They'd have to cross the East Branch of the Potomac at its mouth and then go through the swampy land to the south of here. It's filled with dank, pestilent vapors. Beyond that, the place is inhabited with snakes and other slimy creatures that feed on each other. God knows, no one in their right mind would ever think of living there, and there's only the roughest of trails." He shook his head. "No, they'd take one of several much better roads well to the east of here." He put his hand to his chin. "If you're trying to seek information on such a party, you should go to a place called Hungerford's Tavern, up to the north of here. It's a little farming village, but several roads from the south and east come together there and form the main wagon track up to Fredericktown."

"How far is this Hungerford place?"

"Less than twenty miles and the road is good. You leave here right after dawn, you'll be there by late afternoon." Suter assumed a wistful look. "I've been there a couple of times. It's a good-sized tavern, well kept. There's a right proper village around it." A wistful look came over Suter's face. "I'd like to set up a real tavern like Hungerford's, but this town will have to grow some more before there'll be enough trade for that. We mostly just get the occasional planter delivering his crop who finds he has to stay overnight." He motioned to the men. "This is the biggest party we've had in weeks."

CHAPTER FIVE

HUNGERFORD TAVERN

Suter's estimate had been quite correct. They arrived at Hungerford Tavern with the sun low in the west but still bright; all the buildings were casting long shadows. The tavern was flanked by a substantial village, including a blacksmith shop, a store, a church, and numerous cottages and houses. A ring of farmsteads was visible in the distance.

The tavern itself was actually two structures. The larger was a neat, wooden building, half of which had a second story with dormers protruding from the roof. Three tall, sturdy chimneys rose from the main building, and there was a small, covered porch at its main entrance. The second was a smaller, single-story building. A stable with a fenced paddock stood behind the two structures.

When they were still a hundred yards away, it became clear that something was going on in front of the tavern. There was a crowd of fifty or more people gathered around a large fire. They were watching something happening next to the flames; there was an audible hubbub periodically punctuated by the sound of shouts.

As they closed the distance, Joshua was the first to figure it out. "I'll be damned. They're tarring and feathering someone!"

Then Horner said, "Look up the wagon track. There's a house on fire!"

Wend looked and saw that the apprentice was quite correct; in fact, the burning building was almost fully consumed, a gray-black plume of smoke rising toward the sky. He responded, "Undoubtedly the property of the man receiving all the attention."

Minutes later they pulled up at the edge of the crowd and dismounted. Wend saw a man tied to a stake erected near the fire. He had been stripped naked and one of his tormentors was busy shaving his head. A black iron pot was hung on a tripod over the fire.

Horner exclaimed, "My God, sir, I've heard of this but never seen it."

Wend answered, "Neither have I, but I've heard it described often enough." He pointed to the pot, where a man was stirring the contents with a long wooden paddle. "They're heating pitch pine sap in there. When it reaches the proper temperature to be fully liquid, they'll apply it all over the poor fool with a brush. Then they'll dump feathers over him."

Horner asked, "Won't that burn him permanently? God above, how can he survive?"

"Pitch pine liquefies at a fairly low temperature. It will scorch when they apply it, but I'm told it doesn't scar permanently, at least not all over."

Donegal pointed at a long, round piece of wood laying on the ground. "If I'm 'na wrong, they're going to give him a ride out of town on that rail."

Joshua spoke up. "Look there—over by the tavern. That must be the man's family." He pointed to a spot near the front porch, where a woman stood with a little boy and girl. The woman had a hand over her face and was weeping. The little girl, perhaps four or five, hung on to her mother, her face buried in the woman's skirt. The boy, who was perhaps eight, was staring at what was happening to his father, eyes wide, his face a mixture of horror and anger. Tears were streaming down his face, and his hands had closed into fists.

Wend saw a man in an apron standing on the porch of the tavern, calmly smoking a pipe. He assumed it was the proprietor. A young tavern maid stood beside him. He walked over and said, "We just rode in, sir. My name's Eckert—Wend Eckert from Winchester in Virginia."

The man in the apron took the pipe out of his mouth and said, "I'm Charlie Hungerford. This is my place."

Wend asked, "What's that man done to merit all the attention?"

Hungerford pointed to the victim. "His name's Gil Warfield. He was the town's wheelwright. But he's a well-known Tory , and he didn't have the sense to keep quiet about it, particularly after he'd had a bit of spirits. He got seriously in his cups last night in my common room and began denouncing the Continental Congress and the whole Whig cause. He said that soon enough the king would send his army and put down the whole insurrection and hang the leaders like Washington and Adams and Franklin from the gallows." He shook his head. "That might have been all right if it had been a quiet night, but there was a big crowd, and after Gil stumbled on home, a group of hotheads decided they'd heard enough. So this afternoon, after going around and rousing the village, they marched down to his place with this mob at their backs and pulled him and his family out. Then they set fire to his house and shop and dragged him down here for what you see toward right now."

"Talk is one thing. But did he do anything to support the crown besides bespeaking his loyalty?"

"Not a bit. He just said too much at the wrong time. In these days, that can be a major crime."

Wend looked over at the mob. "Has anyone paused to think that the village will no longer have a wheelwright to keep their carts and wagons in good shape?"

The tavern keeper took the pipe out of his mouth, looked out at the mob, and smiled broadly. "In the frenzy of the moment, I don't believe anyone has thought that far ahead."

"Where's your sheriff? Why doesn't he stop this?"

"Mr. Eckert, this is a damned big county. The government seat is up in Fredericktown, which is a day's ride away. The sheriff don't get down here 'cept maybe once a month, if that." Hungerford shrugged. "And Sheriff Lowell is a staunch Whig and on the Committee of Safety. I seriously doubt he'd do anything if he were here."

"For God's sake, it would be his duty to stop this lawlessness."

"Duty, in these precarious times, is as a man sees it."

Wend was thinking about what to say when suddenly he was aware of Taddy Carlin standing by his side, a crooked grin on his face.

"Well, Eckert, this is a place where they know how to deal with Loyalists. Ain't no one tryin' to keep justice from being served, like you did at the Callow place back in Winchester."

Wend gave the Ulsterman a hard look. "Taddy, by all lights, justice was done at Winchester. Just let it lay."

Carlin grinned broadly. "I'll do that for now, Loyalist, but you'd best watch carefully what's happening here and keep it in mind." He turned and walked back to join the crowd around the fire.

Hungerford, having heard the exchange, looked sharply at Wend but said nothing.

At that moment, Ballantyne came over with Seidal at his side. He called out to Hungerford, "Good afternoon, sir. I take it you are the proprietor of this establishment?"

"Indeed, I am. How can I help you?"

"Sir, I am Captain Jedidiah Ballantyne of the First Virginia Regiment, and this is Sergeant Seidal."

Hungerford's brow furrowed. "Well, Captain, excuse my puzzlement, but what business has brought a military detachment from Virginia north of the Potomac? Perchance are you on your way to join Washington's army?"

"We are on a much more serious mission, sir. We are assigned to stop a party of Loyalists determined to start an Indian insurrection on the border country of Pennsylvania, Maryland, and Virginia."

Hungerford took the pipe out of his mouth. "That would be serious, indeed. And you believe that group of men would come through here?"

"Yes, they traveled by boat to Port Tobacco and are bound for Fredericktown. I'm told that this is the major road to that place."

"You are correct, sir." Hungerford tapped the pipe on the rail to empty it, then put it in a pocket. "Could you describe this party?"

"It consists of at least five people, led by a man named Connolly— John Connolly. He has two compatriots named Cameron and Smyth, and they would be accompanied by at least two servants. Have you seen such a group?"

Hungerford's raised his eyebrows and pursed his lips. He hesitated for a long moment, then looked into the distance over the captain's shoulder and said slowly, "No, I can't say that there's been any party like that here."

Ballantyne quickly responded, "Then it's likely they're still to the south of here?"

The tavern keeper nodded slowly. "That would be the obvious conclusion." He paused a second, then said, "Unless they passed without stopping at the tavern. But given the distance to Fredericktown, along with the lack of any real taverns between here and there, I should think they would have stopped—at least to rest their horses."

The captain turned to Seidal and smiled broadly. "Horst, by God, we've beat them here! We can wait until they come through and then snap them up. I'll wager they'll arrive in the next day or two at the most."

Seidal nodded. "That sounds reasonable, Jedidiah. And in any case, we need to rest our horses. They've had four hard days."

Ballantyne turned back to Hungerford. "Sir, I'm grateful for your information. And with your permission, we'll camp here."

"That would be my pleasure, Captain. You can turn your horses loose in the pasture behind the stable. Now I can also inform you that I have an excellent selection of spirits and my wife puts fine meals on the table. I hope you will avail yourself of our services."

At that moment there was a burst of loud cheering. Wend looked around and saw that a man was brushing Warfield with the pine pitch. The victim writhed and shrieked constantly as the hot pitch was applied.

Another man stood ready with a large bucket of feathers. He was laughing at Warfield's throes.

Suddenly there was a loud wail close to the porch, and Wend saw Mrs. Warfield collapse to the ground. Wend ran over to find out she had fainted and was totally unconscious.

Almost immediately Hungerford was beside him, along with the maid. The tavern keeper said, "Let's get her into the common room."

They carried the limp woman into the tavern, while the maid led the children behind. Once the woman was in a chair, Hungerford got a cup of strong whiskey and placed it under her nose. It soon had the desired effect, and she opened her eyes.

Hungerford asked, "How are you, Charlotte?"

The woman took a deep breath, then a gulp of the whiskey, and said, "I'll be all right, Charlie." Then she shook her head, "Charlie, you know Gil's a good man, and he's been a faithful husband and father."

"Of course he has, Charlotte."

The woman shook her head. "But I've warned him—warned him to keep his mouth closed about all this that's going on. And I warned him again last night when he went off to the tavern. I said, 'Gil, don't you talk politics!'" Tears welled up in her eyes, and she began sobbing. "And now we've lost everything. Everything!"

Hungerford nodded. "It's a shame when a man can be persecuted just for his politics."

Wend asked, "They plan to ride your husband out of town. Is there anywhere you can go? Any place nearby you can seek succor?"

Charlotte looked around with wide eyes. "My brother has a farm in Log Town."

Hungerford said, "That's only a few miles north. You could be there this evening."

The woman shook her head. "But how will we travel? They ran off our horses, and our wagon is in ashes by now."

Just then there was a welling up of sound from the mob outside. Wend stepped out through the door and found the crowd clapping and cheering at the top of their voices. He saw that Warfield had now been covered in feathers. Several men had lifted the rail, and two others were untying the victim from the stake in preparation for mounting him on it.

Looking around, Wend saw Ballantyne and the Carlin brothers at the edge of the crowd, watching with rapt attention to the proceedings. Ballantyne had a stern look on his face. Taddy and Johnny were smiling and laughing outright. Seidal stood beside them, his face expressionless. Nearer to the tavern, Joshua, Donegal, and Horner stood side by side, all three with jaws set and their arms crossed in front of them.

Then Wend heard horse hooves pounding at the gallop from the south. He looked down the road and saw two riders approaching. In the lead was an older man, perhaps in his early fifties. He was mounted on a tall, powerfully built, black stallion, and he was dressed in the clothing of a gentleman of some wealth. He wore a dark green shell jacket, tan leather riding breeches, brown knee-high boots, and a tricorn hat. Behind him, on a fairly nondescript bay, was a younger man of Horner's age, dressed in the clothes of a working man.

The two pulled up a few yards from the crowd, largely unnoticed. The villagers were watching intently as several men were putting Warfield up on the rail; one had a rope in hand to lash him in place.

The man on the black stallion took in the scene at a glance. Then without hesitation he reached down in front of his saddle and pulled a horse pistol from its holster, pointed its muzzle to the sky, and fired.

The sound of the shot reverberated around the yard and produced instant silence. All the people turned *en masse* toward the riders.

Hungerford stepped out onto the porch after hearing the shot. Wend turned to him. "Who is that man?"

"That's Major John Sommers. He's got the largest plantation in the area. It borders Rock Creek just east of the village. He's the head of the local militia and also a member of the Committee of Safety."

Wend looked back and saw that Sommers had slipped his pistol back into its holster and stood up in the stirrups. Towering above the mob, he pointed to the man who had brushed the tar onto Warfield. "Moran, what the devil is going on here? Explain yourself, sir!"

Moran scowled and said, "You can see well enough, Major. We're purgin' ourselves of a damned Loyalist."

"For God's sake, what's Warfield done to deserve this treatment? Put the poor man down, and cease this unlawful mischief."

Moran took a step toward Sommers, wagged his finger at the plantation owner, and said, "Major, I'm warnin' you—don't try to stop us. We had enough of Warfield spoutin' his bile about the Congress and Washington and his takin' the part of the damned king and parliament. We don't need his kind around here."

Sommers waved his hand to take in the entire crowd and shouted, "You all know me! No one here would think I'm of the king's party! But by God, this is cruel and unjust! Gil Warfield has been a good neighbor for fifteen years! I beseech you, cease this insanity immediately, and restore the man to his family."

Moran shook his head. "We ain't listening to you, Major Sommers! Not this time! We're purgin' the village of those what don't think the right way." He quickly took a position ahead of the rail and waved the crowd forward. "Let's get going! Let's take him out past the northern end of town and dump the bastard!"

The pack of people streamed up the wagon track through the village.

Sommers sat back down into the saddle and watched the mob depart. He shook his head in resignation, then dismounted and tied his horse to the hitching rack next to the tavern. His younger companion did the same. He looked up at the tavern keeper and said, "Charles, I damn well need some of that special whiskey you keep."

"Instantly, Major. And I got Mrs. Warfield and their kids inside."

"Oh, Lord, I didn't think of that. Let me see them."

Sommers strode rapidly into the common room, and Wend followed.

The plantation owner exclaimed, "Mrs. Warfield, this is unconscionable! You have my regrets for the whole village, which seem to have lost their mind."

Charlotte Warfield let out a sob. "Those are kind words, Major. But it don't help my Gil none."

"Never fear. I'm going to do what I can for your husband and you, Mrs. Warfield."

Meanwhile, Hungerford brought a whiskey for Sommers. He said, "Major, the Warfields have relations in Log Town if they can get there."

Sommers took a sip, then asked, "Charles, where's the Reverend Gresham? I didn't see him here."

Hungerford made a scornful face. "In his church or his house, I presume, doing his best to ignore the whole damn thing."

Sommers turned to his man who had also entered the room. "James, get down to the church, and bring Gresham here immediately. Don't take any excuses. Drag him along behind you by the collar if he balks. And be sure he brings his medical bag with him."

"That would be my great pleasure, Mr. Sommers."

"And get that woman—Mrs. Parker, I believe it is. The one who midwifes. She's got some doctoring knowledge. We must arrange for some care of Warfield."

After the youth left, Sommers drained his cup and handed it to Hungerford. "Another, Charles." Then he motioned to Mrs. Warfield. "Get her into a separate room. Some of that mob will undoubtedly return here to celebrate. We can't allow her to face that humiliation."

Hungerford motioned to the maid, who led Charlotte and her children away.

Sommers took the second cup from Hungerford and said, "Charlie, as I recollect, you've got a horse cart around here."

"Yes, Major."

"I want to hire it and that nag you call a horse. Have your stable boy get it harnessed up."

"Immediately, Major."

Then Sommers looked at Wend, noticing him for the first time. "Who might you be, sir?"

"Lieutenant Wendelmar Eckert of the Winchester, Virginia militia. Temporarily assigned to the First Virginia Regiment."

Hungerford said, "Major, he and some other Virginians are searching for a party of Governor Dunmore's men."

Sommers looked over Wend critically for a moment, then said, "Well, welcome to our village. I wish it were under more favorable circumstances. I assure, you, sir, we are better people than you witnessed today."

Wend answered, "There's a wildness afoot in the land, sir. We've had similar events in Winchester."

"Yes, Eckert. Chaos has descended and is laying over us like a fog, and I have no idea where it will all end." Sommers gritted his teeth so that the muscles of his face stood out. "Last year myself and two other gentlemen of the area wrote up a Resolve in support of Boston's defiance of the Intolerable Acts. The people cheered it, and we published it in the *Maryland Gazette*. It was strong—in fact, it was more radical in its demands to the king and parliament even than the Resolve published by the   Annapolis Council." He took a sip of whiskey. "Frankly, I would be most satisfied if we could achieve some resolution with the mother country that would allow the colonies to govern themselves in distant loyalty to the crown."

Wend responded, "I think many—perhaps most—people would be happy with such a settlement, so we could all return to the comforts of home and hearth free of the present conflict."

The older man shot back, "Yes, would that could happen! But I tell you, my sense is that things here have gone beyond that happy end. The people here are mightily aroused. They are set against the old government, and I fear only a complete break with the king will satisfy them."

"Mr. Sommers, I submit the Congress must act rapidly in some way to determine our path, be it separation or reconciliation with England. That may provide some unity in purpose."

There was a silence, then Sommers said, "You're quite right. Pray that happens soon."

At that moment, the door opened and James entered, followed by a man dressed in the cloth of a minister. He carried a bag in one hand.

"Here's Reverend Gresham, Major. And Mrs. Farley is on her way."

Sommers glared at the man in black with steely eyes. "Where have you been, Reverend, while all this violence was going on?"

The holy man raised his eyebrows. "Violence? I have been at my desk working on my next sermon, John. I have no knowledge of what you speak."

Now there was pure scorn on Sommers's face. "I was not aware you had become deaf and blind, Reverend. What you are blithely unaware of is that a mob made of most of the villagers just tarred Gil Warfield and rode him out of town covered in feathers. At this very moment, the man is probably laying in agony somewhere north of town."

"My God, sir, we must help him."

"That is precisely the point, Reverend. Now Hungerford is getting his cart and horse ready. James will drive you, Mrs. Farley, Charlotte, and her children out to locate Warfield. I trust you will find it in your heart to minister to both his physical and spiritual needs."

"Of course, John. I will do my best to provide medical assistance and solace."

"Good." Sommers turned to James. "When the reverend and Mrs. Farley have finished, drive the Warfields up to Log Town, and get back as soon as you can."

James nodded. "Yes, Major."

"And make sure to take your pistols, James, in case some of that mob gets the idea of continuing their despicable treatment of Warfield. You won't have to use the things—just show that you've got them and they'll slink away."

Presently Mrs. Parker, a heavyset woman, arrived and Sommers explained what was needed. She immediately agreed to assist, and then she, Gresham, and James went out to where Hungerford and his stable boy were getting the cart ready.

Sommers finished off his whiskey and slammed the cup down on the bar. He looked over at Wend. "What did you say you and your detail were in Maryland for, Lieutenant?"

"I didn't. But we're after a party of Lord Dunmore's allies who are intent on fostering a tribal uprising out on the Ohio border."

Concern spread over Sommers's face. "I marched with Forbes and led a company on the border during the Pontiac business. A wave of war parties sweeping through the backcountry now would be a bloody disaster for our cause!"

"Agreed, sir. That's why we must intercept this party."

"How many of them are there?"

"We believe there are three conspirators and two servants, all mounted. They're led by a man named Connolly who has many connections with the Indian sachems. He's riding with a Highlander lieutenant and a third man we know little about."

Sommers froze and stared at Wend. "What does this fellow Connolly look like?"

"Early thirties, lean-bodied, hatchet-faced, prominent nose, and high forehead."

"My God, I believe those men passed through here two days ago. I encountered them out on the road at an intersection to the south of here in the early evening. They were looking for Hungerford's Tavern. Indeed, there were five of them. And the man who did all the talking fits your description of this Connolly fellow."

"Did they say anything else?"

"They asked me how far to Fredericktown. I told them it would be a day's ride on up to the county seat, and then I explained how to get to Hungerford's."

"Well, we were hoping to intercept them here. But obviously we're now behind them."

Sommers shrugged. "I have a friend who is the master of a trading brig. He has an expression he uses often: 'A stern chase is a long chase.' My friend, I regret to say that's what you've got now."

"It would appear so, sir. And I thank you for your assistance."

Sommers nodded to Wend. "Good luck, Lieutenant. Meanwhile, I've got to ride home posthaste. My good wife expects me for the evening meal, and if I'm too late, she'll have me up on a rail like Warfield." And with that he strode out the front door.

—⚶—

The Virginians' camp was set up between the tavern and the stable. At the Winchester fire, the meal of salt beef was boiling in a pot. Meanwhile appetizing smells were wafting from the tavern kitchen, and Joshua was grumbling. "We been eatin' travelin' rations for ten days. Why don't we go into the common room and have a real meal for once?" He motioned toward Wend. "You got some coin on you."

"Yeah, Joshua, I do. But it won't go far if we start burning it in tavern common rooms now. Who knows how long we'll be on the road."

Baird made a face. "Ballantyne said that the tavern keeper told him Connolly ain't been through here yet. That means we just got to sit here until he arrives. Could be anytime now." He looked up at the evening sky. "Damn, it could even be tonight they come ridin' into the village."

Donegal said, "Joshua's right, Wend. We could be on our way home tomorrow with Connolly in tow."

Wend sighed. "I hate to disappoint you gentlemen, but the truth is, Connolly is ahead of us. Undoubtedly he's in Fredericktown or beyond by now."

Baird stiffened. "Now what the hell makes you say that?"

"Joshua, Hungerford lied for some reason. That planter Sommers told me that he ran into Connolly and his party on the road two days ago and they stayed here overnight."

Donegal made a face. "You told Ballantyne yet?"

"No, I'll tell him in the morning. If I told him now, he might want to ride out tonight in desperation to catch Connolly. And our horses need rest after the way we been pushing them since Culpeper. At least we can give them tonight in the pasture."

Baird laughed. "You're going to have devil to pay when you tell Ballantyne about this in the morning."

"Yeah, but he's got a point about the horses, Joshua," said Donegal. "And I don't relish the idea of ridin' through the night. We need the rest as much as the animals."

Wend added, "Meanwhile, I want to go into the tavern and see if I can get more information out of Hungerford."

Joshua perked up. "Now that's a great idea. Let's eat this damned beef and get on over there."

Wend shook his head. "No, all of you stay here. I've got a better chance of getting Hungerford to talk if I'm alone. Besides, I wager you've got better whiskey here than anything Hungerford's got behind his counter."

After their meal, Wend walked over to the tavern. It was a busy night in the common room. As Sommers had predicted, a portion of the crowd had come back to celebrate the banishment of Warfield, and they loudly occupied two tables that had been pulled together. The man named Moran, who apparently had been the leader of the mob, presided over the congregation. The Carlin brothers, drinks in hand, were standing over the tables, joining in the talk and laughter. Ballantyne sat alone at a corner table, pipe in hand, silently watching the others. Seidal was sitting at the bar, a rum drink in hand, staring into the distance, obviously deep in thought. Other men sat and stood around, partaking of food and drink. Hungerford presided behind the counter while two maids circulated throughout the room, attending to the needs of the patrons.

Wend quietly walked to the bar and sat beside Seidal. "Hello, Horst. I see you're not celebrating with the Carlin boys. And you're not keeping company with your neighbor Jedidiah. A night for quiet reflection?"

The sergeant looked over at the Carlins. "Yes, I see nothing to celebrate tonight. Frankly, I hope we can catch Connolly tomorrow or the next day, as Ballantyne expects, and then we can get back to the regiment. I enlisted to fight Dunmore and the king. We should be drilling our battalion to fight the Loyalist army, not running over the countryside like this. They should have sent someone else to catch this Connolly."

Wend saw an opening in Seidal's words. "Interesting you should be talking about training. That's what an experienced soldier would say. And the word around the First Virginia camp was that you had had time as a serving soldier, not just in the militia."

Seidal didn't immediately answer, and Wend signaled to Hungerford for a drink of whiskey. Then he continued in his question to the sergeant.

"Was it perhaps Washington's old Virginia Regiment, or one of the rifle companies, back in the French war?"

Horst slowly turned and looked at Wend. "Neither. I was in the Royal Americans."

Wend took some of his drink. "My God, the British Army itself."

"Yes, I enlisted in the Fourth Battalion of the 60th in 1755 when I was just eighteen. I was desperate to get off my father's farm west of Philadelphia." He grinned to himself. "And then I learned there are worse things than being a farmer."

Wend raised his cup in salute. "Spoken like a true veteran, Horst. But if you were in the Fourth, you fought at Quebec in the Battle on the Plains of Abraham. The biggest battle of the war—and the one that essentially ended it."

"Yes, that is true. But then after the war, the battalion was disbanded, and we were all drafted into the First Battalion, which was well under strength."

"So you served under Bouquet."

"Yes, but I only saw him once. I was posted to Fort Venango on the border well north of Fort Pitt."

Wend froze with his drink in front of his face and turned to Seidal. "Fort Venango was attacked and burned to the ground in the first days of the Pontiac War in 1763. I heard everyone there died."

Seidal didn't respond immediately. He sat looking into the distance, his drink in hand. "That is true. But I was out of the army just before that happened." He took a gulp. "The fact is, I lost many friends there."

"Well, you were indeed lucky."

"Yes, indeed I was. I think about it all the time."

There was a stir behind them. All the village men were getting up from the table and heading for the door. Ballantyne also got up and signaled for his men to leave. Seidal finished off his drink and took his leave. In a couple of minutes, Wend was alone in the common room with Hungerford while the maids worked to clean up. Wend nursed his drink until the women had finished up and left for their quarters.

Wend was about to start a conversation with the tavern keeper, intending to work up to the questions he had—when Hungerford turned toward him. "Eckert, I noticed something today. Ballantyne and his men think of you as a Loyalist. I heard one of them even call you out while Warfield was being tarred. It seems strange that you are with them."

"I have been drafted—or compelled—to be here, if you will, Charles. They put up with my presence because I personally know and can recognize the object of their search, Colonel Connolly of the British forces."

Hungerford gave Wend a sharp look, then said cautiously, "So are you of the king's camp?"

"Actually, Charles, the fact is we are all still subjects of the king, aren't we? The Congress in Philadelphia still maintains that we are trying to reach an accommodation with George and parliament. Until they make a decision that we should push for some form of independence, we are all Loyalists."

Hungerford laughed out loud. "Try to explain that to the hothead villagers around here, and you might find yourself riding the rail like Warfield."

"Yes, Charles. But I think I find myself in the presence of a real Loyalist who is active in support of the king's cause."

Hungerford froze, staring at Wend. "Eckert, you're crazy!"

Wend said nothing. Instead he got up from his seat. In a deliberate manner, he walked around the end of the bar and approached the tavern keeper.

Hungerford backed up until he was stopped by the wall and said in a shaking voice, "For God's sake, what are you doing, Eckert?"

Wend reached out, grabbed Hungerford by his jacket collar, and slammed him against the wall so hard his head snapped back against the wood. He looked at Wend with the vacant stare of a physically stunned man.

Wend glared at the proprietor silently for a few long moments, giving him time to recover his senses. Then he said, in the most menacing tone he could manage, "Hungerford, I'm as hard a man as you will ever encounter. I've killed men in what they call cold blood with knife and firelock. Now, unless you tell me what I want, I'll inform Ballantyne and the two Carlin brothers where your real loyalties lie. And I vow they'll tie you up to that stake where Warfield was bound, shave your head, and leave you with a sign telling all the people here you're a king's man. And I'd not be surprised if they didn't put a torch to your esteemed tavern. Damn, maybe I'll do it myself."

"For God's sake, you've lost your mind! I tell you—I'm for the cause as much as the next man."

"The hell you say. If you're so loyal, why did you lie about Connolly and his party not being here? I know they were here two days ago."

"I tell you they've not been here!"

"It won't work, Hungerford. Major Sommers told me he spoke with Connolly's party down at the intersection south of here two days ago. He described him perfectly. And he said they specifically asked for the whereabouts of your place."

Wend literally lifted the tavern keeper off his feet and pulled him within inches of his face. "I say they knew your sympathies and had reason to believe you'd help them. And then you lied today to delay us here while Connolly opened his lead on us."

"I tell you none of this is true!"

Wend pulled the pistol from his belt and put it on the counter. "We're wasting time. I know you helped Connolly and that he's ahead of us. I guess I don't need the details. But one thing's sure: You've helped him launch a host of war parties on the backcountry. Have you ever seen a farmstead where the entire family has been murdered and the women raped? You ever seen the people of an entire village lying dead in the road? I've seen all that, and so have the men with me." Wend formed his face into a snarl. He bounced Warfield's head against the wall again. "Forget being tied to the stake." Wend moved his hands upward until they surrounded the man's neck. "I'll strangle you, and your wife will find you slumped here."

Hungerford wailed loudly in total surrender, his face distorted in wild terror. "For God's sake, take your hands away! I'll tell you everything."

Wend continued the pressure on his neck. "Talk now. I'll release you when I'm convinced you're being honest."

"It wasn't about being a Tory. It was about money—that's all. A few days ago, a man rode in. He was a planter from down in the tidewater. He slapped hard coin down for me to help this Connolly fellow."

"What kind of help, Charlie?"

"He said they'd need provisions, and he gave me a list of what to have ready. And he wanted me to put them in rooms where other guests wouldn't see much of them. The rooms in that other building were perfect for that. He paid me in advance for the rooms. Then he told me that somebody would probably come looking for Connolly and his men. Something about dispatches being captured. So I wasn't supposed to tell anyone they had been here."

Wend asked, "And that was all you were told?"

"Yes, I swear, that's all there was to it. Like I said, it was just about money."

"And of course, you couldn't figure out that they were king's spies on a secret mission?"

"It wasn't my business." He shrugged. "Look, I don't make a lot of money here. I wasn't about to turn down cash up front."

Wend thought of another question. "What name was Connolly going by? He wasn't using his own name, was he?"

"Cantrell—John Cantrell. That was the name he was using."

Wend took his hands away. He reached under the bar and pulled out some of the good whiskey and filled his cup. "I'll just have some of this at your expense, seeing as you've been pretty well compensated in this business."

Meanwhile, Hungerford slumped down and began to breathe more easily. He rubbed his neck with a hand. "You're welcome to it, Eckert. Just don't let anyone in the village know what I told you. And keep those border country ruffians with you—Ballantyne and those Carlin boys—away from me."

Wend took a deep gulp of the whiskey. It wasn't bad but not on a par with Donegal's. He turned to Hungerford. "You're calling those fine, upstanding soldiers of Virginia oafish ruffians?"

"You heard me."

Wend grinned broadly. "You know, Charlie, I'd have to say I agree with you on that particular matter."

—m—

The next morning had the cold rawness of impending winter. Wend, bundled in his greatcoat, was huddled close to the fire, just finishing his coffee, when Joshua asked, "When you going to let Ballantyne know that Connolly's ahead of us?"

Looking down at his cup, Wend asked, "Is there more coffee in the pot? I'm not in any hurry."

But just then, the captain himself walked over from the other fire. "Eckert, bring your people over. We need to discuss my plan for taking Connolly and his party into custody when they arrive."

Wend looked around at his friends, then up at the captain. "Jedidiah, you can forget that. Connolly is in Fredericktown by now."

"The hell you say. You heard what Hungerford said yesterday."

"He lied, Jedidiah. That planter, Major Sommers, told me he encountered the Connolly group on the trail three days ago now. They asked the way to this tavern by name. And last night, I shook up Hungerford a little, and he came clean."

"You mean the bastard is a Loyalist who knowingly helped them?"

"He may or may not be that, but he took money to help Connolly with supplies and hid his party in one of the rooms over in the second building."

Ballantyne's face had been getting red as he listened. He spoke through clenched teeth. "You learned this last night?"

"Yes, after you left the tavern. I also learned that he's traveling under the name of John Cantrell."

The captain responded, "And you didn't tell me then? You left this lay overnight?"

"Didn't seem much sense in waking you up. Particularly since we couldn't start for Fredericktown until morning anyway."

"The hell you say! We could have made up some ground by riding through the night."

Baird stood up, pointed toward the pasture, and snorted. "Shit, you're dead wrong about that, Jedidiah. All the horses have been pushed hard for four days since we left Culpeper. And our horses have been on the road for ten days since we left Winchester. The truth be they should have days in the pasture to regain their strength. But we owed them at least the night resting and grazing."

Ballantyne stood glaring at Joshua, his jaw set and the muscles working in his face. He shouted, "Damn it! I'll ride these horses into the ground to get Connolly."

Joshua shrugged. "Well, that's exactly what you would have been doing."

Meanwhile, Wend took the last gulp of his coffee, then said, "There's something else you need to know, Ballantyne. Connolly suspects he's being pursued."

"What makes you think that?"

"Because the Loyalist agent who paid off Hungerford told him they know the dispatches were captured. They assume someone would be sent out to stop Connolly." Wend watched agitation grow on the captain's face. "So we've probably lost any element of surprise. Connolly will be looking over his shoulder and will be taking measures to avoid capture. And undoubtedly he's prepared to fight us off if we catch up."

As the words had become more heated, Ballantyne's men had come over from their fire. Taddy Carlin scowled and said, "Eckert, why should we believe this? I say you're trying to throw us off Connolly's trail."

Wend shook his head. "As usual, you're being absurd, Taddy. We know Connolly must go to Fredericktown, no matter what happens, to join up with allies. Why would I tell a lie to get us there before him?"

Seidal said, "Jedidiah, stop and think. What Eckert is saying is logical. It would be easy for Connolly to have passed through here before we arrived. And if that's true, if we stay here he's getting way ahead of us. If Eckert were trying to help him, he'd be encouraging us to stay right here."

Wend said, "Ballantyne, there's a chance Connolly is still in Fredericktown. His compatriots may not have arrived, and he may be waiting for them. Or they may have to take some time to get fitted out for the journey along Braddock's Road. It's possible we can stop him right there."

Ballantyne put his hand to his chin, obviously working through what he had heard. Then he said loudly, "Break the camp! Saddle the horses! We ride for Fredericktown immediately."

Everyone went to pack up their gear, and Ballantyne turned to go, but Wend put a hand on his shoulder. "Jedidiah, take care to mind what Joshua said about the horses."

The captain turned back. "Eckert, the horses will get us to Fredericktown. It's only twenty miles, and they damn well got that in them."

"Not if you push them too hard, particularly our horses. They're well-bred stock, but like Joshua said, they've been pushed for many days. And they're loaded with supplies and weapons besides the riders. Saving a few hours won't be worth broken-down animals."

Ballantyne snapped. "Leave that to me. You just get packed up and mounted."

—⁂—

They got away from Hungerford tavern just after dawn. And almost as if intentionally defying what Baird and Eckert had told him, Ballantyne pushed the pace and allowed little time for resting or even leading the horses. The only lengthy stop was at a small, mean tavern about fourteen miles north called Dowden's Ordinary, where they watered the animals. But after less than a half hour, the captain had them on the road again.

The horses, loyally trying to do what was demanded of them, actually lasted longer than Wend would have expected. But by midafternoon all the animals were showing signs of exhaustion.

Finally, Joshua pulled his hunter up and slid to the ground. "All right, Ballantyne, you bastard. This has gone on long enough."

Ballantyne, who was in the lead, pulled up and looked back. "What are you doing, Baird? Get back up on that horse."

"No way. I'm leading him the rest of the way. Look at his head hangin' down. He's had it."

Wend also swung down and waved to Donegal and Horner to dismount. "We're all leading out, Ballantyne. We can't be that far from the town. We'll do the rest on foot."

The captain set his jaw and was about to speak when Horst Seidal also dismounted. "They're right, Jedidiah. The horses have done as much as they can. We need to find a place where we can stay a couple of days to rest them. I say they'll need no less than two. Three would be better."

In silent agreement, the rest of the men dismounted and started to lead, leaving only Ballantyne mounted. Finally he surrendered and threw down. His anger was palpable, and no one said anything for a long mile.

Presently a horse cart came into view over a hill, coming toward them down the wagon track. As the distance closed, Wend saw that it was a farmer with a load of feed bags.

When farmer was upon them, Ballantyne held up his hand. "Good day, sir."

The farmer answered in a thick German accent, "*Ja*, the day is good."

Seidal spoke up in German. "Sir, how far to Fredericktown?"

The farmer answered in the same language, "A good four miles."

Horst explained, "We've been traveling hard, sir. We need a tavern with a good pasture for horses. What is the nearest such?"

"You are lucky. There is a very good tavern right on the south edge of the town. It is in open country and has a large pasture. It is called the Red Vixen and is run by a lady; the Widow McGraw. It will be the first place you come to just before arriving in Fredericktown proper. I should say you could make it in an hour."

Seidal nodded. "We thank you, sir, and wish you a good day."

The farmer slapped the reins, and as the cart started on its way, he grinned and called out in English, "I think you men will find the widow's place well to your taste."

Donegal watched the departing farmer and asked to no one in particular, "Now what do you suppose he meant by that?"

A little more than an hour later, they came to the Red Vixen. Situated right alongside the road, it was a substantial, two-floor stone structure, somewhat bigger than Hungerford's place. A large stable with a spacious paddock was behind, and beyond that were a pasture, a vegetable garden, and some hay fields.

They led their horses directly to the fence of the paddock and began unsaddling.

Two Conestoga wagons and a cart were parked together near the stable. Simon motioned toward the wagons. "Looks like the wagoners think this is a good place to stay."

Joshua said, "That may be true, but I don't see any Conestoga horses in the pasture or the paddock. Now that's a bit strange."

Just then Ballantyne called out, "I'll go in and make arrangements for camping and taking care of our horses."

Baird looked over at Wend. "How about getting a room? We been living out on the ground for over two weeks now. My ancient back could use a bed or even just a pallet on the floor. And that old wound in my hip has been achin' with all this cold weather."

Wend grinned back at his friend. "All right, Joshua, just because you're getting so decrepit." He turned to Horner. "Go in and get a room for the four of us."

Horner nodded and followed Ballantyne.

The apprentice was back in a few minutes, and he walked up to Wend with a bemused look on his face. He stood there, biting his lip, as if uncertain what to say.

Wend grinned. "Has the cat got your tongue, Andrew? Is the room all arranged?"

Horner shook his head. "No, sir. It was *most* strange in there. I talked to Mrs. McGraw. I told her what we wanted, and she said no problem. Then she asked whose name she should list it under in her register." He paused a moment, bit his lip again, then continued, "So I gave her your name. And then when she heard it, she put her quill down and gave me a queer look. She asked me if you were a gunsmith and whether you had ever lived in Pennsylvania. And when I said you had, she said, 'You tell Mr. Eckert that there's no room until he comes here and makes arrangement to pay for what he already owes me for services rendered.'"

Wend was stunned. "I don't know any Mrs. McGraw. How could I owe her money?"

Horner shrugged. "Sir, like I said, it's the most puzzling thing."

Baird and Donegal had been listening. The Highlander laughed and said, "You'd better take yourself in there and solve the great mystery!"

Joshua said, "Yeah, git goin'. I can already feel that good mattress, so you better settle matters with the old widow woman. I ain't gonna be in any good mood if I spend another night out on the ground."

Wend said, "This is ridiculous. There's clearly some mistake." Then he strode off, determined to deal with the widow and her confusion.

CHAPTER SIX

THE WIDOW MCGRAW

The interior of the Red Vixen was well lit, cheery, and, Wend noted, exceptionally clean. A fire crackled in the main hearth, dissipating the November chill. His nose perked up to the aroma of savory food cooking in the kitchen. Looking around, he saw that the common room was empty except for four attractive tavern maids sitting at a table near the fireplace, talking and laughing, and a fifth who was stoking the fire itself. A heavyset, dark-haired woman wearing a brown gown and white apron stood behind the bar cleaning the surface of the counter. Wend estimated her to be in her late fifties or early sixties.

Wend walked over and said, "Mrs. McGraw, I'm Wend Eckert. I believe you told my apprentice that I owed you payment for something. I came in to clear up the confusion."

The old lady looked up and said in a sharp tone, "Young man, I ain't been confused about nothin' since I was at my mother's skirts. And I ain't the widow. My name's Edna Farley. You'll find Mrs. McGraw in her office through that door." She pointed to an open doorway just at the end of the counter.

Wend walked over and knocked on the door frame. A husky but feminine voice said, "Come on in."

He stepped in and saw the back of a tall, slim-waisted, straight-backed woman in an apple-green gown. She was staring out a westward window, which looked out at the courtyard and the setting sun, with one hand resting on her desk and the other on her hip. The rays of light highlighted her rich auburn hair visible below her white cap.

The woman turned around, displaying a thin, high-cheekboned face with startling green eyes. A lock of the red hair was down just over her left eye.

Wend stood frozen in stunned astonishment.

His mind went racing back twelve years to a tavern called The Proud Rooster on the outskirts of York. And to the memory of a young tavern maid who, without knowing him, had once shielded him from mortal harm.

Finally he was able to find words. "My God, Colleen Alison!"

"Colleen *McGraw* now, Wend Eckert. And I've been damn well waiting more than a decade to collect what you owe me! I saved your bloody life from two of Richard Grenough's men by lying for you. I told them in front of everyone in the common room of The Proud Rooster that you had been in bed with me at the time they accused you of breaking into Grenough's warehouse. And then I had you make love to me as payment for that because, bless my soul, I took a hankering to you."

"Colleen, I'll never forget that night and what you did for me."

"You'll never forget that night? You ungrateful ass! What I'll never forget is that you left me to wake up alone in bed the next morning without so much as a kiss on the cheek or a simple 'goodbye.' I drifted off expecting to get at least one more *payment* before you rode off."

"I had urgent business in Carlisle, and I felt it would be best to get away before those men came back. I thought it would keep you out of danger."

She slowly approached until her face was a few inches from his, smiled seductively, and said quietly, "So now are you ready make amends for leaving me alone in a cold bed and settle up on the last part of your bill?"

"Colleen, I'm married with four children."

She threw back her head and laughed. "So what? Listen, every night the good, churchgoing, married men of Fredericktown come here to pay money to bed my girls, and once in a while they even pay my own price, which I assure you is quite dear. That fresh-faced apprentice you sent in here said you live near Winchester in the great valley of Virginia, so your wife is hundreds of miles away. How is she to know?"

She took two steps back, put her right hand on her hip, and cocked her head to the left. "Will you insult me by saying I do not tempt you in the least?"

"Colleen, you're as enticing as I remember. And I'll always be in your debt. But I've not violated my vows in ten years, and it's not my intention to start now."

There was a long moment of silence. Finally, Colleen took another step back, and said, "All right, at least you can favor me with some of your time. Give a lonely widow woman some company. After dinner, it's my practice to seek some respite in solitude. Come sit with me before the fire in my room for a while, and we shall talk as old friends."

Wend grinned. "The last thing I'll believe is that you're a *lonely* widow. However, I can't refuse that request; indeed, it will be my pleasure. But you must tell me how you became Mrs. McGraw and how you came to own a tavern here in Maryland."

"That's simple. Georgie McGraw was a widower whom I met a few months after your visit. He was traveling to Philadelphia on business. He wanted to buy a bond slave just off a ship to serve in his tavern. His wife had died the year before, and he was lonely, and when he stopped at the tavern in York, he took a fancy to me and offered to pay for my favors.

In bed, he told me he was childless and that he owned this tavern." She shrugged. "I saw my opportunity and made sure to find him exciting and show him a good time. On the way back from Philadelphia, he stopped at the tavern and offered to buy out my indenture if I came to work for him. The rest was easy. We were married a couple of months later."

"Should I ask if you were in love with him?"

"You know the answer to that. He was near forty. I was going on eighteen. It was enough for me that Georgie was a decent man. But I knew how to give him what he needed in companionship and had the knowledge to help him run the tavern. The truth was, he gave me a better life than I had ever expected. Probably the best thing he did was teach me to read and write a little and enough about ciphering to keep the accounts."

"When did you become a widow?"

She shrugged. "Three years ago. I'll admit I was genuinely sad when he got lung fever in the middle of a cold winter and died."

"And so you took over the tavern."

"Yes, and I knew how to run it to make *real* money. I hired Edna to cook and run the day-to-day work. Then I scoured the countryside and found girls who looked good and didn't mind how they earned their money. Pretty soon we were doing a very good business, better than Georgie could ever have dreamed." She laughed knowingly. "The women of Fredericktown have little regard for me, but the men hasten to spend time with my girls."

Then it was Wend's turn to laugh. "That explains why the farmer who sent us to the Red Vixen said that we would find it to our liking."

"Well, he knew what he was talking about." Colleen grinned, then wrinkled her nose and suddenly turned very businesslike. "Now don't take this the wrong way, Mr. Eckert, but you smell mighty strongly of days on the road. I'm going to give you that room you wanted, and I'm going to send up a tub and have one of the girls draw water. Please avail yourself of it before you come down to join me in front of the fire."

—⚹—

Wend, immersed in water, sat in the wooden tub that a stable boy and one of the maids had carried up to the room and then filled with buckets. It had been placed in front of a fireplace with a crackling blaze, and Eckert luxuriated in the warmth. Meanwhile, Baird lay sprawled in one of the two beds, and Donegal sat in the room's only chair, enjoying a pipe. Horner was on his feet, staring out a window into the courtyard of the tavern.

The apprentice turned to Wend and said, "Sir, I think I'll go down to the common room for a while."

Joshua grinned. "I think the sprout is bored with sittin' around with all the tired old men."

Donegal took his pipe out of his mouth. "He should be, but there's 'na doubt the laddie liked the look of that towheaded maid that was bringing the water. She's a scrawny slip of a girl but comely enough. And one thing's for sure, we've learned the laddie is fond of yellow hair."

Horner blushed slightly. "I just thought I'd sit in front of the fire there. There's no chair for me here." A guilty look came over his face. "And the truth is, she isn't hard on your eyes. And neither are the other ones."

Wend looked around at Joshua and Simon and then said to Horner, "Andrew, I want to tell you something before you get too interested. Looking is all you'll do with those girls unless you've got some coin in your pocket."

Horner scrunched up his eyebrows and said naively, "Sir, I'm not clear in your meaning."

Simon laughed. "Now lad, it's easy enough. He means they're harlots."

The apprentice blushed more deeply. "Even that girl who was here?"

Wend nodded. "Yes, lad. Now listen. The widow told me she searched them out and picked them for their looks and their willingness to earn their keep in bed. You go ahead down to the common, and you'll witness the men of Fredericktown roll in, and soon enough some of them will climb the stairs with those maids."

Horner bit his lip. "But she's so young! The others are older than her."

Baird laughed. "Lad, you've got a lot to learn. For some men, the younger the better."

Andrew's jaw jutted out, and he looked at both of them in turn, then back at Wend. "Well, sir, I'm still going downstairs. There's more going on down there than here."

Wend waved at him. "Do what you want, and enjoy the view, lad. It costs nothing to look. And I have no doubt the girls will be very friendly to you. That's what they're paid to do."

Horner hurried out without saying anything further.

When the door had shut behind him, Donegal smiled slyly. "You know, I was watching that lass's face while she was filling the tub. She was stealing glances at our boy Andrew now and then."

Wend shook his head. "She may be interested in the lad, but if I know Colleen, she'll keep the girl's head on her business."

"Which brings us," interjected Joshua, "to the question of how you happen to know Widow McGraw. You haven't told us much about that."

Wend closed his eyes and enjoyed the feel of the water. "You two know a lot about it. You just don't realize what you know."

"Now the lad is serving us with riddles, Joshua," snapped Donegal.

Baird yawned and stretched his frame out over the bed. "Yes, stop playing games. Tell us what you say we're supposed to know already."

Wend opened his eyes. "Well, do you remember that wagon trip I took in the spring of 1764 from Sherman Mill down to Shippensburg?"

Joshua answered, "Yes, you were going to investigate that new forge to see if they could make rifle barrels."

"Well, I did that, but I also used that time to sneak into Grenough's warehouses at Shippensburg and York to try to catch him with stores of powder and lead for trading with the Indians."

"Bless me, aren't you the tricky devil, Wend Eckert," Donegal said and laughed.

"Not tricky enough, Simon. The night I was at the York place, two of Grenough's men—Price Irwin and Shane Reilly—witnessed me coming out of the warehouse. But they just saw a shadowy figure in the darkness and didn't know who it was. I ran into a patch of woods and was able to get back to the tavern where I was staying before they caught up with me. Later, they came in, armed with pistols, ready to grab anyone who looked suspicious."

Baird raised his head from the pillow. "By God, Irwin would have recognized you from that time he and Grenough bumped into us out at Fort Bedford."

"Correct, Joshua."

Donegal raised his finger. "And Shane Reilly was with those men who were chasing Charlie Sawak after the massacre of the other Conestoga Indians and knew you were helping him get away!"

"That's right. They both knew who I was and put two and two together when they came into the common room. Irwin walked up to my table while Reilly stood at the bar. They had me in a crossfire if it came to shooting. Then, in front of the patrons and the proprietor, Irwin accused me of being a thief who had broken into the warehouse, and he demanded that I leave with them. He said they were taking me to the sheriff, but you can guess what really would have happened." Wend looked at his two friends. "That's when Colleen Alison came up and told them I couldn't have been out at Grenough's place that night because I had been in bed with her."

"So had you been passing time with her?" asked Joshua.

"No. The only previous contact was that she had served me dinner. She just took a liking to me."

Donegal looked at the ceiling. "Oh, Lord above, spare me."

Wend continued, "At any rate, that left them no choice but to leave. Later that night, Colleen slipped into my bed. She joked that I could pay her back by making love to her."

Joshua wrinkled up his face and held up a finger. "Now it's coming back to me. Months later, after you were married to Peggy and we were on the way to Winchester, Grenough had those two ambush us in that pass through the Tuscarora Mountains. And then, when we had killed Price and Reilly was laying wounded, you dispatched him by driving your knife up between his legs. And then you said—"

Donegal's face lit up. He interjected, "By God, you said that was for Colleen Alison! Because Reilly had raped her!"

"Yes. A day after I left the tavern, Reilly came back with Matt Bratton, and they caught Colleen out at the woodpile behind the place. They beat her, then took turns on her, trying to get her to admit I was the one who had broken into Grenough's warehouse."

Joshua said, "So if you had left the day before, how did you learn that Colleen had been beaten and raped?"

"Colleen had agreed to watch out for Matt Bratton and let me know if he showed up at York with his wagon. I knew if he did that, he'd be picking up powder and lead and that he'd soon be heading west to trade with the tribes. But she didn't know how to read or write, so she had one of the other maids write the letter for her. What she didn't know was that her friend included a description of the rape so that I would understand what Colleen had borne for my sake."

Simon looked puzzled. "So where does her claiming that you owed her money come in?"

"It's not money. She's mad that I left her alone in bed the next morning without making love again or even saying goodbye. That's the payment she says I owe her."

Donegal's face lit up. "So now we know why the widow is getting you all cleaned up and having you visit with her tonight. She's aiming to get final payment of your account."

Wend gave the Highlander a hard look. "She may still have that in mind, but nothing is going to happen."

—ɷ—

Wend descended the stairs to the common room and found that with the coming of evening, the place had filled up. Fifteen or twenty men were at the tables, and the girls were scurrying around serving their food and drink requirements. He noted that Ballantyne and his men were relaxed at one table, each with a cup in his hand. Horner was right in front of the hearth, and Wend was surprised to see that the young blond maid who had filled his bath was standing in front of the table, tray in hand, engaged in conversation with Andrew. Both were laughing and giggling.

A stout man was tending the bar, and Wend approached him. "Where can I find Mrs. McGraw?"

"She's in her room. But this ain't the time to see her. She takes this time to herself. She'll be out later tonight."

"She invited me."

The barkeep raised an eyebrow and looked appraisingly at Wend. Then he pointed to a door on the other side of the common room. "Well, if that's true, go through that door, which opens into a hallway. First door on the right. But the widow's a hard woman. If you ain't invited, you'll taste her anger."

Wend smiled. "Like I said, she's expecting me." Then he strode across the common room toward the door indicated. It required him to pass by Ballantyne's table. The captain called out to Wend, "Hey, stop and sit down! We need to make plans for tomorrow."

Wend paused and looked down at the table. "I'm sorry. I've got an appointment to meet with Widow McGraw."

Taddy Carlin leered up at Wend. "And a nice appointment that should be." He looked around at his companions. "You all seen the widow?" Everyone at the table nodded grinned knowingly. Then he asked Wend, "How would that wife of yours back at Eckert Ridge feel about you having an 'appointment' with the likes of Mrs. McGraw?"

"Taddy, it happens that the widow is an old friend of mine from Pennsylvania. We'll just be recollecting old times, nothing more. Get your mind out of the swamp water." He turned to Ballantyne. "Jedidiah, let's meet early in the morning and plan for the day. After I meet with the widow, I'm going up to my room and sleep. I'm already weary."

Johnny Carlin quipped, "And after the widow, you'll be even more weary."

Wend ignored Johnny and said, "The morning, Jedidiah." Then he turned and headed for the door without saying anything further. He entered the hall and knocked on the first door.

Colleen's voice answered, "Come in, Wend."

He opened the door and saw a low fire crackling in the hearth. He smelled the wood smoke and then something else: the sweeter, more pleasing aroma of tobacco. He saw the backs of two tall wing chairs in front of the fire and saw pipe smoke rising from the one on the left.

"I'm here—before the fire."

Wend walked to the chairs and saw Colleen sitting in the chair to the left of the fireplace. She had changed to a pale blue gown and taken off her cap so that her auburn hair gleamed in the light from the fire and the candles around the room. She held a long-stemmed pipe in her left hand, and the smoke was wreathing her head.

She caught Wend staring and said, "Yes, I like my tobacco in the evening. It calms me, and smoking it gives me time to think." She grinned.

"I got into the habit by sneaking it at the old tavern in York. I wanted to see what it was like, and I found I enjoyed the taste." She motioned to the other chair. "Join me in front of the hearth. The warmth is good on a chill night like this."

"Interesting, Colleen, that you've taken to tobacco. Many women find solace in rum or whiskey."

"My father left us when I was at my mother's skirts. Mother despaired and started drinking. It became her whole life. Finally, Mother sold off me and my sister into servitude as indentures to get money. I vowed never to follow her path." She reached down and held up a cup of whiskey. "I allow myself exactly one of these each day." She pointed to a cabinet where a decanter and cups were placed. "Have yourself a libation."

Wend poured himself a drink and sat down. For a moment there was silence between them. Wend broke it by saying, "My apprentice, Andrew Horner, seems infatuated by the young blonde you sent up to draw my bath."

"That's Emily Crider. Lots of men are interested in her."

"Well, Horner doesn't have much experience with women, particularly coquettes, and in any case, he doesn't have the money to pay for her favors. And if my eye is any good, she seems to be leading him on. You might want to speak to her to keep things from going much further."

Colleen exhaled a stream of smoke. "Emily is the youngest and newest of my girls. She's still learning her trade, including how to size men up. Sometimes she lets her heart lead her instead of keeping her mind on the job."

Wend looked over at Colleen and grinned. "I remember a young tavern maid in York who once had the same failing."

Colleen blushed. "Yes, and she paid for it dearly." She looked over at Wend. "Let me tell you something you don't know: I paid for it the day after you sneaked out of my bed. Irwin and Reilly, accompanied by the man you asked me to watch out for—that Matt Bratton—came to the tavern and caught me out by the wood pile."

She paused to gather her thoughts, and Wend interjected, "Yes, and the three of them beat you and then took turns having their way with you until they couldn't get it up anymore. Then they whipped you with a rope. And all the time telling you it was punishment for helping me out. It took you days to recover."

Colleen sat up, a startled expression on her face. "How did you find out? I sent you a letter, but I kept that part out of it."

"You had one of the other maids, named Edith Harrow, write it for you. And she wrote what you told her to—that Matt Bratton had come and picked up a load of goods from Richard Grenough's warehouse. And that you hoped you would see me again." He looked at her for a moment. "But Edith put more in the letter. She told me what had happened to you in detail and then admonished me never to come back because I had caused you nothing but trouble and pain."

Colleen sighed. "Damn that Edith. She was always trying to be in charge. I should have figured she would have done something like that."

"I am sorry for what happened to you."

"Well, I'll make a confession. At night in bed, for a long time, I made you into my hero, like a knight in all those old stories. I cherished a dream that somehow you found out what had happened to me and hunted down those men and took revenge on my behalf. Then, a few months later, it came out that Irwin and Reilly had mysteriously disappeared. It comforted me to think that you had done it, although of course that was merely a young girl's fantasy."

"It may have been your fantasy, but the truth is the bones of Irwin and Reilly lie deep in a snake pit on Sideling Hill."

"My God, you actually did that?"

"I would have done it intentionally if I'd had the time, but actually, at Grenough's orders, they ambushed me and my new wife in a pass through the Tuscarora's on Forbes Road. My friends and I were headed to Virginia because I had killed two other of Grenough's men and destroyed his expedition to provide powder and lead to the tribes. The sheriff of Cumberland County had advised me to get out of Pennsylvania before Grenough pressured the authorities to arrest me."

"You did that also? Everyone was talking about how a brigand had attacked one of Grenough's wagons in the mountains. Its cargo of supplies for Fort Bedford was burned, and the men were killed. But I never dreamed that was because of you."

"Believe me, they weren't army supplies. That was just a story to hide his plot. Grenough was getting rich by illegally trading with the Indians."

"I don't understand. Why were you making such a career of attacking Grenough and his men?"

"In 1759, I discovered evidence of his conspiracy while hunting along Conococheague Creek. My family was traveling Forbes Road to Fort Pitt, where my father was to be the armorer. Grenough's men had a Mingo war party ambush us, and my family was wiped out. I was left for dead lying in the road." He reached up and touched the back of his head. "That's how I lost part of my scalp."

"So you were actually on a mission to seek vengeance on Grenough."

"I had vowed to destroy him and his company. It had been my life since the ambush on Forbes Road."

"What about Grenough himself? He's an important man. His influence spreads across Pennsylvania like a spider's web. You'll never dare touch him."

Wend looked into the fire for a long time, deciding how much to tell her. Then he quietly said, "I thought the same for over ten years. But just a few months ago, on a blustery night in the forest alongside the Shenandoah River, fate put him in my hands, along with Matt Bratton." He raised his hand and motioned toward the hearth. "The bones of both of them are in the mud of the river, and their souls are burning in flames hotter than your fire this very moment."

Colleen reached down, picked up her cup, and took a sip. Then a reflective look spread over her face. "So my first instinct was right. When I first saw you, a youth sitting in The Proud Rooster, I looked at the hard face you show the world and immediately got the sense that you were a man of great determination, a ruthless man who would go to any length to finish what he started. But then I saw the gleam in your eyes and knew you were also a man of intelligence and sensitivity. It occurred to me that those characteristics are a rare combination. That thought is what attracted me to you."

Wend took a bit of his whiskey and responded, "The word *determination* could apply to you. I saw that just knowing you for a day and a night. And look at you today—the indentured servant who now owns a prosperous tavern. We both understand what it cost you to get here. And now you are set for a life of reasonable comfort and security."

Colleen got up and carefully put the pipe down on a rack on the mantle. Then, with the flames behind her, silhouetting the curves of her body, she crossed her arms and looked down at him, a crooked smile on her face. "Yes, I could have the life of a tavern keeper. A life of catering to the needs of travelers and the desires of men for the rest of my life." She shook her head. "That would be enough for many men or women, but it's not enough for me."

Wend was puzzled. "Owning a prosperous place like this is the dream of many people. What do you want beyond where you are now?"

"When I was still a maid at The Proud Rooster, I sometimes rode with the owner on his wagon into York...usually for market day. The road took us past Grenough's estate. I loved the grand look of his house—the stone middle portion flanked by wooden wings on either side, the four tall chimneys rising from the center and wings. The whole of it backed up by the stable and other outbuildings. I pledged to myself that someday I would be the mistress of a great house like that, on wide land holdings, with servants, a carriage, and horses."

"Well, you are still young. You're not yet thirty. I should not be surprised if you find a rich man who wants to marry you and realize your dream."

A flash of irritation crossed her face, and she stamped her foot. Then she picked up her cup and emptied the remnants of her drink in one gulp. "Wend Eckert, you misjudge me. I thought better of you! I tell you I will obtain my dream, and it won't take a life of pandering to some rich bastard to do it! There was enough of that with Georgie McGraw. I'll get that estate on my own."

"I meant no offense, Colleen. One thing I know for sure is that you have a will of iron. But how do you expect to do it?"

"It may surprise you to know that I've already made my plans, and I'm putting them into action. Did you see those two Conestogas and cart out in the yard?" She took a step toward him, her chin held up. "It may interest you to know that those are mine. I purchased them in the last month."

"Are you planning to start a freighting company?"

"Freighting company be damned! I intend to become a sutler to the army. I'm selling this tavern to get enough money. I've already laid in a stock of the goods that men and officers will need. And when the tavern is sold, I'll get horses and hire drivers. And then I'll take my goods and my women and cater to the soldiers' physical needs—their stomachs and the most important thing in their lives, their cocks."

"My God, Colleen. Following the army—do you know how risky that will be?"

She drew herself up to her full height, hands on her hips. "You only get the great rewards when you are willing to take the great risks! And I'll not flinch at taking my chances!"

Wend nodded. "Chance, indeed. You could easily lose all your fortune. But you are throwing into the pot something far more important: your very life. Being with the army can be fatal, even for women."

A defiant look came over her face. "I have thought through all of this, and I am ready to face the hazards, both financial and physical. I tell you this now, and remember it well, Wend Eckert: one day I will be the mistress of a grand estate."

Wend nodded, then said slowly, "I cannot but wish you the best of fortune."

A silence ensued between them, and Colleen returned to her chair. But after a moment, she turned to Wend and said, "We've been talking about me and my plans. But I've been remiss and self-centered. What brings you to Fredericktown? And who are those rough men with you who are camping in the yard?"

Wend quickly explained the mission in general terms.

Colleen asked, "Do you know the names of the people you're after?"

"The leader of the group is named John Connolly. But he is using the name of John Cantrell. He may still be here in town at one of the taverns. We're going to be looking around for him tomorrow."

"Cantrell? By God, now some things that have happened make sense. You're the third person who has asked after him in the last few days."

"The *third* person?"

"Yes, there was a youth here about three days ago, asking if he were here or had stayed here. Then two men came in together this very morning, and one asked if we had seen someone named Cantrell."

"That's very interesting. We know that Connolly's party should have been here in town at least three days ago. If the people he's to meet came asking about him for a second time, it appears that his allies are having a hard time finding him. He could still be here, perhaps in a private house, which would make it a harder time seeking his group. But in any case, it looks like they didn't plan very well for making contact with their allies. Perhaps that reflects the hastiness of their plot."

Colleen looked at Wend in a thoughtful manner. "There's something else you should know. The youth who was here first was maybe fourteen or fifteen. He was fresh faced and roughly dressed like he was from the backcountry. And we were supposed to get a message to a certain party named Munger at Spiegler's Tavern, which is at the northern edge of town, if Cantrell came here. But the man who was here this morning was named Bradley. He was much older—in his thirties—dressed in tailored clothes and well spoken. And he said he was at the Black Ox in the center of town."

Wend sat up straight in his chair, stunned by the meaning of what he had heard. "You mean they were from two separate groups?"

"I *know* they were from two separate groups. When the second man—this Bradley fellow—inquired, I asked him if he was at Spiegler's place with Mr. Munger. He looked puzzled and then said no. That's when he told me they were staying at the Black Ox."

"Colleen, what you've told me is very important. Now we know where to start looking for Connolly and his confidantes here in town. Or at least getting information about them if they've already left to head west. But even more importantly, it also seems that Connolly's plot is bigger than I expected. We figured to find one party of men waiting here to join him. But if he is being joined by two groups, it could be trouble for us if we're outnumbered. Or at the very least, it would make it difficult to round up all the conspirators."

"Yes, I see." Then Colleen looked at him and raised her eyebrows. "Well, you know what this all means to me, don't you?"

"I'm not sure what you're getting at."

She put her head back and laughed deeply. "It means, Wend Eckert, that you owe me even more than when you came here. And someday—God knows when—but someday I'm going to collect in my own way."

—◊◊◊—

Wend took his leave of Colleen and walked out into the common room.

Ballantyne was still at the same table, but only Seidal was with him. Joshua and Simon had come down and were sitting at the fire with Horner.

Pulling out a chair at Ballantyne's table, Wend sat down with the two men. "Jedidiah, we need to talk."

Ballantyne lifted his cup. "A little while ago you wanted to wait until morning. So what changed your mind?"

"I've got some new information about Connolly from Mrs. McGraw."

"What the hell would she know about it?"

"She knows that two different groups of people have come here asking about him. You understand what that means, don't you?"

Ballantyne screwed up his face. Finally, he repeated hesitatingly, "There are two separate parties of his allies here?" Then illumination spread across his face. "My God, there are more men in this damn plot then we knew!"

"For once in your life, Jedidiah, you've hit the bullseye. And it makes sense. Connolly will need a lot of trusted men to reach out to the various tribes and pockets of Loyalists on the border if he's to pull together a big uprising in a short time." Wend looked in turn at the captain and then Seidal. "Mrs. McGraw said that one of the inquiries was by a youth who was dressed in rough clothing. That makes it likely that he and whoever he's with came from the Pittsburgh area to help escort Connolly back along Braddock Road and perhaps bring supplies and fresh horses. The other was by a man who could have been from the gentry, possibly from the Virginia or Maryland tidewater. It occurred to me they may be bringing money and perhaps trade goods for presents to the chiefs."

Seidal nodded slowly. "You know, Jedidiah, he's got a serious point. Connolly might have enough men to ambush us while we're in pursuit of him or outnumber us when we do catch up."

Wend said, "We must do something to even the odds. It would be best if we could stop one of the groups here in Fredericktown. Mrs. McGraw says one of the inquiries she had was this very day, by a man named Bradley. He's the one in gentleman's clothing and is staying at the Black Ox Inn, which is just a few minutes' walk from here. Why don't we send someone over this evening to discreetly find out if Bradley is still there and try to discover how many compatriots he has? Then we can make a plan to capture the lot, perhaps at first light in the morning."

Ballantyne set his jaw and sat thinking for a long moment. Then he shook his head. "No, we'll go right now. *All of us.* We can surround the Black Ox, then send someone inside to inquire about Bradley and his men. If they're indeed there, we'll rush in and snap them up." He looked at Seidal, a broad smile on his face. "We can't wait until tomorrow. They may ride at dawn, and we would miss them."

Wend raised his hand. "Just a minute, Ballantyne. I think we should be a little more circumspect about this. It's still early evening. Lots of people will be out in the streets. This isn't a rough back-country town. The sight of nine heavily armed men striding through the streets and then surrounding the inn is likely to raise concern among the townspeople. Undoubtedly someone will call out the sheriff to ask us some questions." Then, as he spoke, a thought hit Wend. "And I should have realized this long ago. Before we take *any* action here in Fredericktown, we should go talk to the sheriff and tell him what we are about. In any case, he's not going to be amused by a bunch of armed men barging into a tavern and taking someone prisoner."

"I ain't goin' to be bound by no damned local sheriff. We're working for Virginia an' it's all well above some county sheriff's head."

Wend shook his head. "Ballantyne, that's the point. We're on *Virginia* business in *Maryland*. We don't have any real authority here."

"I've got orders from Colonel Henry. That's all the authority I need."

Wend sighed in frustration. "It wouldn't matter much if we caught Bradley and Connolly out on the road in the middle of the bush somewhere. But here in town, the sheriff is going to have a lot to say about us grabbing men who, as far as he knows, are law-abiding travelers. And then there's the local Committee of Safety. They won't be happy about the Virginia military intruding in their territory. We'll at least have to explain our mission to them."

"Look, Eckert. We've got the numbers and the weapons, and we can't take no chance on this Bradley gettin' away. Besides, he may know where Connolly is if he's still in town. We'll deal with the sheriff when he shows up." Ballantyne rose from the table. "Horst, get our men turned out with their arms. Eckert, you do the same. We're leavin' instantly for the Black Ox."

Wend shrugged and walked over to join his own friends. "How much of that did you all hear?"

Baird responded glumly, "Enough to know we ain't gonna have a comfortable evening here in front of the fire."

Donegal said, "Come on, lads. Let's get our pistols. Rifles won't be much good for the work we're lookin' at tonight."

—⚒—

Eight of the nine Virginians stood together on the street in front of the Black Ox Inn; the ninth, Seidal, had been sent around to the back of the inn to check out what doors and possible escape routes existed.

As they waited for the sergeant to return, Wend noted that the inn was an impressive building. It was sandstone and very strongly built. The main part was three stories high, the top floor having dormers out through the roof. A stone addition of two stories had been built on the left side. And then a second, single-story addition extended even further to the left.

Presently Seidal returned and said to Ballantyne, "There's a fair-sized yard and paddock between the main part of the building and the stable. There are three doors in the back. It'll take at least two men to cover them effectively."

The captain bit his lip for a long moment, then barked out, "Right, Seidal. You and Jackson keep the back covered. I'm going in to check out the common room. Eckert, come with me to see if Connolly happens to be there. Bring Horner along as the messenger. The rest of you stay here, ready to come in if I send Horner to get you."

The three entered through the front door of the inn, which opened into a wide hall. Then they saw a doorway on the left that led to the stone addition, the entire first floor of which constituted the tavern common room. About half the tables were filled with patrons. Ballantyne led the way to the counter, which was at the moment unattended. A door behind the counter led into the single-floor addition, and Wend could see that it served as the cook room for the inn. Wend looked around and saw another door at the back of the room, which evidently led to the yard in the rear.

A minute later a stout man came out of the kitchen and approached the three. "Gentlemen, can I help you? Perhaps some spirits?"

Ballantyne said without preamble, "We're looking for a certain man with the name of Bradley. You happen to know if he's staying here? He might have several friends with him."

The barman looked critically at the captain, then at Eckert and Horner. "Might I ask for what reason you are interested?"

Ballantyne cleared his throat and said, "We've got reason to believe—"

Wend interrupted him. "Are you the proprietor of this inn?"

"David Fowler, sir. And I am indeed the owner."

"Well, Mr. Fowler, it happens we're interested in some land Mr. Bradley has for sale. We wanted to talk to him about it and perhaps arrange to go take a look if the price is favorable."

The proprietor nodded. "Oh, I see. I just don't like lettin' out information about my patrons to just anyone." He motioned to a group of men sitting at a table before the heath. "That's him in the green coat."

Wend looked at the table. The man in the green coat was facing them with his back to the fire. He was blond-haired with a high-cheek-boned face and blue eyes. From what Wend could see, he had a spare frame with a shallow chest and bony shoulders. He had an amused look on his face as he talked to his associates. Wend estimated that the man was in his early thirties. And Colleen had been right about his clothing; it had been fashioned by a good tailor to the most current fashion. There were four other men around the table, all of whom were similarly well dressed. Bradley had a cigar in his left hand, the smoke wafting up toward the ceiling, and a pewter cup by his right hand.

Having scanned the men at the table, Wend looked around the entire room. "Jedidiah, one thing's for sure. Connolly's not here."

Ballantyne nodded, then turned to Horner and said, "Go out and get the Carlin brothers. Tell Baird and Donegal to stay out front in case any of these men try to escape that way. Then go around to the back and let Seidal know we've found our quarry and to be on the alert."

Wend put his hand on Horner's arm. "Wait a minute, Andrew." He turned to the captain. "For God's sake, Jedidiah. Do we want those two hotheads in here? I say bring in Joshua and Simon; they'll stay cool if Bradley and his men try to resist. Besides, they're good with pistols, and we don't want some bystander hit if gunfire erupts."

Ballantyne frowned, then growled, "Horner, do as I said."

Wend shrugged, then nodded to the lad, who strode off purposefully.

In a few moments, Horner returned with the Carlins in tow, and the three came to the bar.

Ballantyne nodded in the direction of Bradley's table. "They are our men. Taddy, you get on the left side of the table so you can cover them and block that back door. Johnny, take the right side between their table and the main entrance. Eckert, you and Horner stay here at the bar, but be ready to cover me. When I go to the table and confront Bradley, everyone pull your pistol and come closer so that they see they're in a crossfire."

As the Carlins moved into position, Wend signaled for Horner to move to the end of the bar to provide another angle if it came to gunplay. Then he saw that various patrons around the room had begun to take notice of the movements and the fact that all the Virginia men were dressed in rough clothing and heavily armed. There was a distinct buzz, and heads turned to see what was toward, which increased when Ballantyne started walking to the table.

Fowler also noticed. He asked Wend, "What in the devil is going on?"

"I'm afraid we weren't entirely truthful, Mr. Fowler. We're from Virginia and about to apprehend those men for a plot against the backcountry settlements."

Meanwhile, Wend kept a close watch on Bradley. He had picked up on the fact that something was going on, and after looking around, he whispered something to the men at his table. Wend half expected them to pull weapons or at least make ready.

Instead, they merely stopped talking, and Bradley, taking a deep pull on his cigar, stared at the captain as he approached.

Ballantyne reached the table, looked around to make sure the Carlins were in position, and then, motioning toward the man before the fire, asked, "Does your name be Bradley?"

The blond man carefully exhaled his smoke in a long stream, smiled broadly, touched his right forefinger to his forehead in a casual salute, and said, "Warren Bradley at your service, sir. And to whom do I have the pleasure of speaking?"

Ballantyne instantly pulled his horse pistol from his belt and aimed it at Bradley. "Captain Jedidiah Ballantyne of the First Virginia Regiment. And it won't be any pleasure for you. I'm arresting you and all these men in the name of the Virginia Committee of Safety." He waved his left hand around the table. "Put all your hands where I can see them! If any of you make a sudden move, I'll not hesitate to fire!"

As he spoke, the Carlins pulled out their firelocks, taking aim at the table. Wend pulled out one of his pistols but aimed it at the ceiling, ready to aim and fire as necessary. He nodded to Horner, who then did the same.

Meanwhile, none of the men at the table moved. Bradley, an expression of amusement over his countenance, looked around the table and said, "Gentleman, have any of you given our sister colony to the south cause for legal action? I can say that I've not been to Virginia for at least two years, and even then it was only to visit a friend's plantation to the south of Alexandria. As far as I can recall, my only transgression at that time was getting a little intoxicated on my host's very good sherry." All the men laughed at Bradley's humor and then shook their heads.

Wend was surprised to observe that Bradley seemed not the least intimidated for a man looking down the barrel of a horse pistol. Indeed, still smiling at his own humorous remark, he leaned back in his chair in an attitude of complete relaxation and took another deep pull on the cigar. He exhaled the smoke upward toward the ceiling. Finally he said, "Now my dear Captain Ballantyne, may I ask precisely why it is that your esteemed Committee of Safety wants us apprehended?"

Ballantyne was clearly taken aback at Bradley's cavalier attitude. He snarled, "You bastard. You know damn well what we want you for. You're conspiring to help Dr. John Connolly raise the Ohio tribes against the border settlements!" He waved his pistol over the table. "I've got four other armed men here in this room and four others outside guarding the doors. I demand that you get up and come with us as prisoners to be taken back to Williamsburg! I want no bloodshed, but we won't hesitate to shoot you down if you resist."

Bradley remained unconcerned. In a calm voice he said, "My dear fellow, I assure you that you are making a great mistake. Please allow me to present a document that will convince you of that fact." He started to reach for an inside pocket of his coat.

Ballantyne took a step closer, his pistol aimed directly at Bradley's head. "Don't move any further, or I'll put a ball right between your eyes!"

Suddenly a loud, authoritative voice said, "Nobody is going to do any shooting unless it's me."

Wend looked at the main doorway and saw a large man holding what appeared to be a pair of dueling pistols in his hands. Another man stood beside him, armed with a brace of horse pistols.

Bradley grinned at the new arrival and said, "Well, Sheriff Lowell, you have arrived at a most opportune moment. These gentlemen from Virginia are a bit confused, and I believe your intervention will allow us to clear up matters."

The sheriff nodded and then said, "That we'll do, but right now I want all these bloody pistols back in your belts." He waved his pistol around the room. "Immediately!"

Wend put his pistol down on the counter and waved to Horner to do the same. Ballantyne gritted his teeth but still held his pistol on Bradley. He looked over at Lowell and asked, "You are indeed the sheriff?"

"I assure you, sir, that I am the duly appointed sheriff of Frederick County. Now put that damned pistol down before I lose my patience."

With great reluctance Ballantyne lowered his pistol and then stuck it back into his belt. He nodded to Taddy and Johnny, who did the same.

Bradley grinned. "Ah, now, that certainly relieves the tension." He reached inside his coat and pulled out a folded sheet of paper. Handing it to Ballantyne, he said, "Now, my fine fellow, this should explain the matter of my presence in Fredericktown."

Jedidiah took the paper and opened it. Then he blushed, bit his lip, and looked around to Wend. "Eckert, come here and read it."

Wend walked over, took the paper, and quickly scanned the words. As he did so, a feeling of embarrassment came over him. After he finished, he looked at Ballantyne and said, "Jedidiah, we have entirely misinterpreted the situation." He motioned with his hand toward Bradley. "This is Captain Warren Bradley of the Anne Arundell Light Horse Troop." He shook his head. "And he is under orders from the Maryland Committee of Safety to search out and capture John Connolly and his conspirators. In a word, he's on the same mission as us."

Ballantyne flushed even more. "Dammit, Eckert, are you sure? Is this not some trick?"

"Jedidiah, it looks very authentic to me."

Bradley stood up. "I assure you, Captain, it is quite genuine." Then he called out to the proprietor. "Mr. Fowler, if I may impose on you, could you show us all to one of your meeting rooms? I think we should pursue this matter in private and allow your clientele to enjoy their Saturday night relaxation with no further disruption."

Fowler, an expression of relief written all over his face, came out from behind his counter and started walking toward the door into the original part of the inn. "Follow me, gentlemen. I have a room entirely suited to your needs."

CHAPTER SEVEN

CONFRONTATION IN FREDERICKTOWN

Fowler, accompanied by one of his stable boys, led them to the largest of his meeting rooms. It was quite chilly inside. While the boy started the prelaid fire in the hearth, the proprietor moved around the room lighting wall-mounted candles. He turned to Bradley and said, "This place will warm up fast with the fire and the large number of men in here."

Meanwhile, at Wend's instruction, Horner had rounded up all the Virginians who had been at the front and back of the inn and brought them to the room. A long table with chairs for eight people dominated the room. Bradley took the chair at the head of the table near the hearth, and Ballantyne intentionally went to the chair at the opposite end. The sheriff settled himself at the right hand of the Maryland captain.

As the rest of the men filed in, Bradley looked carefully at Joshua, then Simon, and finally at Wend. He pointed to Wend and said, "When I was a lad in 1756, I marched with a company of Maryland provincials on the Forbes Expedition. Those heavy gray coats you and the other two men are wearing look like the watch coats the regulars used to wear. Did you three spend time in the British Army?"

Wend nodded toward Donegal. "He was in the 77th Highlanders. Mr. Baird was Bouquet's chief scout, and I scouted for the army in Pontiac's War. We picked up the coats along the way."

Bradley stared at Baird for a moment. "You do look familiar, sir. Perhaps I saw you during the campaign."

Joshua shrugged. "I was often riding with the colonel. You could have laid eyes on me then."

The seats at the table filled up, and the rest of the men leaned against wall. Bradley took a final draw on his cigar and tossed it into the fire. "Now gentlemen, let us put our cards on the table, face up."

Ballantyne leaned forward in his seat, his hand grasping the edge of the table. "Yes, and you can start by explaining how you know about Connolly's plot. We found out about it through captured dispatches between the colonel of a Loyalist regiment and Lord Dunmore. We were sent by the Committee of Safety to stop the conspirators a'fore they could get started on their dastardly job."

Bradley raised his eyebrows. "Very interesting, sir. However, we got our information from a much more direct source. Almost from the horse's mouth, if you will. Let me explain. Connolly, at the outbreak of the insurrection, traveled from Pittsburgh down to the Virginia tidewater and met with Lord Dunmore, where they cooked up the plan to raise the tribes in support of the crown—"

Ballantyne impatiently interrupted, "Bradley, tell us something we don't know."

Bradley shot him an irritated look and raised his hand. "Pray, sir, let me relate the entire story. What you probably don't know is that after conferring with Dunmore, Connolly took ship to Boston, where he personally met—in great secrecy—with General Gage to explain the plan. The general immediately agreed and added some additional elements."

A look of suspicion came over the Virginia captain's face. "If this was all so secret, how did you find out about it?"

The Maryland captain sighed and said, "Patience, my dear Mr. Ballantyne. That is exactly what I am about to explain." He pulled out another cigar, and while everyone waited, he took a taper from the mantle and lit it from the fire. When he had the tobacco well lit, he continued. "It happened that Connolly had a servant named Crowley who had come with him from Pittsburgh. However, Mr. Crowley, finding out the sordid details of the plan and its murderous implications for the backcountry, deserted Connolly and, at great hazard to himself, made his way through the siege lines to be received by the pickets of Washington's army. He convinced the guard officers to take him directly to the commanding general."

Wend spoke up. "So this man Crowley was able to give the details to Washington?"

"Precisely, Eckert, and I believe you gentlemen are not fully aware of the great scope and strategic implications of the plan. Let me lay it out for you. First, the part you know about is that Connolly and the men with him are to go to Pittsburgh and make contact with other Loyalists. They have a list of influential men loyal to the king. Now Connolly, having spent much time treating with the tribal chiefs in the Ohio Country, has developed friendships and alliances with them. He is certain they will be quite ready to rise up for the purpose of destroying settlements and farmsteads and generally driving colonists back east. Second, while the Ohio tribes are preparing to raid, Connolly and influential sachems will travel to tribal villages on the Great Lakes to rouse the northern tribes, and then to Fort Detroit, to meet with the senior British officers."

Sheriff Lowell bit his lips. "If they do join together, it will be like Pontiac's War of '63 and '64. It could be damned bloody."

Bradley nodded. "Yes, my dear sheriff, but there's more. The third element is even more serious. As part of the effort, General Gage has sent orders for the detachments of the 18th Foot—The Royal Irish—which man the forts along lakes, to take to the field in support of the tribal insurrection. They are to march with the Indian force, probably in the strength of two or three companies, to provide a disciplined element of the column. The military also has access to powder and lead, which will be used to supply the war parties, and trade goods to provide encouragement to the chiefs. Meanwhile, as the combined Indian and army force is marching southward to join the Shawnees, Mingoes, and Delawares of the Ohio Country, Connolly and his cohorts will be recruiting and organizing companies of rangers from among the Loyalists of the frontier. Crowley told Washington that Connolly believed he knew of enough men ready to join the cause to form several companies."

Baird, who had been leaning casually against the wall, stood up. "By God, Gage has taken a page from the book the French used during the late war!"

The men turned to look at the scout. Bradley raised his eyebrows. "Sir, exactly what do you mean?"

Joshua looked around the room. "Here it be: you send war parties of Indians alone against the border, and they'll be good for one or two raids. But soon as they've captured some useful goods from farms and settlements, they up and head for home to show off to their women and elders. But the French used to send regular officers and militia along with the war parties; they would keep the warriors at their work longer. Plus they brought trade goods as gifts so the bucks didn't need to take stuff from the settlements as booty. It made the war parties much more dangerous."

Bradley looked thoughtfully over his cigar. "Ah, yes, Mr. Baird, I quite take your meaning. It seems Gage has retained some of the lessons from his experiences in that war."

"That be real true, sir," responded Joshua. "Remember, after Braddock's defeat, Gage formed and commanded the 80th Foot, which was all light infantry for use in the border country. And he made a study of Indian warfare."

The Maryland captain nodded. "Quite illuminating, sir. But now let me tell you the fourth part of the plan, which you gentlemen from Virginia may find quite arresting." He gave Ballantyne a hard look. "Once the settlements of the western borders of Pennsylvania, Maryland, and Virginia have been destroyed or cowed into submission, Connolly is to lead the combined Indian and British force down Braddock's Road to the Shenandoah Valley and capture the most important town in the valley, Winchester."

Wend had been slouching in his chair, the effects of the long day making him drowsy as he listened to Bradley's words. But hearing the name of the town, he bolted upright, all weariness banished. He shot a glance at Donegal, Baird, and Horner, who had also been startled by hearing about their own town. He interrupted the captain's words. "You say *Winchester*? Why have they singled that place out?"

"It's part of a larger strategy for which Winchester will be a base of supply and operations. They are assuming that by the time they have subjugated the border country, Dunmore will have defeated or at least have driven back the Patriot forces in the tidewater. Moreover, Gage is expecting reinforcements from Britain, and he has promised to send some regulars to stiffen the governor's Loyalist army. With all that achieved, Dunmore will march northward by land and water, and Connolly will advance southeastward from Winchester to combine with the main column at Alexandria. Thus they expect to reassume control of the heart of Virginia." Bradley looked around the room, waiting for his words to sink in. Then he continued, "And gentlemen, once Virginia is again under the authority of the crown, it will split the northern colonies from the south, precluding unified action by the Patriot forces."

Wend said, "So Connolly is not just fomenting a border war to distract the colonists, as we have believed. In fact, he is setting the stage for the defeat of the entire colonial cause."

"Succinctly stated, Lieutenant Eckert." Bradley took another pull on his cigar. "Now, to continue, once Washington received all this information from Crowley, he summarized it in a dispatch to the Congress in Philadelphia. The war committee immediately realized the import and on the very same day sent orders to the Council of Safety in Annapolis to intercept Connolly and all his allies. That requirement was assigned to me and the men you see here. Further, once having captured the conspirators, we are to deliver them to the Continental Congress for trial and ultimate disposition."

Ballantyne interjected, "And I have orders to capture and deliver Connolly to the Virginia Committee." He looked at Bradley defiantly and added, "And I intend to carry out my orders."

"Most commendable, Captain. However, I submit that since my orders come directly from the Congress itself, I have primacy in this matter." He paused, then continued, "Not to mention that we happen to be in Maryland, not Virginia. It would seem that I have, as the lawyers like to say, *jurisdiction*."

Lowell spoke up. "Bradley's right. If anyone is going to take action against this damned Connolly, it's going to be those who have authority here. Which means these gentlemen from Annapolis or me."

Ballantyne gritted his teeth. "Virginia or Maryland, we can deal with that later. Meanwhile we're sitting here arguing when what we *should* be doing is finding out where Connolly and his friends are. They could be right here in town. That's what we were about when we came to the inn, and we're wasting time."

Bradley looked over at the sheriff and then back to Ballantyne. "Well, as it happens, Captain, we know the whereabouts of Connolly and all his conspirators."

Ballantyne was momentarily speechless. Then he asked, "And how the devil did you find out?"

"Quite simple. We arrived in Fredericktown two days ago, and not being familiar with the town, naturally we contacted the sheriff here. He obligingly assisted us in very discreetly searching the town for strangers. It was easy to determine that Connolly wasn't in any of the taverns or inns. But residences were another matter. The sheriff says there are nearly two hundred houses. However, Lowell had his finger on known Loyalists and with commendable discretion conducted a survey of the list to find out who had strange guests. In fact, the reason the sheriff so fortuitously came into the common room at the moment when you were pointing that very large horse pistol at my head was because he had just found out where Connolly stayed while he was here."

Ballantyne gave Bradley a questioning look. "Stayed while he *was* here? Is he gone now?"

Lowell nodded. "He and his immediate party stayed at a private home owned by a family named Harner, and another party of three men and a young lad from the Pittsburgh area came east and stayed at Spiegler's Tavern on the north end of town. They arrived three days ago. They were heavily armed and had packhorses with supplies. The next day two men with a packtrain of ten horses arrived at Spiegler's, and they were obviously connected with the men from the west. From their conversation picked up by maids, they had come down from York in Pennsylvania. Connolly and his four other men joined the party yesterday, and at dawn today the entire party rode out. Ed Spiegler said they were definitely headed northwestward on the wagon road up South Mountain. I 'spect by now they've made the crest of the mountain and tomorrow will probably get to Elizabethtown, which is in the valley beyond."

Wend spoke up. "I'll wager the packhorse train from York contains powder, lead, and trade goods as gifts for the chiefs."

Bradley nodded. "We rather thought so ourselves. It appears that Connolly and his minions will spend the winter cultivating the tribal sachems, organizing Loyalist militia, and communicating with the British army on the lakes. Then, with the spring thaw, the various forces will move to the attack of the border settlements."

Wend said, "The surest way to stop this plot is to catch Connolly and his party on the road. If they're allowed to get to Pittsburgh, where they have allies, it may become like trying to stamp out a rapidly spreading fire."

"Quite correct, Lieutenant." Bradley raised a finger. "Now, gentlemen, by my calculation, Connolly's party has grown to at least eleven men. Undoubtedly all well armed. My group totals five, and yours, Captain Ballantyne, consists of nine men." He paused for effect. "Only if we combine our forces do we outnumber the Loyalist conspirators."

Ballantyne bit his lip. "So are you sayin' we should work together?"

"Did I not make myself clear, sir?"

Leaning forward, Ballantyne pointed his finger at Bradley. "I'll do it only if you agree here and now that once we catch the devils, they go back with us to Virginia."

Bradley shook his head. "I've already stated my position on that. They come with us and thence to the custody of the Congress. That is *not* negotiable."

Ballantyne partially rose from his chair. "But you be forgettin' somethin' real important, Captain. I'm the one that's got *nine* men. I say that's plenty to take on Connolly—damned if we need you and your gentlemen cavalry." He pulled himself up to his full height. "And the truth is, we're used to livin' and fightin' in the kind of country where we're goin' to find Connolly. So I say be damned to you. Go back to the tidewater and parade around in your fancy uniforms and sleek horses, playin' at soldiers."

For the first time, Bradley's face lost the look of mild amusement and was replaced by a grim visage. He said in a very controlled voice, "Captain Ballantyne, I'm going to ignore those remarks because if I regarded them, I could only consider that you had called into question the honor of my company and my men."

Ballantyne, now standing fully upright, didn't seem to notice the angry tone in Bradley's voice and the import of his words. He started to speak, saying "I don't care—"

Wend quickly interrupted. "If I may speak, I think there is a solution for this standoff regarding how to dispose of Connolly once captured."

Bradley looked at Wend and said, "By all means, go ahead, Lieutenant."

"Look, the fact is that both parties here have some claim to the Loyalists. Yours, Captain Bradley, is from the Continental Congress and your Council of Safety in Annapolis. We have a claim because the plot has been hatched by our former governor and Connolly, a citizen of Virginia. Moreover, the Virginia frontier will bear the brunt of any attacks."

"I'll concede that's a point, Eckert. But you must acknowledge that Congress has primacy in this matter."

Wend raised a finger. "Does it, Captain? It has primacy only by the consent of each of the colonies. Should Virginia not consent to being ruled on this particular matter, how is Congress to compel her to follow its guidance?"

Ballantyne settled back into his chair and grinned. "For once you are making sense, Eckert. So we have every right to keep Connolly once we catch him!"

Wend held up his hand to quiet the Virginia captain and said, "Not so fast, Jedidiah. The point is that since each side has a justifiable claim, only a compromise will settle the matter. Here is my proposal: let us agree that the disposition of the Loyalists should be determined by the location where they are captured. If we apprehend them along the road here in Maryland—that is, say, by the time we get to Wills Creek or sooner—they go with Bradley. But if Connolly is able to get past Wills Creek and on to Braddock's Road before we apprehend him, we Virginians take possession. After all, the land beyond Wills Creek is of somewhat unsettled title."

Bradley squinted over his cigar and looked at the sheriff, then to Wend. "I can accept that. If we don't overhaul them by then, he's yours."

Ballantyne set his chin and glared at Wend. "Eckert, why should I accept something like this?"

"Because, Jedidiah, we need the cooperation of these Marylanders, and we need the blessing of Sheriff Lowell to operate in this colony. And I frankly believe the Virginia Committee of Safety will be just as satisfied if Connolly and his men are delivered to the Congress."

Lowell spoke up. "Your lieutenant is making sense, Ballantyne. I could declare you outlaws if you continue to resist working with us and take you into custody."

Ballantyne sat quietly staring at Wend. Then he slowly turned to Bradley. "All right, I'll work with you." He shrugged and continued, "Anyway, with the lead Connolly's got now, chances are we won't overtake him until he's way up Braddock Road."

Bradley slapped his hand down on the table. "Capital! Let us now make plans."

Lowell said, "I 'spect you'll all be departing at first light."

Wend held up his hand. "Not so fast. Our horses have been going for as much as ten days without rest. They need time out in the pasture before we start pressing them for a chase."

Joshua pushed himself from the wall. "Wend is tellin' the truth. At least a couple of days in the pasture if they're to have any strength at all."

Bradley looked at the sheriff. "Actually, we also need a couple of days to make preparations. We left Annapolis in haste with minimal supplies. We have to gather some provisions, and we need warmer coats for the mountain country." He looked around the table. "This is Saturday. I propose we plan on leaving Tuesday morning, giving time to gather supplies and provide minimal rest to the animals."

Lowell looked around. "It seems to me that's going to put you at least four days—more like five—behind Connolly."

Bradley shrugged. "It can't be helped, but Connolly most certainly will be greatly slowed by that heavily laden packtrain. Traveling light, we should be able to make some time up on him."

The sheriff looked around the table, a thoughtful look on his face. "Perhaps we can help matters a bit. Why don't I mount one of my men on a fresh, strong horse and send him over the mountain to Elizabethtown? It's possible Connolly will rest there. My man can see Jonathan Hager, who's a strong supporter of the cause and is the biggest landholder there. He knows everyone in the town. If Connolly is staying at a public place there, he'll find out easily. And he will rouse the militia to stop him. There's a chance he could have Connolly and his men in hand when you get there." He thought a minute, then continued, "And if Connolly has already flown the coop, Hager can at least tell us when he did leave."

There were nods around the room. Bradley asked, "When could your man ride out?"

Lowell shrugged. "Dawn tomorrow."

The Maryland captain reflected a moment, then said, "Make it so."

—〜—

The Virginians walked back to the Red Vixen through streets now dark, empty, and cold in the raw November weather. There was little talk, the men thinking over what had ensued at the Black Ox and contemplating the hard chase that faced them in the days ahead. When they reached the tavern, the Winchester men filed inside while the First Virginia soldiers went to their camp in the yard.

Except for Ballantyne. Instead he grabbed Wend's arm and said in a rough tone, "Stay here a minute. We have somethin' to settle."

Donegal, at the door, overheard Ballantyne's words. He turned around and asked, "You want me to stay, Wend?"

Wend waved him inside. "It's all right, Simon. I'll be there in an instant."

Once they were alone, Ballantyne stood silent for a moment, his breath visible in the chill air.

Wend noticed that he was fuming, in near rage.

Finally the captain spoke. "I don't like the damned trick you pulled on me back there at the inn. Don't ever do that again."

"What trick do you mean, Jedidiah?"

"You damn well know what I mean: going against me and siding with that macaroni Bradley and Sheriff Lowell."

"For God's sake, Ballantyne, somebody had to find a middle ground to break the deadlock. In fact, you had put yourself in a corner, and now we can work with the Marylanders on an even basis. And I told you right here at this tavern that we were going to have to deal with the Maryland authorities sooner or later."

"Middle ground, hell! You set up a deal that means Connolly will probably go with the Maryland people once we catch him. I figure with them havin' to deal with that packtrain, we'll catch him west of Elizabethtown. Which means we'll go back to Virginia empty-handed."

"But we'll have succeeded in our objective. The plot will be frustrated. Isn't that what's important?"

"I got an assignment to bring back Connolly for justice in Virginia. I will take great pleasure at seeing him in the docket at Williamsburg and to personally testify about the murderous plot he and Dunmore had cooked up. And I intend to be there to witness both that and him hanging from a gallows."

Suddenly a thought formed in Wend's mind. "And as the man who brought him back, to accept the commendation and perhaps some more tangible reward of a grateful Committee of Safety. Like as not a promotion?"

There was a long moment of silence between them. Finally Ballantyne nodded. "Aye, perhaps. And what's so wrong with that? Things are mightily unsettled in these times. Some men are rising, others falling. Last year I was a lieutenant in a border militia company. This year I became a captain by bringing in a whole company of soldiers, even though I ain't some high-and-mighty gentry from down in the tidewater. Now I figure this war is goin' to last a long time, and the man who stopped Connolly just might have a bright future in Virginia's army."

Wend said, "Sure. Why not Major Ballantyne next year and Colonel Ballantyne soon enough?"

The captain set his jaw and glared at Wend. "The truth is, they're making people colonels right now who ain't done anything in their life but be a lawyer or make speeches in the Burgesses. Sooner or later the men who actually done some fighting are going to rise to the top."

"True enough, Ballantyne. But take my word for it—you're not one of them."

"Damn you, Eckert, with your smart mouth." He gritted his teeth. "Just remember this: don't cross me again, or you'll have cause to understand that I'm not a man to be trifled with."

"And you should keep in mind I'm not a man who forgets threats."

"Just remember what I said, Eckert."

And before Wend could think of anything further to say, Ballantyne turned and strode swiftly toward his camp, where Seidal stood stoking up the fire.

—◊—

Sunday was a slow day at the Red Vixen, with most of their normal clientele at home with their families observing the tenants of the Sabbath. Colleen explained to Wend that she had made it a day of rest for her staff, requiring only the minimal domestic work. And after the evening meal, it was also customary for the girls and other workers to get together for musical entertainment in the common room, mostly for themselves but also for whatever guests might be staying in the tavern.

So it was that after cleanup for supper was complete, the Vixen crew pulled out their instruments and began to tune up. A young man named Charlie, who helped Edna in the kitchen, brought out a fiddle, and a tall, raven-haired maid named Susan had a wooden flute. Eva, an auburn-haired girl, played the mandolin.

The common room was empty save for the staff, the Winchester men, and two wagoners who had brought their Conestogas into the yard at sundown, all in all maybe fifteen people. Colleen came and sat with Wend and his friends.

The three musicians sat next to the hearth and played several bright tunes. Then a petite, brown-haired, pug-nosed maid named Faith stood up, and all the Vixen people clapped. "All right, are you ready?" she called out. There was a loud answering shout form all the staff, and she nodded to Charlie, who started a brisk piece of music. Faith began her song, which was a bawdy criticism of the British, starting with the king and running all the way down to the redcoat army. It was obviously a favorite, for all the Vixen people started singing along and clapping rhythmically.

After she finished there were cheers and applause from all in the room.

Just as the applause was dying out, the main door of the tavern swung open, and Taddy Carlin strode in, followed by Ballantyne and the other First Virginia men. Johnny was carrying a large jug.

Horner leaned over and whispered to Wend, "They got that jug earlier today from out in the town. It's very cheap whiskey. And the whole lot of them have been pulling on it in their camp for quite a while. They were at it two hours ago when I went out to grain our horses."

Wend was about to reply when Ballantyne called out, "Is this a private party or a public night in the common room?"

Colleen stood up. Wend looked at her face. She had been relaxing and enjoying the goings-on as much as any of the others. But now her face had turned stonelike, and her eyes narrowed into a frigid glare. However, when she spoke it was in a controlled, conciliatory tone. "Captain Ballantyne, you and your men are certainly welcome. But that jug of yours is *not*. It is my rule that *only* liquor purchased *here* may be consumed in the common room. Whether you buy drinks here or not you are welcome, but leave that whiskey back at your camp."

Silence dropped like a curtain over the room, everyone staring at Ballantyne and his men. It persisted for a very long moment. Taddy spoke up, and it was evident from the slurring of his words that he was feeling the whiskey. "Hell, Jedidiah, the damned jug's almost empty anyway."

Then the captain turned to Johnny. "Go ahead, lad. Take that back and put it by the fire."

Ballantyne turned back to Colleen, and said, "Mrs. McGraw, we apologize for violating your rules. I'll stand a drink for my men."

The proprietress's face softened. "Well, then, come join us for an evening of music." She waved them to a table, then motioned to Faith to continue singing. She did so and went through several more songs, followed by a trio of numbers by the three musicians.

They paused to rest, but after a few moments, one of the girls called out, "It's Emily's turn!" This was echoed by several others.

Colleen leaned close to Wend. "Emily's a gifted singer. You'll enjoy her voice."

Wend watched as the girl got up from her chair and spoke with Eva and the other musicians for a moment. He asked, "How did you happen to bring her into your group?"

Colleen turned to him and said in a low voice, "She came here as a refugee from the Indian uprising last year in Virginia. Her family lived to the south of Pittsburgh, and their farmstead was attacked by a Shawnee war party. She was the only survivor and was taken in by a neighbor family. She had relatives not far from here, and the people she was staying with arranged for her to journey east with a band of other displaced persons who just wanted to get away from the war."

Wend nodded. "Yes, we encountered such a caravan when we were on our way to Pittsburgh last year."

"There were many groups like that coming through here. Anyway, Emily moved in with her relatives, but it wasn't a good match. The man of the family took a shine to her, and although Emily didn't encourage him in any way, his wife figured it out and made clear she wanted the girl out of the house. They hustled her off to service at an inn. That's where I found her on one of my trips to gather the right kind of girls for my purposes."

Wend shot a glance at Colleen. "The *right* kind of girl. Young as she was, did she know what she was getting into when she threw in with you?"

"She wasn't a virgin. That inn was a run-down, dirty place, and the proprietor was scum who had already imposed himself on her. She was desperate to get away from him and that scurrilous place. I made it clear what I was proposing and what was expected of her, and she willingly came along. She is young and in some ways naive, but she does what is required. In the last few months, she has learned what it takes to please a man."

Emily had taken her place in front of the hearth, the flames behind her and perfectly silhouetting her body, which Wend, looking at her closely for the first time, had to admit was lithe and shapely. Her high-cheek-boned face, blue eyes, smooth and pale complexion, and blond locks gave her an angelic countenance that belied her occupation. Wend remarked, "She looks like an innocent child."

Colleen smiled slyly. "Indeed. A major selling point in this trade."

Emily started to sing, and Wend was immediately impressed with the beauty and flexibility of her voice. She started with a rollicking tune but soon turned to more romantic, winsome themes. Wend looked around the room and saw the effect the combination of her voice and childlike beauty on all the watchers, male and female alike. He noted that even Ballantyne and his men, who had been whispering and joking even while the music was going on, had become silent and attentive as the blond girl sang.

As she finished a song, Colleen said, "Oh, please, Emily, you must give us 'Scarborough Fair.'"

It was obviously a favorite, for there was an enthusiastic chorus of agreement from the others of the tavern staff.

Emily nodded to Eva, and an anticipatory hush settled over the room.

She stood silent in front of the fire, letting the quiet linger on for effect, and her face took on a reflective countenance, her eyes half closed and cast downward. Then the flute, fiddle, and mandolin began to play an introduction as she stood there. Wend realized they and the singer had all practiced the song together and performed it many times.

Then Emily raised her head, her eyes sweeping the room as if searching for something, and then began to sing:

"Are you going to Scarborough Fair?
Parsley, sage, rosemary, and thyme;
Remember me to someone who is there,
He once was a *true* love of mine.

Tell him to buy me an acre of land,
Parsley, sage, rosemary, and thyme;
Between the salt water and the sea sand,
Then he shall be a true love of mine.

Tell him to plow it with a ram's horn,
Parsley, sage, rosemary, and thyme;
And sow it all over with one peppercorn,
And he shall be a true love of mine.

Tell him to sheer't with a sicle of leather,
Parsley, sage, rosemary, and thyme;
And bind it up with a peacock's feather,
And he shall be a true love of mine.

Tell him to thrash it on yonder wall,
Parsley, sage, rosemary, and thyme,
And never let one corn of it fall,
Then he shall be a true lover of mine.

When he has done and finished his work,
Parsley, sage, rosemary, and thyme;
Oh, tell him to come, and he'll have his shirt,
And he shall be a true love of mine."

As she sang, Wend glanced at Horner. The apprentice's eyes were flooded with infatuation and longing as he watched the girl perform. He thought to himself, *The lad is going to be lovesick and morose for days after we leave here.*

She finished the song by repeating the initial stanza:

"Are you going to Scarborough Fair?
Parsley, sage, rosemary, and thyme;
Remember me to someone who is there,
He once was a true love of mine."

Then she put her right hand over her heart and lowered her eyes as if in contemplation.

The entire presentation was extraordinarily emotional, casting a spell over all present. There was spontaneous, enthusiastic applause after Emily finished, and once it subsided, Colleen stood up and said, "All right, we've had our entertainment, and it's getting late. Let's finish up the night chores and get a good rest. We'll be busy again tomorrow."

The staff began to break up. The two wagoners headed to the stairs to go to their room. Edna barked out some orders to the cook-room workers.

Joshua sighed and looked at his cup. "I think we could stand one more drink 'afore we go up to the room. What do you think, Simon?"

"I'm thinkin' you're right on the target, Joshua." Donegal turned to Wend. "How about you?"

Wend held up his hand. "I've got some business with Colleen. Maybe after it's finished."

The proprietress had gone up to the bar to talk to Edna, and Wend walked over. "Colleen, I need some advice."

"Of course, whatever I can do. What is it you need to know?"

"We require some provisions before we ride out on Tuesday. We face a long trip, perhaps well up Braddock's Road. Where might I find what I need in Fredericktown?"

She laughed. "Weren't you listening to me yesterday? You need look no further than right here. I told you I was building up a sutler's stock of goods. Come with me to my storage sheds tomorrow, and I'll wager you'll find everything you need." She grinned broadly. "And for you, I'll set a fair price."

Wend was about to reply when he was stopped by the sound of a woman's high-pitched voice protesting in distress, "Please, I said 'no'! I told you we're not working tonight. I tell you, leave me alone!"

Turning, Wend saw that Taddy Carlin was holding Emily's arm while the girl was trying to pull away. "Dammit, my money is as good as the next man! And I saw you heading for the stairs with more than one man last night."

Colleen took a step toward him then stood with her hands on her hips. "Take your hand off the girl. Just like she said, they're not working tonight! And I've been watching you, sir. You're in your cups. I doubt she'd do you any good in your condition."

Taddy's face contorted into a crooked smile. He said with a tone of braggadocio, "There ain't enough drink in this tavern to stop me when I'm ready. And by God, I'll have this little wench tonight! Who heard of any tavern harlot not working when there be good money ready to be paid?"

Carlin started to drag her toward the stairway. A look of horror came over Emily's face, and she looked beseechingly at Colleen.

Before he could get far, Andrew Horner was at him. In a long, smooth motion, he drove his right fist into the center of Taddy's face. Carlin's head snapped back, and he fell like a dropped sack of grain to the floor, where he lay motionless.

Emily sprang away.

Donegal, his drink still in hand, turned to Joshua and said casually, "Na' did you see the lad? That blow was a bolt of lightning."

Joshua nodded. "Damned if it wasn't, Simon. I ne'er had any idea the lad knew how to fight. Ain't ever seen him lift a hand to anyone."

Johnny Carlin, who was into the whiskey as much as his brother, roared like a lion and sprang forward toward Horner, his hands raised and spread wide as if to grab him. Horner took a step forward to receive the soldier's charge, left arm raised to deflect him and right fist back and ready to strike. But Andrew was no match in size or experience for the rushing Ulsterman, who brushed aside the boy's defense, threw him back against the edge of a table, pinned him there with his left hand and pummeled him with the right.

Meanwhile, Ballantyne and Jackson stood up and rushed to the Carlin brothers' assistance. Only Seidal stood back, his arms crossed, a look of disgust on his face.

Wend took a step forward, intent on aiding his apprentice who undoubtedly was about to be overwhelmed and beaten to a pulp. Joshua and Donegal came up out of their chairs. A dagger appeared in the High-lander's right hand.

But then just as it seemed a melee must ensue, with bloody reper-cussions, an earsplitting bang reverberated through the room, startling everyone and freezing the entire assemblage in place.

Wend looked around to see Edna Farley standing behind the bar, a smoking horse pistol in her left hand pointed upward toward the ceiling. In her right was a second pistol, the cock pulled back, it's muzzle pointed directly at Johnny.

The woman said, "You take another blow and I'll pull the trigger. And you won't be the first man has taken a ball in this room."

Colleen stood with her hands on her hips. "She's speaking the truth. And if you survive, you'll nurse your wounds in the sheriff's cells. He's a personal friend, and he'll have no questions for me about this matter." She turned to Ballantyne with fire in her eyes. "Now, Captain, you may take your men out of here instantly!"

Jedidiah's face was smoldering anger writ large. His fists were tightly balled at his sides.

Wend realized the man was on a knife edge trying to decide whether to fight or withdraw. He called out, "Jedidiah, remember you've got a mission you're very keen to complete! You get involved in legal charges here, Bradley will leave without us and you'll be out of the game."

Seidal walked over and grabbed his officer's arm. "He's right, Ballan-tyne. Let it be."

The captain looked around at the scene, first at the woman with her pistol leveled at Johnny and then at Donegal's dagger. He retained wits enough to realize his disadvantage and the truth of Wend's words. He took several deep breaths. The muscles on his face eased, and then he motioned to his men. "All right, pick up Taddy and let's get back to the fire."

Johnny stood hesitating, a scowl on his face. Then he pointed at

Horner. "This ain't finished, not by any long shot. Time's goin' to come when we settle this. You understand, Dutch boy?"

The lad picked himself up. "You just pick the time and place, long as it's just you and me."

Carlin turned and stormed out of the room, followed by the other Ballantyne men.

After the Virginia soldiers had left, the maids worked to straighten up the common room while Edna carefully reloaded the horse pistol. Emily had taken charge of patching up Horner's face.

Colleen and Wend sat at a table by the fire. She had brought them both whiskeys from the bar.

Wend smiled and said, "Unless I'm mistaken, you've broken your rule. That's the second drink I've seen you with tonight."

"Some nights are for breaking rules." She gave Wend a sideways look. "Something you might think about."

She glanced over at where Emily was tenderly ministering to Andrew's wounds, then turned to Wend and raised her eyebrows meaningfully. "If I were you, I shouldn't expect him to spend the night in your room."

Wend looked at the two young people for a few seconds. "Andrew is the most dedicated apprentice I've ever had. He came to me as a redemptioner, supposedly as a field hand. But back in Germany he had been a wood carver. So I took him on to learn gunsmithing, and he is a quick study. For years he has focused single-mindedly on learning his trade, but in the last few months, he's awakened to the lure of females. Though, unless I'm greatly mistaken, Andrew has never actually had a woman."

Colleen grinned at him over her cup. "Then he's found the perfect girl to introduce him to the mysteries of lovemaking."

Wend cocked his head. "Colleen, he doesn't have the coin to pay for her tender attentions."

"I said this is a night for breaking rules. While she was back in the kitchen to get water and cloth to treat Horner, she asked to spend the night with him on her own time, and I couldn't deny her—not after what he did."

—⁓—

Tuesday morning came with a damp chill in the air and an overcast sky. The nine Virginians were in the yard of the Red Vixen, busy saddling their horses. Horner and Jackson were loading the pack horses.

Wend looked to the east. It was time for dawn, but the only sign of the sun was a slight brightening in the clouds above the trees. He said to Joshua, "It's going to be damn cold up on that mountain and colder the higher we get."

"Damn right." He waved toward Horner. "And Andrew's going to feel it. He ain't got no heavy watch coat like us—just that short jacket he brought from Winchester."

Wend looked over at his apprentice. "Yes, he didn't expect anything like this when we left. He'll just have to suck it in."

Joshua looked up toward the mountain. "Gets bad enough, he can drape a blanket over his shoulders like a shawl. I done that often enough when I was young and didn't have no proper coat."

"There wasn't much you didn't do when you were young."

"Yeah, and my bones tell me about it every day." Baird looked over at Horner and said, "I'm going to go over and help him make sure that pack saddle is on right. Be nasty if the thing came loose up on the slopes."

A few moments after Baird left, when Wend was just finishing adjusting his saddle and other gear, Ballantyne came and stood next to him. They were shielded from view and hearing of the others between Wend's and Joshua's horses.

"Eckert, I'm just remindin' you what we talked about the other night: keep your nose out of my business. Don't try to step in between me and

Bradley while we're ridin' with those Marylanders. You just keep in mind what you're along for: to identify that rat Connolly and nothin' else."

Wend shook his head. "That's how it started out, Jedidiah, back in Culpeper. But since Saturday night in the Black Ox, things have changed. It got real personal for me and my friends when Bradley told us that capturing Winchester was part of Connolly's plan. So I thought it over the last day or so. We're in this all the way now, and we're going to make sure that neither Connolly nor any of his allies ever gets to Pittsburgh. So I'm dealing myself in on the planning and decision-making. And after seeing how obstinate you were at that meeting, I think Bradley will like it that way. If you think you can stop me, we'll have it out right here."

The captain laughed. "You think you can take me?"

"I've killed better and meaner men then you, Jedidiah. I don't fight fair, I fight to finish. I learned long ago there's no right or wrong, just winning and losing."

Ballantyne's face flushed red. "You bastard—"

Wend cut him off. "You won't stop me because as strong as Connolly's party is now, you need our numbers to fight them successfully. And think of this: if the chase goes beyond Elizabethtown, we're the only ones who know Braddock Road intimately. Joshua knows all the shortcuts and the hazards. You've never traveled the road. You'll have to depend on us. So just get used to the idea of having me looking over your shoulder."

Wend turned and walked away, leaving the captain sputtering behind him.

He saw Colleen standing alone in the dusk in the middle of the yard, dressed in a long coat, her arms crossed. Their eyes met, and then with her head she motioned over to where Horner stood beside the pack horse. Wend looked over, and saw that Emily was with the apprentice, a shawl over her shoulders, her golden hair down and standing out even in the gloomy light. She had something made up of dark green material in her hands.

Wend walked over to where the proprietress stood. "What's Emily up to?"

"She's got an overcoat for Andrew. It came out during the night that he's only got a thin jacket." She smiled up at Wend. "So I let her give him my husband's old coat, seeing as he's got no further need for it."

He looked at her with a crooked smile. "After two nights with that girl, he's going to be so messed up that he'll be no good for days."

"Don't complain to me about your problems. Now I'm going to have to put Emily's nose back to the grindstone. We'll be busy tonight, and men will be wanting her." She shot him a crooked smile. "Her heart won't be in it."

Meanwhile Ballantyne was calling out for the men to get mounted.

Colleen stared at the officer and then lowered her voice. "Wend, that man hates you. You need to watch out. If I know men, he's the kind that will act upon it when the opportunity presents itself."

Wend stared at the captain for a moment, then turned back to Colleen. "Have faith in me. You called me a hard and ruthless man. It may happen that Ballantyne gets a big surprise somewhere along the way."

She gave him a conspiratorial smile. "I'll count on it, then."

Wend looked at her and sighed. "Well, I guess this is goodbye. Thanks for all your help these last few days."

She moved very close to him, her green eyes looking up into his. "You know my father was Ulster, and my mother was full Irish. That means I'm *fey* if *anyone* is, and right now I've got this strong sense that we'll meet again. I had that feeling about you for more than ten years, and it turned out right, and it's welling up in me now. So I'll 'na say goodbye." She quickly reached up, kissed him on the cheek, and then rapidly walked back to the tavern door and stood watching them depart.

In a moment Emily left Horner's side and joined her mistress at the door. Horner swung up into the saddle, looked back once, and then, leading the packhorse, trotted in the wake of the other men heading up the road. Wend mounted, then swung his mount around so he faced the two women and swept his hat off in as gallant a motion as he could manage, and then he put his spurs to the animal and was on his way.

—⁂—

As they rode up to Spiegler's Tavern, Wend realized that it was the functional twin of the Red Vixen. Whereas the Vixen was the gatehouse of Fredericktown for traffic coming up from or heading to the southwest, Spiegler's provided the same service for the northwest. It was situated just outside the town, and beyond lay the foothills of South Mountain. While the Vixen was stone, Spiegal's was of wooden construction. But like Colleen's place, it had a good pasture and spacious stable. There were numerous horses grazing in the pasture and three Conestogas parked near the stable. A wagoner was hitching up his team in preparation for departure.

Wend saw a line of saddled horses hitched to a fence rail at the edge of the yard. He presumed they were Bradley's, but he saw no sign of the cavalrymen. The Virginians dismounted, and Ballantyne announced he was going into the tavern to find the Maryland captain.

Wend dismounted and, throwing his rains to Horner, said, "I'm going in with him."

Ballantyne looked around and called over his shoulder, "Stay here, Eckert."

Wend laughed. "Not a chance, Jedidiah. The new rules apply." He entered the common room just behind the captain and saw Bradley sitting at a table with Sheriff Lowell.

Bradley motioned with his hand. "Ah, Ballantyne, Eckert, and right on time! Come join us."

Ballantyne shot Wend a scowl, but made no objection as the two of them took seats.

"Now gentlemen," continued Bradley, "The good sheriff has been busy over the last two days. He, eh, *confronted* the gentleman who sheltered Connolly and his companions and has obtained some valuable information."

Wend asked, "How were you able to get him to talk to you?"

Lowell raised his eyebrows. "I simply convinced Mr. Harner that if he didn't, I would see that the extent of his involvement with a plot in support of the crown would become known throughout the town. Obviously, that would lead to rather serious repercussions for him, his trade, and his family. After some consideration, he decided that cooperation was the better part of valor."

Ballantyne waved his hand impatiently. "So cut to the chase. What did you learn?"

"We learned that Connolly has found out that he is being pursued."

Jedidiah shrugged. "That's it? We knew that from the beginning. They realized their dispatches were captured."

The sheriff sighed. "Yes, yes, they *assumed* that somebody would be on their trail, but they didn't have any certainty. However, Connolly found out that the Maryland contingents were here in town looking for him. Someone told Harner about the inquiries they were making at various taverns. Learning that, they accelerated their preparations and left a day earlier than intended."

Bradley said in a reflective tone, "Well, they know they are being followed, but they can't know the strength of our party."

There was a momentary silence as everyone considered that, which Wend broke by asking, "Sheriff, did you learn anything else of value?"

"Between questioning Spiegler and Harned, we learned a lot about the men who are with Connolly."

Ballantyne cocked his head. "So who are these people?"

"This fellow Smyth is a doctor from Pittsburgh like Connolly. He apparently knows—and is influential with—a lot of Loyalists around the

Forks of the Ohio."

Bradley said, "Tell them about Cameron."

The sheriff nodded. "Yes, Harner had a conversation with the lieutenant. He's a professional soldier who served in the French war here in the colonies and before that in Europe, selling his sword to various countries. He stayed here after the peace, living down in North Carolina. Since early this year, he's been helping organize and train Loyalists, particularly the Scots, into a Tory militia. Undoubtedly he's along to do the same with the ranger companies Connolly wants to raise. You know about the other two in the group."

Wend nodded. "Yes, apparently they're simply servants."

"Indeed. Now, the four that came from the west are led by a man named Richard Munger, who was a captain in Connolly's militia during the war last year. Two others were also members of that battalion. The fourth is a callow lad apparently recruited to help with the horses and other chores."

Wend said, "That's all very logical. Presumably Connolly would have recruited Munger and his men before leaving Pittsburgh. What do you know about the men who came down from York?"

"They belong to a mercantile trading company with warehouses and trading posts along Forbes Road. Spiegler said they looked like seasoned backcountry men. Their names are Stewart and Markley. The innkeeper said their horse packs were very heavy."

Wend nodded. "Undoubtedly lead, powder, and trade goods."

Lowell said, "Spiegler didn't get a close look at the packs, but he rather thought the same."

Bradley looked around the table. "So, thanks to the good offices of the sheriff, we've obtained some valuable information on who we're facing." Bradley took a sip of his coffee and then added, "Now, as planned, the sheriff sent a man off on Sunday morning."

"Yes, I sent the very man who was with me at the Black Ox, so you'll recognize him. His name is Paul Kunkel. He knows the road well, and when you get to Elizabethtown, you'll find him at Cotter's Inn, which is not far from Hager's place."

Ballantyne said in a gruff tone. "Well enough. But it be time to stop talking and get moving. We need to get to this Elizabethtown and see if your man Kunkel and this fellow Hager actually have a line on Connolly."

Lowell grinned. "With any kind of luck, Hager has already got the whole lot in hand."

Bradley drained his cup and stood up. "Well, let us hope you are correct, Sheriff. But in any case, let us ride." He turned and waved his compatriots to come along.

When they were in the yard, Bradley looked toward the heights of South Mountain. He turned to Lowell. "Now, if you please, could you appraise us about the road between here and Elizabethtown?"

The sheriff pointed to the mountain. "Today you will do well to get to the crest. There's a good inn at the top, which will be able to pasture your horses and shelter you. It's about fourteen miles to the inn, and the road itself is good. It's the main route for freight wagons and other travelers heading west to Wills Creek, where it connects to Braddock Road. You'll start traversing the foothills soon after you leave here, and by mid-morning you'll be ascending South Mountain itself. The mountain really consists of two ridges. With luck you will be at the first in the middle of the afternoon, then you'll go down into a shallow valley, followed by a sharp ascent to the highest crest."

Bradley bit his lip. "Being mindful of the condition of our mounts, how steep is the actual road once we're on the mountain proper?"

Lowell shrugged. "Good question, Captain. It wanders back and forth to take advantage of the easiest path for the Conestogas, so your horses should be reasonably comfortable. But since it's relentlessly upward, you'll have to pace them to preserve their stamina."

Bradley considered a moment, then said, "That covers the climb. What about the descent into Elizabethtown?"

"A steady downward slope from the inn, followed by a few miles on the flat into the settlement. You should be there in the afternoon of the second day."

"Thank you, Sheriff." Bradley looked around at Ballantyne and Wend. "Well, gentlemen, shall we mount up and get to it?"

—⁂—

Joshua pulled the collar of his watch coat tighter to protect himself from the cold, gusty wind that swept across the mountain. The he reached up to shade his eyes from the bright sun and pointed. "What the devil is happening up there?"

Wend looked up and saw, a couple of hundred yards ahead, two Conestogas stopped on the road. The drivers were standing at the side of the track, looking down a steep embankment. Puzzled, he responded, "Damn if I know, Joshua, but something's got their attention."

As they approached the wagons, they saw that one of drivers was now carefully picking his way down through the trees and rocks of the near-vertical slope. Bradley, who led the column, held up his hand to signal a halt and then gave the order to dismount.

All the men walked up to the wagons to see what was happening and gathered around the wagoner at the side of the road. Bradley greeted him and then asked, "What's toward, sir?"

The driver pointed down the slope. "There be a man lying down there. He's near hidden in the bush. I just happened to look down as we were passing and saw a pair of booted legs. There's no tellin' how long he's been down there, hidden in the bush like that. We stopped and stared at him for a while. Looked like he was dead, sure enough. But just as we were convinced of that, he made the slightest move. So my partner,

Joel, is trying to get down there now."

By this time Joel had reached the distressed man and was on his knees examining him. After a moment he stood up and turned around. With his hands cupped around his mouth, he shouted, "Henry! He's alive, all right, but he's busted up pretty bad. He's got a broken arm and leg and like enough more wrong inside. But that ain't the worst of it."

Henry shouted down. "What's that?"

"The poor devil's been shot, that's what!"

The other wagoner shouted back. "Did you say he's *shot*?"

"You're damn right, Henry. He's been hit in his side. And he's been here a while; his coat's all stained with dried blood. But he's still bleeding; there's also lots of wet stuff."

Henry called down. "Is he awake?"

"Naw! He moved his mouth like he was tryin' to mumble somethin' when I first got down here, but he's passed out again now."

Bradley, looking down at the site, shook his head gravely and said, "Steep as that hill is, he's lucky he didn't fall further."

Wend agreed. "Looks like some underbrush stopped him from rolling after he landed."

Meanwhile, Joel had started pulling foliage away from the man's body to better get at him. As he pulled one bush out of the ground, the man's face became visible.

Wend gasped. "Good God, Bradley, look! It's Kunkel!"

CHAPTER EIGHT

THE INN AT SOUTH MOUNTAIN

Wend and Bradley stood looking down at Paul Kunkel as he lay in the bush on the side of the hill.

The wagoner Joel shouted up, "He moved his leg again, but he's still unconscious!"

Bradley looked over at Wend. "We've got to figure a way to get him out of there. And we've got to do it without injuring him further."

"Yes, steep as it is, and as bad off as he is, we can't just go down there and drag him up."

At that moment Ballantyne joined them. He glanced down at the scene. The wagoner was at the moment kneeling in front of the injured man's head, and the Virginia captain said, "That fellow is in a bad way. Is he alive?"

"He is indeed," responded Bradley. "And since you can't see his face, you should know it happens to be Kunkel, the sheriff's rider."

"Kunkle you say? Well, I'll be damned."

Wend filled him in. "Jedidiah, it looks to me like Connolly left a rear guard behind, and they shot Kunkle off his horse. What's unclear to me is how they knew he was the sheriff's man. Given all the travelers who come by here, they couldn't just assume any horseman was their enemy."

Bradley raised his eyebrows. "That's a good point, Eckert. Hadn't thought that far."

Ballantyne looked at the other two, a glint in his eye and the hint of a smile on his face. "Well, however they figured it out, you know what this means, don't you? So much for Sheriff Lowell's idea of stopping Connolly in Elizabethtown."

Bradley sighed in resignation. "That seems clear enough, my dear sir."

Ballantyne broke into gloating grin, then laughed curtly. "And as far ahead as they are, it surely means that we ain't got no chance of catchin' up to them 'til they're way beyond Wills Creek." Then in a sarcastic tone, he continued, "Well, Captain Bradley of the Anne Arundell Light Horse, I say Connolly's goin' to be *mine* to take back to Virginia."

He turned and stocked off.

Bradley looked after him. "What a most *unpleasant* man. Eckert, how did a man of your intelligence and manners happen to get involved with him? And how is it that you became his lieutenant?"

"War makes for strange associations. And the fact is I am decidedly not *his* lieutenant. But it's a long story, and I'll tell you when we have more time." Wend pointed down the hill. "As you said, right now we have to figure how to get Kunkel out of there and keep him alive. Most importantly, we need to get him some sort of medical care so he can tell us exactly what happened."

Bradley looked down at the man. "Yes, let's get organized. If we send two men down there, they, along with that driver, should be able to ease him up the hill in slow stages. I'll get things organized."

Wend turned to Donegal and pointed to Kunkel. "Simon, how about lashing together a strong litter like I saw you do to handle the wounded after Bushy Run? The way he's hurt in so many places, we'll need that to safely get him into one of the wagons and make him comfortable for the ride."

Meanwhile, Bradley was busy organizing the retrieval of Kunkel. Caleb Jackson and one of Bradley's men, Thomas Farrell, both young and agile, had volunteered to climb down the hill to help move the injured man.

The Maryland captain watched as the two men carefully started to descend. He turned to Wend and remarked, "With three men—one at the head and shoulders, one on the legs, and one in the middle of his body—they should be able to keep him fairly level as they inch him upward."

Wend wasn't sure. "Even so, look at the sharp angle of the slope. It's going to be tricky, Warren."

The two men were slowly picking their way downward, carefully placing their hands and feet. Farrell led, searching out the safe path, with Jackson following behind at some distance, using the same features for support.

Farrell had covered half the distance down to Kunkel when disaster struck. Above him, Jackson missed a foothold and catapulted downward, head first. He plowed right into Farrell, then rolled upright—almost to his feet—but lost footing again and tumbled over and over about twenty feet down the hillside, coming to rest below Kunkel's position. Meanwhile, Farrell had become airborne and landed feet first on an outcropping of rock. Dust swirled all around the men.

The others stood on the road, staring down at the scene, shocked into silence.

Finally Bradley remarked in a massive understatement, "Damn."

Joey worked his way down to Farrell, who was moaning and holding his leg. The wagoner shouted up, "This one's got a broken leg!"

Then, with extreme care, he started climbing down to where Jackson was sprawled out. Wend noticed that Caleb was absolutely motionless, appearing unconscious.

Joey got to where the Virginian lay and examined him for what seemed a long time. Then he looked up and called out, "He smashed his head on a rock! The back is crushed-in and bloody. There ain't no heartbeat, and no doubt in my mind but he's dead."

Bradley lost his composure and exclaimed, "Good God!"

Ballantyne sneered, "You proud of yourself? One of my men is dead. I've known the lad's family since he was at his mother's skirts."

The Maryland captain spun around on his counterpart. "Shut up, Ballantyne. Your man volunteered. And how the hell different would you have done it? If you've got a better idea on how to do this, tell me because now we got two injured men and a body to get up."

Ballantyne said nothing, his face flushing

Wend feared they were about to come to blows. He stepped forward to try to interpose himself between the two captains.

Meanwhile Horner had come over, and now he put his hand on Wend's arm. "Sir, I think I know a way of getting them all up safely."

Bradley heard Andrew's words and turned away from Ballantyne. "Lad, what do you have in mind?"

"We might be able to hoist them up." Andrew walked over to the edge of the road and looked over the area. Then he looked over at Henry, who was standing by his wagon. "You got a good length of rope in your wagons?"

"After doin' this for more years than I care to count, 'course we do."

"Good," said Horner. "We'll need that litter that Donegal is making up. But you can't just drag the litter up over those rocks and bushes. You got to hoist him up into the air clear of them." Then he pointed to a large tree with wide branches that extended over the slope. "When I was on the ship coming across from Germany, I watched sailors rig lines to spars to raise and lower cargo. We need to run the rope over that big limb, like it was a spar on a mast, and then down to where Kunkel lays.

Then we can hoist the litter straight up and sway it back over to the road. Once we get Kunkle up, we'll do the same with Farrell." He looked at the wagoner. "You got enough for that?"

Henry looked up at the tree, then down to where Kunkel was lying. "Yeah, I'm thinkin' between me and Joel, we can make a long-enough length to pull him up."

Horner turned to Bradley. "Captain, I think there's no getting those two out of there safely any other way."

Bradley seemed somewhat stunned by what had happened. He simply nodded acquiescence.

Wend realized he must get things moving. "All right, Andrew. Rig your rope while Donegal cuts saplings and lashes them together for the frame of the litter." He turned to the wagoner. "Have you a strong blanket we can fold to form the bed of the litter?"

Henry said, "Sure enough," and then scurried to get the rope and blanket.

Wend then put his hand on Baird's shoulder and pointed up to the side of the mountain above the road. "Joshua, whoever did this most likely was hiding in the bush from the side of the hill where he—or they— could watch the road and have a clear shot. Try looking around up there and see if you can find any sign that will shed some light on how many of them there were and anything else."

Baird scanned the hill. "Yea, I see a couple of likely spots."

It took the better part of an hour to make ready to hoist the casualties. Henry tried throwing the line over the big branch, but after several tries he could not get it into the right place just over Kunkel. Finally, Horner climbed the tree and very carefully wriggled out along the big limb and ran the line right over where the injured man lay.

Meanwhile, Donegal had cut some strong saplings and lashed together a well-braced litter with the blanket folded around it to support Kunkel's body. Horner, having carefully climbed down from the tree, knotted together a four-legged sling that he attached to the corners of the litter. Then he tied the lifting line to it at the center point so the litter would hang level when suspended. Finally, he fitted two lines each about fifteen feet long to opposite ends of the stretcher to help maneuver it.

When all was set, Horner motioned to one of Bradley's men named Jamie Sedgewick. Andrew, with almost painful slowness, descended the cliff, followed by the Marylander practicing the same care. When they arrived at the wounded man, Wend directed the swaying of the litter out over the hill and then its lowering down to where the two men could grasp it. They gingerly loaded the sheriff's man onto it.

Meanwhile Wend had organized a line of six men to haul on the lifting line.

Andrew waved to Wend. "All right, start pulling in on the line very slowly." He paused. "And try to do it evenly—no jerking if possible."

With great care the men walked the line back, and with Horner and Sedgewick steadying it, the litter rose slowly off the side of the hill and into the air. Each took one of the control lines in hand and crawled up the hill to the road.

Wend kept the men on the line moving back until the litter was several feet above the level of the wagon track, and Horner signaled for them to stop. Then, working together, he and Sedgewick slowly used the handling lines to pull the stretcher over the road surface.

Horner turned to Wend. "All right, while we keep a strain on these handling ropes, ease off on the hoisting line."

After a moment they had the litter and man on the ground.

Wend moved beside Horner. "Nicely done, lad."

Horner sighed in relief. "Well, it worked. I wasn't sure how things would go until we got him right over the road." He pointed up to where the rope ran over the tree branch. "Would have gone smoother if we had a pulley or, as the sailors say, a block."

Wend patted his apprentice on the shoulder. "Nevertheless, Andrew."

Meanwhile Bradley knelt beside the litter and leaned over the deputy. "Kunkel, can you hear me?" He paused and then said more loudly, "Kunkel! It's Warren Bradley. We met at the Black Ox. Do you remember me?"

The wounded man's body moved slightly. One eye opened a fraction and he moved his mouth, but nothing came out. Then the eye closed again.

Wend, now standing beside the stretcher, said, "Warren, look how he's quivering. He's been laying out in freezing cold for the better part of two days. It's a wonder he's alive."

Bradley waved to Henry. "Have you got some blankets?"

"Right, sir." The wagoner hurried to his Conestoga. In minutes he was back with two rough blankets, and he quickly tucked them over Kunkel.

Bradley rose and looked up the road. "We've got to get him some care. What about that inn up at the crest? How far is that?"

Henry waved in the general direction of the mountaintop. "I've traveled this road many times. The inn is indeed your best hope, and it's not far now." He looked up at the sun, which was low on the horizon. "We can make it by nightfall if we get the other fellow up, put them both into my wagon, and get started right away."

Wend nodded. "Let's quick make a pallet for Kunkel and Farrell inside your wagon on top of your cargo."

In a few minutes, they had Kunkel in the Conestoga, and the litter was being lowered for Farrell. Horner and Sedgewick guided it as they again crawled down the side of the hill.

Another few minutes saw the injured Marylander up on the road and into the wagon.

Recovering Jackson's body was another problem because he was too far down the hill to be reached by the same rig. In the end they tied all the rope they had into one long length, and Horner made his way down and tied a loop around Jackson's chest, and the dead man was dragged slowly up the hill to the road.

Ballantyne, who had been standing to one side, not participating in the recovery, walked over beside Wend and said bitterly, "No litter and sling for Caleb? He deserved better treatment than being hauled up like a sack of flour."

Wend shot back, "I didn't see you making any suggestions on a better way to do it." He looked over to where men were loading Jackson's body into the second Conestoga. "And I can assure you he didn't feel any pain coming up the hill." He turned to walk away but then turned back to face Ballantyne, "You didn't do a damn thing to recover him, but given your concern, I'm sure you'll welcome the opportunity to give the lad a decent burial once we get up to the inn."

As he was speaking, Baird came sauntering down the road and joined them. "Well, I found the tracks they made and the place they shot from." He pointed up the mountain to a clump of pines. "There was two of them, and they waited up there in them green pines you can make out." He swung around and motioned up the wagon track. "They hid their horses in trees about twenty yards off the road up there. Found piles of dung and grass chewed down where they were tied."

Wend considered a moment. He turned to Bradley, who had joined them. "Warren, Joshua is mounted on a very strong hunter. Why don't we send him ahead to the inn to warn them we're bringing in injured men and see if they have anyone who can help treat them?"

Joshua grinned broadly. "Oh, yeah! That's a damn fine idea. I'll be waitin' for you in front of the fire with a good drink in hand."

Bradley nodded. "All right, but two will be safer than one. There's some small chance the men who shot Kunkel are still hanging around. I'll send one of my men along." He called out, "Jamie! Jamie Sedgewick!"

After a few minutes Baird and Sedgewick were on their way, and a short time afterward, the wagons and all the other riders got underway toward the crest.

—⁄⁄⁄—

The wagoner's prediction proved entirely correct. The last rays of light from the sun were just visible in the western sky as the cavalcade arrived at the South Mountain Inn. Wend saw that the main building was a two-story, well-built stone structure with tall chimneys at either end. It was situated just off the wagon track in a grove of high trees on a narrow plateau crowning the very crest of the mountain. The horsemen and Joey's Conestoga went straight into the yard, which lay between the rear of the inn and the stable. The inn was busy. Wend could see several other Conestogas and a couple of carts already parked near the stable.

Meanwhile, Henry pulled his wagon up to the front entrance of the inn, the better to offload Farrell and the still-unconscious Kunkel.

Horner and Seidal jumped up into the Conestoga's bed to hand down the sheriff's man, who had been placed on the litter. Wend and Simon stood by at the wagon's rear gate to receive the stretcher, which they lowered to the ground. Then Farrell was carefully eased down and laid on a blanket. Meanwhile, the inn's proprietor, a stout, balding man whom Wend judged to be in his midforties, came out onto the front porch. He was followed by Baird and Sedgewick, both of whom had cups in their hands.

Bradley walked up to the innkeeper. "Sir, I am Captain Warren Bradley of the Anne Arundell Light Horse. We have two men with serious injuries who need immediate assistance."

"Gunther Rheinhardt, sir, at your service." He looked down at Kunkel and then Farrell, meanwhile wiping his hands on his white apron. "Yes, yes, I see what you mean."

Joshua interjected, "He says his wife can do some doctoring. She's on her way out now."

Reinhardt added, "Yes, sir. We called her when we saw the wagons approaching. She will be right here."

Even as the innkeeper spoke, a tall, wiry, horse-faced, dark-haired woman of an age that matched the innkeeper hurried out of the tavern. She was dressed in a sober gray gown and a white apron and cap and wasted no time going to the litter.

Bradley said, "Mrs. Rheinhardt, the man on the blanket has a broken leg. But the man on the litter has been shot in his side and has a broken arm and leg from the fall."

"Yes, young man." She motioned toward Kunkel. "I can certainly see the blood with my own eyes. Now get out of the way and let me look for myself." She bent over the stretcher, examining the arm and leg, then pulled back Kunkel's jacket to look at his wound. She clucked her tongue. "How long has he been layin' out in the weather?"

Wend answered, "Near two days, Mrs. Rheinhardt."

"At this time of year? And he's still alive? It's sure the poor soul's a heartbeat from bein' with the Lord." She turned to her husband. "Gunther, let's not be wastin' any time. Get him to the meeting room and put him on the table. That's the best place for me to work."

Rheinhardt said, "Yes, Greta,"

"And then have Jenny get a pot of hot water and clean rags. And you fetch my bag."

"Yes, Greta."

She pointed to Farrell. "And Gunther, take this man to one of the bedrooms. He ain't in any danger. I'll get to him when I finish with the other one."

But before her husband could say or do anything else, she turned and pointed to Donegal and Eckert. "You two—don't just stand there gawking. Pick up the litter and follow me now."

And without further words, she turned and headed for the front door. Wend nodded to Simon, and the two of them quickly lifted Kunkel and carefully carried the litter after her. Bradley followed behind.

Greta Rheinhardt led them through the common room into a spacious room at the rear, with a long table and chairs in the center. She waved to the table. "You boys put him up on that." She looked around. "Now where's that Gunther?"

As she spoke, her husband appeared, carrying a heavy canvas bag. "Yes, my dear, I've got your medical bag," he said.

"Good. Now put it in that chair, and get the candles lighted and the fire going. And get that lazy Irish girl Jenny heatin' the water."

"Yes, dear." Reinhardt wasted no time scuttling out of the room.

Bradley cleared his throat and spoke up. "Mrs. Rheinhardt, it's vital that when Kunkel regains consciousness, we speak to him immediately. We need to find out exactly what happened to him and see if he has any knowledge of who shot him."

She gave him a withering look. "Young man, look at the poor lad laying there. I'm of the mind it will be a miracle if we keep him alive. And all you can think about is pullin' some words out of him." She looked beseechingly heavenward. "Now all of you just scat! Wait out in the common room, and if by chance I get him to come around, you'll be the first to know." She made a shooing motion with both hands.

Wend, Bradley, and Donegal made their escape. Once back in the common room, Wend talked to Reinhardt and arranged for a room. Then he got a cup of whiskey and walked over to join Bradley, who was at a table in front of the fire. He was talking to Rheinhardt, who stood by the table.

Bradley lit one of his cigars from the candle on the table. "Now, my good sir, I need to ask you some questions, if I may."

The innkeeper shrugged. "Of course, Captain. What do you wish to know?"

"Have you had a large group of men here, say two nights ago?" He described the composition of Connolly's group. Wend added a description of Connolly himself.

The chubby proprietor smiled. "Oh, you mean the group of men sent by the Virginia government to strengthen the militia out in Pittsburgh."

Bradley took the cigar out of his mouth. "That's what they told you?"

"Yes. They said the Virginia Committee of Safety was worried about an Indian insurrection led by the British, and they were taking powder and other supplies to organize companies for protection of the border country."

The captain looked at Wend, then asked, "Now while they were here, did you notice anything out of the ordinary about their party?"

Rheinhardt made a face. "Not a thing. The only occurrence of any note was the fact that they had lost something from one of the packs in their train."

Bradley went on the alert. "Lost something? What?"

"I never learned, exactly, but it was important enough that they sent two men back the morning after they got here to find it." He made a face. "And the rest of the group stayed here until they returned in the afternoon."

Wend sat down at the table, then shot Bradley a glance. "So the party left when the two men got back?"

"Yes. Like I said, it was late in the day, but they were in a hurry. I told the leader—this Cantrell fellow—that they would find it impossible to make Elizabethtown by dark."

Bradley grinned. "Naturally you would have been happy if they'd have stayed another night?"

"Well, I mean, a party of eleven? With a healthy thirst? And using several rooms? Naturally that would please me." Reinhardt made a face. "I pointed out it was likely they'd have to camp out in the bush because the next ordinary is at Elizabethtown itself. But Colonel Cantrell didn't seem the least concerned about that."

Wend said, "Were the men who went back carrying rifles?"

Rheinhardt put a hand to his chin. "Now that you mention it, I believe so. Of course, nothing remarkable about that."

"Of course," Wend echoed in an ironic tone.

Bradley smiled, "Thank you, Mr. Rheinhardt. You've been very helpful." After the proprietor left, Bradley took a long draw on the cigar, then carefully blew the smoke out toward the fireplace. Then he observed, "Obviously most of the brains in the family reside with the good lady working on Kunkel at this moment."

Wend laughed. "Oh, I think Rheinhardt's smart enough—just working *very* hard not to put two and two together and get the right sum."

"Perhaps you're correct. Anyone with a modicum of intelligence would have suspected what happened the moment we unloaded Kunkel."

Wend looked back at the counter where the proprietor was busying himself. "Undoubtedly Rheinhardt now understands everything. But that aside, the important thing is that we now know Connolly is not as far ahead as we expected."

"You're quite right, Eckert. He's only a day ahead now. Probably sleeping tonight in Elizabethtown."

"Warren, if we get an early start, we'll be there by midafternoon. If we pause only long enough to make inquires and then force our pace, there's a chance of overtaking Connolly before he gets to Wills Creek. It's several days' travel with some steep ridges, the most challenging being Sideling Hill. They'll be handicapped with that heavy packtrain, and we can make up some distance each day."

Bradley looked at the fire over his cigar. "You know, your compatriot Ballantyne is going to be sorely disappointed if we do capture Connolly before Wills Creek." He blew out some smoke and then looked down at his cigar. "I should be very grateful if you could enlighten me why the man is so aggressively perverse."

Wend looked down into the fire for a few seconds. "I asked the same thing of Sergeant Seidal a few days ago. He is convinced it's because Ballantyne lost his brother and several friends at the Battle of Point Pleasant."

"I heard of that battle. It was during Virginia's war with the Ohio tribes last year. Quite bloody, am I not correct?"

"Quite correct. The sergeant thinks Ballantyne has grown bitter because he feels that Lord Dunmore didn't properly support the southern column of the army, leaving them alone to be ambushed and suffer severe losses. And then he got home and things got worse. His wife and her baby had died in childbirth, leaving him essentially alone in the world. Seidal thinks the loss and loneliness essentially drove him to a constant, smoldering anger."

Bradley reflected a moment. "Well, perhaps that explains it. But other men have had similar losses and learned to move on."

"Warren, I contented myself with that view of him for a while, but the other night in Fredericktown, Ballantyne revealed something else to me: he has become exceedingly ambitious. The man is obsessed with capturing Connolly and taking him back to Williamsburg because he thinks the acclaim will help him attain higher rank in the Virginia forces." Wend looked at Bradley for a moment, then continued, "I was turning that over in my mind while we rode up here, and it seems to me that perhaps he has filled the emptiness of his life with the need to rise in the world to the point where it has distorted his judgment."

Bradley laughed out loud. "Distorted his judgment? Come now, I believe you are underestimating the effect. My observation is that the man is on the very edge of rationality, if not beyond."

Wend took a sip of his whiskey. "Either way, Warren, it has made him a very dangerous man."

"Indeed, Eckert." A silence followed, and Bradley took a sip of his drink and then a draw on his cigar. Then his face formed into a crooked grin, and he waved at Wend. "Forgive me if I observe that Captain Ballantyne, whatever his other attributes, seems, shall I say, to have a certain lack of esteem for you. Perhaps to the extent of presenting the threat of physical harm."

"Quite correct. The man hates me."

"You promised to explain how you became his lieutenant."

"It begins with the fact that he has accused me of being a Loyalist and spy."

A startled look came over Bradley's face. "And that *somehow* led to you serving under him?"

Wend explained the events of Culpeper and Henry's assignment of him to assist Ballantyne.

After he had finished, Bradley sat examining his cigar for a long moment. Then he said, "Based on what you said earlier, perhaps you should reexamine your thoughts on Ballantyne's motivation toward you. It may actually be more about his *ambition* than *hatred* of you. It occurs to me that he cynically used your alleged status as a spy as a convenient vehicle to curry favor with Colonel Henry and to make himself a hero among his men."

Wend contemplated that for a while, then responded, "You may well be right—or perhaps it's a convenient marriage of the two."

Bradley nodded. "Ah, yes. The two motivations are not mutually exclusive."

A prolonged silence followed as the two men became lost in thought, staring into the fire. After a while, the Marylander reached down, picked up his cup, and took a long sip. Then he changed the direction of conversation. "I wonder how Congress's invasion of Canada is coming."

Wend was surprised. "Invasion of Canada? I had not heard. When did this happen?"

"The word arrived in Annapolis just before we departed. Congress is convinced that our sister colony to the north will join in the cause if they see a force march on Quebec. To that end, they've sent two columns northward. One, under a general named Montgomery, is advancing from

Ticonderoga up the lakes. The second, under a certain Colonel Arnold, left Boston and is marching northward through the Maine wilderness."

Wend was puzzled. "Warren, this is indeed fresh news to me. But I'm puzzled. Where are the men for these expeditions coming from? I thought our rather limited resources were being focused on the British in Boston."

"That's true enough. But both of the columns are fairly small. Less than a thousand men each. It is my understanding that the British have few soldiers in Canada, and Congress is of the opinion that the Canadian yeomanry will flock to our colors as we march on their capital and that the conquest of the weak British forces will be easy."

Wend shook his head in doubt. "I cannot be sanguine about that prospect."

Bradley cocked his head. "Pray tell, why not? Surely the French population will be eager to throw off their recent British conquerors."

"I am skeptical of that. There has long been enmity between the French trappers and traders and our settlers in the northwest of New York and Pennsylvania. But there's something else to think of. At the end of the French War, in the early '60's, soldiers of the Highland regiments—the 77th, 78th, and even some from the 42nd—were given land grants along the Canada border country. The British Army thought it was cheaper to grant them land than to transport them back to Scotland." Wend hesitated a moment and then continued, "And the British government was quite happy to settle them in Canada rather than see them come back to the Highlands where they might cause political trouble."

"Yes, less chance of another Culloden."

"Precisely. But the point is, there exists a strong force of disciplined and trained soldiers likely to be loyal to the crown right along the Canadian border."

"You really think they would fight for the British?"

"Warren, look at the situation in North Carolina. There are a lot of Highlanders there, and they have formed a strong Loyalist militia that has thrown in with Lord Dunmore. I believe they are convinced that the crown will prevail and that they want to be on the right side in the aftermath."

"Now I hadn't known that, and indeed you make a convincing point."

Wend looked into the fire. "I confess that this northern invasion worries me. I think it is an overreach. We should concentrate on getting the British out of Boston before we raise other expeditions."

Bradley drew on his cigar and then exhaled the smoke. "Perhaps you are right about the Highlanders. But then look at the Irish—these rough, bellicose fellows like the esteemed Captain Ballantyne and the brothers Carlin." He continued in a disdainful tone, "They have the opposite attitude from the Highlanders—a positively rabid support for the idea of independence to the exclusion of any reconciliation with the crown and parliament. I find that irrational. We would be far better off if a way were found to secure peace and our full rights as Englishmen under the beneficial protection of the home government."

Wend smiled. "Permit me to ask a question: I suspect you have had little contact with the people you call *the Irish*. Is that not so?"

Bradley shrugged. "I must confess that is true. There are few to be found in tidewater Maryland, and, let me be honest, those present are generally of the lowest class and invariably ne'er-do-wells or servants."

Wend sighed. "Warren, they call themselves the Ulster-Scots or just the Ulster people to differentiate themselves from the true Irish. They're bitter because they were forced to flee Lowland Scotland due to British intolerance for their religion. They initially ended up in Ulster County, Ireland. There they faced poverty and the disdain of the Irish, and eventually many of them took ship here to the colonies. Mostly they came in through New York and Philadelphia and flowed to the border country to settle on cheap or free land. Now many of them are migrating southward along the Great Wagon Road into the Valley of Virginia and the southern colonies." Wend took a sip of his drink. Then he leaned forward and looked into Bradley's eyes. "As you say, some of them, like the Carlins, are perpetually poor and rootless. But others have done well as farmers, shopkeepers, and tradesmen. In Winchester, we have many who have, over the years, become valued members of society."

Bradley stared at Wend for a long moment with a puzzlement on his face. "Now, my dear Eckert, I confess to being mightily surprised at your defense of the Irish, uh, or Ulster-Scots as you call them. It is superfluous to say that that there is not much affinity between the Germans and the Ulster people."

He took another sip from his cup, then said, "Warren, it may startle you to learn that my wife is Ulster."

Bradley raised his eyebrows in surprise. "A German married to an Irish...uh...Ulster-Scot woman? That is unusual."

Then Wend reached up and moved his hair queue aside. "I'm sure you noticed the scarring on the back of my head. In 1759 my parents, brother, and sister were killed in an attack by a Mingo war party on Forbes Road." He looked directly in Bradley's eyes. "I was shot, partially scalped, and left for dead laying on the wagon track. A company of the 77th Highlanders rescued me. The point is, afterward I was adopted by an Ulster minister and his wife, who raised me with great kindness and affection."

Bradley bit his lip, lowered his cigar, and stared at Wend for a few long seconds. Then he said very carefully, "Eckert, I beg that you forgive my remarks about the Ulster, which I made in ignorance. I deeply regret any offense they may have caused."

"Think nothing of it, Warren. There was no way you could have been aware of my background. But keep this in mind: admittedly the Ulster are, in general, a rough lot. However, if our resistance to the British turns into a protracted conflict, make no mistake—we're going to need them. There are a multitude in the border country, and they have long confronted the tribes in defense of their freeholds. They have become stalwart, experienced fighters. Moreover, they have an abiding hatred of the English, and I believe they ultimately will become the core of our army."

"I do see your point."

"And to be honest, I have a question for you, Warren. I've noticed your only weapons are horse pistols; none of your men are carrying carbines or any other kind of long arm. Has the Anne Arundell Light Horse ever seen any action?"

Bradley looked down and studied the stub of the cigar in hand. "You question is well taken. Our duties heretofore have included only escort of the governor at ceremonial functions and similar events. We were sent on this duty because we were the only mounted unit in the colony at the disposal of the Council of Safety."

"You said you were in Forbes's column, so you at least have done some soldiering. But what about the men of your troop who are with you?"

Bradley sighed. "Let me be completely honest. It's true that I marched in Forbes's column, but I never shot my firelock in anger. And none of the men with me have either."

At the moment the Irish maid, Jenny, rushed into the common room, looked around for a moment, then scurried over to them. She spoke to Bradley, "Please, sir, Mrs. Rheinhardt says come quickly. Poor Mr. Kunkel is awake!"

Bradley and Wend jumped up and followed the girl to the meeting room.

Kunkel was covered by blankets and looked to be sleeping. Greta Rheinhardt stood beside the table, a cloth over her shoulder, her left hand on her hip. There were pots of water, rags, dressing material, and a jug of whiskey on the table beside her patient.

The proprietress turned to them and said, "The man's lucky. The ball went right through his body, so all I had to do was clean and dress the wound. But there's no tellin' what damage it did inside. And I got his leg splinted. But that right arm of his is broken in at least two places. I got it tied to a length of wood so it'll stay straight 'til he gets to a real doctor."

She had just finished speaking when Kunkel opened his eyes. He stared up at the people around him, and then a look of recognition came over his face. "Captain Bradley!"

"Yes, I'm here, Kunkel. This good lady says you're going to be all right." He put his hand on the man's shoulder. "But we need to know who did this to you."

"It be that man Munger!" He stopped to catch a breath. "Munger and another blackguard."

"How do you know that? And why did they know you were behind them? Can you tell us that?"

"I was riding up the mountain road when they shot me. Weren't no warning. Suddenly I was hit and fell right off my horse down the side of the cliff. Landed on my arm, and it hurt like hell. Then I hit my head and blacked out for a little time. Next thing I knew I was layin' there on the side of the hill among rocks and bushes." He paused and took a deep breath. "Suddenly I heard them. They was up on the road looking down at me. I kept my eyes closed and laid still. One man said, 'Hey, Munger, you got damn sharp eyes.' Sure enough, that's the sheriff's man who was nosing around Spiegler's Tavern askin' about us, just like you thought."

Bradley said, "So they recognized you from when you were checking out all the taverns for strangers?"

Kunkel nodded. "That Munger said he recognized my hat, the way it was shaped." He let out a groan and shut his eyes. Then he opened them again and said, "Then Munger said, 'He's dead. Sure as hell, Mooney. Let's take his horse and ride back to the inn.'"

Bradley asked, "Did they say anything else?"

"Not that I heard 'cause I passed out again. Next thing I know'd I was looking up at Mrs. Rheinhardt right here."

The captain pressed him on the shoulder. "That's good, Kunkel. Now rest. Tomorrow the Rheinhardts will put you on a wagon bound to Fredericktown." He leaned close to his ear and said, "And I vow to you, we'll get Munger. He and his compatriot will pay for what they did to you."

Bradley and Wend walked out into the hall, followed by Mrs. Rheinhardt. She had her bag in hand and said, "Now I'm going upstairs and work on your other man, the one with the broken leg. I'm going to splint it, and we'll send him down to Fredericktown with this fellow so a doctor can do a right job of setting it."

Then she went down the hall and ascended the stairway at the end.

Bradley sighed. "Eckert, I must admit today has been a disaster. We've lost two men."

"Yes, and now we're only one man stronger than Connolly's party. We lost much of our advantage if it comes up to a stand-up fight."

"Yes, that occurred to me."

Wend said, "Warren, I've been turning the situation over in my mind. Until now, we've assumed that Connolly will be pushing to get as far as possible ahead of us. But with the burden of the packtrain, and now that he's certain that he's being pursued, he may have decided his best move is to turn and destroy us. The events of today may be a precursor to additional ambushes."

"Yes, that's possible, but we don't know that for sure. So what, precisely, are you suggesting, Eckert?"

"Just this: I think we should travel with a vanguard—or point—well ahead of us in case Connolly plans another attack. I would suggest Joshua, who has an almost supernatural ability to sense trouble, and one of your men to assist him."

Bradley put his hand to his chin, then nodded. "Done, starting tomorrow."

—ɯ—

Later, after sitting in the smoke-filled common room for hours, Wend walked out into the inn's yard to clear his head. Ballantyne's men had been given permission to sleep in an open-front shed to shelter against the cold and light wind that was flowing through the trees at the crest. They had built a fire before the open side. Seidal stood before the flames.

Wend joined him. "Having trouble sleeping, Horst?"

"No, I'd damn well like to be in my blankets right now, Eckert. But Jedidiah decided we needed to keep a sentry out on the off chance Connolly's men were still about and that we needed to keep the fire going. I took the first watch."

Wend looked up in the sky. "It's a bit windy, but the sky's clear enough. Lots of stars out."

Seidal nodded, then motioned for Wend to come with him. Together they walked to the western side of the grove, where the mountain started to slope downward. He pointed into the distance. "If you look closely, you can see some lights down in the valley. Used to be several, but I can only see two now."

Wend squinted and soon was able to pick out the lights. They flickered as the wind gusted. "Must be Elizabethtown. Wind's blowing tree branches back and forth in front of them."

"Yeah, that's true. But I'm always impressed by how far even weak lights carry in the dark."

"Indeed, particularly on a moonless night like now."

The two stood wordlessly for a moment, staring out into the blackness, listening to the tree branches rustling in the gusts.

After a while Seidal said, "I've never seen dark nights like we had in the wilderness at Fort Venango. There were no settlers' cabins about, no lights to see at night standing sentry duty. It felt like you were part of the sky."

Wend decided that, with the two of them alone, it was time to clear something up. He said quietly, "Horst, how long before the massacre did you desert the garrison?"

Seidal's head spun around, and he looked for a moment like he was going to deny it, but then his chest heaved and he asked, "How did you figure it out?"

"They weren't allowing many discharges from the 60th in those days right after the French War. It was sorely understrength. That's why they consolidated the third and fourth battalions into the first and second. And when I served as a scout, the officers were always complaining about the number of desertions."

Seidal looked down at his hands, then said, "Soldiering wasn't so bad when we were on campaign. You kept busy, and there was the excitement of being with friends. And I tell you, I was proud to stand in line and trade volleys with the French on the Plains of Abraham." He put his hand to his eyes and then stared out into the night. "But after the war, some of us got sent down to Venango, and I found out how much worse things could get in the army compared to life on the farm. There was supposed to be a full half company in the garrison, but we were so understrength there were only seventeen of us and the lieutenant. There were two wives and three children. All alone there in the wilderness, nothin' but guard mount, boredom, and shitty—sometimes outright rotten—rations."

"So you took your own discharge."

"By spring 1763, after nearly a year at the place, I'd had enough. I stole a supply of rations and new shoes from the quartermaster's stock and took off one night when I was the lone sentry and the only one awake in the place. I'd spent a lot of time hunting when I was on the farm, so I felt pretty good about making my way through the bush. I headed southeast, knowing enough about the map to be sure I'd eventually strike Forbes Road."

Wend thought a second. "May 1763? You must have left just before Pontiac attacks began."

"Yes, couldn't have been more than a day or two. The first indication I had that anything was going on was the second night out. I was bedded down on a ridge, and I looked back to the northwest and saw a faint glow on the horizon. Didn't have any idea what it was at the time, but afterward I realized it must have been Venango burning."

"The tribes destroyed Venango and seven other forts in just a few days during the first attack."

"Yes, but of course I didn't know that at the time. But a couple days later, I nearly stumbled into a war party. There was about fifteen of them, and they were heading eastward. It was clear something was going on." He crossed his arms and sighed. "Then, several days out from the fort, after I had cut Forbes Road and was heading east, I came to an abandoned farmstead. Place was a mess like the people had left in a hurry. But it was a godsend. I found some food and enough clothing to shed my uniform, so I didn't feel so obvious."

Wend commented, "The people must have gotten word of the raids and fled."

"Yeah, late the next day I sighted Fort Ligonier. I planned to sneak around it, but then I saw the area between the stockade and the outer works was filled with wagons and families camping out, so I realized they had gone there to shelter. I decided maybe I could go in without anybody asking questions, and it turned out that way. I found out right away what was happening. And the total garrison was only a lieutenant and seven men of the regiment, none who knew me."

"Yes, Horst, the forts right along Forbes Road had been put into caretaker status and used mostly as supply depots before the war. Baird and I scouted for a company sent out by Bouquet to reinforce Bedford and Ligonier."

The sergeant nodded. "Yeah, I remember when that column came in.

There was lots of celebrating by the settlers. And then not too long after that, Bouquet and his relief convoy arrived."

Wend grinned. "Yes, I was with them."

"Well, I didn't waste no time leavin' after that. I headed east fast as I could go 'til I got to Fort Bedford. By then I decided I had better get out of Pennsylvania before somebody recognized me, and I took the trail south from Bedford to Fort Cumberland at Wills Creek. When I got there, turns out a train of settlers was gettin' ready to go down to southern Virginia, so I joined them. They was glad to have another armed man along." A smile came over Seidal's face. "It happened there was a nice-lookin' German girl with the train who later that year became my wife and has now given me three fine children."

"Horst, with a good family and a farm that has prospered, you are a lucky man."

Seidal looked down at his hands, and Wend could see he was rubbing them together. He looked at the man's face and was surprised to see a look of anguish.

"Yes, Eckert, I used to think that. For seven years I was very happy and had put my days in the Royal Americans—and the way I left it—behind me. Then one day I drove my family in the cart to our local store. While there, we encountered a group of people traveling to the Carolinas. As I was loading the cart with our purchases, I suddenly heard someone say, 'Seidal, my God, is that you?' I turned around, and my heart nearly jumped out of my chest. I recognized the speaker as a man who had been in another company of the Fourth Battalion."

Seidal reached up and rubbed his hand across his forehead. "His name was Shadt. Jacob Shadt. He pointed at me and said, 'I thought you were dead. I was at Fort Pitt in '63, and your name was on the list of men who died at Fort Venango. How the devil did you survive?'"

The sergeant shook his head. "I panicked, Eckert. I denied knowing what he was talking about. I said my name wasn't Seidal, and I denied ever seeing him before or being in the British Army. That was pretty stupid because the man could have asked anyone in the village about me."

Wend asked, "So he left it at that?"

"Yes, I was fortunate. He just gave me a puzzled look and said, 'Well, you're sure a match for a man I knew in the 60th Foot.' Then he gathered his family into a wagon and drove off."

"Even if you had admitted who you were and told him the truth, what could he have done, years later? Hell, Seidal, he would likely have congratulated you on your escape."

"Yes, in retrospect, you're absolutely right, Eckert." He crossed his arms. "But you're thinking logically. Sometimes, the mind doesn't work that way. For seven years I had managed to forget about the regiment, Fort Venango, and how I left. But seeing Shadt brought it all back and aroused a heavy sense of guilt in my mind. I began having trouble sleeping; I would have dreams about the men whom I had known at Venango. Worse, I began to see them laying slaughtered on the ground of the fort or shrieking as they were burned at the stake. Eventually it wasn't just me seeing them, I began to hear them calling out to me for help. Sometimes they screamed damning words at me."

Wend looked at him for a moment. "Horst, it's normal you would have dreams like that. I have nightmares about the attack on my family. Sometimes I wake thinking it has just happened." He shrugged. "It's part of life, and you have to live with it. You can't control your mind during sleep."

"But Eckert, you didn't desert your family. You have nothing to feel guilty about."

"Horst, sometimes I feel guilty just for being alive when they're lying in a grave beside Forbes Road."

"But you feel guilt for what didn't happen to you. I feel shame for what I actually did." Seidal took a deep breath. "That's why I volunteered for the First Virginia."

Wend saw it at once. "Sort of a way of making up for walking away from the 60th?"

"Yes. I was a good soldier once. I want to be able to be so again. I want to have compatriots who know they can rely on me, and when this is all over, I want to be able to truthfully say to my children, 'I have done my duty in the army.'" He hesitated a moment, then continued. "I was content to stay at home in Dunmore's War and missed the action at Point Pleasant, where so many of our men died. But not this time. If I do my duty, perhaps the nightmares will stop."

"You could as easily end up in a grave in some godforsaken place as coming home to the esteem of your family."

"Eckert, either way the nightmares will end."

"I understand, Horst. I hope you do find that peace you desire."

"It's the first time I've ever told anyone, Wend. My wife knows only that I was in the army for a while and that I fought with Wolfe at Quebec. I trust you will keep my confidence."

"Of course, Horst. One German to another and one soldier to another."

CHAPTER NINE

THE WRATH OF AN ULSTER TAVERN MAID

Peggy Eckert sat in her chair in the sewing room, assembling a new gown for Elise. At eight, the child was growing like a weed, and it was proving hard to keep her in appropriate clothing. The room was off the central hall at the back of the house just behind the sitting room. Peggy put her sewing down in her lap, reached over and picked up the cup of whiskey from a table at her side, and looked out the window at the growing, late-afternoon shadows. In the dining room across the hall, she could hear the clinking of plates and eating utensils as Liza set the table for the evening meal.

Then suddenly she heard shouting coming from the direction of the workshop across the drive, followed by rapid footsteps as Liza ran to the front door. Then the footsteps came back down the hall and the maid appeared in the doorway.

"Missus Eckert! The wagon be coming up the drive! They're home!"

Peggy quickly put the sewing down and then stood up and straightened her clothing and hair. Feeling excitement rising inside, she walked out to the front porch. Down at the end of the drive, she saw the Morgans' two Conestogas heading northward along the main wagon track. Their own farm wagon had just begun the ascent up the drive, a single rider leading with his horse at the trot. She squinted and saw that the mounted rider was Bernd, his fowler balanced across the pommel of his saddle and his broad-brimmed hat pushed back on his head. She looked at the wagon and saw that Johann was in the seat, urging the four-horse team up the drive at a fast clip.

Lizza said, "They're comin' up the drive smart like, aren't they?"

Peggy nodded and smiled at the maid, then turned back. A sudden realization hit her: the boys were alone. No other riders followed. She turned to Liza, who had come out with her. "Where are the others?"

"Don't know, Miss Peggy. Can't see no one 'cept the boys. Maybe the men are behind for some reason."

Peggy, feeling concern, shook her head. "I can't think of any logical reason why they wouldn't be with the wagon."

Elise and Ellen arrived from the garden where they had been playing. They were followed by Wilma, who smelled of the food she was cooking for supper.

"Mama, look at Bernd riding in front!" called out Elise.

"Yes, dear, I see. He looks very grown up, doesn't he?"

"Yes, Mama. But where's Father? And Uncle Joshua and Simon?"

Wilma gave Peggy a concerned look. "I don't see nobody but them lads, Missus. Where are the menfolk?"

Suppressing her growing sense of dread, Peggy answered, "That's the question of the moment. But I'm sure there's a good explanation. We'll find out soon enough when the boys get the wagon up here."

Meanwhile, other people came running until a little crowd had gathered. Sally and her daughter came over from their rooms in the barracks, and Alice Downy Baird came hustling up from the house at the end of the drive. She stood beside Peggy and asked, "Where are the men?"

Peggy looked over at the older woman. "I've no idea. There must be some trouble."

Sally walked across the drive and joined them. She said nothing, but distress was written all over her face.

Bernd arrived and quickly dismounted. He smiled at Peggy with the reins in one hand and the fowler cradled in his other arm. With pride written across his face, he said, "We brought the wagon back from Culpeper all by ourselves."

"Yes, I see, Bernd," Peggy responded. "But why? Where is your father?"

He burst out, "Mother, there was trouble. Father and the rest won't be back for a while."

"My God, what do you mean? You must explain, Bernd."

"They think father is a Loyalist, Mother. Some men accused him of being a spy."

Peggy stood stunned for a moment. Then she took a deep breath and queried, "Bernd, how can such a thing be?"

Meanwhile Johann had pulled the wagon to a stop and jumped down. "Bernd is telling it right, Mother Eckert." He looked around at the small gathering, then back at his stepmother. "But there's a lot more to it."

"But what about the others?" Sally called out in a distressed voice. "What's happened to them?"

Johann looked around at the people. "Some of the soldiers accused Father of being a Loyalist because he was an aide with Dunmore last year in the war. And those Carlin brothers—the ones who Father chased away from Widow Callow's place—were there and joined in with the others and said Father had stopped them from punishing a Loyalist spy. They said he was one himself."

Peggy was shocked. "The Carlin brothers? Those scum! How could anyone believe them?"

Johann said, "They were saying the same thing as the others, so no one questioned them."

Bernd chimed in, adding, "And then that Colonel Henry sent Father and the others to stop an uprising of the Indians!"

Peggy was puzzled. "An uprising? I don't understand. If Wend is supposed to be a spy, why is he being sent on an important mission?"

Johann sighed. "Let me explain, Mother Eckert. It's quite complicated." He started from the beginning and related all that had transpired at the camp of the Virginia regiment. Everyone listened with rapt attention. Then after he had finished, he looked perplexed and said, "But I had expected you would know something of this by now."

Peggy said, "Johann, make sense. How would we know? We've heard nothing since you left—all these long days."

Johann said, "I was sure that Mr. Wood would have informed you of the message he got from Colonel Henry."

Peggy shook her head. "I tell you, we've heard nothing. Not from James Wood or anyone else."

Johann looked at Bernd, then explained, "The colonel said he would send a dispatch rider on a fast horse with a letter to Mr. Wood, listing the charges against Father and asking him to vouch for him as a Patriot." He shrugged. "The rider should have reached Winchester days ago."

Alice said, "If he'd received such a message, surely James would have sent a note to you explaining what was going on."

Peggy bit her lip and thought for a moment. "You're right, Alice. There's something amiss about all this."

Sally, fear in her voice, asked, "But what can we do to find out what's going on? Where are our husbands? When will they be back?"

Peggy sought to calm the younger woman. "Sally, they will be all right. There are no better men in the border country, and we must have faith in them." She put her hand on the girl's arm. "Now, I'll send a rider to the Woods' place first thing tomorrow with a letter asking James what he knows." She turned to Johann. "Right now we must get the wagon unloaded and tend to the horses. Take it down to the stable and have Specht help you, but don't tarry, for it is near time for supper."

Alice glanced at Peggy, then sought to reassure Sally. In a comforting tone she admonished, "Yes, the best thing is for us to go back to our homes and be about our normal routine, and we will certainly learn more on the morrow." She took the young woman by the arm and said, "Come, I'll walk with you back to the barracks."

—\m—

After dinner, Peggy wrote the letter to James Wood, putting in a summary of what had happened to Wend and the other men of Eckert Ridge. Then, after settling the children in bed, she retired herself. Satisfied she had done what she could, she soon slept, but her mind would not stay quiet. She soon came awake and spent hours tossing and turning. Finally, in frustration, she got out of bed, threw on a warm wrap, and descended to the sitting room. There she poured herself a cup of whiskey and sat in a chair thinking over what she knew and worrying about what she didn't know and what could happen to Wend. As she brooded, she felt an urgent voice within her saying that immediate action was required. By the time first light was showing through the windows, she had satisfied herself that simply sending a letter to James Wood would not be adequate. She had settled on a plan. She went upstairs to the boys' room and, entering quietly, roused Johann.

He came awake easily and quietly, with no surprise showing in his eyes. She thought, *That's from living in the forest with the Mingo all those years.* Then she whispered, so as not to disturb Bernd, "I'm going into Winchester to see Mr. Wood myself. I want you to come along to help with the chaise and to give a firsthand account to him of what happened in Culpeper."

"Yes, Mother Eckert."

"Get dressed for town, and then run down to the barracks and have Jacob Specht help get the chaise and Boots ready to leave right away."

They were away shortly after dawn, with Peggy driving the spirited animal at a fast pace through the brisk wind. She found that the challenge of handling the reins as the chaise swept over the rough wagon track kept her mind busy and off the dire situation that had engulfed Wend.

They entered Winchester well before midmorning and pulled into the yard of the Golden Buck. After the fast run from Eckert Ridge, Boots needed rest, water, and fodder before they went on to the Woods' plantation, which was southwest of the town. Peggy and Johann had breakfasted very lightly before leaving, so she went into the main room of the inn to arrange for refreshment while the lad tarried momentarily to tend to the horse.

When she entered, Peggy was astonished to see Anna McDonald and Jean Wood sitting together at a table. The two women waved.

Anna exclaimed, "Peggy, what a surprise! We hadn't expected to see you today, but it's always a pleasure. Please come join us." She pointed to a cup in front of her. "They actually have some tea, though God knows where they found it."

Jean smiled and inquired, "Are you in town for some shopping?"

Peggy took a deep breath and said, "Actually, I'm on more urgent business. I've come to see your husband."

"Business with my husband? I don't understand."

Not wasting time, Peggy asked directly, "Has James been visited by a courier from Colonel Patrick Henry in the last few days?"

Jean's face wrinkled in puzzlement. "A courier? If so, James has not confided in me. Why ever do you ask?"

"Wend is in great danger. He has been labeled a Loyalist spy by men in Henry's regiment. The colonel told Wend he would send an officer to discuss the matter with James. I must see him to find out what he knows.

I was going to your house to talk with him."

"That won't be necessary. My husband is right here in the inn. He's in a meeting with all of the Committee of Safety."

Anna spoke up. "Actually, it's quite fortunate you came in. James is leaving today for Williamsburg to attend the next session of the House of Burgesses. That's why Jean has come here with him—to see him off."

Jean nodded. "Yes, the committee meeting is to settle the position of Frederick County on the issues that will come before the legislature. And particularly to discuss the implications of Lord Dunmore's Proclamation and what measures we must put in place. James will take horse right afterward."

Peggy looked at Jean. "What proclamation?"

Jean asked in a puzzled tone, "You haven't heard? My dear, Dunmore has declared martial law and has announced that any slave who leaves his master and joins his force to fight for the king will immediately win his freedom."

Anna said, "Yes, and the slaves of several plantations in the tidewater have already revolted and run off to join Dunmore's forces. People are living in terror of a widespread slave uprising." She waved to an empty chair. "So there are most worrisome tidings, but at least things have worked out conveniently for you to see James. Sit down with us, and have some tea and cakes. As soon as the meeting adjourns, you can talk to him about Wend's predicament."

But Peggy's Ulster blood was up. "No, my dear Anna. This matter is too urgent to wait. And I'm of a mind that confronting the entire committee will be more effective than simply talking with Captain Wood."

Jean was startled. "But my dear, you can't just walk in on them. It's not polite and certainly not proper decorum."

Peggy laughed out loud. "It won't be the first time I've violated the rules of decorum. And that's not something I'm worried about when my husband's reputation and very safety is at stake."

At that moment, Johann came through the inn's front door and strode toward the table.

Peggy waved to him. "Come along, Johann. We have business to conduct." And she turned on her heel and headed for the doorway at the back of the common room that led to the meeting rooms, her stepson dutifully following.

As she entered the hall that led to the back rooms, Peggy realized she didn't know in which one the committee was meeting. *Well, there's only one way to find out*, she thought. So she opened the first door she came to and found two men discussing a paper that lay on the table. She excused herself and moved on to the next, where she interrupted Mr. Satterwhite, who owned a store on Loudoun Street. He was sitting very close to a young lady who was definitely *not* Mrs. Satterwhite. She shut the door without saying anything and moved on to the final room, which was the large one where the luncheon had been held the day that Morgan's company had left.

Without knocking, she swung the door open with rather more force than she had intended. It slipped out of her hand, swung back, and banged loudly against the wall. The heads of nine men snapped around to look at their unexpected guest.

Although unintended, Peggy was rather satisfied with the effect.

James Wood sat at the head of the table before the fireplace, with McDonald, Smith, Rutledge, and Thruston close at hand and four other men seated along the sides. Once they recognized that a woman stood in the door, they all rose.

Peggy quickly took in the scene as the committee members stared at her. All had drinks at hand, and several had either pipes or cigars going. A cloud of smoke floated above their heads. While many women would have felt intimidated under the gaze of so many men, all of whom comprised in essence the ruling clique of Winchester, it was an environment that Peggy McCartie Eckert had grown up in. She was entirely comfortable being the center of attention in a crowded common room. Without hesitation, she announced in a strong confident voice, "James, I have something that must be discussed immediately."

Wood's face displayed confusion at Peggy's arrival. "My dear Mrs. Eckert, it is always a pleasure to be in your presence, but as you can see, the members of the committee are engaged in deliberations of some solemnity and weight. Perhaps we could meet once the committee's business has been concluded."

Peggy drew Johann into the room and shut the door. "Solemnity and weight? There is no more urgent business than that which I have brought you, gentlemen." She looked up and down the table, fire in her eyes. "So take your seats, and listen to what I have to say."

Almost as one, the astonished men did as she said.

Peggy waved her arm in a sweeping motion that took in the length of the table. "This committee sent my husband to the town of Culpeper to deliver firelocks to Colonel Patrick Henry of the First Virginia Regiment. And now, because of your orders, Wend is in serious—perhaps mortal—danger." She had their attention now and hurried to continue. "Immediately upon arriving at the camp, he was accused by a scurrilous group of men of being a Loyalist and confidante of Governor Dunmore. Nay, not just a Loyalist! He was accused of being a traitor and spy against our cause. A *spy*—do you understand?"

Thruston, a look of incredulity on his face, said, "Mrs. Eckert, I find the very idea ridiculous. After all, he was presenting muskets to the army. Are you somehow misinformed, dear lady? Perhaps some baseless rumor has reached you?"

"It is *not* ridiculous, and I am in no way misinformed, Reverend. Wend was accused by soldiers who had witnessed him acting as an aide to Dunmore last year and now hold that against him. But more seriously, two Ulster scum who a few weeks ago attempted to steal Mrs. Callow's farm have enlisted in the regiment, and they falsely vowed they had seen him protecting a Loyalist." She put her hands on her hips. "It was those two damnable Carlin brothers, the ones Wend chased off the Widow's farm, and whom you—" she said, pointing at Sheriff Smith, "—know well because you made short work of driving them out of the county."

Smith nodded. "I did indeed, and no men deserved it more."

Wood furrowed his eyes. "Wend considered a spy? This is astonishing and hardly credible."

Peggy turned on him. "Hardly credible? James, don't play me for the fool! In fact, it is my information that you should already know a considerable amount about Wend's problem. Has not a courier arrived from Colonel Henry to advise you of these events and ask you to vouch for Wend's faithfulness to the cause?"

Astonishment spread across the politician's face. He raised his hands in front of him as if to fend off a threat. "Mrs. Eckert, I pledge that I have been visited by no such individual. Your story here today is the first time I have heard anything of this matter."

For the first time since she had entered the room, Peggy was taken aback and momentarily stumped for a response.

Wood continued, "Dear lady, how did you come by the intelligence that a rider was sent?"

Peggy turned to Johann, who had been standing by impassively, his arms crossed in front of his chest and his face as wooden and stoic as only he and his father could manage. "Here is my stepson, Johann Eckert, who was at the army camp when all this occurred. He arrived back at our farm only yesterday. He can second exactly what I have told you."

Without the slightest change in his expression, Johann spoke in a grave voice that demanded the attention of all present. "Mother Eckert speaks the truth. My father told me that Colonel Henry had vowed to send an officer to Captain Wood. He was to leave immediately and obtain the captain's reference regarding my father."

Wood shook his head. "Mrs. Eckert, as God is my witness, no such messenger has reached me."

McDonald raised his hand and asked, "Mrs. Eckert, is your husband being held as a prisoner?"

Peggy laughed outright. "A prisoner, Angus? Worse. He has been dragooned into a dangerous mission to prove his loyalty under the charge of the very men who accused him." She again turned to Johann. "Explain what happened to your father in Culpeper and what Henry has forced him to do."

Johann told them what was known about Connolly's conspiracy and the men who had been sent in pursuit of his party. Peggy looked at the faces of the men as they learned of the possibility of an Indian uprising and saw real fear in their eyes, for they had all lived through the French War and Pontiac's Rebellion and knew the horrors of tribal raiding.

McDonald interrupted, saying to his compatriots, "By God, Connolly has traveled the Ohio Country extensively. He knows and has treated with all the important chiefs. If any white man can raise the tribes, it is he."

Wood nodded in agreement. "As you know, I was a member of the commission that negotiated the final treaty of the war with the tribes last year in Pittsburgh, as was Connolly. I can tell you he was very much solicitous of them throughout the talks and always took the position favorable to the tribes. So you can be assured they'll listen to Connolly. In any case, they're chaffing at the bit after last year's humiliation at the hands of our militia. They'll have no trouble gathering parties of young bucks who will be eager to take revenge on the border settlements."

There were nods around the table. Thruston was more vocal. "Oh, Dear God, they'll have the settlements in flames."

Smith said, "Gentlemen, with no organized force to stop them between the Ohio and here, it's not impossible we could see them penetrating into Frederick County."

There was a buzz around the table. One man exclaimed, "For God's sake, that's not happened since the Pontiac War over a decade ago!"

The table went quiet as all of them contemplated that statement.

Johann ended the silence by resuming. "You ask if my father is a prisoner. I tell you he is worse off than that, for he is forced to ride with men who wish him evil and would take his life if the opportunity presented itself."

McDonald raised an eyebrow. "But you say that Baird and Donegal are with him?"

"Yes, as is the apprentice Andrew Horner."

"Well, at least we can take comfort in that."

Peggy glared at him. "Angus, I take little comfort. If there is a shooting fight with Connolly's men, Wend could as easily die at the hands of this Ballantyne or the Carlins as one of the conspirators. And neither Joshua nor Simon would have little chance to protect him."

Smith nodded agreement. "Indeed, the lady is correct. Those Carlins are blackguards who would put a ball in a man's back without thinking twice."

Peggy spoke up. "So now, gentlemen of the committee, you understand why I have come here today. My husband is in immediate peril. The man who sent him on this mission—this Patrick Henry—has seemingly lied about informing Captain Wood of his situation. I beseech you to act in some way to pursue this matter and at least demand accountability from Colonel Henry."

Thruston turned to Wood. "By all means, James, we must take some action."

Wood raised a hand. "We are all aware that I ride for Williamsburg immediately after this meeting is complete. It is my understanding that Henry is marching his regiment to that place to complete recruiting and formally take up the colors from the Committee of Safety. I will personally confront him to demand an explanation of his actions, and I will raise the plight of Mr. Eckert before the Burgesses. If necessary, I will seek Henry's condemnation by the legislature for hazarding the life of a patriotic citizen of Frederick County on what I consider a flimsy and unverified accusation by untrustworthy men."

"I appreciate your intent, James," responded Peggy. "However, it is of little immediate help to Wend. And for all we know, he may be at this very moment lying on some forest path with vultures picking at his bones."

Wood shook his head. "I understand your fear, Mrs. Eckert. But on the other hand, he may just as well be safely riding for Williamsburg with his party—and with Connolly as a prisoner. My dear lady, the truth is, we have no way of telling and no way of assisting him."

Peggy grimaced in anguish. "God above, is there not something that could be done?"

There was a long silence, all the men looking down at their hands.

After a long moment, Sheriff Smith looked up. "It has occurred to me that there is one measure we can take that has a chance of stopping the conspiracy before it begins, and incidentally perhaps we could help Mr. Eckert."

Wood looked at Smith. "An intriguing statement, sir. Please enlighten us."

"We know that Connolly and his party are traveling up from the tidewater and thence through Maryland to the Braddock Road. Let me send a courier on a strong horse directly north to Wills Creek, which is the start of Braddock's Road proper, to alert the sheriff there to watch out for Connolly. With luck, they have not already passed through there and can be intercepted before they travel further west. Connolly may be known there, and in any case, they can watch out for any suspicious party of men heading westward. My man can be there in two days of hard riding."

McDonald slapped his hand down on the table. "That's a capital idea. And I know Connolly well enough. I'll prepare a description for the messenger to carry."

Wood nodded. "By all means, let us proceed with that. It's indeed possible they can be cut off, which would allow Wend and his companions to come home sooner."

Rutledge, who was the former county lieutenant and thus in charge of the militia, said, "There's something else we should do now: put the county's militia companies in order in case the attempt to stop Connolly fails and the uprising does materialize."

Wood pointed at Rutledge, "Yes, I agree. But make it as a general, deliberate preparation, not specifically about an Indian war. Nothing incites the populace more than the threat of Indian raids. We don't want to get the people overly alarmed about something that might not occur."

"Yes, I understand, James. But we'll quietly get the companies organized, fully armed, and involved in drilling. In any case, they are in reasonable shape after the war last year."

Thruston turned looked up at Peggy with a smile on his face. "My dear lady, I share your worry about Mr. Eckert, and I shall pray for him daily until we know he is safe. But let me express the gratitude of the committee for your action to alert us to this danger of an uprising. We are indeed indebted to you."

There was a round of agreement from the men at the table.

—⚶—

It was midafternoon when Peggy climbed into the chaise that Johann had brought around to the front steps of the Golden Buck. Jean and Anna called goodbye to her from the small porch, and then they drove away up Market Street and turned onto the road east.

Peggy was exhausted after spending most of the night awake and brooding and then facing the stress of confronting the committee. She would have gone right home, but she felt it necessary to stay long enough to see James off. Then Jean and Anna had invited her to spend some time with them, and she thought it would be impolitic to refuse. In fact, she felt a need to mend fences for her abruptness with them in the morning. Now, having completed the social amenities, they finally drove homeward, Johann handling the reins. Peggy found herself nodding off, but every time she actually went to sleep, some bump or dip in the wagon track brought her awake almost immediately. Finally she gave up, pulled herself upright in the seat, and pulled her coat more tightly around her.

Johann looked over and gave her a rare smile. "Mother Eckert, you were very good with those men in the meeting. I was very proud of you, and I believe Father would be also."

She looked at her stepson and saw that his face had again become impassive. It reminded her of his Indian upbringing. "I guess tribal women are not allowed to speak out to the warriors, who make all the decisions."

Johann shook his head. "Pardon me, Mother Eckert, but that is not correct. Mingo women have a very important part in making decisions that affect the entire village. There is a woman's council that meets very regularly, including any time something important is to be decided. The warriors cannot go to war or move the village or take other actions unless the women agree."

Peggy was surprised. "What about your mother, Abigail? I suppose she was not allowed to participate in this women's council because she was a white captive."

The boy smiled again, very tightly, and replied, "When a village adopts a captive, as they did with my mother, they become a full member of the Mingo tribe. My mother became very important because she knows about medicine and treating sick people. That's why they call her 'Orenda.' It means the woman with magic hands." He stopped talking for a moment as he dealt with navigating a bad place in the road. Then he continued, "If you know my mother, you know that she…" He searched for the right words. "She knows her mind and can be very insistent. Her husband, Wolf Claw, learned not to disagree with her. She soon became very important in the woman's council and in decisions for the village." He thought for a long moment, then said, "What you did today reminded me of when Mother convinced the village to become inoculated against the smallpox."

Startled, Peggy asked, "Your mother knows how to do inoculations?"

"Yes, she got the information from the red-haired nurse who was with the soldiers who wear skirts."

"You mean the Highlanders, like Donegal?"

"Yes. They came to the Ohio Country the year after Pontiac attacked the forts. They took back many of the white people who were living with the tribes."

"That would have been in 1764, when you were no more than five."

"Yes, and I remember Mother arguing with the women and the men of our village that they should take the inoculations. She said because the people of the forest were having much contact with the white men, the smallpox would come again among us. She said there was already pox in a village further up along Slippery Rock Creek, and we would see it soon enough. She kept pressing them until they finally agreed. Then mother brought a sick person to our village and used the fluid from his sores to do the inoculating." He turned and looked at Peggy. "I was the first one she did. That convinced all the people who still doubted. They said if she would do her own child, then it must be safe."

"Your mother, Orenda, is very daring."

"Yes, but I think you are much like her. I saw that today."

A warm glow flowed through Peggy at the boy's words of respect. Then she thought of something. "How did it come that this nurse helped your mother?"

"Mother said it was because of me."

"Because of you? I don't understand."

Johann bit his lips and looked straight ahead for a long moment like he hesitated to tell her.

"Come on, Johann, the nurse must have had a reason to favor you."

The boy sighed. "Mother said it was because she once loved Father."

"Because the nurse loved Wend?" Peggy was momentarily puzzled. Then it hit her. "Do you know the nurse's name? Was it Mary?"

"Mother didn't know her name. But later, after I had left the Mingo village and was camping with the soldiers, I heard Father and Joshua and Simon talking. They thought I was asleep, but I heard them speaking about a nurse named Mary who had given papers to Mother that explained how to do the inoculation. Joshua helped her."

Peggy simply said, "I see." But now she knew without a doubt that the military nurse had been Mary Fraser. She had indeed been Wend's lover during Colonel Bouquet's march in 1763 to relieve Fort Pitt in the initial stages of Pontiac's War. But, before they were married, Wend had told her that Mary had died of a wound to her side received at the Battle of Bushy Run. It had eventually mortified, and she had slowly weakened and then finally succumbed. But the incident Johann had described could only have occurred in 1764 during the invasion of the Ohio Country—more than a year after Mary had supposedly died.

Anger flashed within Peggy. It was clear that Wend had lied to her about Mary Fraser, just like he had not told her about the existence of Johann until he arrived back with him in tow after Dunmore's War. *But why?*

Peggy was determined to find out, and she knew exactly who to ask.

—⚬—

That night there was nothing that could have kept Peggy awake, not even her smoldering anger at Wend's deception. After arriving back at Eckert Ridge, she immediately went to bed, leaving it to Wilma to feed the children the evening meal and for Johann to pass on the information about her confrontation with James Wood and the Committee of Safety. She finally awoke when the sun was high in the sky the next morning.

Then she got up, dressed, and called for breakfast. As she sat eating, she mulled over what Johann had told her and how to find out the full story. By then the edge was off her Ulster anger, and she was rationally considering her best course. There was, of course, one person who would know the background about Mary Fraser, and that was Alice Baird.

In the mornings Alice conducted a school for the children of the farm. That included all the Eckert children, the three of the journeyman gunsmith Wilhelm Hecht and his wife, Amy, and now little Louisa Potter, the five-year-old daughter of Sally by her first husband who had died at the hands of a Shawnee raiding party. Peggy determined she would walk down to the Baird house after lunch. She and Alice usually talked at least once each day, so the older woman would not be surprised at Alice's arrival. But today would be different; instead of the usual gossip about happenings on the farm and in Winchester, she would drag the story about Mary Fraser out of Alice.

It was early afternoon when Peggy tapped on the Bairds' front door and then let herself inside. Alice was in the great room, looking through the clothing which hung on a long rack. The house's interior could most charitably be described as "cluttered." Besides being the teacher of Eckert Ridge, Alice could also be thought of as the sutler, for she provided all sorts of materials necessary to the well-being of the residents, from fabric to a range of cooking utensils. As an accomplished seamstress, she manufactured most of the clothing for the farmhands and the apprentices. In addition, books, slate boards, and papers were stacked on chairs around the room. This was not to mention Joshua's collection of firelocks—rifles, fowlers, and pistols—that were ranged on pegs or simply standing upright in a corner.

Peggy removed the school materials from a chair, carefully putting them on the floor, then sat down.

Alice continued looking through the clothing but asked, "So how did your trip to see James Wood go?"

"I ended up meeting with the entire Committee of Safety at the Golden Buck."

Alice threw back her head and laughed. "I'd have given a fat purse of the king's coin, if I had one, to have seen that! Did you throw a keg of powder into the good gentlemen's laps?"

"Less explosive. I say more like a pan of priming powder. But I got their attention." Peggy then recounted the course of the meeting. She added, "It was fortuitous that I took Johann along. He was able to give them a credible account of what happened to Wend at Henry's camp and what he's been forced to be about now."

Alice finally finished looking at the clothing, then went over to a cabinet, took out a small jug, and poured two cups of Donegal's whiskey. She handed one to Peggy and then took to a chair where she could look at her friend.

Peggy took the moment to raise the subject that was her main objective. "On the way home, I got to talking with Johann about his life in the Mingo village and his mother."

"Well, it's about time. You gave the boy a cold shoulder for months after Wend brought him back from the Ohio Country and forced him to sleep with the field hands and apprentices in the barracks for all that time."

"All right, Alice, we don't need to cover that ground again. It was a mistake, and I've tried to make up for it these last few months. But it was all because Wend kept his existence a secret from me for over ten years."

"Probably because he feared your angry reaction."

Peggy paused and then looked directly at Alice. "Maybe. But now there's another case of the same thing happening."

Alice was in the act of raising her cup. She stopped, holding it halfway to her mouth. "What do you mean?"

"On the way home yesterday, Johann told me that his mother had inoculated the people of his village against the small pox. That was back in '64."

A shadow crossed Alice's face, and she hesitated a moment before responding. Then she spoke slowly and with care. "Well, I'm not that surprised. She is known as the medicine woman of the Mingo."

"That's the point: Johann told me she wasn't sure how to do it until she received information from a nurse in the hospital of Colonel Bouquet's expedition into the Ohio Country."

A look of great wariness came into Alice's eyes, and she avoided looking directly at Peggy by concentrating on sipping from her cup. "Oh, that was fortunate."

"Yes, Alice, it was. And Johann told me the nurse's name was Mary." She paused and then added, "As in Mary *Fraser*. Mary Fraser, who was Wend's lover during Bouquet's march to relieve Fort Pitt."

Alice didn't answer. She looked down at her cup.

Peggy continued, a sharp tone in her voice. "And the point is, Wend told me Mary died in 1763 of the wound she received at Bushy Run. So how was a red-headed nurse named Mary helping Abigail Gibson in late 1764?"

"There are a lot of auburn-haired Highland women, and Mary is a common name."

"Give it up, Alice! Johann told me that the nurse helped Abigail because she knew Johann was Wend's son and that she had been Wend's lover." She looked right into Alice's eyes. "And he also told me that Joshua helped Mary get the directions for inoculations to Abigail." Peggy took a long sip of her whiskey. "So I have absolutely no doubt that Joshua told you all about it."

Alice drained her cup, put it down on her sewing table, and crossed her arms. "All right, Peggy, but the truth is, Wend didn't lie to you. At the time he told you Mary was dead, he thought it was the case."

"So when did he learn she was alive?"

"About four days after you were married. On the way south to Virginia, when you stopped at the Pennsylvania Fort Loudoun located on Conococheaque Creek."

"Yes, I remember that place."

"Well, the commanding officer there was a certain Captain McDonald, of the 42nd. He had been a captain in the 77th, and Donegal was in his company. He knew Simon, Joshua, and Wend from the march to Fort Pitt the year before. He stood the three of them to a drink, and while talking, it came out that Mary had actually survived her wound. The last time Wend had seen her at Fort Pitt, she had been wasting away. The surgeon told Wend she was doomed before he left to scout for a mission into the Ohio Country. When they got back two months later, the 77th was gone, and no one knew anything about Mary. All three of them assumed she was dead."

Peggy stood up and started pacing back and forth. "That explains something I've wondered about for ten years. When we got to the fort, I stayed behind at our camp to make dinner. When they came back, all three of them looked very quiet and didn't say much."

"Joshua says Wend was in shock."

"So how did it come about that Mary lived?"

"Shortly after Wend left Fort Pitt for the Ohio Country, the surgeon made a desperate attempt to cut into her wound to see if he could clean it out and remove the mortification. They figured there was nothing to be lost because the girl was near dead. But they were shocked to find that a large piece of cloth had been left in the wound in that hectic night at Bushy Run. They had been forced to treat her in the light of only a tiny fire. The cloth was what was causing the wound to mortify. They took it out, sewed the wound back up, and in a few days Mary was in full recovery." Alice sighed deeply. "The irony was that Mary spent the winter of '63 to '64 at Carlisle Encampment."

"My God, that's only over the mountain from our village at Sherman Mill! It's not more than ten or eleven miles away." Peggy reflected a moment. "It was sheer chance that Wend didn't run into Mary in all the times he went to Carlisle!"

"Yes, and if he had—"

Peggy quickly finished the sentence. "He would undoubtedly have married Mary!"

Alice stared at Peggy for a long moment. "Yes, so now you know the truth of it."

"Wait a minute, Alice. Something's not clear. Mary knew where Wend lived. Why didn't she find a way to get word to him?"

"Because, Peggy, she thought Wend had brought Abigail back from the Mingo village and married her. She didn't know that our dear Miss Gibson turned Wend down and decided to stay with the Indians."

There was a long moment of silence as Peggy thought that over. "So how did it come about that Abigail and Mary met?"

"It was during Bouquet's campaign against the Ohio tribes the year you and Wend moved down here. You remember that while you were building your first place here on the ridge, and before I came down from Carlisle, Joshua left to act as chief scout for the expedition. Mary was with the hospital of the Black Watch. She stayed behind when the 77th Highlanders were mustered out and sent back to Scotland. As an orphan she had nowhere else to go, and at any rate they recognized that she was a very accomplished nurse."

Peggy stopped pacing and sat down in the chair. "So how did the two meet?"

"It was during the treaty talks at the Indian villages called Waka-tomica on the Muskingum River. Bouquet had marched deep into the Ohio Country and forced the chiefs to sue for peace. All the various Indian tribes had been summoned to come there. While negotiations were in progress, Abigail, with Johann, came to the hospital of the 42nd and asked Mary for instructions on how to inoculate her band of Mingos. When they arrived, Mary suspected that a tall, blond woman with the Mingo who spoke educated English and was interested in medicine must be Abigail Gibson. Then she took one look at the boy and realized he was Wend's, which confirmed her suspicion."

"All right, but Johann said Joshua helped her. How did that come about?"

"Mary agreed to let Abigail read a medical book that explained the procedure, but just as she was starting, the surgeon found out what was going on and sent Abigail and Johann back to the Indian encampment because Bouquet had forbidden Indians in the military camp. And the doctor was scandalized that Mary would help the Mingo."

Alice poured herself another drink. "But Mary was absolutely determined to help keep Wend's son from getting the smallpox. So she tried to contact Abigail in the Indian camp but found that her band of Mingos had left Wakatomico just a few hours before. They didn't want to be forced to send Abigail back to the whites since Bouquet was ordering the release of all captives. Frustrated, Mary thought up a daring plan. She tore the relevant pages from the surgeon's book and convinced Joshua to help her ride after the Mingo band." She sipped her drink, then said, "And Joshua could never refuse anything Mary asked, so he agreed. They slipped out of the military camp on his horse and overtook the Mingo in a couple of hours."

"My God, the woman is resolute."

"Yes, and keep in mind, Peggy, she was only sixteen then—little more than a child." Alice laughed out loud. "But she has the fiery spirit and determination of a redhead." She gave Peggy a meaningful look. "At any rate, when they caught up with the Mingo, she gave Abigail the book pages. Abigail was puzzled that she would go to all that trouble for a band of Indians and asked her about it. That's when Mary told her she was a former lover of Wend's, and that's how Johann came to know about it."

A look of mystification came over Peggy's face. "Didn't Mary and Joshua get in trouble with the military for what they did?"

"They should have, but they avoided punishment by sheer happenstance. On the way back to the army camp, Joshua and Mary spied a packtrain of Richard Grenough's men taking illegal powder and lead to the Indians. They rushed back and told Bouquet, who was able to send a column to intercept and capture the train. After that, Bouquet found it easy to overlook their transgression."

Peggy crossed her arms and sat silently for a while, digesting everything Alice had told her. Then a question formed in her mind. "Alice, why is Joshua so devoted to Mary?"

Alice took a deep breath, and a look of irony came over her face. "Because he was desperately in love with her mother, Lizzie Iverson. He had been since he first laid eyes on her."

"Iverson?"

"Yes. Mary's natural father, a sergeant, was killed in an attack on Fort Pitt in 1758. Joshua was away from the force on a long scout, or he would have asked Lizzie to marry him. Instead, since she had to have a source of rations, she immediately married another sergeant named Iverson. She had no real love for the man, but it was expedient. That's the way of the army. When Joshua got back, he was brokenhearted. And then when both the sergeant and Lizzie died of the fever at the siege of Havana, Mary became a ward of the regiment, taken care of and educated by the chaplain and normally working in the hospital. Joshua visited with her all he could."

Peggy grimaced. "Well, at least Joshua told you the story. He didn't keep it from you like Wend has done with me twice now."

"He told me some of it. Other parts I heard from others. And I've never been jealous about the situation."

"Alice, there's nothing to be jealous about. That Lizzie woman is long dead."

"Well, think about this: Mary is as good as dead. She's in Scotland. Donegal got a letter from her in 1767, saying she was going home with the 42nd. She was planning to be a governess for some rich family. And with her looks, by now it's most likely she's married with children."

Peggy fumed for a long moment, then said, "What you say may be true, but I'm telling you, it galls me that Wend holds these things out from me."

Alice slammed her cup down on the table beside her chair. "For God's sake, Peggy, give it a rest! Have you told Wend about every man you spread your legs for in your father's stable or in the bushes down by Sherman Creek?"

Peggy set her chin and just stared at Alice. Then she said defiantly, "He knows what I did when I was young."

"Look, Peggy, we've been through this before. You keep worrying about Wend's love for you. God above, the man married you even when he knew you were carrying Matt Bratton's child—the issue of his worst enemy in Sherman Mill. He married you even though he knew you had whored yourself. He's been faithful and provided for you and all your children, and he treats Bernd like his own. I'm telling you now, it's obvious he's in love with you. So stop brooding about things that happened long ago."

The two women looked wordlessly at each other for a long moment, then Alice broke the silence. "And there's something else you should keep in mind. Learn to cherish Johann like he was your own because if things go bad out there on this damned mission they're on, Johann could be all you have left to remind you of Wend."

CHAPTER TEN

THE FORD ON
CONOCOCHEAQUE CREEK

The trip down South Mountain turned out to be uneventful, except for the bone-chilling wind from the northwest that was in their faces for the entire trip. By the time they rode into Elizabethtown in late afternoon, Wend's face was burning and his whole body was shivering, even under the heavy military watch coat.

The town was astride a crossroads formed by the intersection of the westward route to Wills Creek and the North-South track known as the Great Wagon Road, which ran from Philadelphia down to the southern colonies. Wend could see two tavern-inns, which served as a nightly haven for freight wagons and packtrains, a store, blacksmith shop, and several houses. There were several buildings under construction. The most substantial structure was a large house on the eastward side, which later proved to be Jonathan Hager's place. Farmsteads ringed the town.

They stopped at the larger of the two taverns, known as Cotter's Common. It had a spacious yard, a large stable, and several other outbuildings, all but the stable of log construction. They rode into the yard and dismounted. They were met by Baird and Sedgewick, who had taken the advance for the day.

The two met with Bradley, Ballantyne, and Wend. The scout and his compatriot were full of information from the innkeeper, a Mr. Harry Cotter. "Connolly and his men left here right at dawn this morning. Their packtrain is indeed ten horses."

Wend sighed. "That's a lot of powder and lead."

Bradley said thoughtfully, "So they're probably a good twelve hours ahead of us."

Joshua responded, "More if they push it and ride right up 'til darkness, which is likely since they know they're being pursued."

Sedgewick added, "They're still using false names and telling people they're on the way to help defend Pittsburgh. Cotter didn't have any reason to doubt them."

Wend thought a moment. "We've a problem. None of us have any real familiarity with the road between here and Wills Creek. Perhaps we can find someone to guide us, which will make it easier to make good time and close the distance to Connolly. If we can engage someone to get us to Fort Cumberland, after that Joshua, Donegal and I know Braddock Road pretty well."

Baird smiled. "Well, the man who could help us with that is right inside the common room. That Hager fellow the sheriff told us about back in Fredericktown."

"Joshua, did you talk to him about our mission?"

Baird wrinkled his face. "Of course. We had a drink with him and told him everything. He knows Kunkel well and is fightin' mad about what the bastards did to him. He's ready to help any way he can."

Bradley nodded. "Well, gentlemen, that's quite reassuring. He's the man who will know someone to lead us. Let's go see him."

The common room was steamy warm, with a crackling fire in the hearth and the air laden with the smell of cooking food. The appetizing smells wafted in from the cook room, reminding Wend that they had eaten little on the road down from the South Mountain Inn. He suddenly felt ravenously hungry.

A round-faced, balding, dark-haired man with a thick waist, whom Wend judged to be in his early sixties, lounged at a table in front of the fireplace.

Joshua waved toward him. "This here is Jonathan Hager."

Hager rose and said, "Well, gentlemen, welcome to Elizabethtown. Mr. Baird has told me all about your quest." He extended his hand to the three officers.

Bradley introduced himself, Wend, and Ballantyne. They all sat down around the table, Joshua standing, drink in hand, nearby.

Hager looked at the men. "I'm ready to help you in any way we can. The last thing we need in these troubling times is an uprising of the border tribes. I've spent years encouraging people to settle here. We have fertile land, abundant water, and all the timber we can use. And situated on this crossroads, we're a perfect place for travelers and freighters to break their journey. With these assets, our town has prospered, but the fear of raids will cause families to flee and set us back mightily."

"We aim to make up time on Connolly before he gets to Wills Creek," Bradley said quietly. With his party burdened with a packtrain, we might be able to actually catch up with him. But we need someone who knows the road, and possibly some back-trail shortcuts, to guide us."

Wend added, "Perhaps you have a likely man who might be persuaded to accompany our party?"

Hager put his hand to his chin, then smiled. "Don't have to think much about that. I know just the fellow. Name is Abel Reimann, a young lad of nineteen."

Bradley said, "Do you think he would be willing to do the job?"

"I think he'd be delighted for the excuse to journey to Wills Creek.

The lad's taken a shine to a young girl there. He rides there with mail at least once a month, sometimes more often." Hager waved to Cotter, who hustled over to the table. "Harry, can I impose on you to send your stable boy over to the Reimann place and ask Abel to come on over posthaste? Have the boy tell him it involves riding to Fort Cumberland."

The tavern proprietor laughed outright. "He'll jump at that, like enough. I'll send my boy right away."

He hurried back to the bar and called out to a light-haired maid, "Helga! Run out to the stable and get Charlie!"

Hager said, "Abel lives with his Pa and Ma and the other Reimann children at a farmstead not a quarter mile away. Charlie will have him here in the time it takes to have a cup of libation."

Joshua looked down at has empty cup and said, "A libation. Now that's a hell of a good idea."

As they waited, Helga served drinks and Hager regaled them about how he had obtained the land rights in the area and his efforts to found a viable town. The name was in honor of his wife, Elizabeth, who had passed away years ago. By Hager's reckoning, there were near two hundred people in the village and the surrounding farms. He was proud that they had a store and that a blacksmith had established himself two years before. He looked around at the men at the table. "With the inns and a blacksmith, we're a good place for the wagoners to stop, either traveling the Great Road, or from South Mountain, or heading eastward. And the Potomac is just a few miles south, so many wagons break their journey here before making the crossing." He waved his hand to take in the common room. "You got four Conestoga men here laying over right now, and I'll wager more will pull in before full dark. Harry's thinking about expanding the tavern next spring."

Soon enough a young man came through the front door. He wore a shell jacket, a scarf around his collar, breeches, and a wide-brimmed hat turned up to the side with a bucktail affixed. He had pushed the hat back jauntily on his head to show a crop of blond hair.

Hager said, "Here's Abel now."

The youth sauntered up to the table and greeted Hager, who introduced him to the men.

Abel Reimann nodded to each in turn and then said, "Charlie said you got some ridin' for me to do."

Bradley nodded. "Riding with us and doing some guide work. We need to get to Wills Creek as fast as possible."

Hagar added, "Abel, they're trying to catch up with and capture a party of Tories who want to start an Indian uprising here in the border country."

Reimann's eyes opened wide. "The bastards! I was only eight during Pontiac's War. We lived in Pennsylvania then, and several farmsteads around us were raided. I was terrified for months and couldn't sleep at night havin' nightmares a raiding party was going to hit our farmstead." He set his chin. "They got to be stopped!"

Bradley grinned. "Indeed, lad. Can you be here ready to ride at first light tomorrow?"

"Captain, I'll do better than that. Give me an hour, and I'll be back with my horse and rifle, and I'll sleep here in the common room tonight. Then I'll be right ready to ride with you soon as you and your men are saddled."

The Marylander grinned. "That's the stuff, lad."

And with that, Abel Reimann touched his hand to his hat, nodded to the men at the table, and strode out the door.

Bradley, Ballantyne, and Wend had a quick meeting, planning for their departure. Then they broke up for the overdue evening meal.

By the time the food was settling in Wend's stomach, between the long day in the saddle and the heat of the tavern, he found himself sinking into drowsiness. He decided to have one more small round of whiskey and then retire to the room he had secured for the Winchester men.

As he was just finishing the drink, young Reimann entered the tavern, a pair of saddlebags over his right shoulder, a blanket under his left arm, and a rifle in his right hand.

Wend eyed the rifle with professional curiosity, then suddenly sat upright, wide awake. "Abel, can I take a look at your firelock?"

The youth look down at the rifle and shrugged. "Sure enough." He handed it to Wend.

Wend looked at the gunmaker's mark on the barrel and then closely examined the lock and fittings on the stock.

"Where did you get this, Abel?"

"My pa bought it from a neighbor, Mathew Heckert, when we lived up the Great Cove, just south of Fort Lyttleton. It's Lancaster County style. Heckert said he bought it back in 1758 from the best gunsmith in Lancaster." Then he continued, "Pa got a new firelock last year, and he gave me this one."

Wend looked down at the rifle, and a wave of remembrance and nostalgia swept over him. "Heckert was right. This *was* made by the best gunsmith in Lancaster at the time. His name was Johann Eckert."

Reimann raised his eyebrows. "Oh, did you know him?"

"He was my father. This is one of the last firelocks he made before he was killed by Mingos on Forbes Road." Wend ran his hand over the stock. "I was his fifteen, his apprentice, and I carved the basic shape of the stock. Then my father finished the rifle."

The lad's eyes opened even wider. "Well, Mr. Eckert, it's been a great gun. But the truth is, its barrel is getting worn now. But if you're used to it, you can still hit a target at good range." He took the firelock back from Wend. "The lock's in good shape, and I was thinking of having a gunsmith put a new barrel on it."

"Or you could get him to grind the bore to make it into a smooth rifle. You'd still get a decent range with ball, and you could also use it with scatter shot. And it would be cheaper than getting a new barrel."

Reimann was about to reply when the door of the common room swung open, and a blast of frigid air swept into the room. Wend looked over to see a traveler had entered and slammed the door behind himself. He was in his midtwenties, and he was dark-haired, thin, and wearing backcountry clothing. He carried a rifle, saddlebags, and a blanket. Walking up to the bar, he ordered a drink from the proprietor and then began talking with him in an animated fashion. As he spoke, other men at the bar turned to listen, and several got up from nearby tables to hear what the man was saying. After a few minutes, Cotter came out from behind his counter, wiping his hands on his apron, and walked straight to where Jonathan Hager still sat at the table before the fire, followed by the stranger and the group of men who had been listening to him.

"Jonathan, this man says he needs to talk to the local sheriff. I told him the county sheriff lived down in Fredricktown but that you acted on his behalf up here."

The traveler looked down at Hager and said, "I got something you sure enough want to hear."

"All right. Who are you and what's your business?"

"My name's Ezra Scarlow. An' I'm on my way to Baltimore to meet my sister who just came over from Ireland. I aim to take her back to Pittsburgh."

Hager nodded. "Fair enough. What is it you've got to tell me?"

"I was at an inn at Wills Creek three days back. They're all aroused 'cause a man named John Connolly, who was Dunmore's agent in Pittsburgh, is on his way back there to stir up the Indians against the border people."

Bradley, who was still sitting at the table and smoking one of his cigars, cut in. "How do they know that?"

"A rider had just come in from the sheriff of Winchester. They had the word about Connolly and warned the Wills Creek people to stop him and his men. There were circulars all over the town with a description of Connolly. And some of the militia had been turned out to watch for him on the road into the village."

Hager pointed to Bradley and Wend as well as to Ballantyne, who had come over to the table. "It happens these men know about the plot and are leading a party to apprehend Connolly. They leave tomorrow at dawn to resume the pursuit. Certainly between these men and the Wills Creek militia, the fugitives will be caught within the next few days."

Scarlow shook his head. "Well, that may be true, but that ain't the main point I want to tell you."

One of the crowd who had followed Scarlow, a tall, heavy-shouldered Irishman, spoke up loudly. "This fellow says Connolly and his party is just a few miles away! He's camped just up the road!"

Hager motioned for the Irishman to be quiet. "All right, McCarthy, keep your peace. Let Scarlow tell the story."

Scarlow took a deep breath and said, "He's right. Connolly and his party are camped at a creek not that far from here."

Wend interjected, "How are you sure it's Connolly?"

"I know him by sight! I was a private in his militia battalion during the war last year! Anyways, just after I forded the creek, I looked over and saw Connolly standing beside the road. There was a bunch of other men and horses in the camp. I called out, 'Hello, Major!' and he looked at me for a moment, then waved and said, 'Hello, Scarlow.'" He looked around at the men at the table. "I just nodded back at him and kept goin'."

Bradley took the cigar from his mouth and in a puzzled tone asked, "Now why do you suppose they've stopped there?"

Scarlow said, "Sir, I think they got trouble with one of their horses. Like I said, I didn't stop 'cause I was a'feared they would take me into custody for recognizing Connolly. But I did see a man beside a horse that was down." He shrugged. "I think maybe they stopped to try to find another horse at one of the farms around there. Can't think of anything else."

Hager raised his eyebrows. "It sounds like he saw them at Conococheaque Creek Ford. That's only two hours ride from here."

"He's right," Scarlow responded. "That's about how long ago I passed there. It was just a'fore dusk."

A thought hit Wend. "Warren, we could roust out our men and take Connolly tonight if he's still there. Even if they left right after Scarlow saw them, they'd only make a few more miles before full dark. Either way, we could catch up with them in a few hours."

Bradley gave Wend a sharp look. "You mean ride through the night? Through unfamiliar territory?"

"We've got Abel Riemann to help. Undoubtedly he knows the road and the lay of the land around Connolly's camp if he's still on the Conococheaque."

Hager agreed. "The lad could take you there blindfolded and help you get them surrounded."

The Marylander nodded. "Eckert, you're right. By God, it's worth the chance. We could end this pursuit tonight."

Wend nodded. "We'll want to travel light, leaving the baggage behind and taking only weapons and a couple days' rations."

Bradley, enthusiasm growing, agreed. "Yes, just the necessities to ride fast."

McCarthy, the big Irishman, suddenly said, "We could help you! There's plenty of men right around the village who'd be willing to go with you to stop this bastard and his men. Nobody wants to see war parties raiding through the territory. I could rouse out a dozen well-armed men within the hour!"

Wend thought, *That's all we need is a mob of excited, ill-disciplined militia with us to complicate matters.* He looked at Bradley and saw dread in the captain's eyes.

The Marylander bit his lip, then said, "Mr., uh, *McCarthy*, I appreciate your willingness to assist, but I fear the time it would take to call out your compatriots and get organized would inevitably cause too much delay. Our party has been specifically assembled for this mission and is used to working together."

Hager spoke up to the Irishman. "Jeremiah, Captain Bradley's right. If Connolly's going to be caught, they must ride almost immediately to catch him in the camp." He motioned to the crowd of onlookers. "The best thing for you men is to go home and get a good night's rest. We may find use for you in watching over the prisoners when they're brought back here."

Meanwhile, Ballantyne, who had been silently staring at Scarlow, stood up. "Damn it, wait just a minute. I say we aren't about to go anywhere this night. The fact is, this whole story stinks like the carcass of an animal that's been dead for three days." He walked over to where Scarlow stood and glared at him. "You *say* you were part of Connolly's militia. Well, how do we know you ain't really part of his crew, sent back to lure us into an ambush?"

Scarlow frowned at the captain. "I ain't no damned Loyalist. I'm as much for the Patriot cause as you are, Mister. What I've been tellin' you is the plain truth."

Ballantyne shook his head. "And I ain't buyin' this. There's some big holes in your story. For one thing, how the hell do the people in Winchester know about Connolly and where he's headed? And for another, what made them send some sheriff's man up to spread the alarm in Wills Creek?"

Bradley raised an eyebrow. "He's got a point. How would they have the word?"

Wend cleared his throat. "I think I know. Colonel Henry sent a courier to James Wood, who is on our Committee of Safety, to have him vouch for my loyalty to the Virginia cause. Undoubtedly he included at least some part of the story about Connolly's plot to explain his inquiry about me. Wood's a smart man. He probably alerted the committee and the sheriff, and they decided to send word up to Wills Creek."

Ballantyne scowled. "Eckert, you're guessing. I say the truth is they ain't got a clue in Fort Cumberland, and Scarlow is tellin' a story made up by that crafty Connolly." He pointed his finger right in Scarlow's face. "Truth is, there ain't no way he can prove what he's sayin'."

All the men stared at Scarlow as they considered Ballantyne's words. Wend would have expected the young man to be intimidated by the accusation, but he stood eyeing Ballantyne with a confident smile on his face.

Then he spoke up in a calm tone. "Actually, I do have proof of what I'm sayin'." He reached inside his jacket and pulled out a piece of paper. He opened it up to show a handwritten note. "This here's a receipt for me buyin' a young colt from a man in Wills Creek. I plan to get the horse from him on my way back with my sister."

Ballantyne laughed. "Shit, that don't prove nothin'."

Scarlow grinned. "Perhaps not, but the other side sure does." He turned the paper around to show all the men at the table. It was a printed handbill. "If you read this, it says to watch out for Connolly and has a description of him. These things are posted all over Wills Creek."

Bradley took the paper and read over it. "He's right about what it says." Then he handed it to Wend.

Wend quickly read the words. "This description of Connolly is quite accurate. It was certainly composed by someone who's familiar with him."

Bradley snuffed his cigar out. "That settles it. Let's ride."

"Wait a damn minute." Ballantyne looked around at the men at the table. "I don't like the idea of riding out in a rush and leaving our packs behind. If we miss Connolly, we'll lose a day comin' back and gettin' the stuff."

Rising from his chair, Bradley countered, "Admittedly it's a chance, but I say one worth taking."

Ballantyne set his chin. "I got a better idea. I say we leave just a'fore dawn, with all our baggage and provisions. We might still find Connolly at the ford, and even if he left we'll be traveling faster than him, and we'll get him, likely by the end of the day or early the next." He shook his head vigorously. "And I don't like the idea of takin' my men out into this cold night. In case you ain't been outside lately, there's a bone-chilling dampness in the air, and the wind's pickin' up. There be some kind of weather comin' in from the west, and we'll be in the middle of it."

Wend gave the Virginia captain a hard look. "For God's sake, Jedidiah, that's all the more reason to move now. If freezing rain or snow does come, it could shut down travel for days. Let's move before it happens."

"Agreed," snapped Bradley. "Ballantyne, I'm ready to ride, and I'm sure Eckert and his men will come along."

Wend nodded agreement. "You can wager on it."

The Marylander said, "With my four, Eckert's four, and Reimann, we'll have nine men. That's enough to do the job, particularly if we catch the fugitives unawares." He shot Ballantyne a sharp glance. "So you and your men can sit here or come along. It's all the same to me."

Ballantyne's face turned red. He looked quickly at Eckert, then back to Bradley. "All right, we'll ride with you. Ain't nobody saying First Virginia men hold back in the face of action. But you just remember I'm the one who told you this could end badly."

And with that he stalked out of the room into the yard.

Bradley turned to Wend with a broad grin on his face. "Well, my dear Eckert, the fox is afoot, and it's time to ride to the hounds!"

—⁂—

Ballantyne was right—right at least about the weather. Wend felt it right away when he stepped out of the inn to saddle up. The northwest wind was frigid and laden with moisture. However, the weather held for the first hour, as Abel Reimann led them westward along the wagon track.

But then the storm enveloped them—first in the form of higher wind and blowing sleet, but in just a few minutes they were riding directly into driven snow mixed with sleet, which bit sharply at their faces. Visibility soon became nil.

In just a few minutes, Bradley, who was leading with Reimann alongside, pulled up and dismounted. The others followed suit. Wend and Ballantyne joined him and the guide for an impromptu meeting. Wend saw that Bradley was shivering in his cloak, which was considerably thinner than the heavy military watch coats.

Bradley pulled the cloak tight about him and shook his head. "I don't think we can proceed further. This weather is unbearable, and my horse is having trouble with his footing."

Ballantyne's laugh was audible even above the wind. "Just like I told you: this has been a fool's errand from the start. Let's head back to the inn. We'll have to lead the horses, but at least the wind will be at our backs."

The Maryland captain looked around, exasperation in his eyes. "Maybe we *should* turn back."

Wend put his hand on the young guide's arm. "Abel, how far from the creek do you think we are?"

"Mr. Eckert, we made good time 'til this storm came on. We ain't but a little more than three miles away from their camp, bein' they're still there."

Wend looked around. Through the darkness and snow, he could make out a grove of evergreens off the right side of the road. He pointed and then shouted, "Listen, Warren, we don't have to give it up. We can lead the horses into those pines. They'll afford a measure of shelter, and we can make a small fire. In the meantime, we could send Reimann and Baird ahead to scout. They can determine if Connolly's party is still encamped and get the precise lay of the land. In the meantime, maybe the storm will ease somewhat. But in any case if it's only three miles, we can push our way there if they haven't left. We could hit them at first light."

Bradley turned to Abel. "What do you think, lad? Are you up for it?"

"Yeah, Captain, I can do it. But what about that Baird fellow? He must be fifty, and he's got a lame left leg. He'll just slow me down."

Wend waved Joshua up to the group. He joined them, traces of ice and snow adhering to his stubbly beard. Bradley told him what they were thinking.

Baird considered a moment and shrugged nonchalantly, "Sounds right to me." He looked at Reimann. "You think you're up to it, lad?"

"Me? Me? I beg your pardon, sir, but what about your leg, Mr. Baird? There will be some stiff walkin'."

"Shit, lad, I was scoutin' on this gamy leg when you were still drooling on your mother's tit. Let's get goin'. And you take care to keep up with me." He wrapped the reins of his hunter around his right hand and started off up the road. Then he looked back over his shoulder and called to Reimann, "You comin', Sprout?"

Wend laughed, remembering how years ago Joshua had egged him on in similar situations.

Abel made a face but led out in Baird's wake. The two soon faded into the storm.

Wend turned back to Bradley. "Let's get into the pines."

The grove proved better protection than Wend had hoped. There was a small knoll, and they took shelter behind it, with the high trees and underbrush breaking much of the snow and sleet. The men gathered wood and laid a fire. Wend picked out some kindling and used a flintlock to ignite the fire. Soon their situation was much improved, with the men huddled in a circle around the flames. Wend looked at the party. All the men from Winchester and the First Virginia were snugged down in their winter clothing. The Maryland cavalrymen, more lightly dressed, were not faring as well. Bradley's face was red, and he was still shaking from the cold and wind. Wend thought, *Welcome to war on the border.*

It was at least three hours before Baird and Reimann materialized out of the storm.

Joshua threw he reins of his horse over a low tree branch and announced, "They still be at the river camp, all snugged down under blankets. Got two fires going and a sentry posted beside one, sittin' up with a blanket hooded over his shoulders and head."

Abel nodded agreement. "You get out from under these trees, you'll see the storm is easing a little. And the clouds are breaking up some."

"Yeah, that's the truth," Joshua agreed. "Now someone here got a drink? I say we let the Sprout here and me get warmed up a little, then we move up on the bastards. We can be ready to take them right at first light."

Donegal pulled a small metal flask out of his coat pocket. "Here you go, Joshua. Just the stuff."

The scout took the container, looked at it longingly, then handed it to Abel. "Here you go, Sprout. Take a pull."

Reimann nodded thanks, took a long draw, and handed the whiskey back to Joshua, who took a gulp. Then the two moved close to the fires.

Bradley looked at Wend. "Sound right to you?"

"Yes, we should be able to get them while they're just rousing or before they're actually up. Perhaps avoid any shooting and get the whole party."

Ballantyne had come over as they were talking. Bradley asked, "Are you with us on this?"

"Yeah, long as we're here. But that's provided the road's in good 'nuff shape for us and the horses."

Joshua had heard and called over from the fire, "It'll be all right! Even without pushing we'll be there in just over an hour from when we start."

—⚏—

They took to the road about an hour before first light was due. Once upon the road, they realized that young Abel was right; the weather was indeed easing. The biting sleet had stopped, and there was only patchy snow falling gently. They made good progress, and before an hour was out, Reimann held up his hand and whispered, "We're 'bout a hundred yards from the creek—just around a bend in the wagon track."

Joshua said, "Let Sprout and me go and take a quick look before we go barging in."

Bradley nodded and signaled for the rest of the men to dismount.

The two scouts were back in just a few minutes.

Joshua shook his head and announced with urgency in his voice, "You got to hand it to Connolly—he's pushing those men hard. They're up and just about ready to ride. All them packhorses are loaded and ready to go."

Abel said, "We'll have to move fast or they'll be across the creek."

Wend looked at Bradley. "Warren, if they're ready to move, there's probably going to be a fight. Everyone needs to check their firelocks and protect the powder in their priming pan against this weather."

Bradley called out the orders to the men, then they moved off with Joshua and Abel taking the advance ahead.

Just as they reached the bend in the road, Abel came back, riding as fast as conditions permitted and waving frantically. "Captain Bradley, they're breaking camp! The packtrain is heading for the creek, and the rest are mounting up!"

Bradley waved his hand "Forward! As fast as your horse can manage in this snow!"

The entire party surged forward. Soon they rounded the bend and had the fugitive party in view.

Wend saw that the packtrain, under the control of two men, was on the road and about to descend into the water of the ford. The creek itself was at least fifty feet wide. The others were still in the camp, but several men were mounted and others were about to take horse.

Bradley pulled up, staring at the scene. He looked back and forth between the creek and the campsite. Wend could see uncertainty on his face. At the same time, Ballantyne stared at the sight, a blank look on his face.

Suddenly Bradley pulled a pistol from its holster and shouted, "Let's get at them! Charge!"

Wend held up his hand and screamed at the top of his voice, "No!" He reached over and grabbed the reins of Bradley's horse. "Warren, this is not the time for a cavalry charge! It will turn into a melee with lots of casualties."

All the others were looking at him now.

"We've got to use our strength." Wend pointed to a small rise off to the left. "I'll take riflemen over there. We can stop the packtrain with well-aimed fire."

Then he pointed to the campsite. "Bradley, your men have pistols only. Work your way along the road under cover of bushes, and try to block the men still in the camp from getting to the ford!"

He shouted to Ballantyne, "You and Seidal, get your men into the woods and try to get on the other side of the camp to cut them off! Then lay down a fire with your muskets!" He looked at Seidal. "Sergeant, you know what I want?"

"Yeah, Lieutenant. We'll keep their heads down."

"Joshua, Horner, Donegal, Abel, come with me."

Wend threw off, dropped the reins, and started running for the top of the little hill. He kept slipping and sliding in the snow and mud, but he finally made it. The other riflemen joined him in a second.

"Joshua, we've got to stop the train from crossing."

"Yea, but take a look. They're already damn near midstream."

Horner said, "Sir, it's a shot of one hundred fifty yards or more."

Wend pulled the cloth off his lock, found a low branch on a bare oak, rested his rifle, and took quick aim at the man in the lead of the pack-train. He pulled the sett trigger, then squeezed the firing trigger. The firelock went off before he expected it, and he was sure he had missed. But after a long moment the man's head slumped down, and he slowly fell off his horse into the water.

Joshua reached over and grabbed Wend's rifle and gave him his. "We'll feed you!" Then he said loudly so the others understood, "Wend will do the shootin'!"

Taking a little more time, Wend sighted on the other packtrain man, who was leading the second half of the horses, and squeezed the trigger. It was a good hit; his head snapped to the side, and he tumbled off his horse.

Joshua passed him another rifle. Wend looked around for a target. He soon found it. Another rider had come from the camp and, forcing his mount into the water, was attempting to get control of the train. Wend swiveled toward him and fired. The man moved as he shot, and Wend's ball took him in the shoulder instead of the head. The man slumped, then slid down and took shelter behind his horse. He led the animal back toward the campsite before Wend could get his hands on another rifle.

Young Reimann, busy reloading a firelock, called out, "Mr. Eckert, the packtrain is still moving toward the other side!"

Wend looked back to the creek. Abel was right. The lead horse was instinctively leading his "herd" onward.

Wend exclaimed, "Shit!"

Donegal called out. "You got to do it, Wend! Stop that horse."

Baird grimaced, hating the idea as much as Wend. "He's right. Put the animal down."

Wend sighed and took careful aim. The ball took the lead horse near the ear. The animal collapsed into the water.

The second horse, whose lead was attached to the dead horse, now shrieked in fright and began trying to pull away from the carcass. The rest of the train also began to panic and whinny in fear, rearing and fighting to get free of their lead lines. The horses stalled midstream.

Turning, Wend looked down to the road. Considerable firing was in progress; obviously Connolly's men were resisting. He said, "We're done here." He then turned to Horner. "Andrew, you and Abel run back and get mounted. Ride out into the stream and retrieve the packtrain." Then he motioned to Joshua and Donegal. "Let's get down to the road and help with the fight at the campsite."

Using the available cover, which was sparse, the three worked their way down to the edge of the road where they found Bradley and two of his men crouching behind trees at the side of the road, directly opposite the camp. Wend looked around and then asked the Maryland captain, "Where's Sedgewick?"

Bradley turned to Wend, a distraught look on his face. "Lying beside the road with a ball in his forehead. When Connolly and his men saw what was happening in the stream, they turned back into the camp, dismounted, and started firing from cover. They got Sedgewick with the first shot as we were moving up."

Wend looked over at the campsite. He could see horses but no men. The musket shots of Ballantyne's men were audible at regular intervals. Their firing was clearly having the desired effect; Connolly and his men were hunkered down in the bush.

Bradley said, "Eckert, we're at a standoff. We must rush them to finish this." He paused, then continued, "Perhaps if we all moved in at once from two sides."

"Yes, that might work. But we'd likely lose more men. Better to wait them out." Wend pointed to the camp. "Connolly is a smart man. He's got to know the game is up. He's lost his packtrain, and he's pinned down in that camp up against the river. If he tries to mount and make a rush to cross, we'll shoot him and his men down like we just did with the packtrain. If he stays there, sooner or later we'll pick off more of his men."

Bradley looked up at the sky. "I don't like the prospect of staying here in the cold and snow for an indefinite period."

"Neither do I, Warren." Wend looked over at the camp. "Listen, I know Connolly personally. Let me talk with him and see if he has the sense to surrender."

Bradley took a deep breath. "It can't hurt."

Wend waited until there was a pause in the musketry from the First Virginia men. Then he cupped his hands and shouted, "Ballantyne, stop firing for now!"

A few seconds later, he heard the Virginia captain's voice, "All right, we'll hold fire."

Wend looked at Bradley and said, "Well, let's see what happens." It had become silent in the woods, and he called out, "Connolly, John Connolly! It's Wend Eckert. Wend Eckert the gunsmith from Winchester! Let's talk!"

The silence persisted for long moments. Then Wend heard Connolly's voice. "All right, Eckert. I recognize your voice."

"John, you're outnumbered, and we've got your packtrain. We can keep you from moving for as long as it takes. And I know you've got at least one seriously wounded man in there. Give it up. For humanity's sake, it's time to surrender."

There was a long silence.

Then Connolly shouted back, "Give us time to talk it over!"

Wend looked over at Bradley and winked. "Certainly, John. But pray don't take too long. I've got a bunch of rabid rebels here who are bent on moving in on you. I don't know how long I can restrain them."

"I understand, Wend. I've got a similar circumstance. The men with me are adamant in their support of the king and governor, as am I."

"We'll wait for your decision. But you must understand there is no way forward for you and your party."

"There is always the choice to die honorably in the service of the king."

"John, think about Susanna and your children. This insurrection isn't going to last forever. She needs a good man to help raise those children."

There was a prolonged silence. Finally Connolly called back, "Wend, we shall give you our answer presently!"

Wend turned and looked at the Maryland captain. "I believe it's just a matter of a few minutes now. Their position is untenable."

"I hope you're correct. We don't need any more casualties."

The minutes dragged on with no sound from the besieged men. Bradley had pulled out a pocket watch. Presently he said, "It's been fifteen minutes. Surely they could have made a decision by now."

Wend grimaced. "You're right. I've started to wonder if they're up to something." He cupped his hands and called out, "Connolly, we need an answer from you! You've had adequate time."

The response came back immediately. "I request a formal truce and a parley to clarify our status if we surrender. I propose Eckert and I meet in plain sight on the road."

Wend pursed his lips. "Warren, I'll talk to him only if you come with me. You are the senior man and have ultimate authority."

Bradley nodded. "Certainly."

Wend shouted, "We agree! But there will be two of us. Our commander will accompany me."

There was no reply for nearly a full minute. The Connolly called, "That's fine! I'm putting down my firelock now and walking out to the road."

The Loyalist colonel appeared from beside a large tree surrounded by thick evergreen foliage. He extended his hands to show they were empty, though a brace of pistols were in his belt, and stepped out on the road. Wend put his rifle down and did the same, and Bradley stuck his pistols in his belt.

They met in the middle of the wagon track, separated by a yard of space, the snow falling around them.

Connolly briefly raised his hat in salute, and a wry look came over his face. "Well, my dear Wend, life is full of strange coincidences. The last time I saw you was at Fort Gower on the Ohio when you were a loyal aide to the legitimate governor of Virginia."

Wend touched the brim of his own hat in response. "John, the world has turned since then." Then he continued, "I trust Susanna is in good health."

Connolly smiled. "Indeed, she was when I left her. She is with her brother at his inn in Pittsburgh."

Wend motioned toward the Marylander and said formally, "This is Captain Warren Bradley of the Ann Arundell Light Horse. He is the senior officer of our party and the man authorized by the Continental Congress to treat with you." Then to Bradley, he said, "Captain, this is Colonel John Connolly of Lord Dunmore's military force."

Bradley raised his hat. "Colonel, I compliment you on your skill in advancing this far on your mission. However, it must be obvious that the time has come for you to surrender in company with your men."

"Clearly we have the option of resisting until the end, Captain. We have sufficient ammunition to make any attack costly for you."

"Colonel, why waste lives? And if necessary, we *will* attack. A raising of the tribes for border war cannot be permitted. I vow we are ready to suffer whatever casualties are necessary to preclude such an undertaking."

Wend added, "Connolly, you need to be aware that Wills Creek and other settlements ahead of you have been informed of your scheme and furnished with your description. Even if you should, by some chance, escape us you will face interception at the hands of militia along the way."

The Loyalist said nothing immediately, but Wend saw a change in his posture; his shoulders sagged slightly and his entire body seemed to relax, as if he were accepting the inevitability of failure.

"All right, Captain Bradley. We will place ourselves in your hands but only if it is clear that we will be accorded all the legal courtesies of prisoners of war. I must request your promise as a gentleman that all of my men will receive humane treatment and protection from the rabble."

Bradley nodded. "Of course, sir. You have my assurance."

"Then, sir, I am at your service." Connolly reached down and pulled his pistols from his belt, then presented them to the Maryland captain. He turned toward the camp and called, "Doctor Smyth, have the men put down their arms and come forward!"

Bradley asked, "Colonel, how many men do you have surviving?"

"There are Doctor John Smyth and Lieutenant Cameron, who is gravely wounded, and two more, Ridgely and Fallow, our servants. Another man is dead, shot by the musket fire."

Wend was alarmed. "What about the rest? We killed the two pack-horse men in the stream. We know you had three others, including a man named Munger."

The thinnest of smiles came over Connolly's lips. "I'm afraid Munger and the others, all from Pittsburgh, chose to depart at the onset of your ambush. They did not consult with me."

Wend's anger flared. Now he realized why the colonel had been stalling. "That's a bold-faced deception, Connolly. You helped them go, and you've been delaying things to give them time to get away."

Now Connolly's smile broadened, and he spread his hands wide. "Deception? I would characterize it as a legitimate stratagem of war, my dear Wend. In any case, they are gone into the snowstorm and beyond your reach."

Wend looked behind Connolly and saw that a man had emerged from the trees of the camp. He was tall and thin faced with dark hair, and he was dressed in a heavy, dark gray overcoat and tri-cornered hat. There was an expression of disgust on his face.

Connolly motioned to the man. "This is my associate, Doctor John Smyth."

Smyth nodded. "There's a wounded man back in the camp being tended by my servant Ridgely."

"He's a lieutenant in Dunmore's militia named Alan Cameron," added Connolly.

Smyth motioned back to the camp. "He needs care—more than I can give him here in the cold and snow."

Bradley asked, "Can he ride?"

The doctor sighed. "He's lost a lot of blood. He's been fading in and out of consciousness."

The Marylander nodded. "We'll find a way to get him back to Elizabethtown. Doctor, please return to the camp and get him as ready as possible to travel."

Meanwhile Joshua, Donegal, and Bradley's men had left cover and come up to the group.

Wend told Joshua about the escape of the three men. "They escaped to the northward just as the action began. How about getting mounted and seeing what you can find out about their movements?"

"Yeah, I'll do that, but it's goin' to be hard in this snow." He pointed to the west. "In case you ain't noticed, the clouds are gettin' damn dark over there. I 'spect the snow's going to get heavier very soon."

Bradley looked westward and grimaced. "I dare say Baird is right." He turned to Connolly. "If you and your men will give me your word not to attempt escape, I suggest we work together to get Lieutenant Cameron ready to transport and we make haste to return to the shelter of the tavern in Elizabethtown."

"You have my word on behalf of all of us."

In a few minutes, Baird, having mounted, picked up the trail of the escapees and headed northward along the creek, disappearing into the snow as he followed their trail.

Meanwhile, Donegal set to work constructing a litter that could be carried between two horses.

While the Highlander worked, Horner and Reimann had led the packtrain back to the camp. Bradley, Ballantyne, and Wend examined the contents of the packs. Most of the horses were carrying powder and lead. There was also a substantial amount of knife and hatchet blades along with some standard trade goods such as beads and fabric.

Wend made a quick estimate. "I'd say there's well over two thousand pounds of goods in these packs. The ammunition is certainly enough to fuel a season of raiding all along the border. The Ohio tribes would be extraordinarily grateful to whoever delivered this material to them."

Horner and Reimann had also been able to recover the bodies of the two men Wend had shot. Altogether there were four bodies to be transported back to Elizabethtown: the two packmen, Sedgewick, and the Loyalist who had been hit by Ballantyne's men with their musket fire. The bodies were laid out next to each other and covered with blankets.

Wend stood looking at the blankets, reflecting that it was an expensive bill for so small a skirmish.

John Connolly was leaning against a tree, his arms crossed in front of him as he watched the activity in the campsite. Then he spoke up. "Well, Eckert, it might interest you to know that those two men you shot and the packhorses are from Richard Grenough's company."

Wend was startled. He responded suspiciously, "I don't understand. Grenough went missing earlier this year."

"His wife has retained control of the company and hired an overseer to manage it." He gave Wend a sly look. "Certainly you are aware that Northcutt and Lord Dunmore are convinced you killed him."

Bradley, who was standing nearby, heard Connolly's words and gave Wend a sharp look. "What is he saying, Eckert? That you killed someone in cold blood?"

Wend explained, "Richard Grenough was an influential merchant and Indian trader working out of York. He had the ear of important officials in Pennsylvania, and he was a major supplier of provisions and military supplies during Virginia's war against the Ohio tribes last year."

Connolly added, "Indeed, and he was on his way to Williamsburg last April to settle accounts with the governor when he disappeared while camping on the Shenandoah. Camping, I might say, very near Eckert's place."

Wend said very evenly, "Connolly, his disappearance was investigated by Sheriff Smith of Frederick County. All the evidence is that Grenough was killed by a roving band of highwaymen who had been operating in the county for several months. He concluded that the band attempted to rob Grenough at his campsite near Ashby Ferry and that he died resisting them. His remains were never found, and the sheriff thinks the rogues dumped his body and that of a man with him into the river."

Connolly laughed. "How convenient for you, Eckert. It is well known that you held Grenough and some of his men responsible for the death of your parents and siblings. I'm afraid that Northcutt doesn't believe there's any coincidence that Grenough's death should happen just a few miles south of your farm. He told me when I was at his regimental headquarters that he intends to exact the full measure of justice from you when this rebellion has been put down."

Wend looked at Connolly and permitted a small smile to cross his face. "Well, John, you've just given me a very personal reason to make sure that this *rebellion* does succeed."

Chapter Eleven

PRISONER CONNOLLY

The entire party finally rode into the yard of Cotter's Common at Elizabethtown in the late afternoon. The storm had waxed and waned throughout the day, but some respite for the horsemen had come from the fact that the wind was at their backs. However, their progress had been greatly slowed because the litter Donegal and Horner rigged between two horses often needed adjustment. This and the requirement for Doctor Smyth to attend to Cameron had necessitated frequent stops.

Joshua Baird had returned from his scout within a half hour to tell them that the three men had gone a short distance northward, then crossed the Conococheaque at a shallow ford, and it was useless to try to overtake them in the prevailing conditions.

Meanwhile, Bradley had dispatched Abel Reimann to warn the tavern keeper and Hager about the need to accommodate prisoners and care for the wounded man. Thus, when the party arrived at the inn, Hager, his son, Jon, and the proprietor stood on the front porch.

Hager called out to Bradley, "We've got rooms set for the prisoners! Bring them right into the inn."

Bradley and Wend escorted the captives into the common room and then up the stairs to the second floor. Two rooms had been set up. A rather large room accommodated Doctor Smyth, Cameron, and Smyth's servant, Ridgely—who was trained to act as a medical orderly—so that Smyth could minister to the wounded lieutenant. Connolly and his servant were put into a smaller room next door.

Wend escorted Connolly to his room. Horner brought the colonel's baggage up to the room and laid it out on the bed.

Wend turned to Connolly and said, "You will understand that we must go through your belongings."

The Loyalist waved a hand in resignation. "Do what you must."

Just as Wend was getting started, Bradley and young Jon Hagar came in. Hager was carrying a long chain with a shackle attached.

Connolly's eyes opened wide. "Pray tell, what is that for?"

Bradley said, "I'm taking no chances. You'll be shackled to the bed."

"For God's sake! Does the word of a gentleman carry no weight with you? I gave my parole!"

Bradley gave Connolly a wry look. "You tricked us at the parley this morning to allow some of your men to escape. From here on out, I'll trust you in my sight, but otherwise you'll live under restraint." He shrugged. "Besides, I don't want to have to post a man in the hall or in the rooms to watch you."

"There's enough chain," said Hagar, "to allow you free movement around the room."

The colonel responded sarcastically, "I suppose I should be grateful for that generous concession."

Hager connected the shackle to Connolly's leg and the end of the chain to the frame of the bed. Then he stood up. "I'll go check on Doctor Smyth to see what he needs to care for Cameron." He nodded to Bradley and then hurried out of the room.

As he left, Ballantyne walked in. Hands on hips, he took in the scene and Connolly's chains. "Now we're dealing with this Tory in the proper manner."

John Connolly looked down at his shackled leg and then back up to Bradley and Wend. Then, ignoring Ballantyne, he smiled and said in a confident manner, "I am at a loss to understand why two gentlemen such as you are involved in this ill-conceived insurrection. Eckert, I know you are well off in your trade, and you have profited mightily by performing musket work for the Virginia royal government. And you, Captain Bradley, I assume have substantial land holdings in tidewater Maryland."

Bradley raised an eyebrow and said, "I'll make no secret that I have a plantation on the West River south of Annapolis."

Connolly shrugged. "Exactly. Now how is it that two men of intelligence and substance are siding with a mob of rebellious rabble? Mostly Ulster Irish?" He nodded at Ballantyne and smiled. Then he continued, "A mob led in rebellion by a few connivers like Washington and that despicable Samuel Adams. You must recognize what the ultimate outcome will be."

Bradley responded, "I don't know, Connolly. The rabble seem to be doing rather well in besieging the British forces in Boston."

"And," added Wend, "your commander, Governor Dunmore, doesn't seem to be particularly successful at the moment, bottled up as he is in a bit of coastal territory and on some ships on the Chesapeake."

Connolly grinned broadly. "Clearly a temporary situation as we recruit our forces. We hold Norfolk, the most important city and harbor in the colony. Northcutt's Loyal Virginia Regiment will be magnificent and well armed. Militia are flocking to our colors. A body of Highlanders is being raised in North Carolina to join us. Beyond that, you must realize that the king will not let the current state of events persist."

Wend asked, "What do you believe he is going to do? What do you think he *can* do?"

"My dear Eckert, let me confide in you. A few weeks ago, I had very illuminating discussions with General Gage in Boston." Connolly smiled with pride. "He took me into his full confidence. Rest assured that preparations are already in train that will deal with this uprising. Gage has been informed that the government in London is planning a massive expedition for the next year, which will utterly crush this so-called *Patriot* cause. We are speaking of tens of thousands of disciplined soldiers landing here in the colonies. Washington's undisciplined, poorly trained, ill-equipped army will be swept up and destroyed, the rank and file chased down like dogs." He gave each of them a grim look, then said, "And when that happens, the leaders will be dealt with severely. Men such as you will feel the brunt of the king's wrath."

Bradley laughed. "Right now, Colonel, it seems you are the one who has much to lose. I have orders to deliver you to the Continental Congress, which will make the decision as to what justice will be dealt out in your case." He crossed his arms and considered for a moment. "You must realize how people of all classes consider your plan to unleash the savages totally despicable and how severe the punishment will be for the man who conceived such a plan."

Connolly gave them a defiant look. "I am proud to stand with my king and to do whatever is necessary to preserve his rightful sovereignty over these colonies."

Wend shot Bradley a look, then turned to Connolly. "If we're talking of loyalty, I'd say that the matter of four thousand acres at the Falls of the Ohio would have a lot to do with yours. If the colonies are successful, your grant from Dunmore will be worthless, and you will have lost a fortune."

"You accuse me of being a mercenary? *You* of all people, Eckert? *You* who have taken the king's money for years? It is the very basis of your wealth. And I am quite aware that you are in receipt of a land grant from Dunmore far larger than mine—ten thousand acres. And that you were given a captaincy in Barrett Northcutt's new regiment." He shook his head "And yet you repay the governor and the king by standing with the rebels. Undoubtedly you plan on taking profit in their need for arms."

Ballantyne's eyebrows rose and his face lit up. "Well, Eckert, I find that very interesting. Ten thousand acres and a commission in Dunmore's army? I think some people in Williamsburg will be intrigued with that information."

Wend ignored Ballantyne. "Connolly, if you know so much, you must also be aware that I rejected Northcutt's offer of a commission and informed him of my intention to join the insurrection. My loyalty cannot be purchased."

Just then a young maid appeared in the doorway. She carried a tray bearing a plate of steaming food and a cup. She smiled at all the men, then said in a heavy German accent, "Hello. My name is Helga. I bring a meal for Colonel Connolly." She walked into the room and placed the tray on the table by the bed.

Connolly smiled at the girl. "Thank you very much. I'm indeed quite hungry."

"*Ja*, my Colonel. If you need anything else, please call for me. I take care of you and Herr Doctor Smyth."

Bradley said, "We'll leave you to your meal, Colonel Connolly, and a peaceful rest. However, I'll want to talk with you tomorrow."

Connolly laughed and reached down and rattled his chain. "Obviously I will be at your service."

They left Connolly and walked down the hall to the stairway. Bradley, hand on the stair rail, turned and said, "I'm planning to rest men and horses here tomorrow and then escort the prisoners down to Fredericktown the next day if Cameron is ready to travel."

Ballantyne gave him a sly smile. "With only the three men you have left?"

"Jonathan Hager is going to recruit several militia to come with us and assist. When we get to Frederick, Sheriff Lowell, I have no doubt, will provide men to help us escort them onward to Philadelphia."

"And what about that packtrain full of powder and lead and blades?"

"Why, it goes with us. We will send those supplies on to Washington at Boston. It's no secret that the army there is critically short of ammunition."

Ballantyne raised his hand. "Not so fast, Bradley. The Virginia forces need powder just as desperately as Washington to help drive out Dunmore. I say our fight is as important as what's going on up at Boston. If Dunmore succeeds, he'll split the colonies."

"Do I need to reiterate, Ballantyne," the Maryland captain said, "that I am operating under orders from the Congress?"

"That was about capturing Connolly. Those orders can't have nothin' to say about a packtrain 'cause nobody knew anything about it." He looked at the cavalryman. "I ain't got a doubt in the world you'd love to arrive in Philadelphia with all them supplies, Bradley. But it ain't happening! I'm takin' half the packs with me when I go. I need somethin' to show for all this time, and you ain't stoppin' me."

Wend looked at the two men. Both had stiffened into aggressive postures. Bradley was gripping the stair rail so hard that his hand was turning white. Wend actually felt that Ballantyne had a good point for he knew how short military supplies were in Virginia. But he would be damned if he'd support him after all the acrimony of the days since Culpeper. He crossed his arms and stayed silent, determined to remain neutral.

Bradley's eyes showed a flash of anger. He looked over at Wend for assistance but found none there. There was a long silence. Finally the Marylander took a deep breath. "All right, Ballantyne. I accede to your position. We will divide the packs precisely in half."

Ballantyne grinned broadly. "That's a smart decision, Bradley. There's enough glory to go around. You'll still get lots of credit for bringin' in over a thousand pounds of military supplies for Congress's army. And so will I when we ride into Williamsburg."

Bradley relaxed, then said, "I'm not concerned about what happens in Williamsburg, but I am sure you'll be received with approval."

Ballantyne grinned. "Yes, and even more so when I bring this traitor in."

Bradley shot a quick look at Wend, then turned back to Ballantyne. "You're not still planning on accusing him of being a Loyalist, are you? Not after what he did at the ford?"

"It ain't what he *did*. It's what Connolly *said*. It proves everything I've been sayin' about Eckert. He's been given a land grant by the governor, and he was in line for a commission in the Loyal Virginia Regiment. That's enough to prove him guilty."

Bradley shook his head. "For God's sake, Ballantyne, he turned all that down."

"That don't mean nothin'. What do you think he would say? I'll wager he's been keepin' Dunmore and his crony Northcutt informed of what's goin' on up in the Shenandoah Valley. That's exactly what I'm goin' to tell Colonel Henry and the Virginia Committee of Safety."

Wend made sure his face remained blank. He said to Bradley, "I'm not worried about Captain Ballantyne's fantasy. He has no proof, and by the time we get back, Winchester's representative to the House of Burgesses, James Wood, will have responded to Henry's inquiry about my loyalty. I have no doubt Henry will be completely satisfied that I am as true to the cause as any man."

Ballantyne simply snorted and brushed past Bradley on his way down the stairs.

The Marylander commented, "I hope things go as you expect. In the meantime, it's been a long day. How about joining me for supper and a cordial libation?"

—⚏—

The two men sat at a table near the hearth and had a dinner of rather stringy chicken and vegetables that had been in the pot too long. However, after the cold and wet of the preceding night and day, even such fare was palatable and welcome. Far more welcome were the tumblers of whiskey that Bradley ordered for them.

As the food and whiskey settled and the heat of the fire added to the general feeling of well-being, Wend saw that Bradley seemed uncharacteristically morose. Gone was the facade of jocular confidence that he habitually exuded. Nor was he particularly communicative. Wend spoke up. "Well, Warren, you have achieved the objective of your mission. You should be looking forward to delivering Connolly to Philadelphia and then returning to your plantation and family. But you seem rather subdued."

"Yes, my friend, the mission is successful, but at what cost?" Bradley stared at the fire. "I've known Jamie Sedgewick since he was a youth. His family owns the place next to ours. Now he's lying out in a shed until they can bury him, and I shall have to tell his parents and young wife— who is with child, by the way—what happened. And then there is Tom Farrell, who is injured and now back at Fredericktown. That innkeeper's wife up on South Mountain, Greta Rheinhardt, told me his knee was smashed. I doubt he will ever have full use of that leg again."

The Marylander took out one of his cigars and lit it.

When he finished, Wend responded, "Warren, war inevitably has its costs. Sometimes victory comes very dear. When I was only nineteen, I fought at Bushy Run with Bouquet."

Bradley said, "That was a hard-fought battle and a great victory."

"Yes, a great victory, but the cost to me was also great. I lost the closest friend of my youth in Lancaster. He was a sergeant in the Royal Americans. He died in my arms after helping drive back the Indians' last charge." Wend looked into the fire and continued, "So today, you won a battle but lost a close friend. But like my loss at Bushy Run, you must take solace that he died for an important cause—the safety of the border country."

Bradley stared into the fire for a long time. Then he took a deep breath and spoke on a different tack. "I've been thinking all day during the ride back about the fight this morning. Let me be honest: when the time came to make a decision about how to proceed, my mind was frozen. I couldn't think of anything except to charge into the camp. But you were ready. You evaluated the situation in a second and had a plan, and then you saved me from making a costly, perhaps disastrous, mistake."

"Warren, remember that I've been involved in this kind of fight since I was fifteen. I lost my family in the very first fight when I didn't even get to fire a shot before a Mingo warrior clubbed me into unconsciousness. Since then there have been many skirmishes, and so now when things begin to happen, my instincts take over."

"That's what I've been thinking about, Wend. Let me confide in you: my troop has about twenty men in it, all of substance from the tidewater. As I told you, we've never seen action. But the Maryland Council of Safety has been informed that Washington has a desperate need for cavalry. We have been told to prepare to march north to join his army in due course." He set his mouth and chin, then said quietly, "After this morning, I wonder if I am the right man to lead them."

Wend looked Bradley in the eye. "Warren, your instinct is correct; at the moment, *you* aren't that man. But neither is any other person in your troop. The truth is you must grow into it through experience. And in so doing, you will almost certainly see more of your friends killed or maimed, perhaps in some cases through your mistakes. You will have to live with that."

Bradley stared back at him, and Eckert could see the meaning of what he had said playing in the captain's eyes.

Finally, the Marylander nodded slowly. "I will take aboard what you have said." Then he took a deep pull on his cigar, exhaled he smoke, and changed tack. "In fact, today was the start of that education for me. I have heard stories about the extraordinary skill of border riflemen—and forgive me, Wend, but I was very skeptical. But from my position I saw you take down that packtrain, firing at a range I would not have thought possible. Today I became a believer."

Wend shrugged off Bradley's words. "Warren, there are many men with the same skill throughout the backcountry. Winchester recently sent a company of them to Boston." He thought a moment, then said, "But there is something else you should have learned today."

"Pray tell me."

"The value of rapid *musket* fire. Despite what we think of Ballantyne and the Carlin brothers, they did manage to put down an effective fire against the camp. I believe Sergeant Seidal was a strong influence there for he did time in the Royal Americans and can load and fire three or four times a minute. I listened during the action, and while their speed was certainly not up to that of British infantry, they did fire rapidly enough to force Connolly's men to stay behind cover, where they could not return fire effectively."

"Yes, I see what you mean."

"And Warren, there's something else you should think about. When you get back to Ann Arundell, you might want to see if you can procure carbines for your troop."

Bradley straightened in his chair and in a puzzled tone said, "But we are not heavy dragoons. Light cavalry fight mounted in the saddle with sword and pistol."

"Perhaps that is the way things are on the battlefields of Europe, but here it will be different. You fought on foot today, and you suffered because all you had were pistols. I believe you will often ride to battle but end up fighting on foot or performing scouting on foot. You'll want carbines for such work. If you can't get purpose-built carbines, procure fowlers or muskets and shorten the barrels."

The captain sat thinking for a few moments. Then he sighed deeply. "My dear friend," he said, "I thank you for your counsel. And I shall remember it as we prepare to join the army." He took a drag on his cigar and stood up. "But now I am suddenly very, very weary. It is time for me to retire."

Wend laughed. "It's time for both of us to retire. And thank God we shall have a long, quiet day tomorrow to recover from our travails since we left Fredericktown."

"Yes, indeed, Wend. But thankfully the days of our turmoil are over."

—ᴍ—

During the night the storm passed on and gave way to a clear dawn and a bright day. By midmorning, it became clear they would have unseasonably warm weather. The snow began to melt and give way to mud on the roads and soggy pastures for the horses.

Near dusk, after a day of recuperating, the Winchester men gathered in the inn's stable to tend to their animals. Wend said, "It's time to make plans for going home."

"I'll 'na argue with that," responded Donegal. "My bonnie lady has been without a man for over three weeks now. The poor woman, takin' care of everything herself."

"Shit!" exclaimed Joshua. "She escaped a Shawnee war party all on her own, herding two children at the same time. She can take three weeks without you, Simon. The question is, can you do that time without her? I'm embarrassed to think we got a lovesick Highlander on our hands!"

Wend smiled, then said, "We're in a good place to head straight for Winchester. I talked with Abel Reimann, and he says there's a road that will take us right to a ferry across the Potomac, which is only a few miles from here, and then the road takes us to join the wagon road on down to Winchester."

Joshua screwed up his face. "Once we get across the river, can't be more'n fifty miles to Winchester. We could be there in an easy two days' ride."

Horner said, "Two days if the roads were good, but this mud is going to make things hard for the horses."

Wend nodded. "We'll leave tomorrow, right after Bradley leaves with the prisoners. So let's get everything ready."

"Ain't you forgettin' something, Wend?" Joshua asked the question with a puzzled look on his face. "That bastard Ballantyne wants to take you back to Henry. He ain't goin' to take kindly to us headin' straight out for home."

Donegal said, "Joshua's right, Wend. The asshole is going to demand that you go with him. We got to be prepared to keep him from doin' that."

Wend smiled and shrugged. "I've been thinking about that. We'll talk about it tonight, and when the time comes, we'll be ready to deal with Ballantyne."

Horner asked, "Sir, you have a plan?"

Wend was about to speak when a voice interrupted.

"And just how do you expect to deal with me, Eckert? I'd be very interested in hearing what you have to say!"

Wend turned to see Ballantyne leaning up against the rails of a box stall near the door to the stable. With him were the Carlin brothers and Seidal.

Suddenly a palpable tenseness settled over the stable.

Taddy Carlin was grinning. "You ain't goin' nowhere, Eckert, unless it be the camp of the First Virginia. You still got a lot to answer for."

Donegal, incredulity all over his face, exclaimed, "What the hell are you talkin' about, Carlin? Wend killed two men and near killed another stoppin' Connolly's party at the ford. He didn't hesitate a minute to take all them Tories down. That's proof enough he's loyal to our cause. It's time to give it up, the lot of you."

Jedidiah Ballantyne laughed out loud. "Not by a long shot, Highlander. I got plenty of evidence on Eckert that is going to settle things with Henry and the Virginia Committee of Safety. He's been playin' a long, sly game, just like a spy would. It's sure he was tryin' to slow us down at Hungerford. And he's sided with these Marylanders every chance he gets just 'cause he knows it will keep us from takin' Connolly back for justice in Virginia. And just yesterday, Connolly himself put the finger on Eckert, tellin' about how he's got a big grant of land in Ohio from Dunmore and he's been offered a commission in the Loyalist forces. Henry's going to have a lot to say about that."

Wend was about to respond when Horst Seidal spoke up. "Jedidiah, for God's sake, it's time to let Eckert be. You know he organized the whole action at the ford yesterday. If he hadn't taken over, that fool Bradley would have had us rushing madly into the camp on horseback. Then he drove the whole lot of them back into the camp where we were able to take them without losin' our own men."

Ballantyne turned on the sergeant in fury. "Horst, why are you siding with this bastard?"

"It's less siding with him than worrying about you, Jedidiah. You are letting your anguish over Point Pleasant and your family's death take over your mind. It's distorting your judgment. For God's sake, stop trying to use Eckert as a stepping stone to makin' a name for yourself. You ain't gonna get Connolly to take back to Virginia, but you were in at his capture and got all that ammunition from the packtrain. That's enough to earn you the gratitude of the Committee of Safety, which is what you're thirsting for."

Ballantyne's face flushed red. "What the hell has gotten into you, Horst? I've always been able to count on you for support."

Baird laughed and said, "He is supporting you, Ballantyne. He's tryin' to keep you from makin' a damn fool of yourself."

Seidal said, "I say let's take the ammunition and get back to the regiment and do some real soldiering. I joined up to drive Dunmore out of Virginia and fight the Redcoats up in Boston, not chase around the backcountry. We've done what we was ordered to do; it's time to leave it be and let Eckert go home. All he wants to do is build muskets, and God knows we need them."

The captain glared at Seidal and was about to speak when suddenly everyone's attention was drawn to the sound of shouting by many men. Horner strode to the stable doors and looked out for a moment. Then he turned back to the men inside. "Good lord above! There's a mob of men gathering in front of the tavern just down the way! There's near thirty of them!"

Wend joined Horner to look out on the scene. The tightly packed group of men were right in front of the tavern that was up the road from Cotter's place. Several were carrying torches, and others were grabbing wood from a stack of firewood. As he watched, they piled the wood high and someone lit it with a torch. All the while men were shouting. Wend listened and made out that they were shouting threats against Connolly and his men. He could see that at least a few of the mob were armed with various types of firelocks—some pistols, fowlers, even a musket or two.

Horner turned to Wend. "My God, sir, they're calling for the hanging of Connolly!"

Everyone else in the stable rushed to the door.

Donegal pointed to the inn. "There's 'na doubt they're aimin' to rush down the road and into Cotter's place and seize Connolly and his mates. They just got to spend some time buildin' up their courage to do it."

Wend realized that the Highlander was right. As he watched, the door to Cotter's inn opened and Jonathan Hager came out, accompanied by his son and Bradley and his men. The Marylanders had their pistols displayed prominently in their belts.

Wend turned to his friends. "They're going to try holding off the mob. We've got to help."

Donegal shook his head. "We'll need our firelocks up in the room."

Wend thought quickly. "Andrew, make for the back door of the inn. Get up to the room and get our guns, then meet us on the porch."

The lad nodded and ran for the rear of the inn.

Wend looked at Baird and Donegal. "Come on, let's make for the porch."

Joshua scowled. "Shit! You're right, but look at the size of that crowd. This ain't likely to end well."

"We've got to try." Looking at Ballantyne, Wend said, "Jedidiah, a mob like this will balk at attacking a reasonable number of armed and determined men. With your men we'll have eleven. Will you join us?"

The captain stared at the crowd for a long moment. Then he said, "Now Eckert, why should we help? Bradley wants the credit for takin' Connolly to the Congress. Let him defend the bastard. If they ain't goin' back to Virginia, I'd just as soon see Connolly and Smyth die now."

Taddy Carlin looked over at his brother. "Hell, Jedidiah is right. Justice can be served this here minute. Them damned dandies up in Philadelphia will waste weeks or months arguing over what to do. Connolly wanted to set the border settlements aflame. Makes sense for the border people to send him to the fires of hell!"

Johnny Carlin smiled broadly. "Can't help but agree with that. Instant justice is the sweetest!"

Seidal said quietly, "I'm with you, Eckert. A hangin' won't be justice—it will be murder." He started for the shed where the Virginia men were camping. "I'll get my musket."

Ballantyne yelled after him. "Horst, I never thought you'd betray me like this!"

The sergeant ignored his captain.

Wend motioned to his friends, and the three of them quickly strode to the porch and joined Bradley and Hager. Bradley, the stress showing on his face, said, "There's the devil to pay here, Wend. I'm glad you're with us. But I fear you'll need your weapons."

"Warren, they'll be here momentarily. Does anyone know how this got started?"

Hager said, "My son got some word of this starting earlier in the afternoon. A good friend who had been at that inn told him there were people agitating about seizing Connolly and the others. Some who were from town and some travelers. We thought it would never amount to more than drunken talk."

Wend looked at the mob and said ironically, "Well, it does seem to have gotten a bit beyond that."

Bradley looked around. "Where's Ballantyne and his men?"

"They're sitting this out. But Seidal is with us." He pointed to the yard where the sergeant was approaching with his musket in the crook of his arm.

"Good man. How the hell did he happen to get hooked up with that scurrilous lot?"

"Warren, I just thank God he's there. He keeps them reasonably straight."

Wend turned to the elder Hager. "Mr. Hager, will they listen to you?"

"We must hope, Eckert. Normally they will, but somebody's got them inflamed over the prospect of an Indian uprising. That's not hard to do; the older ones remember the horrors of the Pontiac and French Wars, and the younger ones have heard grim stories that have lost nothing in the telling. Apparently these people have been meeting for some time up at the other tavern."

Donegal looked along the wagon track. "There's more coming in from the countryside to join the mob."

Bradley pointed to a heavyset, broad-shouldered man in front of the crowd around the fire. "Look who seems to be the leader of this lot. It's that big Irishman who wanted to help last night."

"I'm not surprised," commented Hager. "McCarthy's a loudmouth and a bully who fancies himself a leader of the popular crowd in the village, particularly after he's had spirits."

Jon said, "Be honest, Father. He's a drunkard who is always causing trouble."

Wend shook his head. "I've no doubt that spirits are fueling most of them over there."

Meanwhile Horner arrived with the weapons. Wend said, "Everyone check your priming after being out in the weather so long."

Bradley bit his lip. "Eckert, do you really think it will come to using firelocks? Won't a show of force do the trick?"

"It may if Hager can't talk them out of it. But look," he said as he motioned toward the far inn. "They're getting ready to move. And some of them have weapons."

Almost immediately Horner said, "Look, Mr. Eckert, they're coming."

Wend saw more men were lighting torches, and McCarthy was motioning in the direction of Cotter's place. Then, as he watched, the entire pack surged down the wagon track toward Cotter's Common.

It took the crowd only a couple of minutes to arrive in the yard, where they stopped about thirty feet in front of the porch.

Baird pointed to a tree at the side of the yard. "There's a couple of men runnin' up a rope with a noose over that big limb."

Young Hager, fear in his eyes, looked at Jonathan. "Father, you must speak to them. You're the only one they might listen to."

Wend observed that the elder Hager was breathing heavily, his chest heaving. He clutched his left shoulder with his right hand. The old man stood looking at the tree with the noose, seemingly mesmerized by it. Then he finally said, "Yes, yes, I will do so immediately."

He raised his arms. "People of Elizabethtown! Hear me!"

The pack of men quieted within a few seconds.

Hager said, "Men, I understand your anger at the Tories held inside, but you must not take the law into your own hands." He put his hands on Bradley's shoulder. "This officer represents Maryland and the Continental Congress. He is here to take the conspirators to Philadelphia to face the judgment of Congress. You must trust the functioning of lawful authority!" He stopped to catch his breath, then said, "I beg you, disperse immediately! Go home and attend to your business and farms, secure in the knowledge that justice will be served to these men in a legal way."

There was a silence in the crowd as they looked at their town founder and considered his words.

But the silence was brief for it was soon broken by the loud voice of McCarthy, shouting out, "Don't listen to him! How are we supposed to trust some bunch of rich dandies with their plantations and carriages and fine clothes to impose justice on this Connolly? He's one of them! They ain't goin' to punish one of their own in a proper way."

Several men shouted agreement, and others joined in until the whole crowd was again shouting.

Then McCarthy stepped out in front of them. "All them so-called 'gentlemen' are just goin' to give Connolly is a slap on the hand. Then in a little while they'll parole him on nothin' but his promise of good behavior. And later they'll exchange him for some macaroni friend of their own who's in British hands! I tell you, we got to take care of justice right here."

The mob erupted in loud, unanimous agreement, torches waving in the night.

McCarthy pointed to the noose dangling from the tree limb. "We need to give Connolly permanent justice! Send him to hell! I tell you, no one else will do the job right!"

Hager bowed his head, breathing deeply to catch his breath.

Wend noticed the older man was shaking and his forehead was wet with perspiration.

The town founder, a look of defeat on his face, said resignedly, "They aren't going to listen to me. They're too worked up, too full of liquor."

"We've got to do something!" Bradley's voice was laden with anxiety. "I fear they're just moments from rushing the inn!"

Joshua gave Wend a fierce look. Then he spoke loudly so all the men on the porch could hear. "They got to understand we'll use our weapons! They got to know somebody will die if they rush us. There ain't no other way."

Wend cocked the pistols in his belt. "Baird is right, gentlemen. We have no choice but to use our firelocks."

Hager looked at Eckert with horror in his eyes. "My God, how could it come to this? These are good men. Many I've known for years. We can't shoot at them! Think of their families!"

Wend ignored him and picked up his rifle from where it leaned on the porch rail. "Bradley, we need to fire a concerted volley." He turned to the others. "But a volley aimed just over their heads. Over their heads, you understand? With luck it may panic them and make them scatter."

Bradley stared at Wend. "Damn, Eckert, are you sure? You're asking me to fire at fellow Marylanders."

"No, damn it, I'm not sure it will work. But I am sure nothing else has a chance of stopping them."

The cavalryman still hesitated, doubt in his face.

Wend could wait no longer. He shouted, "All right, level your fire-locks!"

There was the briefest of hesitation, then everyone followed his command. For a moment Bradley remained hesitant, but in an instant he made ready with his pistol.

Wend held up his rifle and shouted to the mob. "Disperse! Disperse this instant or we will fire! Hear me—we *will* fire!"

There was a momentary silence, broken by McCarthy's voice. He was facing the mob. "Don't listen to him! They ain't goin' to fire at us."

He pointed back to the porch. "Hager won't let them fire at his own townsmen!" Then the Irishman turned and faced Wend, a defiant snarl on his face.

Wend suddenly realized what he must do. He put down his rifle and took out his pistols. He turned to the others and shouted, "Ready!" All took aim. "Now fire!"

There was a ragged volley, all the balls flying close over the heads of the rioters. Except for one ball. It came from the carefully aimed pistol in Wend's right hand, and it struck McCarthy in his right leg, just below the hip.

The big man collapsed to the ground, his hand on the wounded leg. He stared down at the wound, astonishment written over his face. Then he screamed in pain.

For a brief instant, the mob of men stared in silent shock at the big Irishman. Their eyes took in the bright blood flowing out onto the snow and the agony on his face.

And then, as one man, they turned and fled.

Some ran back up the wagon track. Others were scurrying in whatever direction they thought would keep them out of a second volley.

Wend screamed, "We must keep them running! Everyone fire a pistol!" He immediately fired the one in his left hand, and the others joined in.

But it was merely the icing on the cake for there was nothing to see now except the backs of running men and McCarthy lying in the muddy snow and his own blood, writhing in pain.

Bradley looked at him. "My God, Eckert, you did that intentionally!"

Wend shrugged. "You're damned right. McCarthy was the spirit behind the whole affair. I realized that if he went down, the rest wouldn't have the guts to carry on."

The Marylander said, "God help us for this night's work."

"Yes," replied Wend, "God, in his benevolence, is going to have to see his way clear to forgive me in particular. But in the meantime, I suggest we get Doctor Smyth down here to take care of McCarthy."

Suddenly Jon Hager called out. "Father, what's the matter?"

Wend looked at the elder Hager and saw that he had sagged down to the planking of the porch, his back up against the rails and his hands over his chest.

Jonathan Hager looked pasty white. "I can't breathe! Oh, My Lord, it's so hard to breathe!"

Jon said, "We must get him inside! Please help!"

With the son on one side and Donegal on the other, Hager was assisted into the common room and seated him at a chair near the hearth.

Meanwhile, Baird, Horner, and Seidal picked up McCarthy and carried the groaning Irishman to the common room, where they laid him out on a long table. Once there, he wriggled in pain, the leg still oozing blood.

Bradley called out to one of his men, "Parsons, get upstairs and bring Doctor Smyth posthaste! Tell him we have two men who require medical attention."

Parsons ran up the stairs. Meanwhile Cotter brought a cup of water for Hager and had one of the maids press a towel over McCarthy's wound.

Just as they were doing so, everyone in the common room was frozen by the loud bang of a pistol shot sounding from the upstairs hallway. All eyes went to the top landing of the stairs, where Parsons suddenly appeared, clutching his shoulder. He stumbled and fell, rolling down the stairs to the middle landing of the stairway.

The injured man groaned loudly but retained consciousness. He then shouted out, "There's armed men in the hall upstairs!"

Wend and Bradley rushed for the stairway, pistols drawn, followed by the Donegal, Baird, Horner, and Seidal.

Wend reached the top landing first and, shielding himself along the wall next to the door, peeked into the hallway. A tall, black-haired man with a heavy beard stood just outside of Connolly's door. Smyth's assistant, Ridgely, stood further down the hall, near the door to the back stairs.

As Wend peered down the hall, the bearded man stared at him. His eyes were deep blue and seemed to pierce right into Wend, as if instantly taking his measure.

After a second, the black-haired man turned his head and shouted into the room, "For God's sake, get him free! They know we're here! We must hasten!"

Wend shouted to the other men on the stairs, "It's Connolly's men—the ones who escaped! They're trying to rescue the prisoners!"

Wend pulled out a pistol and peered into the hallway again, and he nearly took a ball in his head as the black-haired man fired at him. He pulled back out of sight on the landing. Turning to the others, now just below him on the stairs, he shouted, "We must rush them!"

He lowered himself to the floor, where the gunmen would not be looking, and peaked into the hall. Now the man had been joined by a blond-haired, fresh-faced youth, who had a pistol in one hand and, Wend noticed, a thick packet of paper in the other. As he watched, the youth and Ridgely ran for the back stairs. The black-haired man fired another shot and then followed them. Wend squeezed off a shot at the man's back, but he missed the rapidly moving target.

In an instant all three were gone down the stairs. Wend jumped up and ran down the hall to the back door. Below he saw four men riding off into the night.

Momentarily Bradley was beside him. "Eckert, only Ridgely is gone. The rest are still here. Smyth told me he stayed to take care of Cameron."

Wend nodded, and the two of them went to Connolly's room. The colonel was sitting calmly in a chair at the desk, his arms crossed in front of him. His servant stood against the wall on the other side of the room. The bed was partially broken apart, but Connolly's chain was still firmly attached.

Connolly looked up at Bradley, then pointed to the chain. "Well, Captain, your precaution served its purpose." Then he laughed and remarked, "To paraphrase a well-known literary phrase, 'For want of an ax the endeavor was lost.'"

At that moment, Donegal looked into the room. "Doctor Smyth has agreed to go down and treat Hager and Pearson—and that bastard McCarthy."

Bradley said, "That's good. Thank God the doctor is favoring his medical duties over his political ones."

Wend stared at Connolly. "Yes, Warren, we can be thankful for that. But what I want to know is what Connolly has been up to all day." He walked over to a basket beside the desk and pulled out bits of cheap writing paper that had been torn up so the words were not decipherable. Then he looked at the desk and saw a container of ink and a quill. "Where did you get these writing materials?"

Connolly grinned. "That young maid, Helga, was most sympathetic and accommodating. I wanted to write a letter to my poor wife so that she would know what happened to me. She got me the materials and also said she would send it to Pittsburgh with a traveler."

Wend, still holding the scraps of paper, thought a long moment. "Damn, I saw a packet of paper in the hand of one of the rescuers."

Connolly raised his hands. "Eckert, I told you I wrote a letter to my wife."

Wend shook his head. "He's lying, Warren. That was a big packet of papers in the boy's hand. There was more than one letter there." He turned back to Connolly. "The fact is, you wrote a bunch of dispatches. Undoubtedly to your allies in the Ohio Country."

"I wrote a letter to my wife and family. That's all, Eckert."

Wend turned to the servant, a young man leaning up against the wall. "What's your name?"

"Me, sir? My name is Henry Fallow."

"Henry, you were here with him all day. What did he write and who was it to?"

The youth bit his lip, looked at Connolly, and said hesitantly, "Far as I know, it was a letter to his wife, just like he said."

Wend strode quickly to Fallow, grabbed him by his jacket, and dragged the startled youth across the room, depositing him on the floor in front of Connolly. He put his knee on the lad's chest, pulled a pistol from his belt, and without hesitation smashed the barrel hard across his face once and then a second time. Blood flowed from the boy's nose and the side of his cheek.

Fallow screamed in agony, and a tooth fell out.

Horror spread across Bradley's face. "My God, Eckert. You've broken his nose! You've sliced his cheek open! Have you gone crazy?"

"Shut up, Warren. I'm going to find out what Connolly's been doing."

He looked up at the Loyalist colonel. "Connolly, I'm going to keep beating him until you or he tells me the truth. If that doesn't work, I'm going to kill him in front of you. I'll jam the barrel of this pistol up his mouth and blow his head apart. Do you want him on your conscience, John?"

Connolly scowled. "You expect me to believe you'd execute him in cold blood?"

"You're the one who claimed I killed Richard Grenough precisely that way. If you believe that, you must know I'll do what is necessary here."

Wend cocked the pistol and pointed it at Fallow's face.

Bradley, his face a study in shock and anguish, said, "Eckert, I must demand that you stop this bloody insanity instantly. You are violating all the rules of Christian humanity and the treatment of prisoners. Cease this, I order you!"

Wend continued to glare at Fallows but said between clinched teeth, "Bradley, if you're too damned squeamish for this, go down to the common room and have a drink. Otherwise, keep your silence."

At that moment, Joshua Baird came to the room. He took in the scene at a glance, then leaned up against the door frame and crossed his arms. He remarked nonchalantly, "Wend, I believe you're going to have to shoot the lad. He seems to value his loyalty over his life. Might as well get it over with and move on to Connolly."

Wend made a show of gritting his teeth. "You're right, Joshua. The boy's too stupid to save himself." He put the pistol to Fallows' forehead. "You've got a moment to say your prayers, Henry!"

The youth made a primal scream, blood spraying out of his mouth, and then shouted, "Stop! Oh, God, please stop. I don't want to die!"

Connolly raised his hand. "Yes, for God's sake, stop terrorizing the lad. I'll tell you what you want to know."

Wend released Fallow and stood up. "Who were those letters to?"

"As you suggested, they are to men ready to stand by their king. One letter explains the precise details of the plan as worked out by myself, Dunmore, and Gage. Another letter provides the same information to the commander of the British garrison in Detroit so he and other army forces around the lakes can cooperate. There's also a list of the tribal chiefs who are sympathetic and ready to take the field."

Wend motioned toward the hallway. "Who was that black-haired man and the boy who were here?"

Connolly shrugged. "He's Munger. Richard Munger."

Joshua, still leaning on the door frame, stiffened. "I know Munger by reputation. He's a trader who works the Ohio Country, based out of Pittsburgh. They call him 'Black Dick Munger.' His company ain't nearly as big as Grenough's operation, but he does a good business with the tribes."

Connolly added, "That's right. He's called Black Dick for his raven hair and beard." He paused then continued, "And the boy is named Tom Harley. He's just a simple farm lad who is loyal to the crown."

Wend slid his pistol into his belt. "John, did you know Munger was coming back to attempt rescuing you and the others? Did you plan that out before he escaped back on the Conococheaque?"

"No, Eckert. I vow it was all a surprise to me. Dick Munger worked it out on his own." Connolly leaned back in his chair, a satisfied smile on his face. "You see, the fact is, it doesn't really matter that they couldn't free me, Eckert. Dick Munger is a resourceful, capable, and ruthless man. He's a captain in my Pittsburgh militia, and he knows all the chiefs in the Ohio Country. He helped me with the final treaty negotiations after the war last year. I can assure you the Indians know and trust him. With the information in those dispatches, he's quite as able as I to put the plan into operation. So I am confident that whatever happens to me, all will go on as before." He shook his head. "I just regret I won't be there to be part of it."

Wend turned to Baird and pointed to Fallow. "Joshua, get the lad downstairs so Smyth can patch his face up."

Then without another word, he strode from the room, walked down the hall, and descended the stairway.

He found the common room in disarray.

Smyth, medical bag by his side, was bent over McCarthy, examining his wound. A serving maid was assisting him. The Irishman was grimacing and making low groans. Wend looked over and saw that Jonathan Hager had been laid on another table and covered with a blanket for warmth. His eyes were closed, and he was deathly pale, his chest heaving as he gasped for breath. His son sat beside him, hands to his head. Cotter stood by with his hand on the younger Hager's shoulder. Parsons was slumped in a chair, and Helga was holding a cloth over his wound.

Wend asked the doctor, "What's going on with Hager?"

Smyth looked up from McCarthy's wound and shook his head. "It's his heart. I can't do anything for him except make him comfortable. I told his son he probably won't last out the night. Young Hager wanted to take him home, but moving the old man now will likely finish him immediately."

At that moment, the front door of the tavern swung open, and the tavern's stable boy, Charlie, hurried in, followed by a young, brown-haired woman in a heavy dark blue cape. Wend estimated that she was in her mid twenties. She hurried to the side of Jonathan Hager. "Good God, Jon! I came as soon as possible. What has happened to Father?"

Young Hager stood up and hugged the woman. "Rosanna, thank the Lord you're here in time. It's Father's heart." He then whispered to his sister, explaining what had transpired earlier.

She sobbed and took off her cape. Then she leaned over the old man and said, "Father, it's Rosanna. I'm here with you."

Jonathan Hager's eyes opened briefly, and he reached out with a feeble hand to take that of his daughter. She sat down beside the table, holding tight to his hand.

Wend saw that no one was tending the bar. He was about to go over and pour himself a drink when a thought hit him. He turned back and went to McCarthy's side. "Doctor Smyth, I need to talk to this man a minute."

Smyth shrugged. "If you must."

Wend leaned over the Irishman. "McCarthy, can you hear me all right?"

"Damn you. Of course I can hear you! What the hell do you want?"

"I've just got one question: Why did you start that riot? Last night you wanted to help us round up Connolly and his men. What made you think he wouldn't get justice at the hands of Congress?"

"It weren't all my idea. It was that man who rode in early in the morning along with two other travelers. He was tellin' everyone that Congress wouldn't do anything serious to Connolly. It made sense to everyone. The gentry take care of each other."

Wend's mind was racing. "What was this man's name?"

"Didn't really get no name. He was just a traveler, but he was from out west and he was mightily upset about the prospect of an Indian uprising. And mad at Connolly when he heard what he planned to do. He started stirring everybody up, sayin' we should go down and get him and hang him and the others."

"So you were convinced to lead the mob."

"Somebody needed to do it. By damn, I saw my duty!"

"And did the traveler come with you?"

"Well, he left the inn with us, but that was the last I recollect of him or his friends. I was busy, but I'm sure they must have been in the crowd."

"I see, McCarthy. And what did this man look like?"

"He was tall, and he had real black hair and a thick black beard."

Wend sighed deeply. "Thank you, McCarthy. You've been very helpful."

Then Wend walked over to the bar, found a jug of whiskey, and poured himself a cup of the spirits. He had never felt the need for a drink more. He was full of loathing for what he had just done to young Fallow upstairs, a lad who had committed no sin beyond being faithful to his employer.

He took a gulp of the whiskey and then looked up to see Bradley standing in front of him. The captain was staring with disdain in his eyes. Wend ignored the stare and pulled out a cup and held up the jug. "Well, Warren, that was nasty business up in Connolly's room. Here—do you want a drink?"

Bradley just continued to eye Wend. Finally, in a grave voice, he said, "No, Eckert, I have no stomach for a drink right now. And I must tell you this: over the last few days, I had come to respect and even admire you.

But what you just did to that youth is beyond the pale. Damn, sir, it was despicable! No gentleman would ever behave in such a manner!"

Wend couldn't suppress a laugh. It came out of his mouth sounding like an insane cackle. "Gentleman? Bradley, I've been accused of many things, but being a gentleman isn't one of them." He took another big gulp of the spirits, welcoming the bite of it as it went down. "Look, I'm a mechanic and a gunsmith, and I'm quite satisfied to be just that and nothing more. But life in this country has forced me into war and conflict, none of which I asked for."

Bradley stared at him. "I respect that you've seen hellish things. You told me about the death of your family on Forbes Road. But does that justify beating that lad, perhaps disfiguring him for life?"

"Warren, you've lived your life in the security of a tidewater plantation, and you have no idea what war is like out here. Listen carefully: when I was a youth living in a Pennsylvania village called Sherman Mill, I witnessed a close friend and his whole family burned to cinders by a war party at the beginning of Pontiac's War. In '74 Simon Donegal's wife watched her first husband die under a Shawnee hatchet and fled in terror through the night to save herself and her children. In last year's war with the Ohio Indians, I had the duty of burying an entire village of settlers massacred by a big war party of Shawnees and Mingos. An entire village! More than thirty men, women, and children." Wend took a deep breath. "I tell you, I'll do whatever it takes to stop another Indian border war. I won't see my family and the people of Winchester living in the terror of rampaging war parties."

Bradley bit his lip and looked down at the bar, digesting what he had heard.

Wend took another gulp of the whiskey, then continued in a calmer tone. "Warren, when I saw that packet of papers in the hand of that other boy—Tom Harley—in the hall upstairs, I knew at once that I had to find out what was in them. And I realized that Connolly would never tell us if I simply interrogated him. Even at point of violence against him. But I suspected that a man with his sense of honor would yield if a subordinate was being tortured. The only way to get information was to make him watch his young servant suffer. I tell you, I'm as disgusted with myself as you are, but in the end, it worked. We found out what we needed to know."

Then a voice interrupted. "And just what is it that you found out?"

Wend looked up to see Ballantyne standing a few feet away. Horst Seidal was with him, standing with his arms crossed in front of him. Obviously the two had been listening.

"I found out that our mission isn't over, Jedidiah. Far from it."

"What the devil do you mean, Eckert? We've got Connolly, Smyth, and Cameron. That was the mission."

"Connolly gave Richard Munger letters with the details of the plan and the people who are ready to help with it. He wrote dispatches to the military leaders around the Great Lakes, explaining the movements they must make. In short, he has to be stopped, or the uprising will still go on. The settlements along the border remain in mortal jeopardy. We've got to catch Munger and the three men with him, even it means riding all the way to Pittsburgh."

Ballantyne frowned, then turned to the Marylander. "Where do you stand on this, Bradley?"

"From what Connolly said, Munger has got the information he needs to carry out the plot, and he's a man who can do it. Look at how he organized this rescue. He needs to be stopped. But my written commission was to capture Connolly and deliver him to Congress. I intend to carry out those orders." He thought a moment. "In any case, I have only one fully fit man left, and we are not equipped for the mountainous, bitter conditions along Braddock's Road. In reality, we have no choice but to go eastward with the prisoners tomorrow."

Ballantyne stood thinking, obviously trying to calculate what to do.

"Jedidiah," Wend said, "understand this: my friends and I are riding for Wills Creek at dawn tomorrow. Winchester is not safe until Munger is hunted down and those dispatches captured. I don't give a damn whether you come along. You can ride for Williamsburg with your pack-train of ammunition and undoubtedly will be welcomed with acclaim. But if you have any regard for the people in the Virginia settlements, you'll ride with us."

Seidal spoke up. "He's right, Jedidiah. This Munger must be stopped."

Ballantyne turned to his sergeant. "Horst, you're the one who wanted to go back to the regiment, as you said, to do 'real soldiering.' Now you want to go on?"

"For God's sake, Jedidiah, can't you see things have changed? Eckert is right. I've got a wife and children on the border. They and a lot of other families–your neighbors–are in danger. We're the only ones in a position to prevent this uprising of the tribes." He shrugged. "Besides, Jedidiah, if you bring those packs of powder and Munger *and* the dispatches to Williamsburg, you'll have made your reputation." Then he added, "That's what you're really after, isn't it?"

The captain stood quietly for a few seconds, considering what had been said. Then he took on a look of determination. "All right, Eckert, we'll resume the pursuit tomorrow. And remember, I'm not just taking packs and dispatches back to Williamsburg. I'm taking you also."

Wend looked at the captain and permitted himself a thin smile. "That, Ballantyne, remains to be seen."

Ballantyne ignored Wend's words and turned to Seidal. "Come on, Sergeant; we must make preparations to ride."

As they had been talking, Joshua had helped young Fallows, still unsteady on his feet, down to see the doctor. Now he came over to join Wend and Bradley.

"You gonna share some of that whiskey with me, or are you hoardin' it for yourself?"

Wend pulled out a cup and poured him a drink. "Joshua, we need to ride after Munger and the others tomorrow at dawn."

"You had to bring that up, with me about to enjoy Cotter's spirits." He took a sip. "But you're speaking the truth. I talked with Donegal and Horner upstairs about what Connolly told us, and they're expectin' it."

"Good," said Wend. "We'll need young Abel Reimann to help us make up time between here and Wills Creek. I'll ask Cotter to get in touch with him."

Meanwhile, Bradley was standing quietly with a thoughtful look on his face. Then he spoke up. "You know, Eckert, the timing of that riot outside was a fortunate coincidence for Munger and his men. It created a distraction which made it easy for them to get close to the inn and slip upstairs undetected."

Wend laughed. "It was no coincidence. Munger started that riot."

"What do you mean, Eckert?"

"Just what I said. While you were still upstairs, I dragged the information out of that Irishman over on the table. Munger and the other two got back here this morning; then he spent hours at the other inn, stirring up the men in there. Then, when they were drunk and had reached a fever pitch, he duped McCarthy into leading them to this place. Meanwhile he and his men slipped away to rescue Connolly while we were preoccupied. It was an orchestrated diversion."

A shocked look came over Bradley's face. "Munger's obviously a very clever man."

Joshua looked between Wend and Bradley. "You got that right, Captain. I've heard stories about Black Dick over the years. He'll keep his party on their business and travelin' hard. I wager he'll make no mistakes and he'll take advantage of any mistakes we make in the pursuit."

Just at that moment, there was a great sob from Rosanna Hager. Wend looked over to see her put her hand to her mouth and sob again, "Father, father!"

Jonathan Hager was gasping for breath, his body writhing in pain, his eyes and mouth wide open. Then, in another instant, his body jerked a final time and then he lay perfectly still.

His daughter shrieked in grief. Jon put his arm around his sister.

Doctor Smyth quickly joined them, and put his ear to the elder Hager's chest, then checked for breath at the man's nose and mouth. He looked over at the brother and sister, shook his head, and then gently, respectfully pulled the blankets over Jonathan's Hager's face.

Junior took his sister's arm. "Come, Rosanna, I'll get you home."

Cotter motioned toward the table where Jonathan lay, and quietly said to Junior, "Don't worry, I'll get your father's remains moved to the house immediately."

Rosanna looked over at the counter, directly at Bradley, Wend, and Joshua. The grief on her face became overlaid with anger. She pulled away from her brother and walked defiantly to the bar, confronting the three of them.

"This is all because of you! You and those despicable men from Pittsburgh. You rode into our quiet town, and in two short days destroyed the peace! We were living in harmony and prosperity, and your presence has led to riots, our people being shot at, and," she broke into another sob, then continued, "And the death of our father and the founder of this town. This all broke his heart! For God's sake, I say go! Go and take your conflict and violence with you!"

Bradley bowed his head slightly, and said formally, and with great sympathy, "Miss Hager, we are profoundly sorry for the death of your father. We apologize that our mission has led to such disruptive events. However, your father understood the importance of our quest, and greatly assisted us in completing it. When your grief subsides, I truly hope that you will understand and feel pride that his last acts were in support of the cause of our province and the Continental Congress."

With tears streaming down her cheeks, Rosanna replied, "You speak to me in such fine, gentlemanly words, Captain, but they won't bring back my father, nor restore the tranquility of Elizabethtown." She turned on her heel and began to walk toward the door.

Wend called out, "Miss Hager!"

She turned and looked at him, the anger still burning in her eyes. "And what is it that you have to say?"

"Miss Hager, as you desire, we will indeed *all* leave in the morning. Bradley and the prisoners to the east, and the rest of us to ride westward in pursuit of the remaining conspirators. But be aware that our departure will not bring a return of peace, for there is none. There is *war* throughout the land; war at Boston, war in the tidewater of Virginia, and war is spreading like a contagion to other places in these colonies. Militia are drilling in every town. Regiments are forming and marching. Neighbors are turning against each other. People are being burned out of their homes just for what they think. And if the men we seek escape, you will soon enough see the flames of war right here; war such has not been seen since we fought the French or the Ohio Indians in the days of Pontiac and Guyasuta. So when you go home, indeed pray for your father's soul; but I beg you, pray hard also for our success, for in doing so you pray for your own safety."

Rosanna Hager stared at Wend for a long moment with dread in her eyes, but said nothing. Then she turned on her heel and quickly strode out the door, followed by her brother.

They all stared after her in silence.

Then Bradley turned to back to the bar. "I'll have that drink now, Eckert."

Wend poured a measure of the whiskey. "Warren, I hope we can part on a note of respect. I certainly wish you luck in your journey with Connolly, and good fortune when you take your troop to Washington's army."

Bradley took a deep breath. "Wend, I can't condone your treatment of that lad upstairs, but I regretfully must admit you got important information from Connolly. I'll not allow us to separate in anger and recrimination. And knowing the urgent cause you ride for, I will offer my wish for success." He held up his cup. "Your health, sir."

Wend did the same, "And yours, Captain."

After they had tasted the whiskey, Bradley said, "Wend, let me repeat what I have said before: You must be wary of Ballantyne; take care to sleep with an eye open and a pistol at hand. I suspect the man has no intention of taking you back to Williamsburg alive."

Wend put a hand on Bradley's shoulder. "The truth is, Warren, I must play a delicate game; we need Ballantyne and his men to assure victory against Munger, but I vow to you the day will come when those blackguards will face a reckoning."

Chapter Twelve

BRADDOCK ROAD

The nine riders started to descend a long slope, came round a curve of the road, and immediately had the town of Wills Creek in sight. It was situated in bowl-shaped valley formed where Wills Creek itself flowed into the Potomac. The walls of the valley were a panorama of tree-covered mountains.

The remains of Fort Cumberland, an abandoned artifact of the French War, were a dominant feature of the landscape perched on a high bluff near the mouth of the creek. Wend reflected that like Fort Loudoun in Winchester, undoubtedly much of its timbers were being absorbed by residences and business establishments of the growing town.

Abel Reimann said to Ballantyne and Wend, "I recommend we head for the Stockade Inn, run by a man named Hurley. It's the biggest and is just by the old fort, right up from the bridge across the creek. They keep a good stock of hay, which we'll need for the horses."

Ballantyne asked, "Can they handle caring for our packtrain when it arrives?"

"Yeah, they got plenty of room. They can stable the pack horses and stow the packs when Richter gets here."

The guide was referring to a man who had been hired to follow them with the Virginia share of Connolly's train of ammunition trade-good packs. The plan was for it to be held in Wills Creek until the party returned, hopefully with the remnants of Connolly's men as prisoners.

Donegal, riding near Wend, said, "Well, young Abel here has got us here in very good time. Those back trails he took us over saved a goodly number of miles. There's 'na doubt in my mind we've made up some time on Munger and his crew."

Seidal said, "Look ahead—there's a campfire up there at the side of the road. Who could that be?"

They rode onward, and in a few moments the question was answered. Two men in rough clothes and rifles in hand walked out onto the wagon track and signaled for the party to pull up.

Ballantyne called out, "What's toward?"

"We're from the Will's Creek militia. We're lookin' for a certain party." The speaker signaled toward the fire, and another five men, all armed with firelocks, came out onto the wagon track.

One of them, a man in his late twenties, said, "I'm Ensign Shockley. We're askin' you all to dismount." As he spoke, his men spread out so as to have the riders in a cross fire if any resistance were offered.

Ballantyne laughed. "Let me guess: you're lookin' for a man named Connolly?"

"Yes. How did you know?"

"We're from the First Virginia Regiment. We was sent out by the Virginia Committee of Safety to hunt down and capture Connolly and his men. Fact is, we got him just outside of Elizabethtown. He's on his way to Philadelphia right now as a prisoner."

The ensign looked doubtful. "How do I know the truth of what you're sayin'? Could be you're in with Connolly and tryin' to distract us from our work."

Ballantyne waved to Seidal. "Horst, show him the papers from Colonel Henry."

Seidal dismounted and pulled out the letters from Henry and the committee. "Here are our orders. Can you read, or do you want me to read them to you?"

"I can damn well read," responded the ensign. "Let me see those papers." He took the orders and motioned to the man who had initially flagged them down. "Sergeant Hannah, look at these with me."

The two men went over the papers, their mouths moving silently as they read.

Presently Shockley looked up. "These seem in order."

He called out to the others. "Hey, boys, it looks like we can go home. They got that bastard Connolly!"

Wend said, "Before you go, we've got a question for you. Some of Connolly's men escaped capture and are heading west for Pittsburgh. That's who we're after now. There were three men and a young boy. Their leader has raven-black hair and a heavy beard of the same shade. You seen them pass by here? It probably would have been sometime yesterday."

"We relieved another squad of men this morning. We wouldn't be able to tell you 'bout yesterday. But ain't nobody like that came by today."

The Stockade Inn was a prosperous establishment that obviously benefited from being at the starting place of Braddock's Road and thus a stopping place for traffic going to or coming back from the Forks of the Ohio. The inn itself was a substantial, two-storied building situated next to the old fort, and it was, to a large extent, constructed of timbers reused from the walls. And Abel was right about its facilities for their mounts; there was a large stable and ample pasture. A shed was used to stow a great amount of hay and oats. There was a spacious yard where several wagons were parked.

The proprietor, Kent Warden, was a tall, spare man in a crisp apron. In fact, walking into the common room, Wend was immediately impressed with the clean and neat appearance of the place. Preparations were underway for the evening meal, and pleasant smells of cooking food permeated the room.

Both Eckert and Ballantyne had come in together, and the proprietor greeted them cordially. Ballantyne explained their mission and asked if Munger and his men had stayed at the inn on the previous night.

Warden shook his head. "No, we had no group meeting your description. But there are two other inns and several taverns in and around the town. You'd best send someone to inquire at those other establishments."

Ballantyne nodded and looked at Wend. "All right, I'll send Seidal around to make inquiries at the other places."

Wend thought of something. "Jedidiah, we certainly should do as Mr. Warden suggests. But it's possible they didn't stay here in the town last night. Perhaps they rode through continued traveling right up to nightfall and then camping along the road. That would help open their lead on us."

"If Seidal can't find anyone who saw Munger and his men, we'll know that's what they did."

Wend nodded. "Good point, Jedidiah, but let's have Joshua go with him."

"Eckert, you think Seidal can't do the job?"

"I'm sure he can. But Joshua has a better knowledge of the town and people around here. He may be able to find out more than Horst alone and see if anyone's seen a suspicious group who didn't stay at a common establishment."

"All right, fine. Send him along."

Ballantyne made arrangements to camp in the yard and then left the common room without further comment. Wend took a room for the Winchester men and then ordered a drink from Warden.

The proprietor looked after Ballantyne and said, "I may be off the mark, but it seems that relations between your captain and you are perhaps not the most cordial."

Wend laughed. "Very observant. We are thrown together solely for this mission, and we see eye to eye on very little."

Warden grinned in response, then reached up to a post that supported a ceiling beam next to the counter. He pulled off a handbill that had been posted there, crumpled it in his hand, and said, "We don't need this any longer now that this fellow Connolly has been taken."

"Well, it was a smart move by the Winchester Committee of Safety to send the information up here."

The proprietor laughed again. "Indeed. And I had a long talk with the rider who brought the information to our sheriff. He stayed here overnight before riding back." He shook his head. "There's an amusing story behind it. It seems the wife of one of the men in your party—she's the wife of a gunsmith—literally burst in on the committee at one of their meetings and shamed them into the action. She must be one formidable woman." He motioned toward Wend. "Undoubtedly you know the man." He shook his head. "Confidentially, I don't doubt that he treads lightly around his wife."

Wend grinned, took a deep drink, and said, "She is truly formidable, and indeed I tread lightly and with great tact on all matters with her."

Understanding flowed quickly into Warden's eyes. He chuckled, then picked up the whiskey jug and poured Wend another drink. "This one, my friend, is on the house."

—⚊⚊—

After downing Warden's whiskey, Wend headed back to the stable to help the others finish putting up the horses and get their kit up to the sleeping room. As he approached the stable, he heard voices shouting angrily and hurried to see what was causing the ruckus.

He entered just as a roar of several voices went up, and he quickly saw the cause of the disturbance. A fight between Horner and Taddy Carlin was in progress. Horner was looking stunned on the ground, a hand to his cheek, blood oozing between the fingers. Carlin was standing over him with clenched fists. As Wend watched, Horner sprang to his feet and catapulted himself at Carlin, butting his head into the soldier's midsection and then wrapping his arms around him. He knocked Taddy off-balance, and both went to the ground. The Ulster man landed with his back down in the dirt but smashed his hands against Horner, pushing him away. Andrew swung and hit Carlin in the face, then again grabbed him, attempting to get him flat on the ground and pin him with a knee. He failed, with Carlin slipping away and lurching to his feet. The two began circling and exchanging punches.

Joshua and Simon stood at one side, and all the First Virginia men stood on the other. Wend called to Baird, "What led to this?"

"In case you ain't noticed, them Carlin brothers have been baitin' Andrew since the fight at the Red Vixen." He motioned toward the fighters. "These two were both workin' on the horses a little while ago, and Carlin insulted that blond maid Emily and told Horner he ought to check his crotch because he probably got a pox from her. Horner answered by smackin' Carlin up against the side of the stall. Taddy punched back. This has been goin' on now for a couple of minutes."

Wend said, "Horner isn't a tavern brawler. I'll wager Carlin has lots of experience."

Donegal, leaning against the rail of a stall, said, "Horner ain't doin' too bad. He's bleedin' a little from his nose, and there's that cut on his cheek. But he's gettin' his licks in on Carlin. Taddy's goin' to know he was in a fight."

Wend turned to Ballantyne. "We don't need this, Jedidiah! Why don't you call Carlin off?"

The captain gave Wend a sly look. "This has been buildin' up for days. And now Horner started it. Let it play out. It'll teach that apprentice of yours not to interfere in another man's business, particularly with harlots."

"Wrong answer, Ballantyne! We don't need anyone nursing injuries on this ride. I'm going to break it up before someone gets really hurt."

Ballantyne threw back his head and laughed. "Going to stop it before your man gets the worst of it, are you now?"

Wend said, "He's my apprentice, and it's my responsibility to look out for him." He stepped in between the two men and grabbed Horner by the arm. "It's over, Andrew. Get on over to the inn. We'll get you cleaned up."

Taddy shouted, "Get away from him, Eckert! I'm goin' to finish teachin' him a lesson." He stepped toward them, fists raised.

But as he took his first step, Seidal stuck his leg out, tripping Carlin, whose momentum sent him face down into the dirt. The sergeant stood over Carlin and remarked, "Eckert's right, Taddy. It's over."

Ballantyne spat. "Damn it, Seidal! Whose side are you on?"

"I ain't on anybody's side in a personal fight. Like I been tellin' you, I just want to finish this job." Seidal eached down and picked Taddy up off the ground by the scruff of his collar. "You ain't helpin' things any, Carlin."

Wend gave Horner a shove on the shoulder, and the lad walked off toward the main building without saying another word.

"Jedidiah," Wend said, "it's getting late. Let's get Seidal and Baird off on a look around town to see what they can find out about Munger and his crew."

Joshua smiled. "Yes, indeed, Horst. Let's go. I'll show you the town—

what there is of it."

Wend and Donegal headed for the inn.

They found a morose Andrew sitting at a table before the hearth staring into the fire. There were still streaks of blood on his face.

Wend got a rag from the bar, dipped it in a bucket of water, and handed it to the apprentice. "Here, Andrew, finish cleaning your face." Then he waved to a maid and had her deliver three drinks.

"Joshua says the Carlin brothers have been baiting you over Emily ever since we left the Red Vixen," Wend said. He took a sip of his drink. "You've got to let the words of bullies roll off your back like raindrops."

"I don't mind what they say about me, but he called Emily a filthy harlot. Said she was likely carrying a pox."

"It's simple envy because they know she rejected Taddy's money and then slept with you by her own choice."

Horner was silent.

Donegal smiled slyly and said quietly, "You're makin' sense, Wend, but the truth is the lad isn't going to listen. He's smitten with the lass."

Horner blushed, then looked around at the other two, took a deep breath, and said, "I've never known a girl like Emily."

Wend said softly, "Horner, no man ever forgets the first time he's with a woman. And despite her youth, Emily knows how to please a man and make him feel special. And she felt obligated to you because you defended her." He looked into his apprentice's eyes. "I wouldn't read too much into your time with her."

"It wasn't like that, sir."

"Of course it was. Regardless of how you feel, Andrew, you'll probably never see her again. And Widow McGraw is taking her and all her other girls up to the army. Think what she'll be doing every day and how many men she'll be with. And Emily, young and sweet as you think she is, has agreed to that life."

Horner bit his lip and stared into the fire.

"Now, Andrew, once we deal with Munger and his men, we'll be going back to Winchester. I know you've been spending time with a pretty farm girl there, a German like us." Wend asked, "What's her name, Andrew?"

"Freida, sir. Frieda Haldorf. They have a farm just west of the Battletown Inn."

"I know the Haldorf family. They're very good, industrious people. You should get back with Frieda and consider how she or another girl like her could fit into your life. You'll be finished with your apprenticeship in just over a year, and you know you'll have a job with me—or if you choose, you can go out on your own as a journeyman. A girl like that can be a great help and comfort to a man as he makes his way in trade."

"Sir, I know your counsel is wise and you have lived the way you advise me. I should want to make a life with a wonderful, *virtuous* woman like Mrs. Eckert, whom I admire very much."

Donegal rolled his eyes and burst into a paroxysm of coughing. He put his hand to his mouth, then patted his chest, and said, "Pay me no heed. Some of the whiskey went down the wrong way."

Wend frowned and shot him an angry look, then turned back to his apprentice. "Andrew, finish your drink. It will settle you. Then go up to our room and get a good night's sleep. We'll be starting out on Braddock's Road early tomorrow."

After Horner had ascended the stairs, Simon gave Wend a wry look. "Interesting advice I see you given' the lad. Seems I recall a young gunsmith in the town of Sherman Mill who once defended the honor of a tavern tart, using a log to beat the man who insulted her until he was never the same in the head again. Then he married the girl to keep her from the shame of havin' a bastard son by the same man." He put his hand to his chin and looked at the ceiling as if searching his memory. "Now am I remembering that all proper and correct, or has twelve years' time corrupted my recollections?"

"Shut up, Donegal. It's not really the same."

"Ah, now, laddie, it sounds damn similar to me."

"It's all water over the dam. And once we get home, if that girl Frieda knows her business, she'll soon make Horner forget all about Emily."

"I'm 'na so sure, laddie. You should know that our young Andrew was thinkin' of goin' to follow the army as a gunsmith once he finishes his apprenticeship. Lookin' for a way to find that little maid again."

"Good God, I thought he had more sense than that!" Wend shook his head. "At least for the moment, he's besotted with the girl." He took a deep breath, then continued, "In any case, that's more than a year away. God willing, he'll get over his infatuation. Besides, after a year following the army, Emily won't be the same girl—if she's even alive. You know that's true."

"There's 'na denyin' that, but you'll never convince the lad of that right now. But maybe you're right. Perhaps he'll settle down and find himself satisfied with the charms of a Frederick County girl."

"I'll make sure of that. When we get back, I'm going to keep him so busy he won't have time to moon around about dear Miss Emily."

—⁂—

Baird walked into the common room just under two hours later, called out for a drink, and sat down with Wend and Simon. "Well, our fugitive friends didn't stay at any of the other inns or taverns in the town."

Donegal asked, "So you didn't find any word of them here?"

Joshua grinned. "Didn't say that. Just said they didn't stay at a public house."

Wend pursed his lips in irritation. "All right, stop playing games, Joshua. What have you got?"

"They sure 'nuff came through yesterday. They went directly to a horse trader's place on the west side of town and exchanged horses."

"Oh, shit! You mean they've got fresh mounts?"

"Yeah, they went to see a man named Holloway. Keeps a farm at the base of the mountains to the west. He's got good-sized herds of Conestoga horses, farm horses, and riding animals. Anything that might be needed along the road here." Baird looked at his two companions. "Holloway said they tried to trade even for new horses, but he looked at their mounts and said they'd have to give him some extra."

Wend cocked his head. "They had enough hard coin to do that?"

"Yeah, more than enough. Holloway said they didn't even try to dicker. A man who fits Munger's description went to a saddlebag, pulled out a purse, and gave him the money straightaway."

Donegal said, "So did they camp at his place last night?"

"Nope. Holloway said they had a bit of an argument among themselves. Some wanted to stay overnight, but Munger quashed that idea. He had them transfer their gear to the new animals and ride out just a'fore dusk. Said they needed to make a few more miles to the west before they bedded down."

Wend looked into the fire. "Munger obviously knows the road and is going to push them hard. Now with their fresh horses, we're going to be hard put to catch them before Pittsburgh. And there's no telling what we'll be able to do if they get there. They're liable to go to ground or continue out into the Ohio Country, and we'll never find them. They undoubtedly have friends who can hide them from us once they get to the forks."

Joshua raised his finger. "That's true, but that ain't the worst of it. I got to talkin' with Holloway, and he said the word he got is that after Connolly left Pittsburgh months ago, Pennsylvania was able to take control of the town back."

"Damn," said Wend, "that means we won't get much help from the local authorities when they understand we're from Virginia."

Baird laughed. "Yeah, after last year, they ain't gonna be too friendly with any Virginians."

Donegal raised an eyebrow. "Don't tell them you was on Dunmore's staff. They're liable to throw you in the jail."

Wend shook his head sadly. "This is wonderful. Just bloody wonderful."

Donegal said, "Seriously, if they get to Pittsburgh, I'm thinkin' we'll 'na ever get them."

Baird took a deep drink from his cup. "Well, we'll just have to get them before Pittsburgh." He gave them a thoughtful look. "Now, when we traveled Braddock's Road last year, we had two Conestoga wagons with us. That meant we had to stay on the road the whole way."

Wend perked up. "What are you saying—you can bypass parts of the road?"

"Sure enough. The road mainly follows the path of the old Nemacolin Trail, which was for people on foot and riding horses. But when Braddock and his troops cut the wagon track, they had to straighten the road and find easier grades that would allow Conestogas, carts, and the army's artillery train to pass. Years before that, I traveled the old path and I can recall a goodly number of horse trails that are more direct." He shrugged. "With reasonable weather that keeps them trails passable, I think we can make some good time up."

Simon raised an eyebrow. "That's bonnie news, but now all we got to do is convince Ballantyne to let Joshua pick out the way. Way he feels about us, that might not be very easy."

Wend thought a long moment. "You're right. He'll be suspicious, but I think he'll agree in the end. The man wants to catch Munger and take him back to Williamsburg more than anything else in his life." Wend stood up and said with heavy sarcasm, "Come on, Joshua, let's go talk this out with our most benevolent captain."

Baird stood up. "Yeah, I'm with you, but you got to tell me one thing before we go: What the hell does 'benevolent' mean?"

———w———

When the sun was just past its zenith three days later, the eight Virginians, all muffled against the cold, gusty wind that blew from the northwest, pulled up on a low ridge and looked down on a small settlement
mostly made up of log buildings.

Joshua Baird smiled and announced, "There she be—Ransome's
Tavern."

Wend added, "The village seems to have grown a little since we were
here last year."

"That's 'na lie," said Simon. "There's a couple more cabins. Looks
like one of them's got a blacksmith shop attached."

Ballantyne growled, "You people seem to know a lot about this place."

Wend answered, "Donegal's wife lived here for several months with
the people who run the store across from the tavern. That was last year
after Shawnees killed her first husband and burnt her farmstead down."
Wend looked over at Simon. "Simon married her right in the store last
winter."

A warm look passed over the Highlander's face. "That I did. And I've
no regrets."

Joshua laughed and said, "Just wait until some time passes." Then
he said, "Let's get the horses into the tavern stable. And hurry into the
common room and get ourselves warm." He paused and then remarked,
"Ransome will be able to tell us when Munger and his crowd came
through here."

Ballantyne screwed up his face. "What makes you think they stopped
here?"

Wend answered, "This is the only tavern or inn for miles. It's almost
certain they will have stopped, at least for a while, if only to rest their
horses."

Wend, Joshua, and Ballantyne entered the common room, which felt almost oppressively hot after days out in the weather. Ransome, a man in his early forties with a thickening waist and receding hair, looked up from the bar to look at his new patrons. Suddenly recognition spread across his face. "Eckert! Joshua Baird! God above, what brings you here in this time of year?"

Joshua laughed. "We'll talk about that presently. Right now, we need some good spirits!"

"I've got some tolerable whiskey. But I'm having trouble getting good stuff in the winter."

"As long as it's got a punch, I'll drink whatever you got!"

Wend smiled. "Yes, three drinks, Paul, of whatever you do have." He motioned toward the captain. "This is Jedidiah Ballantyne, a captain in the First Virginia Regiment."

As he poured drinks, Ransome repeated, "What brings you here?"

Wend responded, "We're looking for some men who should have come through here yesterday."

Ballantyne spoke up. "It's four men led by a man with black hair and a full beard of the same color. He's got two other men and a young boy with him."

Ransome didn't hesitate. "They were here for about an hour yesterday afternoon. Rested and grained their horses, then rode out bound for the ferry on the Youghiogheny. Why are you looking for them?"

Wend explained the conspiracy.

"My God!" exclaimed Ransome. "We don't need another Indian War."

Ballantyne frowned. "How far is it to the river, Ransome?"

"About fifteen miles to what they call the Great Crossing, where a Scotsman named Caldwell runs the ferry."

"Shit!" the captain snarled. "They're undoubtedly over the river by now."

Ransome put his hand to his chin. "Just hold on, Captain. That ain't necessarily true."

"What do you mean?" Ballantyne retorted.

"In the winter, Caldwell doesn't run a regular schedule. He just crosses when he's got enough trade to make it pay with that big scow of his. It's sized to take a couple of wagons at a time. He needs ten men to row it across." The tavern keeper shrugged. "So they might have had to sit waiting for a while until he's ready to make a run."

Wend was suddenly fully alert. "Ballantyne, do you understand what this means? We have a chance of catching them today or early tomorrow. We need to water and feed the horses and then take the road."

"Eckert, the horses are tired, and the sun will soon be going down. And ain't you the one who is always for lookin' out for the animals?" Ballantyne gritted his teeth. "Besides, we don't know they're still held up at the river. It could just mean blowing the horses for nothin'."

"Yes, Jedidiah, I like to care for the horses. But the chance of ending this race is worth the gamble. And as for darkness, remember, we know this part of the road well. I say we leave as soon as possible."

"All right. I don't like it, but there is some sense to it. But if this ends in naught, I'm holding you responsible." Ballantyne downed the rest of his drink and then headed for the door. "I'll tell the men what we're planning."

Ransome watched the Virginia captain leave. Then in a voice dripping with sarcasm, said, "What an estimable man."

Just then Donegal came in. "We got the horses watered, unsaddled, and into the barn." He looked at Ransome. "You're a sight for sore eyes. Give me a wee bit of drink, and then I'll be going over to the store to say hello to Ma and Pa Kertin."

Wend smiled. "You need to make it fast, Simon. We're riding for the Great Crossing within the hour."

"'Na don't be playin' games with me."

"It's true, Simon." Wend explained the situation to the Highlander.

Donegal listened, a serious look on his face, and then said to the proprietor, "Well, Ransome, me lad, if we be ridin' into the darkness, you better make that a big cup of spirits!"

After Donegal had finished his drink, Wend and the Highlander walked over to the Kertins' store, which was directly across from the tavern.

Paul Kertin was standing behind the counter facing the shelves, his finger moving as he counted through some of his merchandise.

Donegal called out, "Pay attention now, Paul! You've got some customers."

"Oh, now, you've made me lose my count." He turned to see who had entered, then his eyes opened wide. "Simon! Wend Eckert! The last people I expected to see. What are you doin' here?"

Wend said, "We're on a mission for the Virginia Committee of Safety. There's treachery afoot." He explained about Connolly's conspiracy and the pursuit of Munger and his crew.

"My God, let me call in Lizzie. She'll want to hear about this." He pointed to Donegal. "And about Sally and little Louisa and baby Henry. They're like our own grandchildren."

Wend nodded. "By all means."

Kertin went to the door that led to the living quarters in the back of the store. "Ma! Ma! Come on out here right away, and see who's in the store!"

A voice answered, "Now why are you callin' me when I'm in the middle of cookin'?" A heavyset, round-faced, dark-haired woman appeared at the door, beads of perspiration on her checks and forehead from working in front of the hearth. She stood wiping her hands on the well-worn, food-spotted white apron that she wore over her gray gown. Then she saw who stood in the store, and a look of pleasure came over her face. "Simon, my boy! Wend!" Then she asked, "How's our beautiful stepdaughter and precious little Louisa and the little baby?" She waved her finger at the Highlander. "I tell you, the place feels so empty after you came and stole them from us."

Donegal grinned. "They're all in great health, last time I saw them. They love livin' on the farm, and Sally is a great help with the whiskey makin'."

Paul said, "Ma, they're here on serious business. They're chasin' a party of the king's men who aim to set the Indians to raidin' the settlements again."

"Oh, no! Not after last year. I can't stand the idea of seeing the smoke of burning farmsteads and buryin' people we know." She shook her head. "The blackguards! Who are these men?"

Wend said, "They're Loyalists and were organized by John Connolly."

Kertin said, "That bastard."

Donegal nodded. "The truth is we caught him back in Maryland. But there's still a bunch of his crew headin' for the Ohio Country to stir up the tribes. They were here yesterday. Three men and a young boy led by a man named Dick Munger."

"Munger? I know him. He's an Indian trader, works out of Pittsburgh. Got a black beard that covers most of his face." Kertin shook his head. "He's been through here before. Never did like the look of the man. Always seemed to be hidin' his true feelin' behind all that hair on his face."

Wend nodded. "That's the one. He's carrying orders to rouse all the tribes who fought in the war last year and any others he can get to take up the hatchet. And a detachment of the king's foot is preparing to come down from the forts up around Detroit and the lakes to help."

Ma Kertin frowned. "Did you say a young boy?"

Donegal nodded. "Yes, a fair-haired lad no more than fourteen or fifteen."

Lizzie said, "Why, indeed, there was a youngster like that in here yesterday afternoon. A fresh-faced, innocent-lookin' lad. His name is Tom. He talked with me for a while and said he was anxious to get home. And then he bought some molasses candy. He couldn't wait to take a taste of it, even before he left."

Wend answered, "That's him."

Ma Kertin shook her head. "He should be at home with his mother, tendin' the farm animals. Not ridin' on some murderous scheme like this. How did he get mixed up in the plot?"

"I don't know how or why they recruited him, but he's been in the middle of it all."

Lizzie shrugged. "It's the times. Well, if there's the chance of another war with the tribes, I'm glad Sally and the children are safe in Winchester."

Wend and Donegal exchanged glances but remained quiet. Wend thought, *There's no purpose in worrying Lizzie by telling her about the full scope of Connolly's plan and that Winchester is a prime target.*

They stayed for a few minutes more, Donegal filling in the Kertins about the new house he was building for his family and their life on Eckert Ridge and in Frederick County. Then the two explained that they must ride out to continue the pursuit.

Ma Kertin said in a bitter voice, "Yes, you must stop them. You must run them down for the sake of all in the border country."

Wend looked into her eyes. "Lizzie, from everything I know, Munger is a hard man. But we are harder. We *will* get the job done."

The woman smiled tightly. "I know you will. Pray God goes with you both…and even that scoundrel Joshua Baird."

—⚬—

The night was cold but clear, with stars bright overhead as they made the long descent down to the Youghiogheny River. A small village surrounded the ferry landing at the Great Crossing, which included a combination tavern-inn that served as the headquarters for the ferry service, along with numerous houses and a store. Bright light flooded from the windows of the common room of the inn.

The Virginia party dismounted in front of the building. Wend could make out the large, square-ended scow tied up at the ferry landing and several small boats also moored at the dock or run up on the riverbank.

Ballantyne called out, "We need to be cautious, and keep your pistols at hand! It's possible that Munger and his men are inside the ordinary if they couldn't get across today."

Wend said, "We should send some men around to the back in case we surprise them and they bolt."

Ballantyne nodded. "Seidal, you and Johnny go around back and stop anyone coming out that way until I tell you different."

Then he led the rest of them into the tavern.

There were only three customers in the room, and Wend quickly saw that none of them were the conspirators.

Ballantyne went up to the counter, where a young man was working. The lad asked, "Gentlemen, can I help you with something?"

"We need to see Caldwell, the ferryman. Where can he be found?"

The youngster stepped to a door that led to the kitchen and called, "Pa, there's a man wants to see you!"

In a few seconds a tall, wiry, man with red hair who was dressed in a white shirt, vest, and breeches walked out through the door, wiping his hands with a rag. He looked at the group of bundled-up men standing together before the counter, raised an eyebrow, and said in a heavy Scots accent, "And 'na who is it that wants to be seeing John Caldwell?"

Ballantyne cleared his throat. "I'm Captain Jedidiah Ballantyne of the First Virginia Regiment. My men and I are here on business of the Virginia Committee of Safety."

"Virginia? Now sure, and this is Pennsylvania, at least ways this year it is. What do Virginians want here?"

"We're looking for four men led by one named Munger. He's got black hair and a heavy beard."

"You don't need to describe Black Dick Munger to me. Known him for four years, maybe five. He's a trader out of Pittsburgh. Travels the road here now and then." He shrugged. "You got business with the fellow?"

Wend thought, *The man's playing games with us. And he's stalling.* Wend looked over at Ballantyne and saw impatience and anger coming over his face.

The captain's voice took an edge. "That's not important at the moment. Just answer the question: Have you seen Munger and his men? Did you take them over the river today?"

Caldwell took the rag and wiped imaginary dirt off the counter. "Took him and his men over, along with a farm cart and some pack horses. Then brought a wagon over from the other side. Just two hours hence."

Ballantyne smacked his hand on the counter. "We need to go over immediately. It is urgent we overtake him."

The proprietor stopped wiping the counter. Then he shook his head as if in sadness and looked at his son. "Take them over *immediately*, says the man. Two hours from midnight and in the midst of all this cold and the dark of night."

"You heard me. It's of the most pressing necessity that we overtake Munger and his crew."

Young Caldwell spoke up. "Mister, in winter, traffic really slows down. We only run the ferry when there's a full load of paying passengers or cargo. You're only six horsemen. That ain't close to covering what it will cost to roust out the oarsmen. Ten of them, we need. And they just got back from makin' a round trip. And like Pa said, we had a payin' wagon on the way back."

Ballantyne said, "We're eight and two packhorses. Two men are outside."

Caldwell shook his head. "All this hurry. I'll tell you the same as I told Dick Munger: I ain't movin' the ferry until I've got a payin' load. Like my boy said, it takes ten oarsmen, all of whom get paid by the trip. You expect me to take a loss just 'cause you're in some great hurry?"

Young Caldwell said, "Munger had to wait until Harry Fitch and his son, with his cart and a string of packhorses, came along. And we still held them until that other wagon showed up on the west bank. Five hours he waited, and he was lucky. Harry hadn't come along, they'd still be waitin'."

Caldwell nodded. "Now, my son Donald is speakin' the truth of matters. So you all will just have to stay here until enough fares gather for it me to make a payin' trip." He held up his finger. "A payin' trip both ways." The proprietor rubbed his hands and said, "The good news is that we can put you and your horses up until then. And we got good food and drink. The best for miles around. You might as well make yourselves comfortable."

Baird laughed. "Jedidiah, first in Alexandria, now here at the Great Crossing. You sure have your troubles with ferrymen!"

Ballantyne slammed his fist on the counter. "Now listen, Caldwell. This isn't a matter of your profit. There's a conspiracy afoot! A conspiracy to raise the Ohio Indians against the settlements. Munger is a Tory who is bound to unleash the Shawnee, Delaware, and Mingo to raid the border country. We've been chasing him for days, and he's nearly in our hands. You don't want to be the one who holds us up."

A look of puzzlement came over Caldwell's face. "Raise the tribes? I don't believe it! They just signed peace treaties with the Crown and Virginia." He shook his head. "Anyway, Dick Munger makes his livin' selling goods to the Indians. I dunna' think that he would want to spark a war."

As he was speaking, a dark-haired woman of about the same age as Caldwell came out of the kitchen, wiping her hands on her apron. She asked him, "John, what's all the ruckus about?"

It was young Donald who answered. "Ma, these men say there's a plot afoot to raise the Ohio tribes. They say Dick Munger is behind it."

Wend said, "We just don't say it. There's written proof." He turned to Ballantyne. "Instead of arguing, show them the dispatches and the orders from the Virginia Committee of Safety. Get Seidal in here. He's carrying them."

Ballantyne nodded and motioned for Taddy to get Horst.

Ma Caldwell bit her lip. "We don't need any more Indian raids around here—not after last year. That devil Laughing Eyes of the Mingo came through here and burnt out three farmsteads. They killed people we knew well."

Young Donald Caldwell grimaced and stared down at the counter. He said, almost to himself, "They killed Jeanie Boatwright and her whole family, not a mile from here."

Ma Caldwell put her hand on her son's shoulder. "Indeed, and she was a pretty lass. The boy was sparkin' her."

Wend said, "I'm sorry for your loss, lad." His thoughts went to the years he had mourned the loss of his own first love, Abigail Gibson, mother of Johann, who had been captured by a Mingo war party and sentenced to a life with the tribe.

His recollections were interrupted by Donegal, who pointed to the wall and asked, "Caldwell, where did you get that broadsword you've got hangin' up there? Was that in your family? Or did somebody trade that to get transported in your scow?"

Wend saw that Simon was pointing to a blade on brackets above the door into the kitchen. It was indeed in the fashion of a Highlander's broadsword with a basket guard over the hilt and grip.

Caldwell glanced up at the sword and said, "Family? Barter? I'll have you know I carried that in the 78th Highlanders, fightin' the French under good Colonel Fraser."

Donegal put his hand to his cap, sliding it to a more rakish angle. Then he laughed out loud. "Fraser's Highlanders? Now what I heard was what you lads did was march around a lot up in the New York lake country, puttin' on a grand show. But fighting? Not so much." He grinned broadly. "Now in the 77th, we fought the Cherokee in Carolina and the French at Ticonderoga, and everyone knows we put the savages to flight at Bushy Run. There's a fightin' Highland regiment for you."

Caldwell stared at Donegal with anger in his eyes. "Fightin'? We did our share and then some! And I'd hardly credit the 77th with bein' a Highland battalion." He scowled at Donegal. "Everyone knows Colonel Montgomery filled out his ranks with a passel of Lowlanders when recruiting got slow. Think on it—*Lowlanders* wearin' the tartan, ha! The truth is, you should have been wearin' breeches and gaiters like an English regiment, not the kilt!"

Wend saw Donegal's face turn red and his jaw stiffen. For a moment he thought the Highlander was about to reach across the bar and grab Caldwell. But then Ma Caldwell, who had been going over the papers with Seidal, spoke up and broke the tension.

"John, you'd better look at these! These men aren't makin' up no story." She read a couple of sentences to her husband.

Caldwell listened, then said, "But all this talks about is catching that Major Connolly, the man who used to run things out in Pittsburgh while the Virginians held it. Where does Dick Munger come in?"

"John, listen to me. Sergeant Seidal explained it to me while you silly men were arguing about whose regiment did the most fighting." She looked at her husband. "Dick Munger was workin' with Connolly and is on his way to raise the tribes. He's got letters from Connolly. And you know those Ohio Indians have got to be nursing their anger after they got beaten last year."

Baird said, "It ain't just the Indians—that would be bad enough. But Munger's carrying money to raise Loyalist ranger companies, and there are plans for detachments of the 18th Foot to come down and back up the others. Those are General Gage's orders!"

Caldwell said, "The 18th Foot? Those damned Royal Irish coming down to Pittsburgh?"

Donegal laughed. "Not just to Pittsburgh, Caldwell. The plan is for the whole lot to march over Braddock Road and then down to Winchester. If Munger isn't stopped, you're going to see those bloody Irish assholes parading right through here." He gave the Scotsman a wry look. "You want the people of this settlement holding you responsible for that?"

Wend gave Ballantyne a sly look and then turned back to Caldwell, saying sardonically, "Yes, John. You want to be careful, or you'll be accused of being a Tory. I can tell you that can be a very uncomfortable situation these days."

Ma Caldwell took hold of her husband's arm. "John, we can't let it happen. You've got to get these men over the river as soon as you can."

The ferry proprietor sighed deeply. "Yes, yes, dear." He thought a moment. "Look, I just sent the oarsmen home. I'll get the word to them to be back here an hour before first light. We'll have you on the far bank by morning dusk. That's the best I can manage."

Wend thought a moment, then nodded. "Yes, that will do. Our horses need rest and fodder in any case."

Caldwell said, "You won't lose much time on Munger and his men by stayin' overnight. The fact is his horses are tired also. I saw the animals hangin' their heads down on the trip across. I'm wagering that he had to put up for the night just a short distance from the river."

Wend turned to Ballantyne. "Jedidiah, Caldwell's right about Munger. This will work. The road ahead for miles is almost all upward—successive ridges leading to Highlands and then after a few miles an even higher crest. Munger will find the going hard. If we press things—really force the horses hard—we can have him in hand tomorrow or the next day."

Ballantyne chewed on his lip. "That or we'll be stuck somewhere along the road with dead horses."

—⚏—

Caldwell was as good as his word.

With the faint light of early-morning dusk, the Virginians led their horses down to the landing. Caldwell and his oarsmen were already on the scow, making their preparations, fixing the long sweeps into the oarlocks. As they approached, the proprietor waved them onto the boat's deck and positioned the horses advantageously to distribute the weight. Shortly they slipped their mooring lines and were off across the swift-flowing Youghiogheny, the oarsmen stroking their sweeps in synchronized rhythm. Caldwell steered the boat into the strong current, deftly managing to keep them moving in the right direction.

In the sparse light and morning mist, Wend could just make out the western bank a little over one hundred yards away.

It was but a few minutes until they grounded at the ferry landing, and two of the rowers jumped up, looped lines around mooring cleats, and heaved the scow tight to the ramp.

Caldwell left his steering sweep and walked forward and up the ramp. "All right, lads!" he called out. "Get your mounts ashore!"

After they had all gotten off, Wend thanked the ferryman. For his part, Caldwell waved them on and called "Godspeed!" Then he shouted to the men at the lines, "Go ahead and let them ropes slip—it's back across and a good breakfast for us!"

Ballantyne watched the boat push off, then ordered, "All right, tighten your cinches and let's get mounted."

Joshua raised his hand. "Hold on, Ballantyne." He pointed to the wagon track. "Take a look at the road ahead."

All the men turned to where he pointed.

"Look at that slope ahead of us. I say we lead the horses up the hill to the crest—we'll spare them the weight of men. They're tired enough. Let's save them for the more level places."

Wend seconded him. "Baird's right. We're going to have to walk as much as ride today to conserve the animal's strength for when we really need it. I'll wager Munger is having to do the same." He looked over at Ballantyne. "You said it last night: if we play things wrong, we'll end up with broken-down animals."

The captain stared up the hill, scowling. But after considering for a long moment, he slowly nodded. Then he started out leading his mount and striding briskly up the slope. He looked back over his shoulder and called out, "Let's get started, and you all better be able to keep up with me!"

Thus began a grueling day. They stopped only a few times, and that was at streams where they could water the horses. After they climbed the initial hill, they went over several smaller ridges, then they found themselves on a high plain, which extended for several miles. They rode for much of that distance, periodically leading to rest the animals.

Luckily, they had a bright sun that produced moderate temperatures as they pressed on hard through the hours. It was early evening when they passed Great Meadows, the site of Fort Necessity and Washington's battle in 1754, which had been the start of the French War.

It was shortly after that that Baird pointed to the next steep incline and called out, "This is the climb to the final ridge line, Chestnut Ridge! The valley of the Monongahela is beyond. When we reach the crest, the road turns northward and runs along the ridge for miles until it descends toward Stewart's Crossing."

The Carlin brothers, not true border country men and not nearly as physically hardened as the others, had for hours been lagging behind in near exhaustion. As the party climbed toward the top, Wend looked back to see they were falling even further behind in the growing dusk.

An hour later Ballantyne reached the crest and stopped to look ahead. In the near darkness, he stared down into the valley, his eyes filled with awe. "My God, look how high we are." Then he examined the side of the mountain. "What a hell of a drop-off!"

Wend and Baird joined him. Baird, breathing a little heavily, pointed to the northward turn in the road. Then turning back and pointing at the steep decline of the mountain side into the Monongahela Valley, he said, "That's why the wagon track runs northward following the line of the ridge. It leads to a much more gradual descent into the valley."

Ballantyne turned and looked down at the struggling Carlin brothers and gritted his teeth. They were just visible on the trail and moving very slowly. "We'll have to stop here to let them catch up."

Joshua said, "Can't say that I'll mind that too much."

Wend had been worrying about the scout for hours. It had become apparent that the old wound in his left hip had become increasingly painful to him as the day advanced. Joshua hadn't said a word of complaint, but his brow was wet and his jaw had been set hard as they walked. Now he dropped the reins to his hunter and settled on the ground, relief spreading over his face. He stared down at the Carlins. "They'll be a while, and then we'll have to wait for them to catch their breath."

It was a half hour later, and full darkness had settled in when the brothers finally stumbled to the top of the ridge and collapsed on the ground.

Taddy Carlin was sweating even in the growing night chill. He looked over to Ballantyne. "Jedidiah, I tell you we're through. We're through, do you understand? We got to stop. And besides, these horses are done in. They're goin' to drop if we keep on going."

Joshua spoke up. "We can keep movin' for a while, and these horses—even the nags the regiment provided you—ain't goin' to collapse yet." He motioned along the ridge. "Less than two miles down the road there's a good, well-used campground with water at hand. The road's level and well marked, so we can travel in the darkness. We'd best try to make that spot."

Donegal added, "He's talkin' about a place from Braddock's day, known as Dunbar's Camp, after the colonel who took over when the general was wounded. It was where the army retreated to from the massacre down at the Monongahela. We've stayed there a couple of times in the last year."

Wend nodded. "We can make it easy enough in about a half hour. That's a good place for us to stay."

Johnny Carlin cried out, "Hell, no! I can't go no further. No further, do you understand?" He pointed to his right leg, which was quivering. "My legs has given out! We got to make camp right here."

Taddy joined in. "Johnny's right. We done enough for the day. And how do we know we're even makin' up time on Munger? The truth be they're probably pushing things the same way we are. I'm sayin' this could last all the way into Pittsburgh, no matter how hard we march!"

His brother nodded. "We might as well just plan on trying to round up Munger and his crowd in the town. We ain't never gonna' catch them this way."

Ballantyne looked at his compatriots and scowled in frustration. Then he sighed and said, "We've made good progress today. But it is true the horses are pretty near done in. Perhaps we should camp here for part of the night and get started well before dawn." He waved toward the Carlins. "Could be we'll make up more time if they rest for a few hours."

Taddy nodded in relief. "Jedidiah, that's the right idea. I tell you the men need it too. We need to stop right now."

Suddenly Joshua's voice interrupted them. "You know, I've changed my mind. We do need to stop here for a while."

Surprised, Wend looked at Baird. The scout had risen to his feet, and he had his water bottle in hand, having just taken a gulp. But now he was standing rigidly still, staring intently northward along the ridge. "Yeah, we've gone far enough for right now 'cause the truth is, we've done caught up with Munger."

Wend sprang to his feet and joined the scout. "What do you see, Joshua?"

"There's a fire up to the north."

Wend shook his head. "I don't see anything."

"Wait for the next gust of wind."

The two stood for a moment, and then the breeze freshened briefly, and Wend suddenly glimpsed it: a distant point of light momentarily visible. Then all was dark again.

Wend looked back at the others. "He's right. Someone's camped up ahead."

Joshua nodded. "Yeah, I'm thinkin' they may be layin' over right in Dunbar's Camp. Seein' as Black Dick knows the road, he was probably heading for it today."

The others—even the Carlins—jumped up and crowded around. Eight men, huddled together, all stood deadly still and silent, peering intensely into the blackness.

Finally, Ballantyne said, "I don't see nothin'."

Wend said, "It's there, all right. Just wait 'til the wind moves the tree branches the right way."

The words were barely out of his mouth when suddenly the light flickered into view and then disappeared almost instantly.

There were low gasps from the others. They had all seen it now.

Ballantyne made a face. "How do we know it's Munger? Could be another party, a Conestoga wagoner, or maybe even a cabin."

"There be little traffic this time of year. And there ain't no cabin on this ridge, leastwise not around here," said Joshua.

Wend looked over at the captain and spoke in hushed tones. "No,

Jedidiah, it's not a Conestoga, and it's not a party of innocent travelers. I feel it in my bones. That is Munger. *That is our quarry.*"

CHAPTER THIRTEEN

DUNBAR'S CAMP

Joshua had gone northward along the wagon track to scout out the distant campfire. The other seven of them waited beside the road in the darkness and the night chill that was being aggravated by a freshening breeze. Ballantyne sat on a log, wide awake. His arms were crossed as he stared down into the valley, a calculating look in his eyes. The Carlin brothers were dead asleep exactly where they had settled after climbing to the ridge. Donegal and Horner had found a comfortable pile of leaves and were stretched out in peaceful repose, their coats snugged up tightly. Wend couldn't find sleep, so he sat behind a tree's broad trunk to shelter from the wind. The horses grazed, looking for whatever grass still had some life.

Baird returned after a couple of hours. His report grabbed every man's attention: "Yeah, sure enough, it's Munger and his gang there in Dunbar's Camp. While I was watchin' them, they was warm and snug, sittin' around their fire having supper of boiled salt pork. I saw Dick himself, Smyth's man Ridgely, that boy that's with them, and one other—I guess the one named Mooney."

Ballantyne jumped up. "All right, it's time to move. We're going up closer. I want to take them alive and without a fight." He looked over at Wend with a sneer on his face. "We don't need no cocked-up mess like happened back at the Conococheaque."

Wend asked, "So what's your plan?"

"We'll go into a cold camp not far from where they lay, then surprise them before dawn while they're still asleep."

"Yeah, you ain't got no argument from me that we want to take them unawares," responded Joshua. "But there ain't no cause to freeze ourselves tonight while we're waitin'. I found a cove with shelter formed by a rocky cliff. It be no more than a quarter mile from where they sit. We can go there, have a fire they'll never see, and spend the night warm and well fed out of the wind. Then, a'fore the mornin' light, we can creep up on them on foot with the horses left behind all safe in the cove."

Taddy vigorously agreed. "Damn, that makes a lot of sense, Jedidiah. Why lay out by the road for hours shiverin' while those bastards are sleepin' comfortable? We can get warmed up and well rested. Then we'll be in good shape to move in on them before they're up."

Wend looked at Ballantyne. "Baird's idea sounds good to me. And it should be easier to take them just before morning dusk. That's when they'll be in their deepest sleep."

The captain put his hands on his hips, then paced back and forth for a few moments, thinking it over. "All right, Baird. Lead us to this cove of yours."

—⁓—

The cove was as secure as Joshua had described it; the high upcropping of rock, in reality a stone hillock, formed a barrier against the wind and a visual barrier shielding them from the sight of the fugitive camp. They set to work gathering wood and soon had a small fire burning at the base of the cliff and were able to boil some salt beef for a welcome hot meal. The horses were secured to a picket line and provided with feed.

After eating, everyone settled in for a few hours' respite. Seidal drew the first watch, stationed atop the rocks in a cluster of advantageously located bushes where he could survey the cove and at the same time keep the distant fire of the conspirators in sight.

Wend climbed through the boulders and rocks up to the sergeant's position.

Seidal, looking out at Munger's fire, said, "You can see it all the time now. Looks like they built it up a'fore they took to their blankets."

Wend stared at the point of light and whispered thoughtfully, "Munger has undoubtedly set a watch, just as we have. And they must have little doubt that somebody is pursuing them, although they can't know who we are or in what strength."

"Yes, I'll not argue with that." Seidal bit his lip. "They've made the right moves at every step of the way." He looked over at Wend and added, "Ballantyne is confident we'll easily scoop them up tomorrow. I'm not so sure."

"Yes, I'm also wary about what happens in the morning. I've never seen an action that has gone precisely as expected. No matter how well you plan, the enemy always has a say in what occurs."

There was a long pause, then Seidal responded thoughtfully, "Yes, I remember something that happened back with the 60th. On one patrol,we was following a party of Seneca's, just to watch them and see what they was up to. There was no hostilities at that time. We thought we was bein' real sly, and they didn't know we was behind them. But then one night we made camp and they walked in on us, just appearing without warning out of the bush. Their leader, a young buck, sat down at our fire and grinned broadly at our sergeant. He asked why we were pursuing them since there wasn't no war. The sergeant made friendly, sayin' we were just on a routine patrol, but it was clear to me they could have just as easily taken us down a'fore we knew what happened."

Wend stared at the fire for a moment. "Yes, Horst, this country is full of surprises. We'll just have to be on our toes tomorrow morning."

Seidal asked, "This Dunbar's Camp. What's it like?"

"The ground is good for laying over. Like Joshua said, it's flat and there's water from springs." Wend reflected a moment. "But in some ways, it's a sad and grim place."

"Grim? What do you mean?"

"It's the place to where Braddock's defeated force retreated after the massacre. They fell back on the camp of Colonel Dunbar, who had been leading a supporting column behind the main force. Although mortally wounded, the general remained awake and in command. He ordered Dunbar to burn much of the supplies, their ammunition, their artillery, and some wagons to lighten up the remnants of the army to speed their retreat. There's still much of the charred wreckage left there." Wend looked at the shadowy form of Seidal. "And it's also a graveyard. They buried a number of soldiers of the 44th and 48th who died of their wounds."

The sergeant responded, "You know, when I was in the 60th, there were a lot of stories about that battle. How the men stood up in ranks firing volleys into the trees, to no effect, and were shot down by Indians and Frenchmen hiding out in the bush."

"Yes, Horst, that was before the army learned how to fight in the forest."

"Well, the soldiers did their best, what they had been taught to do. But they had been trained the wrong way, at least for America. We knew better in the 60th."

"Yes, after the defeat, men like Bouquet and others worked out new tactics and taught their men how to fight from behind cover. The British learned to use rangers and light infantry and rifle corps. When Bouquet marched into the Ohio Country during the Pontiac War in '64, he had a completely different kind of army that could match the tribal warriors."

Seidal considered a moment. "Well, at least the men who were killed with Braddock didn't die in vain. The army learned something from it all."

"Yes, Horst, there is that. But such a waste of lives."

They sat quietly for a while. Then Wend changed the subject. "Horst, you've supported me on several occasions. I've appreciated that, but obviously it's opened a serious rift between you and Jedidiah."

"He's changed so much since we joined the regiment. I hardly know him now. The man's become so obsessed with making a name for himself that it's clouded his thinking. I've just been tryin' to keep him dealing with the real business of this mission." He sighed deeply. "But you're right. There's too much bad blood that has passed between him and me since this started, and now he is showing me real anger. Doesn't hardly speak to me except on business. Once we get back to the regiment, I'm going to ask to go to another company. I doubt he'll object."

"Probably the best thing for you, Horst."

They talked for a few more minutes, and then Wend went back down to the fire. Presently, Horner went up to relieve Seidal on watch.

Soon the entire party settled in for a few hours' rest. The divisions were clearly evident: Wend, Donegal, and Baird lay close together, their feet to the fire, bundled up in their heavy coats and blankets against the bitter cold that had descended as the night advanced. Ballantyne and his men huddled on the far side of the fire.

Wend whispered, "I've been watching Ballantyne. He's been brooding ever since it became clear that was Munger's fire up ahead."

Donegal replied, "Aye, I've seen it too. And while you were up there visitin' with Seidal, he and the Carlins were havin' a very serious discussion in low voices. Couldn't hear a thing they was talkin' about."

Joshua said, "Could be our friends have more planned for tomorrow than just takin' Munger and his men. We're four and four—might be if there's shootin' in the mornin', their only targets won't be Munger and company."

"I wouldn't put that past them." Wend thought a moment, then said, "If Munger's men resist and there's gunfire, try to keep one of your fire-locks with a load at the ready. Reload the ones you do fire immediately. And keep your eye on all three of them, whatever happens."

"What about Seidal?" asked Baird. "Where does he stand in all this? You were up there talkin' with him. Did you learn anything?"

"He isn't happy with Ballantyne, and he has no love for the Carlins. But if it comes down to a fight, I don't know where he'll be."

Donegal said, "I'll 'na be surprised if we don't have two fights on our hands tomorrow—or on the way back once we get Munger and his men."

There was a long silence.

Then Wend looked at his companions. "We need to be ready for anything tomorrow morning, particularly once we have dealt with Munger's men. Keep your eye on me as things develop."

—⁓—

In the darkness before morning dusk, the eight men felt their way along the side of the wagon track toward Dunbar's Camp. Joshua, most familiar with the way, led the single-file column. He was followed by Ballantyne and then Wend, with the others trailing behind and Horner bringing up the rear.

As they crept along, Wend looked at the sky above. The stars were few and far between, indicating significant cloud cover. The damp cold cut right into his bones; the heavy, wet air had the feeling of weather coming on. He thought, *Just what we need—snow or freezing rain while we're up here on this ridgeline.* It was obvious that winter was much further along up here than in the Shenandoah Valley and Winchester.

Presently Baird turned around and quietly said to Ballantyne, "We be less than one hundred yards from the camp. Their fire's down to embers; there's just a glow I'm seein' through the trees." He turned and looked ahead for a second, then said, "I'll go ahead and do a final scout."

Ballantyne whispered, "I'm going with you. I need to get the lay of things before we move in on them." He turned around and looked back at Wend. "You stay here, Eckert, and for once don't give me any damn back talk."

With that he tapped Baird on the shoulder, and the two men moved out. Wend settled to his knees, frustrated. He hated the prospect of going into action without seeing the ground himself, but he felt loathe to argue at a time when maximum silence was required for success.

In a short time, the two were back. Ballantyne, in a hushed voice, said, "They're all there sleeping around the fire."

Wend was astonished. "There's no watch?"

Ballantyne shook his head. "We couldn't see any. They must figure we're too far behind."

"Joshua, are you sure?" Wend asked.

"Yeah, sure as I can be. Looked hard—couldn't see no lookout. And there's four figures spaced out around the coals of their fire."

"Stop wasting time, Eckert. We've scouted as carefully as possible." Jedidiah motioned everyone close to him. "Now listen. We got to make sure they can't bolt. So Baird, Donegal, and Horner, work your way around to the other side of the camp, and the rest of us will approach from the road itself. We'll keep them between us and in a cross fire if they want to try any shootin'."

Wend instantly felt suspicion. He would be alone with only Ballantyne's men. He spoke up immediately. "I want Horner with me. Send one of your men with Baird and Donegal."

"What are you tryin' to say, Eckert?"

"Just that I want my apprentice with me. You can read anything you want into it."

"All right, I ain't got time to argue. Johnny, you go with Baird. Now listen. We'll give the three of you a few minutes to work your way around to the other side, then we're going into the camp. We'll steal up on them while they're still asleep." Then he turned to Wend. "Eckert, you always want to be in the middle of things, so here's your chance. When we reach the camp, you go in and try to get their firelocks without disturbing them. You think you can manage that?"

Wend could faintly make out Ballantyne; there was a tight grin on his face. "All right, but I want Horner to come along and stand in a position where he can cover me with his pistols in case one of the Tories comes awake and tries to resist."

Ballantyne stared at Wend for a long second, then shrugged. His mouth formed a crooked smile. "Any way you want it, Eckert." Then he said, "Once Eckert has collected all their weapons, we'll wake them up and take them into custody."

As he spoke, Baird and the other two men quietly moved off along the road, almost instantly disappearing into the blackness. Ballantyne waved the remaining four to follow him along the wagon track. Soon they were at the very edge of the camp. The glowing coals of the fire were in plain sight, with an occasional flare of flame from one or another part of the embers. The captain waved them to crouch down and wait while he allowed time for Baird and the others to get into position.

Wend examined the campsite and was able to make out four blanketed forms arranged around the fire. All were very still. He peered into the darkness around the camp, searching for some sign that a sentinel lurked in the darkness, but he found none. All appeared as Joshua and Ballantyne had described it.

They waited for a few moments, then Ballantyne rose to his feet. He turned and waved for Wend and Horner to enter the camp.

Wend rose to a semicrouch, took out one of his pistols, and crept forward. Horner followed, keeping about ten feet behind, with pistols in both hands. Every nerve in Wend's body was screaming, "Danger!" and his skin seemed to be crawling as he advanced into the camp. He approached the first sleeping figure. It was Ridgely, who had a rifle and pistol beside him. He bent over and reached down to gather up the weapons.

Suddenly a scream broke the silence. "Eckert! Watch out!" It was Seidal's voice. "Drop down!"

Wend went to his knee and instantly saw the shape of a bearded man come out of the bush to his right, a pistol in his hands.

Munger! And he was aiming the pistol directly at Wend.

Suddenly a shot rang out. Munger jerked and went down to one knee. Wend spun around and saw that it was Seidal who had fired. Then he heard Munger, wounded but not disabled, shouting, "Alarm! Alarm! They're among us!"

He turned back to Munger and saw that he had aimed his pistol at Seidal. Instantly flame spouted from the muzzle, and the sergeant screamed in pain and went down.

Wend snapped off a shot and put a ball into Munger's chest. He fell back against a tree, then slid to the ground, blood flowing down his front.

Wend spun around to look at the fire again. The other men were throwing off their blankets. Wend looked at Ridgely just in time to see him pick up the pistol that lay beside him. But it was for naught. Horner fired and hit him in the head. His body went limp and fell right back into the blankets.

The other Tory, Mooney, jumped up, but he was taken down by a shot from behind Wend. He looked around to see Ballantyne standing with a smoking pistol in his hand.

Wend looked around the camp. No one else was visible. He could see only bodies and empty blankets. Then he realized that someone was missing. He shouted to Horner, "Where's the boy? Where's Tom Harley?"

Andrew responded, "He bolted, sir, while the shooting was going on. Ran into the bush!"

"The lad won't get far. Joshua will run him down soon enough." Wend took a deep breath. The whole fight had taken but seconds. Wend searched for Taddy Carlin and saw him sheltering behind a tree. Clearly he had taken no part in the fight. He called out in scornful tones, "It's all over now, Taddy! You can come out."

Then Wend went over to Seidal. The sergeant was gasping in pain.

"The bastard got me good, Eckert—right in the chest."

Wend saw a trace of blood on the sergeant's lips. "Try to lay quiet. I'll get Donegal to look at you as soon as he comes in. He's got some experience with wounds from his time in the army."

"It's no use. The ball's finished me."

"Come on, Horst. We'll get you back to Caldwell's place and a doctor. Just hold on." Wend went to his knees beside Seidal and smiled at him. "I owe you my life. Without your warning, Munger would have got me."

Seidal reached up and pulled Wend down until his ear was close to the sergeant's mouth.

"Eckert, you don't understand. I wasn't warning you about Munger. He rose up out of the bush *after* I called out. I was trying to alert you to *Ballantyne*. He had cocked his pistol and aimed it at your back. He would have shot you if Munger hadn't suddenly appeared."

Wend put his finger to his lips. "Shh! And God bless you, Horst. But not another word about this. I'll deal with Ballantyne in good time and in my own way. You just concentrate on husbanding your strength."

Wend looked back toward the camp. "Horner, come here! Help me get Seidal to the fire."

They settled him into blankets, and Horner threw some wood on the fire to generate more heat.

Ballantyne came over and stood looking down at his sergeant as he reloaded his pistol. Then he asked in a casual, almost disinterested voice, "How is he?"

Wend responded, "The ball's in his chest, and he's bleeding badly. I'm going to try to staunch the flow." He looked up at Ballantyne and said, with as much irony as he could manage, "I'm sure glad this all went so well and things didn't get cocked up like at the Conococheaque."

The captain scowled, then turned and walked away.

Horner found a shirt in one of the dead men's saddlebags and tore it up for use as bandaging. Wend took some of it, wadded it up, and used it to press down on Seidal's wound.

Just then Baird and Donegal came out of the bush, followed by Johnny Carlin. Joshua was half leading, half dragging Tom Harley behind him. He pulled the boy to the fire then deposited him in a heap beside it.

"Found this little sprout runnin' like a crazed bear cub through the trees. Makin' enough noise to be heard all the way back to Caldwell's place. Didn't even have a firelock with him."

Wend looked at young Harley. He was sitting on the ground, sobbing, with tears streaming down his cheeks.

Ballantyne looked at the boy and called out to Taddy, "Take care of him! Tie him to a tree so he ain't no trouble to us."

Wend laughed. "That lad isn't going to be any trouble to anyone. Look at him."

"Don't interfere, Eckert. Carlin, do what I told you." Then Ballantyne motioned to Andrew and Johnny. "You two: drag the bodies out of the way and lay them out together."

Taddy grabbed Harley by the collar and hustled him over to a tree, and the other two began their grim task.

Wend turned his attention back to Seidal. "Donegal, can you look at him and see what we can do? There's a ball lodged in his chest."

Simon nodded and went over to kneel beside Horst.

At that moment, Horner called out, "Hey, Munger's still alive!"

Wend hurried over to the tree where the trader was slumped. The man's hunting shirt was soaked in blood from one wound in his shoulder and another in his chest. But his eyes were open, and he was staring at Wend.

Munger said, "Who are you?"

"My name is Wend Eckert."

With difficulty, Munger smiled. "By God, the Scalp Stealer himself! I've heard of you. All the Mingo hate you for taking some dried scalps from the trophy rack in a village up on Slippery Rock Creek. And you're the one who shot up Wolf Claw, their war captain, last year during the war."

"The scalps were those of my family, Munger. And Wolf Claw's the one who killed them."

Munger chortled but then coughed up blood. "Don't matter none—they still hate you." He swallowed hard. "Well, you caught us. I thought we were a little further ahead. Would have pushed harder if I'd have known you were so close. My mistake."

"You didn't make many mistakes, Munger. It was a hard chase, and our horses are close to being finished."

A painful smile came over his face. "Damn, another two days would have seen us having spirits at Semple's place in Pittsburgh." He suffered a long fit of coughing, then said, "You think you won, don't you, Eckert? But I'm tellin' you now if this colonial insurrection keeps going, the Indians will seize the chance to push back the settlements. May take a couple of years, but mark my words, you're going to see the border in flames."

"Perhaps your right, but they won't have the help Connolly's plot would have afforded them."

"Just mind what I said, Scalp Stealer." Then he shook his head as if trying to throw off the pain. "Is everyone else dead?"

"Tom Harley is alive—taken as a prisoner."

"That's good. Sorry I got him mixed up in all this. He's a fine…"

Munger stopped talking and stared into the distance.

Horner reached down and gently shook him on the shoulder. His head fell over to one side, the blank eyes still open. "He's gone, sir."

Wend nodded, then walked back to the campsite and started to go through the conspirator's baggage.

Ballantyne called out, "Now what are you up to, Eckert?" He grinned slyly. "You looking to get their money?"

"I'm searching for the dispatches. They're the most valuable things we'll get from this day's work."

In just a few moments, he had found the packet of papers. The fire was now flaming up with the new fuel, and Wend sat down beside it to read the letters.

"So what have you got?"

"Be patient, Jedidiah. Give me some time to read through them." Wend grinned at the captain, adding sarcastically, "Or would you rather do it yourself?"

"Go ahead, Eckert. Look through them and then tell me what they say."

Wend spent a half hour reading through the papers.

"All right, Ballantyne. There are five dispatches, and the powers that be in Williamsburg are going to find them very interesting. Three are for the British deputy Indian commissioner, describing Connolly's detailed plan for the attack on the settlements and then for the march south to the Shenandoah Valley. There's a list of the tribal chiefs who Connolly think would be ready to cooperate and an estimate of the number of warriors each could put on the war path. Another identifies influential Tory sympathizers in Pittsburgh and the Ohio Country who are ready to participate in the conspiracy, including some men he thought could lead ranger companies."

Wend turned to Joshua. "You might be interested to know that it's got our old friend Simon Girty listed as a possible collaborator—says he would make a good ranger leader or chief scout."

Joshua smiled. "That ain't no surprise to me. Girty will go with whoever he thinks will do the best by him."

Wend answered, "I'd agree with that." He looked down at the papers again. "The fourth dispatch is to a Captain Hugh Lord of the 18th Foot, The Royal Irish. It contains instructions for both him and Captain Richard Beringer Leroult—he's the senior officer of the 8th Foot, The King's Regiment, in Detroit. It discusses the necessary military movements and some recommendations on cooperating with the tribes and particularly the militia units to be raised." He held up another packet. "The last is a personal letter to Connolly's wife."

Ballantyne's face broke into a broad, self-satisfied smile. "Yes, all that's going to make quite a stir with Colonel Henry and the committee." Then he pointed to Johnny Carlin and Horner. "You two—get on back to our camp and bring up the horses and all our gear. We need to be ready to get out of here. I intend to make haste back to Virginia."

—⬥—

By the time Horner and Johnny Carlin got back with the horses, dawn was well advanced and light was spreading over Chestnut Ridge. But it was a gloomy daybreak for clouds obscured most of the sky, and wet ground fog hung over much of the land.

Simon, who had been sitting with Seidal, rose and came over to Wend. "He ain't goin' to last much longer. I've been tryin' to staunch the blood, but I've just been able to slow it down."

"What about trying to probe for the ball? If we got it out, could we stop the bleeding?"

"Laddie, it's right next to his heart. I'm 'na sure even a regimental surgeon, with all the proper instruments, could get it out without killing him." Donegal shook his head. "The truth be, all we can do is comfort him until the end."

"Is he awake?"

"In and out, Wend."

"I'll go sit with him. It's the least I can do." Wend walked over and knelt beside Seidal. Donegal followed and stood above the dying man. Seidal, eyes closed, had sweat all over his face and was breathing heavily. Wend took a cloth and mopped his brow.

The sergeant opened his eyes. "Ah, Wend. I'm glad you're here. Will you do something for me?"

"Of course. Whatever you need."

"My wife needs to know about me. Will you write her and let her know what happened here? The woman is young and strong. She will remarry a good man, I'm sure. But she and my children should have some memory of me. They need to know about the story of this ride and that I died fighting to protect them."

"I'll do it, Horst. But right now, you need just to be quiet. It will go easier that way."

Seidal took a deep, gasping breath. "My regret is that I didn't get to fight with the regiment and redeem myself for what I did at Fort Venango." He closed his eyes and breathed more easily for a moment.

Donegal asked in a puzzled voice, "What's he talking about? What does he think he needs redemption for?"

"He was in the 60th and deserted from Venango just before it was attacked by the war parties in '63. It's been eating at him ever since that he wasn't with his mates when they were massacred. He wanted to go into battle with real soldiers again to wipe out the stain."

Seidal heard and he opened his eyes again. "Yes, Donegal, now you know the truth. I'm a deserter. But perhaps I made up for some of it on this trip."

Simon dropped to one knee by the sergeant. He laughed quietly.

"Why, you're an old fool, if you been worryin' about that all these years. Why, the best fightin' soldier I ever knew—a man named Bob Kirkwood—deserted twice from the 77th. He would have been hung when they caught him if they hadn't been so desperate for men to fill the ranks back in the French War. And so many men deserted from the boredom of those little outposts like Venango that we used to say it was worse than an epidemic. Why, I might have even gone on the run if I'd been posted to one of those places."

With his remaining strength, Seidal reached up touched Donegal's arm. "Thank you for that, Highlander." He coughed and dropped his arm. "Wend, will you do me one other favor?"

"Sure, Horst. Name it."

"That graveyard you told me was hereabouts with all those men from Braddock's army—put me in the line with them. At least I can spend eternity with soldiers." He closed his eyes.

Donegal answered, "Now are you sure 'bout that, Horst? The 44th and 48th was filled with Irish. Do you want to spend the ages with them devils? There be a lot of pretty spots around here where we could put you by yourself."

Seidal actually smiled at that and forced his eyes open again. "No, they stood their ground and did their duty. Don't matter to me if they were Irish or English or German. That's where I want to be."

Wend said gently, "Don't worry, Horst. We'll put you beside them."

"Bless you, Wend." Then Seidal sighed deeply. "Lord, it's so cold, even under these blankets. And so dark. Shouldn't it be dawn soon?"

Wend looked up at the sky, and although there was an abundance of cloud cover, the campground was well lighted.

Wend and Donegal exchanged glances.

"Yes," said Eckert. "We'll soon start to see dawn. Then maybe it will be warmer and you'll be more comfortable."

"Indeed, Wend, that will be most welcome."

And then Sergeant Horst Seidal's chest heaved. There was a sucking sound, and he was gone, his sightless eyes staring up into the gray sky.

—⚏—

Wend, Baird, Donegal, and Horner set to work to bury Seidal. Although it was November, the ground still had not frozen hard, so digging was not prohibitively difficult. They only had one small shovel, so Wend, Donegal, and Seidal took turns opening the grave. Baird worked on carving an inscription on a weathered plank of scorched wood that looked like it had survived the burning of a wagon two decades before. He asked a lot of questions about spelling the words. They laid Horst in the grave buttoned up in his overcoat and with a blanket over his upper body and head to keep the dirt out of his face.

After filling in the grave, they gathered stones and piled them over it to keep the varmints at bay. Then Joshua placed the marker at the head. It read:

Horst Seidal

Sgt 1st Virginia Regt

Culpeper Cty Militia

60th Regt of Foot

When that was done, they stood at the foot of the grave, and Donegal said some things about God and being a soldier. Wend spoke directly to Seidal's spirit, thanking him for saving his life, and then asked the Lord to seat Seidal at his side in heaven.

And then the four of them walked back the hundred yards or so to the campsite.

To a sight that brought them abruptly to a halt in astonished shock.

Tom Harley, hands tied behind his back, stood upon a wide tree stump. A rope was looped around his neck and then led over the branch of a large tree.

The end of the line was in the hands of the Carlin brothers, standing ready to hoist the boy into the air and eternity. The two were looking at Ballantyne, who stood, hands on hips, a few feet in front of the stump, staring at Harley with a sinister grin on his face.

The boy was shivering all over, and his countenance was twisted into a look of abject terror.

Wend shouted out, "What the hell are you doing, Ballantyne?"

The captain turned and looked at the four men standing at the edge of the camp. He waved at the youth. "What does it look like, Eckert? We're hanging this Tory spawn!"

"I thought you wanted to take him back to Williamsburg as a trophy of your success."

"The boy ain't worth the trouble of feedin' and guardin' him for days. The truth is, no one's going to be impressed with a sniveling youth. The dispatches and packtrain will more than serve my purpose."

Taddy pulled on the rope, taking all the slack out of it and tightening the noose around Harley's neck, so the boy was up on his toes and gagging. Then he called out, "Jedidiah, let's get on with it! This place gives me the shivers. We need to take to the road and get back to Caldwell's and some good spirits to warm our souls."

The captain nodded. "Yep, you boys go ahead and hoist him right up!"

The Carlins heaved on the rope. Tom Harley's feet were jerked off the stump, and he started to swing back and forth, his legs flailing the air wildly.

Wend's rage boiled over. "All right, this stupid game has gone on long enough!" He reached down and pulled his pistols from his belt. "Ballantyne, it's over! Tell the Carlins to drop the rope."

"The hell you say, Eckert!" Ballantyne's hand flew to his belt, and he grabbed his own pistol.

Wend raised the firelock in his right hand, the barrel pointed at the captain.

"Drop it, Jedidiah, or I'll fire."

Without hesitation Ballantyne cocked the pistol and whipped it up toward Wend.

Wend fired.

The ball hit the captain's hand, sending the firelock spinning to the ground. Blood from the wound sprayed over Ballantyne. Jedidiah looked down at his hand in astonishment.

Horner exclaimed in admiration, "Sir, that was a great shot!"

Wend shook his head. "The hell it was, Andrew. I was aiming for his chest. The hand just got in the way."

Ballantyne sank to his knees, shrieking in agony and holding his right hand with his left. Blood was oozing from the wound and covering both hands.

Donegal sprang over to where he kneeled and kicked him over, then pinned him to the ground with his foot. "Na' stay still, you bastard, or I'll kick you again. And then I'll step on your bloody right hand just for the pleasure of it."

Meanwhile, Baird had leveled his pistols at the Carlin brothers. "You assholes, drop that line instant like or I'll serve you each with a ball. I been wantin' to do that since I first set eyes on you back at Widow Callow's place."

The Carlins didn't hesitate. They immediately let go of the rope and raised their hands in surrender. Young Harley tumbled to the ground in a heap, gasping for breath.

Wend called out, "Horner, get all their weapons!"

Wend walked over to Tom, gently took the noose off his neck, and then pulled his knife out and sliced the rope tying his hands. "You all right, lad?"

The boy stood up, still gasping. But he shook himself all over and replied, "Feels like it, sir."

Wend nodded. "Good. Now go over by the fire and fetch all your kit."

"Sir, I don't understand."

"Get everything that belongs to you."

"Yes, sir."

Joshua shot Wend a puzzled glance. "What are you going to do with the sprout?"

"Send him home to his mother."

Wend gathered up the rope intended for Tom Harley's hanging and tossed it to Horner. "Andrew, when you get finished picking up the weapons, tie all three up, hands and legs."

Taddy called out, a tremor in his voice, "What are you going to do with us, Eckert?"

"I haven't precisely decided. Just bide your time, Carlin." Then Wend gave him a devilish grin. "Make the most of the time you do have."

A look of extreme anxiety came over Taddy's face, which was mirrored in his brother's.

Wend walked over to where the boy was gathering his belongings. "You got it all, son?"

"Everything but my firelocks."

"Good. Now go over and saddle your horse. And don't try to play any tricks on me. When you're done, bring him here so we can load all your stuff."

When the lad came back leading the animal, Wend helped him get everything securely in place.

"Now, Tom, come along." Wend led him over to the stack of the conspirators' weapons. "Show me your firelocks."

Harley pointed to a fowler and a very worn horse pistol. Wend picked up the long gun and fired it into the ground. Then he removed the flint and handed the weapon to the boy. He did the same with the pistol.

Wend took the reins of the horse. "Come along, lad." Then he led the horse and boy out to the wagon track.

"Tom, how did you get involved in this affair?"

"Sir, Mr. Munger said we'd be helping the king. My father was very loyal, sir. He was friends with Munger, but he died last year and left my Ma and me and my younger brother and sister to work our farm. Munger visited us and said if I came along, I'd get some money when we got back to Pittsburgh. We sure could use that."

"Well, I don't have any money to give you, but I can give you your life. Think about what just happened. You were about as close to death as any man should ever be before his time."

The boy instinctively reached up and touched his neck, where there was a red bruise from the rope. "Yes, sir. I'll never forget what happened back there."

"I want you to go home to the farm. Go home and stay there. Do you understand?"

"Yes, Mr. Eckert."

"But on your way, I want you to go to Pittsburgh and find Semple's Tavern. It's the biggest in the town."

"Yes, I've been to Pittsburgh, and I've seen it."

"Good. Now listen close. Go to Mr. Semple and ask where you can find his sister, Susanna Connolly."

"You mean Colonel Connolly's wife?"

"Yes." Wend handed him Connolly's letter to Susanna. "Give this to her, and tell her that it is courtesy of Wend Eckert with his compliments and his deepest appreciation for the fine supper and gracious hospitality she showed me last year. Can you remember that?"

Harley repeated the words exactly. Then his eyes turned westward. Concern came over his face, and he bit his lip. "There's a big storm coming, sir. Look at those dark clouds."

Wend looked over and saw that the horizon to the west was indeed

covered with black, foreboding clouds that were moving in fast. He noted that the air was heavy, and he thought, *We're going to get snow later
today.*

As he looked at the darkness and massive clouds spreading across the
entire horizon, a startling vision formed in his mind. Wend put his hand
on Tom's shoulder. "Yes, lad, indeed we are about to have a great storm.
The biggest storm we've ever seen. It's going to spread over all of the
land, and it's going to last a long time. No one will be able to tell how
long. I wager it's going to do more damage than any storm ever has. And
no matter how it ends, the world will be different when it's over."

The boy stared at the clouds in the west, then back to Wend. A puzzled look spread over his face. "Sir, you're not talking about the weather,
are you?"

"You understand what I mean."

"Yes, I think I do."

"Now listen to me. Like I said, go back to your farm and stay there
until the storm is all over. Don't let yourself be drawn out into the cat-
aclysm. Whether our future is under the king or we somehow gain the
right to govern ourselves, Virginia and all the other colonies are going
to need strong, honest men to shape the future. You take care to be one
of those men."

Tom stood staring into the clouds, and Wend could see he was thinking hard about his words.

Wend slapped the boy on the shoulder. "Now get mounted." He
helped him up into the saddle, then, looking up at the young face, he
waved down the wagon track. "Push as hard as you can along the road.
If you do that, you have a good chance of making Stewart's Crossing before the storm in those clouds to the west becomes too severe. And when
you get there, you can seek shelter at William Crawford's plantation. It's
right at the river."

"Major William Crawford? I heard about him. He led a raid on the

Indians last year."

"Yes, that's the man. I know him well. He'll not hesitate to give you shelter and food. And don't forget to remember me to him."

"I will, Mr. Eckert." He looked down at Wend. "And sir, I'll never forget what you've done for me."

And with that he spurred his horse and was off, quickly bringing him up to the trot. Wend watched until the lad and horse disappeared around a bend in the track.

—⁓—

Jedidiah Ballantyne lay on the ground beside the fire, bound hand and foot. Donegal had tended to his right hand. Wend's shot had in fact sliced off the last two fingers as well as some of the flesh in the palm. Now it was wrapped in a blood-soaked dressing. The Carlins lay beside the captain, similarly bound with their hands behind their backs and their feet tied together.

It had taken an hour after Wend had sent Tom Harley on his way for the Winchester men to load up the horses with all the baggage, supplies, and weapons belonging to both the conspirators and the pursuers. Now the campsite was entirely bare except for the three men laying around the fire, which had burned down to the coals.

Wend stood in front of them, the reins to his horse in hand, his rifle on its sling over his shoulder. Baird, Donegal, and Horner were mounted, sitting their horses behind him.

Ballantyne, his forehead covered in perspiration, spoke out through teeth gritted in pain. "So, are you going to kill us now, Eckert?"

"No, Jedidiah. I'm not going to kill you. I thought about it very hard, and the prospect of putting balls in you and your compatriots was very appealing. But there's been enough killing on this trip. In the end, I decided to let Braddock Road deal with you."

Taddy Carlin screamed, "For God's sake, Eckert, what do you mean?!"

But Ballantyne saw it right away. "Carlin, don't you understand? He's going to leave us here tied up to face the weather. Look at that sky. There's a snowstorm coming."

Wend smiled broadly. "That's right. I'm leaving you here just the way you are."

Johnny Carlin's face teared up, and he whimpered, "Oh, God, we're going to freeze."

Taddy shouted, "You bastards! You heartless bastards!"

Joshua grinned down from his horse. "You know, lads, freezing ain't a bad way to go. You just sort of drift off like going to sleep." Then he pulled his pistols out of their holsters and cocked the hammers. "Now if you ain't happy with the present arrangement, just give me the word, and I can end it for you instantly. It would be my pleasure."

None of them took him up on his offer. Instead they simply stared into the distance.

Wend went to his horse and then turned back to the three men. "Actually, I'm going to give you a chance." He pulled a knife from his saddlebag and threw it into the ground about twenty feet in front of the captives. "If you can wriggle over to that blade, you can cut yourselves free. Then you can try to walk out of here. It's about twenty miles back to the Youghiogheny and Caldwell's place. We'll leave your horses and saddlebags there in case you make it. And it's a few miles less to Stewart's Crossing the other way. The choice about which way to go is up to you."

Ballantyne scowled. "Twenty miles in a snowstorm? That amounts to a death sentence!"

Wend laughed. "Jedidiah, I'm giving you better odds than you planned for me. Before he died, Seidal told me you had your pistol aimed at my back this morning when I was disarming the fugitives, and only Munger coming out of hiding stopped you from putting a ball in me.

So I suggest you stop complaining and start planning your best course." Then he added, "You could also build a shelter here and wait out the storm." He shrugged. "But it's your decision. Hell, Jedidiah, you might actually make it. But If you don't, they'll find your bones when the snow clears in the spring, and you can take consolation that some traveler with more charity in his heart than you ever had will probably take the time to bury what's left of you."

A paroxysm of pain came over Ballantyne. He closed his eyes and gritted his teeth. When it had passed, he took a deep breath, opened his eyes and said, "You won't get away with this, Eckert. Colonel Henry will call you to account. And if I do survive, I will personally come for you. There will be no hiding from my vengeance. I'll pursue you to the ends of the earth."

"Well, you won't need to go as far as that. Just come to Eckert Ridge in Frederick County. It's a few miles south of the Battletown Crossroads on the Ashby Ferry Road. Anyone will give you directions."

While he had been talking, Baird and Donegal had ridden out onto the wagon track, and Horner followed, leading the string of spare horses.

Wend swung up into the saddle. The horse, impatient to join his mates, tossed his head and pranced in front of the prostrate men. Wend reined the animal in, then took off his hat and bowed to Ballantyne and the Carlins. "Well, gentlemen, I will leave you to your own devices." He looked over to the west. "We must hurry to get ahead of the storm."

And with that, Wend snugged his hat back down on his head and trotted off after his friends, eastbound for Wills Creek and then south to Winchester.

CHAPTER FOURTEEN

JANUARY EVENING
AT ECKERT RIDGE

The crowd in the Eckert house was composed of a diverse slice of Frederick County's social strata. All the members of the Committee of Safety along with their wives were present. They represented the elite of the community. But there was also a strong strain of tradesmen and some of the neighbors from nearby farms. A number of the Winchester shopkeepers whom Wend patronized for trade supplies were there, and he had especially requested to Peggy that Widow Callow be invited.

The entire affair had, in fact, been Peggy's idea. Wend would have been quite happy sending a simple note in to the committee informing them that the first lot of new muskets manufactured at Eckert Ridge had been completed and that they were ready for delivery to the Virginia military forces. But when he had informed her of the development, Peggy had put her hand to her chin, and then her eyes had lit up.

Wend had long ago learned the meaning of that expression: Peggy McCartie Eckert had an inspiration.

"Wend! We'll make a celebration out of presenting the muskets! An occasion! I've been looking for an excuse to have the important people of Winchester here to the farm. We'll have James and Jean Wood, the McDonalds, the Thrustons, and all the rest of the committee. And we'll have all the people who contributed materials for making the muskets. The Zanes from the Iron Plantation and that leather smith Hauck and his wife."

Wend mentally groaned, dreading the thought of all the preparations that would be necessary. But he knew that when Peggy got this excited about something, protesting would be a futile endeavor. So he simply smiled and said, "Yes, dear. It sounds like a lovely idea."

Peggy's countenance changed to one of great concentration, then she smiled again. "And this is important, Wend. After we show them so much hospitality, it will be hard for the committee to drag their feet in paying you, even if they have to dig into their pockets again!"

Now the event was well underway. Every fireplace was lighted to fend off the cold January temperatures. Even though full darkness had not yet fallen, the house glittered with every candle that could be mustered for the purpose. Peggy, looking devastatingly beautiful in her best gown and carefully coiffed hair, floated through the rooms performing the role of hostess with verve and great relish. Wend, watching her progress, was not surprised to see most of the men in the room surreptitiously eyeing her as she moved from group to group.

Sally Potter Donegal sat on a settee talking with Mrs. Callow, her eyes wide as she looked around the room. A year ago she had been living in a tiny cabin, caring for two young children and helping her husband carve a farm out of the Pennsylvania forest. Then a Shawnee-Mingo war party had changed her life. Now, with her golden hair put up, she wore one of Peggy's former gowns, which Alice had modified for her, in the midst of a social setting she had never dreamed of experiencing.

Then Wend saw Andrew smiling broadly as he stood close by and talked to a pretty girl with straw-blond hair and a well-endowed bosom. Her clothing was attractive but clearly homemade. Immediately he realized it must be Miss Frieda Haldorf, whom Wend had insisted Peggy invite. He fervently hoped Miss Haldorf had the stuff to drive the memory of Emily Crider out of Horner's head.

Meanwhile, Wend was moving around doing his best to play the genial host. It was a role for which he had little experience, and he felt more than a touch of awkwardness as he circulated to exchange pleasantries with all the guests.

Thus he felt a measure of relief when James Wood, whom he passed in the hall, pulled him aside. "Wend, can we talk privately?"

Wend nodded and led Wood into Peggy's sewing room. Wood had just returned from representing Frederick County at the legislature. "James, does this have something to do with events in Williamsburg?"

Wood took a sip of his drink. "Yes, I wanted to tell you that the Williamsburg Committee was most gratified with what you did in the Connolly matter. They were particularly pleased when I delivered those dispatches you captured. The names of some of the men on the list of Loyalists in the Pittsburgh area were a revelation."

"I'm glad they'll be helpful." Then Wend had a thought. "Did you happen to encounter Colonel Henry while you were there?"

"Of course. I made a point of seeing him about you. Wend, I can't forget that I was the one who thought it would be a good idea for you to personally take the muskets down to Henry in Culpeper."

Wend said wryly, "Yes, you said it would help me improve my chances for payment. What it did was get me sent on a long chase with a man named Ballantyne who wanted to kill me for his own aggrandizement."

"That's my point, Wend. I wanted to confront Henry and find out what he was thinking and particularly why he never sent that courier to me for a reference on your loyalty." Wood made a wry smile. "What I found out was surprising, to say the least."

"Nothing you might find out about Henry would surprise me. The man is as much a schemer as Northcutt or Richard Grenough."

Wood gave Wend a wry look. "Indeed, that is beyond question. But what you should know is that Henry told me he never had a doubt about your loyalty."

Wend was stunned. "What? Are you serious, James?"

"Absolutely. That's why he never sent the courier."

"Then why the hell did he send me after Connolly, if not to prove my loyalty?"

"He sent you along with that Captain Ballantyne because he didn't trust the man. Henry gave him that mission to get rid of a burr under his saddle. From the moment he reported to the regiment, Ballantyne had been a troublemaker, stirring up the border men about various issues." Wood smiled. "Henry was impressed with you immediately and figured that you would be able to keep that rogue under control and get the job done."

Wend felt a flash of irritation. "So Henry was using me from the beginning!"

"Indeed, he was."

Wend couldn't resist asking, "Did Henry mention what happened when Ballantyne reported back to the regiment? How did he deal with him?"

Wood raised a finger. "As a matter of fact, now that you bring it up, he did say something. He told me it was curious that, as of last month, neither Ballantyne or any of the men with him had returned." Wood laughed and said, "He also said he had neither the time nor intent to delve into the matter." He shrugged. "Do you have any idea of what might have happened to them?"

Wend cleared his throat. Setting his face with a blank countenance, he stared over Wood's shoulder and replied, "Well, two men were killed in the pursuit. As for Ballantyne and the Carlins, the last I saw of them they were at a camp up on Chestnut Ridge, sitting by the fire discussing the best route to use for their return journey."

"Well, no matter. Perhaps some misfortune befell them on their way back. Anything can happen in these times. And in any case, Henry's days as a military officer are practically over. The Virginia Committee of Safety has recognized his inefficiency and in fact has already replaced him as colonel of the First Virginia. As a face-saving measure, he's been appointed commander of all of Virginia's forces, which is a purely ceremonial job with little real effect on troops in the field."

"That's a move in the right direction. The First Virginia was ill disciplined under him."

Wood held up his hand. "Restrain your bitterness, Wend. Nobody really holds his ineffectiveness with the regiment against him; he had little military experience. But I can tell you that his oratorical and political skills are as much admired as ever. Informed opinion around Williamsburg is that Henry has a good chance of becoming the governor once the Virginia Convention finalizes the structure of the new government."

"You're not joking with me, are you James?"

"Of course not. It's undeniably a job for which he is much more suited than military leadership." Wood put a hand on Wend's shoulder. "And you should be happy if that comes to pass."

"I should be happy? For God's sake, James, why?"

"The fact is, Henry told me he is grateful for what you did in the Connolly matter, and he pledged to me that he will make it a matter of priority to get your request for payment approved once he is in a position of authority with the new government."

"Can we believe what he says?"

"We shall see. But in any case, it is always wise to hedge one's bets. I have also made it a point of ensuring that many of the legislative representatives are aware of what you did and the fact that you have established a viable musket manufactory here in Winchester. And remember,

I shall be there to push the issue with the Burgesses and Committee of Safety and to remind Henry of his promise."

"I'll grateful for that."

"Yes. So you see, although you went through much travail, things seem to have come out right in the end."

"I thank you, James, but please understand that my optimism will be tempered until I see the actual documents of payment."

"Of course, Wend, of course." Wood waved back toward the party. "Well, my friend, I'm sure you are anxious to return to your guests."

As Wend followed Wood out into the hall, Peggy intercepted him. "Ah, there you are. All our guests are here now. You can start the ceremony to present your muskets."

This was actually the moment Wend had been dreading. The prospect of standing up in front of the crowd and speaking filled him with trepidation.

Peggy saw the concern in his face. "Don't worry, dear. You'll do fine. After all, you'll be talking about your favorite subject—firelocks—and of course the people in your shop."

Wend got the attention of Wilhelm Hecht and told him to assemble the apprentices and prepare for the ceremony they had scripted. Wend took his place in front of the parlor fireplace and clapped his hands to draw the attention of the guests.

Peggy circulated, shushing the talking groups and then ushering people from other rooms into the parlor. Soon the entire assemblage was crowded tightly into the room. Meanwhile, Hecht had lined up the apprentices to one side of the hearth. Wend waved to Zane and Hauck, summoning them to his side.

He cleared his throat and said, "Ladies and gentlemen, it's time to proceed with the main business of the evening. Could we have the members of the committee come to my side?"

Wood, Thruston, McDonald, Rutledge, Smith, and the others came forward and formed a tight group to Wend's right.

Wend looked out and saw that Peggy stood in the center of the crowd, glowing with a proud smile on her face. Jean Wood and Anna McDonald were on her right, and Abbey Morgan stood to her left. Just behind her were Alice and Sally. Wend made a tight smile to Peggy and then began to speak.

"As you all are aware, we have been working since spring of last year to begin the production of new muskets for use by Virginia's forces. It has been a challenging effort, I can assure you. We had to fabricate so many parts with which we had no experience. And now I can say that work has come to fruition. We have completed our first lot of twenty-five muskets, following the King's Arm Short Land Pattern."

He paused and was gratified with a round of applause.

Then he said, "And with the help of my compatriots, Mr. Zane and Mr. Hauck, we have ensured that each musket is equipped as a complete stand of arms with bayonet and cartridge box."

There was a second round of clapping.

"And now, we have a presentation to make." He motioned to the door of the parlor, and Horner advanced into the room, holding before him a gleaming musket. The maple stock had been oiled to a fine sheen, and the metal fittings reflected the light of the candles.

Horner handed the firelock to Wend, and he raised it to shoulder height to ensure it was visible to all in the gathering. And a new round of clapping broke out.

When the applause had subsided, he pointed to a brass plate affixed to the butt, midway between the neck and the shoulder piece. "The inscription says, 'Eckert Musket Number 1, Presented to the Frederick County Committee of Safety. Jan 1776.'"

Wend turned to the men of the committee and handed the firelock to Wood.

James examined the musket, then passed it on to Thruston, and it was thence passed from member to member in turn.

Wend realized he was at a loss for words to finish, but Wood saved him.

He reached over, put his hand on Wend's shoulder, and then turned to speak. "Let me say a few words on behalf of the committee. We greatly appreciate what Mr. Eckert and his associates are doing in providing arms for our soldiers. This lot of muskets will be dispatched to supply our brave men even now battling Lord Dunmore in the tidewater. I can say that the Virginia Committee of Safety in Williamsburg will be extremely grateful toward the citizens of Winchester, which will undoubtedly stand us in good stead in future matters."

He nodded to Wend and his men. "But there's some other things for which we need to thank our host. Not all of you may be aware, but he is responsible for eliminating the threat of a major Indian uprising that would have been assisted by the British Army. And most importantly, their ultimate objective was Winchester."

There was a buzz around the room.

"Yes, my friends, Winchester was the target. But the threat is now over due to Wend and his companions Simon Donegal and Joshua Baird and young apprentice Andrew Horner."

Wood paused for a round of applause and then said, "And in the course of that mission, they captured a packtrain of military stores—powder and lead. You know how precious those items are in these times. Mr. Eckert has delivered it to the committee, and I assure you we will put it to good service with our county militia."

Wood was about to say something else, but he never got to it. Everyone stood silent, listening for his next words, but what they heard was a loud banging on the front door out in the hall.

Every head turned, and Wood stood silent. Albert, performing the duty of butler and truly looking the part in an old but well-cared-for black coat and white gloves, rapidly made his way to the door and swung it open. A blast of cold air pushed into the hall and then swept through the parlor. Then, after a brief moment, Albert led in a man, well bundled up against the wind with a heavy overcoat, a wool scarf, and a floppy hat pulled down nearly to his ears. Wend recognized him as Elisha Workman, one of Sheriff Smith's men.

Workman pulled off his hat and looked around the room. Then, seeing Smith, he said, loudly, "Sheriff, I just rode down from town. I got a message. It's urgent. There is a dispatch from the Virginia Committee of Safety in Williamsburg!"

Smith pushed his way past the other members of the committee and went up to Workman, who handed him a small packet. The sheriff carefully opened it and then moved over to where some candles burned to better see the words.

As he read, a look of distress rapidly grew on his face. In a short time, he looked up at the guests. "There's been a disaster! A disaster with our army in Canada!" He bit his lip and looked around the room.

Angus McDonald called out, "For God's sake, man! Tell us what happened!"

Smith took a deep breath. "It was on New Year's Eve. They tried to take Quebec by a surprise night attack, with two columns assaulting the city. But the surprise failed, and the commanding general of the army was killed leading one column."

Wood called out, "Which general?"

Smith checked the dispatch. "A brigadier named Richard Montgomery. It says he was killed by a blast of cannon grapeshot while personally directing the advance. Then the British counter-charged and drove off his whole column, which took heavy casualties."

Wend looked at the crowd. They stood in stark silence, shock in their eyes.

Smith resumed speaking. "But I'm afraid that isn't the worst of it—not for us here in Winchester. The second column was led by a colonel named Benedict Arnold." He paused and looked around the room. "And our company, Morgan's Riflemen, was part of that column." He stood biting his lip, his eyes drawn to Abbey Morgan.

Peggy quickly turned and took Abbey's arm, pulling her close.

Smith shook his head, then reluctantly continued. "It says that Morgan's company led the advance and penetrated the furthest into Quebec, but they were surrounded by British troops and militia and cut off." He looked at Abbey. "Here's the worst of it: the better part of Morgan's Company was killed or captured."

There were muffled cries around the room, and then all eyes turned to Abbey. She stood tall, staring at Smith, the muscles of her face tight and standing out, her mouth set firmly. She said in a calm, strong voice, "Does it say what happened to Daniel?"

"Yes. He is among the captured."

Reverend Thruston quickly pushed his way to stand with Abbey.

Peggy looked at Abbey and hugged her arm tight and looked into her eyes. Everyone else was staring at her to see how she would take the news.

Peggy said quietly, "Abbey, at least he's alive."

Abbey looked quickly at Peggy and nodded, then she looked around the room, a half smile, half grimace on her face. She straightened to stand even taller, if that was possible. Then she said in a measured tone, "Well, God help the British if they're holdin' Daniel. They ain't got no idea what trouble they've latched onto."

There were a few nervous laughs at her words, but most people stood silent, reflecting on the situation.

Then Thruston broke the silence. He exclaimed, "We cannot let this stand! Winchester must send another company to the army!"

For once in his life, Angus McDonald spoke in agreement with the reverend. "Yes, by God! We must immediately recruit another company of riflemen and send them northward to join Washington's force! Winchester must be represented in this great struggle."

There was surge of voices saying, "Hear, hear!" and other expressions of agreement with the two men.

James Wood raised his arms to quiet the assemblage. "Listen, dear people. Be of good cheer. Rest assured we *will* send a new company to Boston. The committee will soon meet to discuss arrangements and initiate recruitment. But tonight let us continue the evening in commemoration of the good men of Frederick County who served honorably and have now won lasting acclaim for their valor in Canada."

Wend signaled to Albert, then turned to the guests. "Gentlemen and ladies, we will have your cups recharged, and that being done, let us raise them in salute to Captain Daniel Morgan and the brave men under his command!"

—⋘—

Wend and Peggy stood on the porch, bidding farewell to the last of their guests, the Woods and the McDonalds. The two couples, along with Abbey Morgan, had stayed after the party to partake of a hot toddy before starting home. Now the Woods' rig was on its way down the drive, and Angus and Anna had just climbed into their carriage. Wend had handed up Anna and also Abbey, who was traveling back to the Morgan home with the McDonalds, and then returned to the porch to stand beside his wife.

Peggy waved goodbye and looked over at Wend. "It was fortuitous that Abbey came with them. Despite her brave show in front of the crowd, once the other guests had gone and she was alone with us, I could see the trepidation and tears in her eyes."

"Yes, and it was very thoughtful for you to suggest she stay here with us tonight."

She responded, "It occurred to me that it would be comforting for her to spend the night with adult friends. All she has at home are Betsy and Nancy, and I thought it might have been painful for her to explain what has happened to their father so soon after she received the news herself."

"Well," answered Wend, "she told me she would indeed have stayed, but she didn't want to take the chance the children would get the word from someone else if she didn't get home until tomorrow."

They stood silently watching as the two rigs drove down the drive and then turned northward along the road.

Peggy asked, "What do you think about the call to form a new company for the army?"

Wend shrugged. "They won't have any trouble. There are plenty of men who will volunteer. There were many good marksmen who just missed out on qualifying to go with Morgan, and now there will be a thirst to avenge him and his men."

Peggy took Wend's arm, snuggled close, and then looked up to him. "You must be aware they're going to ask you to be the captain."

Startled, Wend looked down at his wife. "Me? God above, what makes you say that? Did someone mention something to you?"

"While Wood was talking about recruiting a new company, I watched all the members of the committee. The eyes of every one of them went to you. It was a silent but undeniable signal."

"That's poppycock. My role is to stay here and build muskets. They all understand that."

"Wend, most of those muskets we just presented to the committee were finished while you were off chasing Connolly. The fact is, you settled all the problems with getting the materials before you left for Culpeper. And Wilhelm Hecht is quite competent to make muskets. It doesn't take the skill required for your special pistols or delicate rifles. And while you're gone to the army, I can handle all the record keeping and accounts as I do anyway."

"Look, there are plenty of other men who could be the captain of a new company."

"None who have your reputation. None who were with Bouquet at Bushy Run. None who were successful in two fights against war parties last year. None who stopped a Loyalist conspiracy. And you are the right age. Angus and Smith and Rutledge are too old for the rigors of commanding a company."

"James Wood is the right age, and after Dunmore's War, he certainly has the experience."

"He's needed in Williamsburg. No one else is influential enough to properly represent Frederick County."

"My God, Peggy, listen to you! You sound like you want me to go! Just last year you fought tooth and nail against me going off to fight the Shawnee and Mingo in the Ohio Country. You practically shunned me over it. What has changed your thoughts?"

"You know that was about Abigail Gibson. And I'm not proud of it now."

"But it would mean being gone for at least a year. I just don't understand why you suddenly are in favor of me marching off to the army."

"This is a different war. It's a war is to put the English in their place and secure our rights. After all, I *am* Ulster. Father and grandfather hated the British and told stories of how they persecuted our people simply because we worshiped differently. And how our family fled to Ulster, where the damned Irish didn't treat us much better, and then we finally came to the colonies." She looked up at Wend with a fierceness in her eyes. "To tell the truth, I want to be free of the British! Were I to have a vote, it would be for independence from England, not just some accommodation with the king and parliament."

Wend sighed in resignation. "Yes, over the last few weeks, I have come to the belief that events are indeed driving us toward independence. From what I saw in Virginia, Maryland, and Pennsylvania, a lot of people are determined on it. But in my heart, I fear what such a war will entail. Pursuing Connolly, I saw the best and the worst in people." He paused and bit his lip. "And especially in myself." He sighed deeply and looked into his wife's eyes. "Peggy, to stop the conspiracy, I did things to people that will hound my conscience and plague my dreams forever. And I fear what leading a company of men will force me to do and what I will become by doing it."

"Wend, I know you have great inner strength. You have never shied away from doing what is necessary to prevail, whatever confronts you. But I know you will still be the man I married, even after the rigors of war. And above all, if we are to win our independence, you are the kind of man who must lead the fight."

Wend was about to respond when the sound of trotting hooves coming up from the stable became audible.

Peggy looked out and said in a startled tone, "Why, that's Andrew in my chaise with Boots! And that blond girl—that Freida—is with him!"

Wend smiled sheepishly. "I didn't get a chance to tell you. I let him borrow the chaise to take her home. You know, give her the thrill of riding in that instead of a farm wagon." Wend cleared his throat. "He's been sparking her for a while, and this will give him a chance to make an impression on her."

Peggy stared at the chaise as it swept by and then headed down the drive. The occupants were preoccupied with each other and didn't even look over at the house as Boots trotted by. She turned back to Wend. "And why, my husband, are you taking so much trouble to encourage this romance?"

Wend grinned. "That's easy. They'll make a suitable match, and it'll help keep Andrew working for me when his apprenticeship is over."

His wife turned and looked at him with a sly smile on her face, and she put a hand to her chin. "Oh, I rather thought you were trying to wash the memory of a golden-haired tart from the Red Vixen Tavern out of his mind."

Wend stood speechless in shock. He had told her nothing about the Red Vixen. Finally he gathered his wits and asked, "Uh, how did you happen to find out about that?"

"Men talk to their wives, and the women of Eckert Ridge talk to each other."

"Well, it was Andrew's first time with a woman. The truth is, he is besotted with that girl, and I don't want him doing anything foolish when his apprenticeship is over."

"Very commendable and very calculating, my dear."

"Peggy, I was meaning to tell you about it, but it kept slipping my mind."

She smiled at him and then said in her sweetest voice, "And now, when were you planning to tell me about a certain sultry, auburn-haired seductress named Widow McGraw? Whose first name is Coleen? The one with whom you spent several hours alone in her room at that same tavern? Did that also slip your mind?"

Wend felt rising panic and beads of perspiration forming on his forehead. "Peggy, she's an old friend, and I vow nothing happened."

"Yes, that is what I have been assured of by both Alice and Sally." She paused a moment with a steely look on her face. "And the reason you haven't been sleeping in the parlor or in your shop is because I have chosen to believe it."

Wend struggled to find words.

But before he had a chance to say anything, Peggy picked up her skirts and turned to go inside. She glanced back over her shoulder with her most coquettish look. "Now, my dear husband, I'm going to see that the children are properly abed, and then it would please me greatly if you would promptly join me in our room."

The End

of

Pursuit Through Chaos

Historical Notes and Acknowledgments

As readers of the previous *Forbes Road Series* novels will recall, my *modus operandi* is to wrap a fictional story around a specific historical event, particularly those that are lesser known but significant to the period. *Forbes Road* itself was built around the outbreak of Pontiac's Rebellion and the Battle of Bushy Run, *Conestoga Winter* highlighted the massacre of the Conestoga tribe and the Paxton Boys insurrection, *The Camp Follower Affair* told the story of Colonel Henry Bouquet's march into the Ohio Country, and *Lord Dunmore's Folly* was about the Virginia royal governor's war against the Ohio Indians in 1774. The *Rebellion Road Series* will follow the same format into the Revolutionary War era.

This initial novel of the new series covers events in Virginia, Maryland, and Pennsylvania that occurred in the aftermath of Lexington/Concord and the subsequent investment of Boston by a colonial militia army. As the narrative shows, it was an unsettled, turbulent period as the colonies transitioned from royal control to self-government. Most histories dealing with the first year of the war focus on the events in New England and Canada, as well as the workings of the Second Continental Congress. The conflict between Lord Dunmore's Loyalist forces and the Virginia Patriots is often ignored or at best treated as a sideshow. But the fact is, had Lord Dunmore and John Connolly prevailed in reestablishing royal control over Virginia, thus dividing the colonies, it is unlikely that the Patriot cause could have succeeded, at least in the form with which we are familiar.

Throughout the *Forbes Road Series*, it was my practice to addend notes expanding on the background history behind the events portrayed in the novel and to identify the major departures from actual history that had been taken to dramatize the story. This new series will follow the same policy. Accordingly, the following notes are relevant.

The importance of Connolly's plot. The plan to foment an insurrection by the Ohio Country tribes, which was hatched by Dunmore and John Connolly and then sanctioned by General Gage in Boston, was an integral part of the strategy to retake Virginia. Its main elements were essentially as laid out in the body of the novel: Dunmore would reconquer the tidewater and southern Virginia, while Connolly with his mixed force of Loyalists and tribal warriors would sweep down from the northwest, and the two forces would meet at Alexandria. General Thomas Gage, the British commander in America, had at least two reasons to endorse and expand on the plan: (1) If fully successful, it would take the largest colony out of the war, and (2) Even if that objective was not attained, it would force the rebelling colonists to divert substantial forces to protect the frontier settlements. So essentially the plan was a win-win for the British high command, assuming it actually got off the ground. This is illustrated by the fact that while Connolly's plot was nipped in the bud, the British didn't give up on the idea. Two years later, encouraged by the assiduous work of British agents, the tribes of the Iroquois Federation launched a war against the more northern colonies, sweeping eastward in widespread attacks on settlements in New York and Vermont. The impact forced Washington to detach a strong force of troops from the Continental Army, commanded by General Sullivan, to quell the uprising and stop the raids. Glenn H. Williams's award-winning book, *Year of the Hangman* (Westholme Publishing, LLC, 2005), is a detailed account of that tribal war and Sullivan's punitive expedition. In fiction, Walter D. Edmond's 1936 novel, *Drums Along the Mohawk*, and the 1939 John Ford movie based on it were inspired by this event.

Daniel Morgan and the first rifle companies. On June 14, 1775, the Continental Congress voted to raise ten companies of riflemen, six from Pennsylvania and two each from Maryland and Virginia, to support the New England forces besieging Boston. The Burgesses assigned Frederick and Berkeley Counties to each raise one company, and the Committee of Safety in Winchester chose Daniel Morgan to recruit a company of one hundred men. There seem to be as many versions of how Morgan selected his men as there are people telling the story. It seems clear that he chose them by shooting contest, but its not clear at what range they shot; some say two hundred paces, others two hundred fifty, and some don't specify the distance. The size of the reported target is also variable, but several speak of seven inches in diameter. Its also not settled whether it was done at one site or at several. Regardless of the manner of selection, the muster roll of the company shows a total of ninety-six men. To expedite the flow of the story, I synthesized various elements of the stories into one dramatization, placing the shooting contest and recruiting at Winchester's Fort Loudoun, an appropriate and conveniently central location. The dramatization of the company's departure from Winchester in the narrative is probably fairly accurate. The late Professor Don Higginbotham reports, "Before leaving Winchester, Morgan paraded his men by the courthouse, the Anglican church, and Philip Bush's popular Golden Buck Tavern amidst fanfare. . ." See *Daniel Morgan: Revolutionary Rifleman* (University of North Carolina Press, Chapel Hill, NC, 1961) Don Higginbotham

Patrick Henry's regiment and his military record. In reality, instead of Culpeper, the regiment's principal recruiting camp was Williamsburg. For the novel, I moved it to the northern town to facilitate the pacing of the story and to place Henry in a proper location for the Virginia Committee of Safety to delegate him to organize the pursuit of Connolly. As a matter of fact, Henry did recruit troops in Culpeper at an earlier date when he was putting together a militia unit to stop Dunmore for removing powder from the Williamsburg magazine. The famous Culpeper Minutemen, who later played a key role in the Battle of Great Bridge, did rendezvous and organize in the field described in the narrative. It's also true that Henry was "kicked upstairs" in late 1775 to administrative command of all Virginia military forces because of his tactical leadership limitations. A short time later, he became the first elected governor of Virginia.

James Wood, Jr. of Winchester. Wood (1741-1813) was the son of the man who, as a surveyor and agent of Lord Fairfax, was essentially the founder of Winchester. Like his father, James became a central figure in the cultural and political life of the town and Frederick County, and any story about the area would need to include him as a character. Wood was appointed Deputy Clerk of the County Court in 1766, elected to the Vestry of Frederick Parish in 1766, and in that year was first elected to the House of Burgesses. He would represent Frederick County in the legislature until taking a commission in the Continental Army in 1776. During Dunmore's War of 1774, he was a captain in Angus McDonald's militia battalion that carried out the raid on the Shawnee villages at Wakatomica in the Ohio Country (He was not at the Battle of Point Pleasant, as many biographies indicate. His company was assigned to Dunmore's northern force, not Colonel Andrew Lewis' southern brigade that was attacked by the Indian force at Point Pleasant). After the war, he was appointed to the commission which met in Pittsburgh and finalized the peace treaty with the tribes. In 1776 was appointed a militia Lieutenant Colonel and in 1777 became a colonel in the Continental Army and commander of the 12th Virginia Regiment (later reorganized as the 8th) which he led at the critical battles of Brandywine, Germantown, and Monmouth Court House. In 1779 he was appointed to command the "Convention Army," which was the organization that managed the custody of the Hessian soldiers captured at Saratoga, and was based at Charlottesville (later moved to Winchester). After the war he became a brigadier general in the Virginia militia and in 1796 was elected governor of the state. Obviously I have fictionalized his words and relationship with Wend Eckert, but his role in the novel as a key leader in Frederick County during the period is clearly valid.

Pursuit of Connolly. The route followed by Connolly and his compatriots from tidewater Virginia and then through Maryland as described in the narrative is essentially correct. However, rather than being pursued by a dedicated party of soldiers from Virginia and Maryland, the conspirators were actually captured by a group of local militia. Maryland officials had been alerted about the plot by Washington and the Continental Congress. They in turn warned local militia commanders to be on the watch for the conspirators. Connolly and his companions were traveling under assumed names, but, as in the story, a member of the Pittsburgh militia traveling eastward recognized Connolly beside the road just west of Elizabethtown and alerted officials in the town.

Pursuit beyond Hagerstown and the dispatches. After being captured, Connolly did indeed write dispatches to his fellow conspirators at Pittsburgh and in the Ohio Country, informing them of his capture and the details of the plan. He also wrote a letter to his wife explaining his situation. However, for this segment I took my literary license out of the desk drawer and put it to liberal use. In real life, the dispatches were actually carried by his associate Dr. John Smyth instead of the fictional Munger and crew. The doctor was able to escape shortly after the conspirators were taken into custody and head for Pittsburgh along Braddock's Road. He was pursued and finally caught just shy of Pittsburgh, as in the case of the fictional characters.

John Connolly in history. Connolly (1742-1813) was well known to prominent Virginians. It is accurate that Patrick Henry knew Connolly and had indeed been in a meeting where Dunmore granted him the four thousand acres at the Falls of the Ohio. George Washington was well acquainted with him, initially meeting him on a trip to Pittsburgh in 1770, where the two dined with a group of other men at Semple's Tavern. Connolly was actually still corresponding with Washington as late as spring 1775. James Wood worked with Connolly during negotiations with the Ohio tribal chiefs in spring and early summer 1775. Connolly's seizure of Pittsburgh for Virginia in January 1774 and leadership of a battalion in Dunmore's War made him a hero to the Virginia colonists until it became known that he sided with the king's party in 1775. Connolly's obsession with the Falls of the Ohio lasted throughout his lifetime and was well justified from an economic point of view. As he predicted, an important town eventually developed there, and the man who owned the land would have been in a position to make a fortune. That town subsequently became the city of Louisville, Kentucky. After his capture, the Continental Congress and Washington deemed Connolly too dangerous to be exchanged. He was held in limbo under varying levels of detention throughout the war. Afterward, the Loyalist traveled to England but later returned to America and ended up living in Canada. All along, he continued his battle to get title to the land around the Falls of the Ohio, often citing obscure and highly doubtful legal arguments. In the end the obsession cost him his wife, Susanna (he later remarried), and led to his being in bankruptcy at the time of his death. Connolly's saga is succinctly described in *The Other Loyalists: Ordinary People, Royalism, and the Revolution in the Middle Colonies, 1763–1787* (State University of New York Press, 2009), edited by Joseph S. Tiedermann, Eugene R. Fingerhut, and Robert W. Venables.

Jonathan Hager. The location of Connolly's capture near Hagerstown naturally led to my researching the history of that town as background for the manuscript. In the course of those studies, it turned up that the founder, Jonathan Hager, actually passed away on November 7, 1775, at the age of sixty-one. This was coincidentally the general period when the conspirators passed through the town and were apprehended. I had already planned to use him as a character playing a role in the story, but it was an easy step to dramatize his death in connection with the fictional riot of townsmen and Munger's attempt to free the conspirators. Hager christened his settlement "Elizabethtown" to commemorate his cherished wife, Elizabeth Kirschner. She died in 1765 at the age of forty, leaving Hager with two children, Rosanna and Jonathan Jr. Subsequent to the elder Hager's death, the town was called both Elizabethtown and Hagerstown, until 1813, when the latter name was formalized.

Dunmore's military forces. In his attempt to regain control of Virginia, Lord Dunmore assembled a diverse collection of military units. In addition to some Loyalist militia, he formed the Queens Own Loyal Virginia Regiment, made of volunteers mainly from the tidewater area. When he finally conceded defeat and sailed from Virginia in 1776, the members of this unit went with him and eventually were merged into the well-known Queen's Rangers. In addition, Dunmore had a detachment of marines from units of the Royal Navy squadron, which had been assigned to support his efforts. General Gage sent several companies of the 14th Foot to provide a backing of regulars for the provincial forces. Despite significant royalist support in tidewater Virginia, Dunmore had trouble recruiting colonials in the numbers required, and this was the primary factor that led to his proclamation of November 7, 1775, which declared martial law and offered freedom to slaves who agreed to fight for the king. This was a drastic and desperate measure, which Dunmore had to know would alienate many members of the landed gentry who otherwise would have supported him. But it is a clear indicator of his desperation for soldiers. The proclamation led to uprisings on several plantations in the tidewater area and slaves simply fleeing from others. Eventually between five hundred and eight hundred black recruits joining Dunmore's force. These men were formed into the Ethiopian Regiment. Elements of the unit fought at the Battle of Great Bridge in December 1775 and other skirmishes. But there was a tragic ending: the regiment was struck by a severe epidemic of small pox, and several hundred soldiers and dependents died. Those who survived were transported by ship with Dunmore when he left his final base in Virginia, Gwin Island, in June 1776 and apparently were used in supporting roles with the British forces.

The regiment commanded by the character Barrett Penfeld Northcutt, described in the narrative as the "King's Loyal Virginia Regiment," is fictional, but readers are should not be surprised if they encounter it and its commander in subsequent books of the series.

Actions of royal governors. The reaction to the onset of the revolution by crown governors in the middle colonies was diverse. Virginia's Lord Dunmore, of course, chose to fight the insurrection and attempt to reclaim power. But in Maryland and Pennsylvania it was a far different story.

Governor Sir Robert Eden was popular with Marylanders and had in fact married Caroline Calvert, the daughter of Charles Calvert of the proprietary family of Maryland. Although fundamentally opposed to the growing insurrection against the mother country, he took a passive attitude toward the rebels, allowing the Annapolis Convention and the Maryland Council of Safety to gradually become the de facto governing bodies while he retreated to the role of figurehead. He performed ceremonial duties while providing status reports on the progress of the revolution to the English government. He was finally requested to leave by the Annapolis Convention in June 1776, just before the Declaration of Independence, and he did so still on rather cordial terms with the colonials. In fact, he and his wife returned to Maryland after the war and took up permanent residence.

In Pennsylvania, the proprietary governor, John Penn, also assumed an increasingly detached position and low profile as revolutionary events gathered steam, ceding powers to the various governing entities set up by the Patriots. Because the Penn family, having founded the colony, had extensive land ownership and other monetarily valuable holdings in the colony, he attempted to wait things out, hoping that the tide would turn in favor of the crown. However, as British forces advanced on Philadelphia in 1777, Patriot authorities took he and his family into custody and moved them to an estate in New Jersey owned by his wife's family. There they were held in benevolent exile while Philadelphia was occupied by General Howe's army. Subsequent to the British evacuation of Philadelphia in 1778 and retreat to New York, the Penns were allowed to return to a family estate in Pennsylvania, where they remained until the conclusion of hostilities. Late in the war, the former governor signed a pledge of loyalty to the Patriot government of Pennsylvania and the United States in an attempt to preserve his assets. However, the state eventually confiscated his property and provided a monetary compensation that was a mere fraction of the actual value.

Places named Frederick. As it happens, this story deals with a plethora of places containing the name "Frederick." Winchester and Wend's home, Eckert Ridge, is located in Frederick County, *Virginia*. We also have the city that is now called Frederick located in Frederick County, *Maryland*. To avoid confusion, I have used the name Fredericktown throughout the narrative for the Maryland location, based on research that shows that that title was used at least some of the time in the colonial period, although it was also often referred to simply as Frederick. Just for additional complication, in very early days, Winchester was also called Frederick Town! And of course, we can't forget the existence of Fredericksburg, Virginia.

Acknowledgments. I am indebted to many people for their assistance in preparation of this first book in the Rebellion Road Series. Bryant White extended permission for use of his painting, *Loading in a Tempest*, for the cover and for promotional purposes. Bryant's portfolio of work, as well of that of his wife, Pamela Patrick White, can be viewed online at www.whitehistoricart.com. They both specialize in colonial, Native American, and Revolutionary War-era artwork. Tony Rozwadowski, of K Art and Design here in Culpeper, worked with great diligence to make my very rough and inexpertly drawn maps look professional. His website is www.k-artanddesign.com. Mike Shade and Chris Charboneau performed a most important and helpful function by reading the draft manuscript and making very cogent commentary. As usual, I am most grateful to readers of the Forbes Road Series who have contacted us through the Sunshine Hill Press website, www.forbesroadbook.com, and expressed their interest in the Wend Eckert adventures and shared both their comments on the stories and ideas for future plotlines.

Robert J. Shade
September 2019

Printed in Great Britain
by Amazon